Praise for the Bromance Book Club series

"Nothing about Adams's novel is simple, as it unfurls its catchy premise with surprising wisdom and specificity."

—*The New York Times Book Review*

"*The Bromance Book Club* is a gloriously tongue-in-cheek celebration of all the things that make romance so entertaining."

—*Entertainment Weekly*

"Adams's words help you believe that the right people find the right people." —Shondaland

"A fun, sexy, and heartfelt love story that's equal parts romance and bromance." —*Kirkus Reviews*

"Sweet and funny and emotional. I zoomed through this one Sunday, totally compelled by the romance (and the bromance!). I'm so looking forward to seeing more of this book club."

—*New York Times* bestselling author Nalini Singh

"*The Bromance Book Club* is a delight!" —Alexa Martin

TITLES BY LYSSA KAY ADAMS

The Bromance Book Club

Undercover Bromance

Crazy Stupid Bromance

Isn't It Bromantic?

A Very Merry Bromance

A Very Merry *Bromance*

LYSSA KAY ADAMS

BERKLEY ROMANCE
New York

BERKLEY ROMANCE
Published by Berkley
An imprint of Penguin Random House LLC
penguinrandomhouse.com

Library of Congress Cataloging-in-Publication Data

Names: Adams, Lyssa Kay, author.
Title: A very merry bromance / Lyssa Kay Adams.
Description: First Edition. | New York: Berkley Romance, 2022. | Series: The Bromance Book club; 5
Identifiers: LCCN 2022014818 (print) | LCCN 2022014819 (ebook) | ISBN 9780593332795 (trade paperback) | ISBN 9780593332801 (ebook)
Subjects: LCGFT: Love stories. | Novels.
Classification: LCC PS3601.D385 V47 2022 (print) | LCC PS3601.D385 (ebook) | DDC 813/.6—dc23
LC record available at https://lccn.loc.gov/2022014818
LC ebook record available at https://lccn.loc.gov/2022014819

First Edition: November 2022

Printed in the United States of America
1st Printing

Book design by Elke Sigal

To Meika

Thanks for talking me out of that tattoo
of mashed potatoes

A Very Merry
Bromance

THE BACKSTORY

Last December

Now *this* was how Colton Wheeler liked to wake up.

Naked, warm, and pressed against a woman who'd blown his fucking mind.

His groomsman's tuxedo was a mound of black-and-white fabric on the floor of his hotel suite, tangled up with a silky green dress that had been discarded in a flurry of frantic kisses, heated whispers, and desperate pleas to hurry.

He'd always heard about people who met *the one* at a wedding, but that was for, like, other people. He was Colton Wheeler, after all. Multi-platinum country star. But last night, after standing up along with his best buddies to watch their friend Braden Mack marry the love of his life, he'd fallen under the spell of the most unlikely woman.

The groom's ex. It made no sense. They made zero sense. But she'd kissed him, and even though he'd been kissed by a lot of women before—often without warning—this one had been different.

No doubt about it.

Colton Wheeler was smitten with Gretchen Winthrop, esquire.

It would be complicated, of course. She was Mack's sort-of ex-girlfriend. They'd dated for three months before he met his now-wife. There was always a risk when you dated someone in your own social circle. But here he was, watching her sleep and writing songs in his head, his mind afire with the promise of *This could be something good.*

Sometime in the wee hours of the morning after they'd finally fallen into an exhausted sleep, the sheet had slipped from her torso, leaving her bare to his gaze. Colton pressed his lips to her shoulder. The deep breath she took brought the soft curve of her stomach more fully against his hand. He still couldn't believe what she'd been hiding beneath that sensible dress she'd had on last night.

She inhaled deeply again, but this time it was followed by a long stretch of her legs against his. She was waking up. Colton slid his knee between both of hers, and she made space for him. The toes of her right foot caressed a path up and down his shin.

Colton nuzzled her jaw with the tip of his nose. "Good morning."

Gretchen let out a little sigh and snuggled into his chest. But then she froze. Her eyes flew open. "What time is it?"

"Time to wake you up properly."

He leaned in to kiss her but met blank air instead. She rolled away from him like a rabbit evading a predator. "Oh my God . . . it's light outside."

Colton chuckled and rose on one elbow. "Do you turn into a pumpkin soon?"

"I—I can't believe I slept all night there. I didn't mean to."

"Well, I sure didn't mind." He sat up fully and reached out his hand. "In fact, I'd love it if you came back to bed for a few hours more."

"I can't. I have to go."

He reclined on the bed and folded his arms behind his head, satisfied for the moment to just watch her naked body as she skittered about the room. Until he realized what she was doing.

Looking for her clothes.

"Are you actually leaving?"

Her head swiveled until she spotted her dress. She threw it on, covering her nudity. Colton kicked away the blankets and rose from bed. "Come on," he said, holding out his hand for her. "Slow down. We have plenty of time before brunch, and—"

She jumped as if he'd just suggested they leave the room naked. "I—I'm not invited to that. That's just for the wedding party."

"And I'm the wedding party, which means I can bring anyone I want." He finally succeeded in getting his hands on her again. His hands lightly stroked her hips over the green silk. "And I want to bring you."

"No, I—I can't. I have a lot of work to catch up on today."

Well, that was a relief. For a moment, he was starting to worry that she might be evading him because she didn't actually like him. "Then let me take you somewhere."

Her head swiveled again in search of God only knew what. "You don't have to drive me. I drove my own car here."

He chuckled, reaching again for her. "No, I mean away. Let's go somewhere. Spend a week just talking and getting to know each other and—"

She laughed quietly, but whether it was with him or at him remained to be seen. "Sure. Where should we go?"

"Belize."

She finally met his gaze. "Belize?"

"Ever been?"

She laughed again. This time definitely *at* him. "No."

"Well, believe me when I say you're going to love it." He watched as she located her bra. He remembered the precise moment when he'd taken it off her and flung it across the room. "I'm serious, Gretchen. Come away with me. I'll tell my pilot to get my plane ready, and we can just get away—"

Her mouth dropped open. "You're serious, aren't you?"

"Hell, yes."

"I can't go to Belize with you." She found her purse and shoved both her bra and panties into it.

Colton stepped in front of her and gripped her shoulders. "Hold up. What's going on here?"

"I'm leaving. I have a lot to do today."

"When can I see you again?"

She blinked.

Well, this was a first. "I—I can see you again, right?"

She chewed on her lip. "I don't think that's a good idea." She stepped around him, searching the floor again. She let out an *ah* at the sight of her shoes. She bent to pick them up, one finger hooked through the sexy black slingbacks that had damn near given him cardiac arrest last night.

"Wait. Just wait. Can we start this over, please? I feel like I've screwed something up, but I have no idea what."

"You didn't screw anything up. It's me. I shouldn't have done this. I'm sorry."

"Shouldn't have done what?"

"I started this. I shouldn't have kissed you."

"I was a willing participant. More than willing." He set his hands on his hips and was instantly, painfully aware of his own nudity. And not in a good way.

She stopped her frantic searching and hugged her things to her chest. "Look, I know everyone felt sorry for me last night. Even though I never had anything serious with Mack, and I mean, I was actually at the wedding for Liv because she and I have become friends, but still, I felt everyone looking at me as if I was about to break or something, and I know you only approached me to dance because of that—"

It was his turn to laugh. "You think I asked you to dance out of . . . pity?"

"Maybe." She shrugged.

"I asked you to dance because you had the same reaction to Liv's mother that I did when she almost fell out of her chair."

Her lips quirked finally with a smile.

Thank *God*. He took advantage of her stillness to creep closer, lowering his voice as he approached. "And then I kept asking you to dance and pretty much never left your side after that because you might be the most amazing woman I've ever met."

Her cheeks flushed, and he had the most delicious flashback to that very color on her face when she arched her back and shuddered his name.

But that wasn't the look she was giving him now. She shook her head and pressed her warm hand to the center of his chest, right above the spot where his heart was gearing up for a game of brink of death. "You don't have to do that."

He quickly covered her hand with his. "Do what?"

"Soothe my ego. I'm a big girl. I know what last night was."

"You mean incredible and the start of something that could be amazing? I agree."

Her blush deepened. "Look, I had fun too. But this would never work between us."

"It worked pretty well last night."

She started rapidly backing away from him. "But now it's today. And you're you and I'm me, and—"

"And we could be a pretty damn good we."

She smiled softly. "That sounds like one of your songs."

"Gretchen." He held out his hand. She stared at it with unmistakable longing.

But then she snapped out of it and walked to the door. "Thank you," she said, looking over her shoulder. "For everything."

Colton crossed his arms. "You can say anything you want except that. Just don't thank me."

She paused once again before turning the handle. "Can I count on you to keep this between us?"

"Trust me, my lips are sealed."

Then, without a single backward glance, she walked out the door.

For the first time in his life, Colton Wheeler was someone's dirty little secret.

CHAPTER ONE

One year later

Colton Wheeler lived by very few hard and fast rules, but one of them was when someone asked you to keep a secret, you took it to your grave. So it was with no small gut punch of betrayal that he realized that *these* guys, of all people, would go back on their word to him. They were supposed to be his best friends.

Colton adjusted the strap of his duffel bag on his shoulder with an annoyed jerk. "You swore you wouldn't tell anyone."

"Come on, man," said Gavin Scott, a yoga mat tucked under his arm. He wore a sleeveless training shirt that showed off the line across his bicep that separated pasty-white shoulder from perpetual farmer's tan. "It's not like we told total strangers."

"It doesn't matter who they are. I promised her I would keep this quiet."

"We didn't mean to put you in a bad position," said Del Hicks, jumping in. "Honestly."

"And we didn't even think you'd be here anyway," Gavin added, officially pouting.

"Why wouldn't I be here?"

"Because of the meeting. Isn't that today?"

Ah, yes. The Meeting. It had taken on such infamous significance that it was now preceded only by *the* followed by a capital M. The Meeting in which he would find out if he still had a career left. But his friends didn't know that. They only knew he was meeting with the music label to discuss his next album after a two-year recording hiatus.

And now *he* was the one who felt guilty, an emotion he'd become all too familiar with in the past year. How could he expect these guys to live up to some standard of friendship when he was betraying them every single day with the things he'd been keeping from them?

For a global music star, true friendships were hard to come by. The more famous he got over the years, the lonelier life became. It was hard to trust who really wanted to be in his life and who just wanted the bragging rights of being associated with a superstar.

But these guys, they were the real deal. The best friends he'd ever had. And they'd met in the unlikeliest of ways—through romance novels. They called themselves the Bromance Book Club, a group of men who read romance novels to learn how to see the world through a less toxic lens than the ones that all cisgender heterosexual men are taught to look through. Braden Mack was the one who had started it all and pulled Colton into it. He'd been skeptical, as most of the guys were when they first joined the book club. But Colton quickly learned it was about a lot more than books. It was about camaraderie and brotherhood. The lessons of romance novels had taught them all how to be better men, better partners, and better friends to one another.

"It's okay," Colton finally sighed. "I'll talk to—"

"Mr. Wheeler, what is the meaning of this?"

—her.

Shit. Colton steeled himself as he turned around and looked straight into the eyes of one of the most intimidating people he'd ever met. Peggy Porth. Retired elementary school principal. Certified ballbuster.

Silver Sneakers instructor.

"Hey, Mrs. Porth." Colton's voice squeaked like the time in fifth grade when he'd been caught selling Pokémon cards during recess for twice their market value. In his defense, he'd needed the money for Christmas presents for his siblings.

Mrs. Porth stood just five foot three but somehow managed to look down at him when she spoke. "Need I remind you, Mr. Wheeler, that when you asked if you and a couple of friends could attend our classes, I agreed to just a small group. This class is supposed to be for people over fifty exclusively, but you talked me into it. But now I see three others standing by the door waiting to come in."

The *others* in question were huddled in a nervous circle a few feet away, occasionally casting furtive glances as if to gauge whether they were about to be tossed out by a bouncer. Colton knew them, of course, but not well, and only because they were Gavin's and Del's teammates on the Nashville Legends professional baseball team. His circle of friends included several athletes. Besides Gavin and Del, there was Yan Feliciano, another Legends player. And Vlad Konnikov, a player for the Nashville NHL team, and Malcolm James, who played for the city's NFL franchise. Which was why Colton had invited them in on this secret in the first place. Silver Sneakers was the most effective workout he'd ever had. He'd never been as strong, fit, or flexible, and it had all started by accident. He'd thought he was taking a Six-Pack Abs class but had gotten the room wrong and instead found himself sweating his balls off as he tried to keep up with the sixty-something-year-old women who made step aerobics look like a mere jaunt through the park. He'd been sore for days but kept coming back because, damn, but also because no one in the room gave a single flying fuck who he was.

Turns out, he was sort of into not being fawned over because he was Colton Wheeler.

It was one of the things that had attracted him to . . . Fuck. The *Number of Days Since I Thought About Gretchen Winthrop* board in his mind went back to zero.

"It's our f-fault, Mrs. Porth," Gavin said, his lifelong stutter emerging in fear of the woman. "We just wanted to share it because our teammates are getting jealous of how flexible we've become."

To prove it, he dropped his yoga mat and sprang into a deep lunge that would've sent Colton straight to the emergency room.

"See," Gavin grunted, voice strained. "I could practically play first base now if I wanted."

Mrs. Porth pursed her lips. "Stand up, Mr. Scott. You're making a fool of yourself."

Del grabbed Gavin's elbow and helped him up. Mrs. Porth sighed and looked again at the men waiting nervously by the door. "Fine," she said. "They can join. But let me remind you that if you disturb anyone—"

"They won't," Gavin said quickly. "I mean, we won't. Thank you, Mrs. Porth." Gavin raced to the door and gave the guys the good news.

A moment later, Gavin returned with his teammates in tow, all wearing variations on the standard professional athlete uniform—basketball shorts, moisture-wicking shirt, and kinesiology tape on whatever body part hurt today. After depositing their yoga mats and duffel bags, they shuffled over to Colton.

One of them extended his hand. "Hey, man. Thanks for letting us join. Jake Tamborn. We met at Gavin's birthday party last year."

"I remember," Colton said, accepting the handshake because it was the polite thing to do. He still wasn't thrilled about them being here, but he repeated the gesture with the other two men—Brad Eisenberg and Felix Pinas. Both men were in their midtwenties and had the confident posture of two dudes who had no idea what they were in for.

"Did you warn them?" Colton whispered to Del as the three men walked away.

"That they're about to get their asses kicked? Yeah."

"Did they believe you?"

"Nope."

Colton grinned for the first time since arriving at the gym. "This is going to be fun."

The door to the fitness room opened, and Vlad ran in, flustered. He dumped his yoga mat next to Colton's and shoved a Santa hat on his head. "How does this look?"

"Surprisingly good. Why?"

"Elena says I have to dress up as Santa for our Christmas party to hand out presents to all the kids."

Vlad and his wife, Elena, were hosting their first-ever Christmas party in a couple of weeks. Normally, Vlad would never have had time because of his hockey schedule, but he was still recovering from a broken leg suffered during last year's Stanley Cup playoffs.

So when the guys decided to organize a Bromance family holiday party, Vlad jumped at the chance to host it because it might be his only chance.

"I've never played Santa before," Vlad said. "We don't do Santa in Russia."

"No Santa?" Gavin gasped and looked up from stretching his quads as if Vlad had just admitted to barking at the moon on Christmas Eve.

Del smacked the back of Gavin's head. "Damn, dude. Get out of your American bubble every once in a while."

"We call him Grandfather Frost," Vlad said.

Gavin sat all the way down, crossed his legs under him, and began to bounce them butterfly-style. "How is he different from Santa?"

Vlad started stretching as he spoke. "Well, he has a white beard, so that is the same. But he does not wear a red suit. He wears long robes. And he does not have reindeer. His sleigh is driven by three horses. And he is not just about giving gifts. He is about good deeds. He gets cold when he is around bad people."

"I like that. Maybe you should play him, instead," Colton offered. "No reason to change your own traditions."

"But Elena says that will confuse the kids and make them question if Santa Claus is real."

Del shrugged. "Tell them that he and Santa are friends and help each other out."

"I don't know," Gavin said. "I do kind of want to see Vlad in a Santa suit."

Vlad got a panicked look on his face. "What if I screw it up?"

Colton patted him on the back. "You'll do fine. We'll help you get ready. Just practice saying 'Ho, ho, ho.'"

Mrs. Porth clapped her hands loudly and walked to the front of the room. Next to her stood a woman about ten years younger. "Those of you who are new to the class," she said, staring directly at Jake, Felix, and Brad, "can follow a modified version of all of our exercises."

As predicted, the three new guys snorted because, of course, professional athletes would have no reason to follow a modified workout routine. They had no fucking idea what was coming.

The guys spread out in a long line extending from one side of the room to the other. In front of them, roughly thirty-five other exercisers took their places next to their own mats and bottles of water. Later, they would all grab an aerobics step for the part of the class that truly separated the women from the men.

"All right, everyone. We're going to start with some light stretching and warm-up," Mrs. Porth said. The speakers began to play a quiet, calming music, like the kind you'd hear in a day spa. "Let's get those arms loosened up with some nice, easy shoulder shrugs . . . That's it. Now start to roll them back and forward . . . Very good. Now some arm circles."

Colton spread his arms out wide and smacked hands with Felix. Colton gave him a sharp look, and Felix inched sideways with a quiet *Sorry.*

"Okay, everyone," Mrs. Porth said. "Now for some easy yoga poses to get those legs nice and ready to work."

Colton followed her instructions into goddess pose and several others. A moment later, he looked up from his mat to a disturbing sight. "Dude, get your downward dong out of my face."

"Isn't it called downward dog?" Brad whispered back, his face upside down between his legs.

"Not when you do it."

Brad crab-crawled a few inches away.

"Okay, everyone, excellent job," Mrs. Porth said. "Now, everyone grab your step and place it in front of you. Remember that you can adjust it to whatever height is most comfortable for you."

Mrs. Porth had the highest setting.

A moment later, Jake groaned. "Shit, you didn't tell me it would be this hard."

"What did you expect?" Colton snorted. "This is the Jazzercise generation. They've been kicking asses in leotards since the dawn of MTV."

"So what time is the meeting with the label?" Noah grunted.

"Three."

"You worried?"

Colton glanced over quickly. Did they suspect something? "No. Why would I be worried?"

Noah shrugged. "I don't know. I mean, just that you've never had a meeting like this since I've known you."

"It's just a formality," he said, adopting the *no big deal* attitude he'd perfected at ten years old. No one wanted to see him worried. Or mad. Or anything other than the carefree, aw-shucks playboy who had sold millions of records around the world.

Because Colton Wheeler had one job, and one job only. To make other people happy.

Even if it killed him.

CHAPTER TWO

"Your honor, may I approach?"

Gretchen Winthrop fought to keep her tone neutral as she waited for the federal judge to respond to her request. Inside, however, she was raging. It never ended, the indignities that her clients were forced to suffer. The judge nodded and waved his fingers in an annoyed *make it quick* way, and both she and the attorney for the government left their respective tables. The judge looked down from his desk, hand over the microphone that recorded the deportation proceedings of the Memphis Immigration Court.

"Your honor, my client is ill. She has a fever of 102 degrees and can barely sit up."

Judge Wilford raised an eyebrow and looked at Assistant U.S. Attorney Justin McQuistan. "It would seem Ms. Winthrop is correct. Why is the defendant in court sick?"

"Your honor, it is my understanding that—"

Gretchen cut him off. "My client cannot possibly be expected to contribute to her own hearing without proper healthcare. I request a postponement until Ms. Fuentes can be treated properly."

The judge waved them back to their tables. A moment later, he spoke into the record. "The court grants defendant's request for a postponement pending proper medical treatment for Ms. Fuentes."

He banged the gavel, and Gretchen let out the first full breath in over a half hour. She sat down next to her client, Carla, a fifty-six-year-old woman who'd crossed the southern border with her parents at the age of seventeen. Carla's parents had already been deported, and the court had denied her request to stay even though she'd lived in the United States nearly all her life. But she had children now. And grandchildren. A boy and a girl, both under three. An American family who loved and needed her.

Gretchen squeezed her hand. "It's going to be okay. A postponement is good. We're going to get you healed up, and I will bring you proper clothes and shoes."

Tears leaked down Carla's cheeks. "My babies . . ."

"I will request a visitation."

Too quickly, deputies took her away through the door at the side of the courtroom. Back to the detention facility where countless others waited their fate. People who came to the United States out of desperation and found the Land of the Free did not always live up to its ideals. The clerk called the next case as Gretchen shoved her files back into her bag. As she walked out, another lawyer waiting for another client took her place. An endless cycle of cruelty that tore parents from their children, wives from husbands, friends from friends. And for what reason? Because they weren't lucky enough to win the lottery of birth? Because they wanted a better life for the people they loved? Because they were too desperate to stand in the impossibly long line for legal entry while they watched celebrities and athletes and supermodels cut to the front of the line?

Gretchen paused outside the courtroom and leaned against the wall, letting her overloaded bag fall to her feet. She closed her eyes and sucked in a deep breath. She'd been practicing as an immigration attorney for nearly ten years, and it never got easier. If anything, it had gotten harder. When she'd started, she'd had the benefit of idealism, that naive hope that she could make a difference. Now she knew better. The only thing that never changed was how hard certain Americans would fight to wall out the most vulnerable, who simply wanted a chance at a better life. Sometimes she wondered if she was doing any good at all, if maybe she'd be better off using her experience and expertise to push for better laws. But who was she kidding? She was never leaving Nashville, and the reasons had nothing to do with her career.

Gretchen peeled away from the wall and headed toward the lobby of the courthouse. She had a three-hour drive back to Nashville, her hometown and the location of her law clinic. The federal immigration court in Memphis was the only one in the entire state of Tennessee—just one more hurdle for her deportation clients, who barely had reliable transportation to get to work, much less the other side of the state. After waving at the security guards, she pushed open the heavy, thick glass door and braced herself against the blast of wintry air. People up north would laugh at what southerners like her considered cold, but she was a Tennessee girl to the bone. Anything under fifty degrees was an assault.

As she drove, she dictated notes into her phone for the next steps in Carla's case, stopping only when she reached the exit that would take her back to the office. December had puked its merry contents all over the city's streets and buildings. Massive wreaths hung from streetlamps, their red bows flapping wildly in the wind. If she opened her window, the scent of roasted pecans from the nearby Christmas market would soften the earthy tang of the river. Orange road barricades blocked entire lanes to direct the masses of tourists in town for the annual Christmas on the Cumberland display, where more than a million lights were strung along the famous Cumberland River Pedestrian Bridge and the two parks it connected.

Few cities did Christmas as big as Nashville.

Few people despised it as much as Gretchen.

Which is why her office was the only one on its block without a wreath on the door or a string of lights outlining the front window. She had a no-decoration rule at her clinic, which was located on the first floor of a three-story building in the city's east side, an eclectic neighborhood of artsy stores, quaint restaurants, and historic brick buildings. In the ten years since Gretchen had opened her doors, the neighborhood had undergone a revitalization that bordered on gentrification. But she couldn't afford to keep up with the revival. Immigration was a civil matter, not criminal, which meant that the defendants were not guaranteed the right to counsel. The vast majority of deportation defendants never sought attorneys to help them, and the ones who did rarely had the money to pay. Gretchen's cases were nearly all pro bono, which meant she couldn't afford a fancy office. At least her friend Alexis owned a café up the street, so quick lunches and hits of caffeine were just a block away.

Gretchen parked in the small lot behind her building, grabbed her things, and walked in the back door. Her assistant, Addison, pounced the minute she saw Gretchen coming up the hallway toward the front. "It's freezing in here. Can't we please turn the heat up today?"

"Not until the end of the week. Put on a sweater."

"I'm already wearing a sweater," Addison grumbled as she reached for Gretchen's coat to hang it up. "And he called again."

Gretchen set her bag on the floor. "Who?"

Addison thrust a stack of pink message slips at her. "You know who."

The sigh that left Gretchen's lips could have powered a small steamboat. Her friend and law school classmate Jorge Alvarez had been calling for six weeks now, asking her to consider joining his refugee resettlement nonprofit as a staff attorney.

"I told him you already had his number, but he insisted on leaving it again. Just in case."

Gretchen knew the number by heart at this point. She retrieved her bag and slung it over her shoulder. "I'll call him back tomorrow."

"Just call him now and get it over with," Addison said, trailing Gretchen down the short hallway to her office. "What's so hard about telling him you're not interested in the job?"

Gretchen answered honestly as she flipped on the light. "I don't know."

"Maybe because you actually *are* interested."

Gretchen scowled at Addison lounging in the doorway. "I have clients who need me here."

"That's a non-denial denial." Addison gave Gretchen a knowing look.

"I'm not looking for something else," Gretchen said, sitting down in her ancient desk chair.

"Yes, you are. The problem is you just aren't sure what it is." With that, Addison turned on her heel and sauntered out with all the swagger of a prosecutor who'd just nailed a defendant on the stand.

"Hey!" Gretchen called. "What the hell does that mean?"

"I can't tell you that. It was meant to be cryptic."

"It's bullshit, is what it is."

"But it's *good* bullshit," Addison called back. "Because it's true."

"It's *not* true. I am perfectly happy where I am. I love my clinic. I love my job. I love my life."

"Who are you trying to convince?"

One of the clinic's case managers, a college intern named Joey, entered her office. "You know, when you told me working here would be like joining a family, I didn't know that would include stupid arguments."

"Shut up," Gretchen grumbled under her breath.

"See? Just like family. My sister used to say the same thing to me every day."

"That was meant for Addison," Gretchen said, followed by a pointed look at the chair across from her desk.

He got the message. He clicked his pen and looked at his legal pad. "Okay, tell me what to do."

Gretchen spent the next fifteen minutes giving him instructions on what to do next with Carla's case. Just as they were wrapping up, an instant message popped up on her screen from Addison. **Your brother is holding for you on line three.**

She quickly typed back, **Which one?**

Evan.

Alarm sent a jolt of adrenaline through her veins. Of her two brothers, Evan was the oldest and the one who pretended the hardest that Gretchen didn't exist. If he was calling her—on her office line, no less—something must be wrong.

She nodded toward the office door, and Joey once again got the message. He rose and walked out, shutting the door behind him. Gretchen picked up the phone and hit the blinking button. "Hello?"

Her brother's voice was muffled, as if he'd pulled the phone away from his mouth as he waited for her to pick up.

"Evan," she said sharply.

Her brother came back to the phone. "One second."

"You called me, remember?"

But he'd already gone back to barking orders at whichever lackey was unlucky enough to be called before him. Gretchen's jaw jutted sideways as she considered hanging up on him. If something was wrong, he was taking his sweet time telling her about it.

He finally came back to the phone. "Hi, sorry about that."

"Why did you call me on my office phone?"

"I couldn't find your cell number."

Of course he couldn't. Because why would she be saved in his contacts like any normal sibling? All their lives, he'd treated her like a pesky brat who needed a good talking to, but now that they were adults, that had morphed into a detached formality that was even more annoying. Not that they'd ever been close. She used to blame their twelve-year age difference, but the chasm between them went beyond age. "What's up?" she asked.

"I need you to come out this afternoon."

"Out where?"

"To Homestead."

Homestead. A warm word for a cold place. The corporate headquarters of Carraig Aonair Whiskey had certainly never felt like home to her. More like a dirty little secret. Rather, she was *their* dirty little secret. She was one of *those* Winthrops, a bona fide heiress from one of Tennessee's richest and most influential families, but they rarely liked to claim her and her inconvenient politics publicly.

None of them had ever forgiven her for daring to deny the family legacy—their words, not hers—and forge her own career path. Which made Evan's summons both suspicious and worrisome.

"Why?" she asked.

"I need to talk to you about something important."

"Is everyone all right?" The entire family flashed before her eyes. Uncle Jack. Their parents. Her nieces and nephews. She didn't get along with Evan, but she loved his kids.

"Everyone's fine. Can you make it in the next hour or so?"

No. She had a shit-ton of work to do and an aversion to being summoned like a naughty kid to the principal's office. But when she opened her mouth, all that came out was "Sure."

She quickly answered some pending emails, stuffed several folders into her bag to work on later, and told Addison to call her cell if anything came up. Then she ducked out before Addison could pepper her with questions. Or, worse, offer more amateur psychoanalysis about why, even now, when her family whistled, she came running like a starving puppy in search of scraps.

Because that would be pathetic.

The first time Colton had walked through the doors of the Nerve Music Group Nashville twelve years ago, he'd felt a twinge of *This is it?* This unremarkable office building in the most boring part of the city was home to some of the hottest acts in country music, the place where stars were made?

But unlike the neon-glowing party of Music Row, the offices of the industry's major record labels weren't meant to inspire. They were designed to intimidate, to remind starry-eyed artists that music was a business, first and foremost.

If Nashville was a party, these buildings were the chaperones.

And today, Colton had the sinking feeling he was about to be dragged off the dance floor by his shirt collar.

The staff in the lobby greeted Colton as they always did—with warm deference. He was, even still, one of their top-selling artists, after all. Photos of him and his album covers decorated the walls of the lobby, the hallways, even the goddamned bathrooms. An escort—maybe an intern from the nearby Belmont School of Music or, more likely, some executive's nephew—met him at the door and offered him a bottle of water before showing him to the elevators that would take him to the top-floor suites where the label's executive offices were located. The young man bade him goodbye as Colton entered the elevator, and another one was waiting for him as he got out—a young woman this time, who smiled and called him "Mr. Wheeler" in a way that made him want to duck into the restroom to check for gray hair.

She led him to the large conference room where his dreams had come true all those years ago. Back then, he'd walked in to find everyone already there, waiting for him with smiles and congratulations.

Today, the room was empty. "Am I the first one here?"

"You are," the girl said, still smiling.

That was a first. Rock star time, and all that. But anxiety had a way of violating the speed limit. Colton declined the young woman's offer of a beverage from the well-stocked mini-fridge and instead strode to the bank of windows overlooking the city. The first time he'd looked at this view, he'd seen nothing but opportunity, fame, fortune. It was different this time, filtered through the lens of age and experience. Now, he saw all the cracks in the pavement, the roofs in need of repair, the tired cab drivers in need of a break. He still saw the city's shine. But he also saw its dirt.

"I thought you superstars were always late."

Colton turned around. His A&R guy, Archie Lovett, walked in with a cocky grin and a Starbucks cup. A&R stood for artist and repertoire, and it was the division at every record label that handled the artists and their music. Archie had been his A&R guy from the start, and it was his job to act as a liaison between Colton's team and the label.

"Good to see you, brother," Archie said. They shared a backslapping half hug. "I just about forgot how ugly you are."

Colton flipped him off, and Archie laughed as Colton knew he would. Their relationship had always been like this—as much a friendship as a professional one. It was one of the things Colton had always loved about this label. It felt like a family. The downside of that kind of relationship was that Colton felt like he was disappointing a friend when he didn't live up to their expectations.

His manager, Buck Bragg, walked in next, with a smile that conveyed calm confidence but a grip on a bottle of antacids that said he'd had a rough day so far. He quickly greeted Archie before joining Colton at the windows. "I don't think you've ever beaten me here since that first contract."

Colton shoved his hands in the pockets of his jeans. "I haven't been this nervous since then."

"We're going to get things worked out," Buck said. "Don't worry."

"*Don't worry?* What the hell does that mean?"

Buck shrugged. "It means *Don't worry.*"

"Except you've never told me not to worry before, so now I'm officially shitting my pants."

The drumbeat of footsteps behind them brought them both around to stare at the door as label executives walked in single file, each carrying leather folios, cellphones, and iPads. The last to walk in was the most important, Vice President Saul Shepard. A former college wrestler, Saul had stumbled into the music industry after a brief career as an entertainment attorney. He was intimidating without trying, gave nothing away with his expressions, and shook hands with more force than was necessary. The man was three inches shorter than Colton, but Colton always felt like he had to look up when speaking to him. Today, he seemed like a giant.

"Good to see you," Saul said, shaking Colton's hand with a finger-crushing squeeze. "Glad you could make it in to get this thing figured out."

Nervous sweat pooled under Colton's arms. *Get this thing figured out?* What the hell did that mean? Before he could ask, though, Saul directed everyone to sit with a stern, "Let's get started."

Buck gave Colton a reassuring pat on the back as they walked to the table, but it had the opposite effect. As soon as they sat down, Colton held out his palm. "Give me some of those."

Buck dumped a half-dozen chalky tablets into Colton's hand.

Saul cleared his throat. Everyone else sat. Executives opened their notebooks. Archie projected something onto the screen behind Saul. And not a single one of them met Colton's eyes.

"Just so we're on the same page as we get started, let's review where we stand," Saul said.

The twinge of alarm became a knot in his stomach. That wasn't the kind of language someone used when they were about to congratulate an artist for their future chart-topper.

"Archie, take us through Colton's latest contract and where we're at."

What? Why the hell were they reviewing his contract? Colton's eyes narrowed as the screen displayed a bullet point of the major terms of his last deal. "I'm sorry, but what the hell is happening here?"

"I'm sorry?" Saul asked.

"I'm well aware of the particulars of my contract, and so is everyone else in this room. What are you leading up to?"

Archie cleared his throat. Saul leaned back in his chair and smoothed his tie. "Colton, we are all invested in your success."

Invested in your success. A phrase that somehow conveyed the opposite. "Stop dancing around the damn point. Did you like the new stuff or not?"

"No."

The word was like a broken string in the middle of a song. A sour note followed by the sting of the thin wire against your arm. Next to him, Buck shot him a practiced look of *Don't freak out.*

Too late. How the fuck was he supposed to not freak out over that? Colton's mouth was suddenly dry, and he wished he'd taken them up on their repeated offers of water. "Would you mind telling me what you don't like?"

Buck tried to interject. "Can I have a minute to talk to Colton—"

"It's boring," Saul said.

"*Boring?*" Indignation wrenched the word from Colton's mouth like a pair of pliers.

"Colton," Buck said, setting his hand on Colton's arm. "Let me do the talking."

"No," Colton said. "I want to know what *boring* means."

"Colton, you've always stood out as a distinctive talent in a sea of long-haired wannabes. But this—" Saul shook his head. "What you gave us sounds like you plugged some angsty keywords into songwriting software and added a few riffs for fun."

The air whooshed from his lungs as if Saul had literally punched him in the stomach. He must have made a noise because Buck gave him a look that said, *Shut up before you blow up your entire career.*

Colton wheeled his cushy leather chair away from the table and stood. "I've given you everything. For twelve years, I've produced hit record after hit record. I've brought in untold millions of dollars to this label, sacrificed everything—"

"But what have you done for us today?" Saul interrupted.

"Excuse me?"

"Your success is our success," Saul continued. "But that means your failure is also our failure. And we cannot afford for you to put out something that is going to lose money. And to put it bluntly, there is not a single hit on this demo."

Colton pinned Archie with a glare. "Did you know about this?"

"I did."

Betrayal stole what was left of his oxygen.

"Saul is right," Archie said. "I'm sorry, Colton. It pains me more than you know to say this to you. But what you've given us isn't going to work. And I think you know that."

"Airtime matters," Saul said, as if Colton didn't already know that. "There's nothing on this demo that is going to get the airtime necessary to break into the top five."

"Okay, let's dial this down a notch," Buck said. "Colton, sit down and let's talk this out."

He crossed his arms. "What's there to talk about?"

"We're not saying that these are not salvageable," Archie said in a placating tone.

Colton rolled his eyes. "Gee, thanks."

"What are you suggesting?" Buck asked. "Because Colton is very passionate about his songs, and if you're going to start dictating what an artist can and can't say in his music, then we've got a bigger problem."

"It's not what you're saying," Archie said. "It's how you're saying it."

"How do you want me to say it?" Colton's voice rasped against his dry throat. Because he already knew the answer. They wanted easy. Meaningless. They wanted the barefoot, beer-guzzling beach bum. They wanted the country bro, the one thing Colton couldn't be anymore.

"Let's talk about solutions," Archie offered.

The only solution Colton could think of was to take these songs and go indie. But, of course, he couldn't do that. Because going indie meant breaking his contract, which meant returning millions in advances. Indie meant financing his own tours, his own recordings, his own distribution. It meant negotiating his own terms with streaming services. It meant money. Colton was rich, but there were a lot of people who depended on him now. Too many to risk it.

"Colton, what do you think about that?"

He blinked out of his thoughts. "About what?"

"We have some new songwriters we want you to work with."

Colton ran his hands over his hair and bowed his head. It had finally come to this, then.

"We think you're going to like them," Archie was saying. "You know I wouldn't suggest anyone to you that I hadn't personally vetted. They're excellent at taking raw material and crafting it into something better without losing the originality of the demos."

"I thought you didn't like the originality of the demos."

Archie ignored the petty remark. "We're going to give them the songs today, with your permission, and we can set up studio time after the New Year to start recording."

"What if I say no?"

Saul answered, "Then you'll be in violation of the terms of your contract."

"Just like that? Write the same old shit, or I'm out of the family?"

"This isn't a family," Saul said. "This is a business."

"For fuck's sake," Buck snapped. "Was that necessary?"

"Just making it clear that this is a business. A business that has invested millions of dollars into a product, and we expect that product to be delivered." Saul stood up, signaling an end to the meeting.

It felt like the end of something else to Colton. His career.

"Take some time to think about it," Saul said.

"How long?" Buck asked.

"We need an answer by January first."

"What?" Colton shouted. "You're giving me less than a month to figure out the future of my entire career?"

"You've had two years."

Colton stormed out. Behind him, he heard Buck trying to settle nerves and reassure Archie. Colton didn't wait for him. He bypassed the elevators and took the stairs. Buck caught up with him anyway in the parking garage.

"Colton, wait."

Colton set his hands on his hips. "Did you know?"

"Know what?"

"That they didn't like the new songs?"

"No." Buck sighed. "But I had an inkling. When Archie didn't respond, I wondered if maybe there were some conversations happening behind the scenes."

"And you never thought to warn me?"

"I didn't want to worry you unnecessarily."

"Instead, you let me be ambushed."

"I'm sorry. I was hoping I was wrong."

Colton turned away and stared at nothing.

"Do you remember what I told you after that first meeting when we signed your first contract?" Buck asked. "I said there would come a time when the realities of this industry would start to steal the shine from the promises of it. So I need you to be honest with me. Do you still want to do this?"

Colton whipped his gaze so quickly to his manager that he swore a bone cracked in his neck. "Still do what?"

"This," Buck said, gesturing vaguely at nothing and everything. "Make music. Tour. Be a rock star."

"Are you high? Of course I still want to do this!"

"Then give me something to take to them. Anything."

"I gave them something. They threw it back."

"Then work with the songwriters."

"What's the alternative?" The question was dry and sour on his tongue.

"You tell them you want out."

"Break my contract?"

Buck's answer was a blank stare.

"I don't want out." His mouth was dry as he dug the keys from his pocket. "Tell them I'll do it. I'll give them exactly what they want."

He stormed away.

"Where are you going?" Buck yelled.

"To find my fucking muse."

CHAPTER THREE

The road to Homestead was long and winding, lined with farm fields, stone fences, and bad memories.

Everywhere Gretchen looked was Winthrop land, where generations of her family had lived and built an empire. As she pulled into the mile-long driveway that would take her to the corporate building, she passed the original house, the place where it all began when an Irish immigrant named Cornelius Donley sold his first batch of whiskey in a roadside stand. The farmhouse was now a tourist spot on the whiskey trail and had been expanded over the years into a tasting room. She imagined Uncle Jack inside, charming the ladies as he pushed the whiskey. On a whim, she whipped into the lot. She had fifteen minutes before her meeting with Evan, and a dose of Jack's humor was just what she needed to prepare.

Gretchen's high-heeled boots crunched on the white gravel of the parking lot until she reached the original cobblestone sidewalk to the porch. The tasting room was technically in the big red barn next to the farmhouse, but visitors had to enter through the front door of the house itself. In warmer months, tourists could sit in one of the many rocking chairs on the wide wraparound porch to wait for room at the bar, but in December, most people chose to wait inside.

The porch was now decorated for Christmas in a simple, old-fashioned style, as if welcoming visitors to step back in time. Swaths of fresh garland draped elegantly along the roof, and a large fresh wreath with a plain red bow hung from the peak of the gable. Each rocking chair was adorned with plaid blankets and pillows. Flanking the door were two potted evergreens decorated with nothing more than strings of fresh cranberries.

Inside, Gretchen was greeted by the soft murmur of tourists wandering the rooms of the first floor of the house, where sepia-toned photos of the family going back to Cornelius Donley himself lined the walls in mismatched black frames. In the back of the house, the old kitchen had been preserved and turned into an exhibit describing life in the 1870s. One of the most prized artifacts was one of the original barrels Cornelius used for his first batch, now protected within a climate-controlled glass case. A dozen tourists were gathered in the kitchen when Gretchen walked through, some silently reading the information placards as others tried to lean closer to read the faded inscription on the barrel.

"Why does it say Donley's Dare?" a woman asked. The man next to her shrugged.

"Because that was the name of the original whiskey," Gretchen said.

Everyone in the room turned to look at her. "I don't think that's true," a man said. "Where did you hear that?"

"From my grandfather."

"Did he used to work here?" a woman asked.

"You could say that."

Anyone else from the family probably would have been recognized on sight as a member of the Winthrop clan. Gretchen was never recognized. Her photo appeared exactly once in the entire house and tasting room, and it was from when she was fifteen years old.

"I still don't think that's true," the man said quietly as Gretchen walked on. She didn't care to correct him.

Outside, a long, paved walkway took visitors from the house to the tasting room. It, too, had been decorated for Christmas. A collection of rustic antique lanterns lined the path. At night, the candles within would be lit, casting the whole place in a soft, warm glow for visitors as they approached the barn. A Google search of romantic spots in Nashville would include this very pathway near the top ten. At least once a day between now and the end of the holidays, someone would stop on this walkway and propose to their partner.

Inside the barn, the old-world ambiance continued with rough wooden floors and a large wrought iron chandelier, which was now draped with more fresh greenery and cranberries. A twelve-foot Christmas tree covered in white lights and red ribbon was the only other decoration in the tasting room.

Every tall table was filled with visitors, each sampling flights of the company's various whiskey offerings. More tourists circled the barn. And that's where she found Uncle Jack, right where she knew he'd be. Flirting with the line of women who flocked to him with interested smiles. He wore a pair of jeans and a T-shirt with the company logo. This was his domain. Gretchen's father—Jack's older brother—controlled the business side of the empire, but Jack was most at home here, surrounded by the craft itself.

She inched closer to the bar and elbowed her way through a group of women who had "fiftieth birthday party" written all over them.

"Hey, Uncle Jack."

He looked up and grinned. "Well, this is a surprise." He walked over to his left and lifted the hinged counter so he could come around. She walked into his embrace and breathed in the comforting scent of wood barrels and spice that always clung to him.

"What're you doing here?" he asked, pulling back.

She grimaced. "I've been summoned to see Evan."

"For what?"

"No idea. I was hoping you knew."

Jack shook his head. "Not a clue." He started patting her sides as if frisking her. "You got any weapons?"

"Just my killer wit."

"That's my girl," he said with a final pat.

"That I am."

He made the sad expression she'd come to know as Jack's regret face, and not for the first time, she wished she knew why he'd never married and had children of his own. He would've been a great father. Instead, he showered all that love and attention on her.

She glanced around. "It's crazy busy in here."

"Christmas tourism." He shrugged, then nodded to an open stool. "You got time to sit?"

Gretchen glanced at her watch. "Just a couple of minutes."

He took the stool next to her. "How's the clinic?"

"Good."

He tilted his head. "*Good?*"

"What?"

"The only time I worry about you is when you're not bitching about something."

She shrugged. "It's good."

Jack shook his head again. "You're not leaving until you tell me what's going on."

He could always see right through her. Gretchen sucked in a deep breath and let it out quickly. "I've been offered a job in D.C." She quickly explained the job and everything else Jorge had told her.

His eyes flickered with concern before he reeled it back in. "Are you going to go out for the interview?"

"No. I mean . . ." She shook her head. "No."

"You don't sound sure."

"I am."

"Then why are you telling me about it?"

Jack was the only person in the world she could be truly honest with, so she decided to unburden herself. "I wonder if I'm actually making a difference here."

"Of course you are."

"But for every client I help, there are ten more I can't. It's this never-ending cycle of bullshit and cruelty, and the only way to change it is to change the laws."

As she talked, he nodded, his expression pensive. "Sounds like an incredible opportunity, Gretchen."

Something akin to panic shot through her. He was supposed to be talking her out of it. "You think I should consider it?"

"I think you should always consider opportunities when they come your way."

She forced a grin. "You sound eager to get rid of me."

"You *are* a pain in the ass."

She looked at her watch again. "I gotta run."

They both stood, and Jack pulled her back in for another hug. "Keep me posted, okay?"

"I will." She kissed his bearded cheek and turned around, the weight of his gaze heavy on her back as she walked out.

She drove to the corporate building farther up the road and parked in a visitor spot near the entrance, where a group of tourists in winter hats and gloves listened to a company tour guide explain their history. Gretchen waved as she ducked around the group. The tour guide blinked as if she recognized Gretchen's face but couldn't quite place her. She got that a lot. Any other member of the Winthrop family would've been treated like royalty, but Gretchen barely earned a second glance. Her reception wasn't any warmer on the executive floor. Evan's secretary, Sarah, greeted Gretchen with about as much enthusiasm as a museum docent facing a group of sticky, hyper kindergartners. She'd only been there a year but had quickly adopted Evan's attitude toward Gretchen.

"His meeting is running late," she said, barely glancing up from her computer. "I'll let you know when you can go in."

"He's expecting me," Gretchen said.

Sarah offered a brittle smile.

Gretchen bit back the hot retort on the tip of her tongue and instead sat down in one of the leather club chairs that flanked a large window overlooking the lush landscaping behind the building. Winthrop land stretched as far as she could see. Dense woods hid her parents' home and, a little farther away, Evan's house. Jack and her other brother, Blake, had homes on the other side of the property. There was land there set aside for Gretchen, too, but she would never use it. She wasn't going to waste money on a monstrous mansion when she could use it to help people instead.

A half hour ticked by before Sarah finally looked up again. Gretchen could've sworn her lips actually pulled tight into a disapproving grimace as she peered over the top of her reading glasses. "He's ready for you now."

Gretchen stood without a word to the woman and stomped down the hallway. The plush carpet absorbed her footsteps, which only annoyed her more. She at least deserved an angry *click-clack, click-clack* after being forced to wait.

"Gretchen, come in. Sorry for the wait." Her brother stood up behind the mahogany desk, his reflection blurry in the shiny surface like a wispy ghost of the men who'd sat there before him. He had the same lean build and imposing height of their father and grandfather, but that was where the similarities ended. He brought none of the light and laughter that had once filled this office when her grandfather was still alive. And her father's capacity for at least making people feel welcome had apparently skipped a generation when it came to Evan. He exuded cold severity.

"Thanks for seeing me," Evan said, smoothing his tie. "I know you're busy."

"I am. Don't ever summon me like this again, Evan, and then make me sit outside for a half hour."

"Sorry," he said, sounding anything but. "It couldn't be helped."

"You said this was important." Gretchen adopted a businesslike tone, the one she used on judges and government attorneys who thought they could railroad her.

Evan rounded his desk and headed toward a wet bar against the opposite wall. "Thirsty?"

"No." She sat in one of the chairs facing his and began to shake her foot back and forth with impatience.

"Well, I could use something." He took his time, picking out ice cubes from a waiting ice bucket and dropping them into a glass. Then he removed the stopper from a crystal decanter and poured a hefty splash of whiskey over the ice.

Evan finally turned around and walked to the front of the desk so he could lean against it and look down at her. She lifted her eyebrows. "Am I supposed to guess what this is about, or . . . ?"

He took a long sip before answering. "Ronald Washburn is going to be leaving the foundation board after the holidays."

Gretchen schooled her features in something akin to polite disinterest, but her heart had suddenly found the pace of a squirrel crossing the road. "What does that have to do with me?"

"It means there will be an open seat." He lifted his eyebrow at her as she absorbed the information, because Evan couldn't just come right out and say what he wanted to say. He had to play mind games with her.

"And you're offering it to me?"

"It's not entirely up to me. The board will need to approve your appointment. But if you're interested—"

"You know I am." She might not have chosen to join the Winthrop corporation, but the family charitable foundation was another matter. It had always been the one thing she wanted to be part of. But every time a seat had opened up before, she'd been told that it wasn't the right time. She'd heard every possible excuse.

"There are legalities, of course," Evan said, "so you'll need to file some conflict-of-interest paperwork for tax reasons."

"I know what I have to do." Her voice came out in a breathless rush as she perched on the edge of her seat.

"Probably better than I do," Evan said with one of those patronizing nods that he seemed to reserve for her. As if he were still just humoring her and her silly little law career. But she didn't care this time. He was finally giving her a chance. The foundation oversaw millions of dollars in annual charitable gifts. Maybe she could finally start to use some of those gifts for the causes that mattered to her and people like her clients.

Gretchen stood. "I'll fill out all the paperwork and send it to Sarah. Do I need to do anything else?"

"For the board seat? No. But there is something else I'd like to talk to you about." Evan motioned for her to sit again.

Gretchen hesitated but then slowly returned to her chair.

"I understand you know Colton Wheeler."

What. The. Fuck.

A foghorn wouldn't have been as loud or alarming as the inexplicable mention of the man she had spent the better part of a year pretending not to think about. His name caused a wicked splash and drenched her in bewildered panic, as if she were floating in a swimming pool and someone dropped a piano in it. No one was supposed to know about them. No one.

"I—why?" she finally stammered, throat dry.

"We want to sign him as our next brand ambassador."

She shook her head, mostly to clear it. "I'm not following."

"He's not an easy get. He's notoriously picky about who he works with."

Understanding began to settle in her chest like a bad case of bronchitis. The sweet thrill of landing a spot on the foundation board became sour disappointment.

Evan continued, oblivious to her growing discomfort. "He's the perfect face of the new CAW."

The new CAW? What the hell was he talking about?

"I've already had marketing put together an entire promotional concept for him to consider. If we can get him, we will grow this company's bottom line further than anyone ever imagined."

She finally found her voice. "You want me to talk to him."

"We think he might be more open to an official negotiation if the initial offer comes from a friend."

"We're not friends." It was all she could manage to say, and it was at least true. They *weren't* friends. They'd had one amazing night of hot passion after Mack and Liv's wedding, but that was it. She'd ignored all his calls and texts afterward. And, by some miracle, she'd managed to avoid him since then despite their many mutual friends.

"Acquaintances, then," Evan was saying.

Gretchen sank into the back of the chair. "I can't believe you."

"What do you mean?"

"You offered me a spot on the board just to soften me up for this, didn't you?"

He dismissed her words with a flick of his hand. "The timing is a coincidence."

"And I fell for it. I actually thought—" No. She wasn't going to finish that sentence. She wasn't going to give him the satisfaction of knowing that after all these years, he still had the power to reel her in like a fish on a hook. She stood on shaky legs and hated her body for the weakness she still felt around him.

He laughed. "Are you actually suggesting that I somehow masterminded a vacancy on the foundation board just to get you to have a single conversation with someone?"

"I wouldn't put it past you."

He shook his head and made a noise of disapproval. She'd been hearing that noise all her life, and it still managed to sting.

"For God's sake, Gretchen. You've been wanting to take a more active role in the family foundation for years. This is your chance to prove you're ready. If I was wrong, then I'm sorry for wasting your time."

She pointed at him. "Don't do that. Don't act like you're doing me some big favor for making me earn a place that should be mine by birthright."

"Gretchen," he sighed again. "Why does everything with you devolve into hysterics?"

"Stop. Your gaslighting doesn't work on me anymore, Evan."

"Gaslighting? That's a big word."

"It's what you've always done. You accuse me of being hysterical just to get a rise out of me so you can prove your own false point about how I'm some kind of rebellious teenager."

"It's not like you've never given me a reason for that impression."

She swallowed back the sting of self-recrimination. "I'm not that person anymore. I haven't been for a long time."

Evan stood, apparently feeling that he'd won this round in their unending boxing match. "Gretchen, you know I have always admired your passion."

She snorted.

He spread his hands. "Fine. I haven't always admired your passion. Your little teenage rebellions cost us a lot of money and embarrassment in the past. But I thought you had at least grown out of some of your more radical tendencies. You should be grateful."

"For what? Being born?"

Something vicious flickered through his eyes. "Yes, dammit. You were born into one of the most prominent families in Tennessee. The whole damn country, for God's sake. You never wanted for anything."

Except respect and acceptance.

Evan let out a long, weary sigh. "I don't have time for this. Are you going to talk to him, or not?"

Gretchen's pride told her to flip him off and walk out. The starving puppy inside her spoke instead. "When do you need an answer?"

"By the end of the year would be preferable. If at all possible, we'd like to get this squared away in time for the annual gala."

"That's less than a month away," she protested. The family hosted a fundraising gala for the foundation every year just before Christmas.

"Then you'd better work fast," Evan said, returning to his seat, a dismissal if she'd ever seen one.

Gritting her teeth, Gretchen turned and stomped toward the door. She didn't know who she was angrier with—Evan for putting her in this position, or herself for going along with it. But she was going to do it. She was going to willingly talk to the man she'd sworn to avoid for the rest of her life just to prove something to her brother.

Turns out, she really was that pathetic.

"Gretchen."

She turned around against her better judgment.

Evan smiled, and it sent a shiver down her spine. "It's nice doing business with you."

CHAPTER FOUR

Old Joe's had all the ambience of an armpit, but the dank, musty pub was one of the only places in the entire state of Tennessee where Colton could sit in peace and listen to some music without someone exclaiming, "Holy shit, you're Colton Wheeler!"

In here, no one gave a shit who he was. This was a locals-only bar, a songwriter's bar, right down to a scuffed stage wedged into a small corner, an unremarkable address far from Honky Tonk Row, and a grizzled bartender named Duff who'd met everyone and was impressed by no one. Especially Colton. The first time he walked in a year ago, Duff plunked a light beer he hadn't requested in front of him and said, "There's only two reasons someone like you starts hanging out at a place like this. You're hiding from something or you're looking for something. Which is it?"

Tonight, he was definitely hiding.

Duff's back was turned when Colton sat down, and the man pretended to not hear Colton behind him.

"You gonna give me a beer, or what?" Colton finally said.

"Fuck off, princess."

That was Duff's nickname for him. Colton no longer reacted to it. "It's looking festive in here," he said instead.

It was a lie. Duff's attempt at decorating was more terrifying and depressing than cheery. The fake wreath on the door had faded from green to gray, and there was enough dust on its bow to cause an asthma attack. Limp tinsel that had long ago lost its shine framed the dusty mirrored shelves where Duff kept "the good stuff," as he called it. His standards and Colton's about what constituted "good stuff" were apparently quite different, because the only bottle Colton recognized was a brand of vodka his grandfather used to affectionately call "rotgut." He'd tried it once and puked for three days.

Duff finally turned around. He grabbed a bottle from under the counter, twisted off the cap, and set it in front of Colton.

"I don't drink Budweiser," Colton said.

"You do tonight."

This was part of their game. Duff was one of the only people on the planet, aside from his friends, who didn't fawn over him. Colton tipped back the bottle and choked down the beer. "You got any peanuts or anything? I'm starving."

"Does this look like a fucking restaurant?"

"You know, some could argue that it's irresponsible for a bar to offer liquor without anything to soak it up."

Duff turned away for a moment. When he returned, he had a bowl of lemon wedges. "Suck on that."

The place was deserted tonight, even by Old Joe's standards. Colton was the only person at the bar, and the only other two people in the place were huddled together in a back booth as if they were conspiring to rob the joint. On the stage, a young man with longish hair and a well-loved six string was warming up. Colton had never seen him here before, but the way he ran through a complicated fingerpick with ease told Colton that he at least knew his way around a guitar.

"Who's the kid?"

"Name's J. T. Tucker."

"For fuck's sake, please tell me that's made up."

"People used to say the same thing about you."

Colton flipped him off. Duff was right, though. A lot of people assumed Colton Wheeler wasn't his real name. It was too perfect for a country star to be anything but a stage name, but it was real. He was named after his great-grandfather.

"How was the meeting today?" Duff suddenly asked.

Colton spit-choked. "How the hell do you know about that?"

"I know everyone and everything in this town."

"It was fine. Super."

"Bullshit. They told you to get your shit together or get the fuck out."

Colton pointed with indignation. "That is *not* what they said."

Duff shook his head. "Keep telling yourself that."

On the stage, the kid adjusted the microphone and winced at the screechy feedback. Eager to get the attention off his own career woes, Colton nodded toward the stage. "He got any talent?"

"None. I just let any old idiot with a guitar wander in off the street."

"Where'd you find him?"

Duff actually answered without sarcasm for once. "He found me. Sent me a demo and asked if he could play."

J. T. shifted nervously in his chair and then spoke to his nonexistent audience. "This is, uh, this is something I wrote myself."

Those words might normally have made Colton cringe, but if

Duff had cleared him, the kid had to have something worth listening to. Within seconds, his assumption was confirmed. The quiet voice that had spoken into the microphone unfurled into a deep, clear tenor, and he used it to convey the kind of emotion that normally took performers years to perfect. Colton couldn't help it. He breathed out a slow *Damn* and leaned on the bar.

The kid was pure, raw talent. Colton looked back at Duff. "How old is he?"

"Eighteen."

A year younger than Colton was when he had started playing in bars around Nashville. It took three years of paying his dues, working his way up to bigger and bigger gigs, before he finally got noticed by the right people. Something told him it wouldn't take that long for J. T. "Who's his manager?"

"Doesn't have one. He's not sure he wants to go that route."

"He's thinking of staying indie?" More and more artists were abandoning record labels in favor of producing and selling their own music. They could maintain creative control and earn more profits without having to first earn out an advance from a label. It was the dirty little secret of the music industry. Artists were paid an advance on an album, and few ever sold enough to pay off the advance in order to start earning royalties. So it made indie seem great.

The downside was that you were also responsible for all the up-front costs. The production. The distribution. All costs associated with gigs. Hell, even the album artwork. Few artists got rich anymore from the sale of their songs. The money came from touring, endorsement deals, and all the other extras of being a rock star. Most indie musicians never got big enough for that. But not every artist wanted that either. Some were content to just make music. Nashville was full of singers and songwriters whose work ended up being performed by someone else.

But this kid?

This kid could go places.

"Reminds me of you at that age."

Colton tore his gaze from the stage to stare in shock at Duff. "Was that a compliment?"

"Don't let it go to your head. I know talent. He has it like you once did."

"I'm still talented."

"Lotta good it does you anymore."

"What the fuck does that mean?"

The door creaked open to the right of the bar, and Colton would've paid no attention to it if not for the surprised look on Duff's face. "Now that's something you don't see in here very often."

Colton glanced over his shoulder. And fumbled his beer. It landed on the bar with a dull thud and then tipped on its side. Beer sloshed onto his jeans, and he jumped back with a yelp. Duff wheezed out a laugh and tossed a rag at him. "Never thought I'd see you flustered over a woman."

"Fuck off," Colton said under his breath, but Duff was right. He was flustered. Because standing just inside the door, looking as out of place as a metalhead at a Luke Bryan concert, was Gretchen Winthrop. The only woman who'd ever flustered him this much.

Her eyes were pinched at the corners, as if they were adjusting to the darkness. She wore a black wool coat over a sensible black suit, and she carried a scuffed leather messenger bag on one shoulder. He had the split-second thought that maybe she was lost and had wandered in by sheer coincidence to ask for directions. But then she turned her gaze directly on him, and he realized she was here on purpose. She was here for him. Colton's heart became a snare drum.

Gretchen adjusted the strap of her bag and started toward him. The heels of her boots drummed a purposeful beat on the rough hardwood floor. He'd barely had time to regain his senses before she stopped next to him and said with absolutely no fanfare, "I was told I would find you here."

"Who told you that?" Great. Real smooth. The woman who'd been a permanent resident in his dreams for a year announced that she was looking for him, and that was the best greeting he could come up with?

She stared at the front of his jeans. "Having some trouble there?"

He glanced down and realized the beer had spilled directly on his crotch in a wide dark circle, as if he'd pissed himself. "It's beer," he stammered. He grabbed the rag Duff had tossed him and began wiping madly at the spot, which did absolutely nothing except make things worse because he was actively rubbing his dick in front of her.

"Christ," Duff muttered. "Stop before you embarrass yourself." Duff then lifted his chin at Gretchen in the universal bartender language for *What'll you have?*

"Got any CAW 1869?"

Duff's eyebrows met his hairline. "That's a hard whiskey for a woman."

Gretchen shrugged. "What can I say? It's in my blood."

Colton and Duff looked at each other with equally stunned expressions of *Is she for real?* Colton finally cleared his throat and dropped the wet rag on the puddle of beer on the counter. "Duff here doesn't believe in anything of quality. He prefers to send you to the hospital by poisoning you the old-fashioned way."

Duff smirked. "Wait here."

Wait here? Colton watched Duff disappear through a door to what Colton always assumed was the entrance to Hell. Where the fuck was he going?

"So, how've you been?"

Blinking, Colton looked down at Gretchen. "Fine. You?" Jesus. What the hell was wrong with him? Where was his swagger, his stage presence? He leaned a hand on the bar. "You're looking good."

Her face remained expressionless. "Thank you."

The door to Hell reopened, and Duff came out with a bottle of the exact whiskey Gretchen had asked for.

Colton made a whiny noise. "What the fuck, man? You've been torturing me with weasel piss while hiding shit like that back there?"

Duff plunked the bottle down. "This is only for people I like."

"Single shot, please," Gretchen said, not even bothering to hide her smile, which was so dazzling that Colton forgot for a moment that he'd just been insulted.

Duff whistled appreciatively. "Yes, ma'am."

Ma'am? Who the hell was this man? Not that Colton could blame Duff. Gretchen had the same effect on him. He forgot who he was around her. As Duff poured the whiskey, Colton attempted to regain some semblance of his dignity. "What, uh, what brings you by?"

"I was hoping to talk to you."

"Yeah? Well, here I am, honey." Colton spread his arms wide.

Duff snorted and set the whiskey in front of Gretchen. "You're too good for him."

"Can we sit?" Gretchen picked up the glass and nodded toward a booth.

"Yes. I mean, yeah, sure." He tried to wink, but he was pretty sure it looked more like he had something in his eye.

Duff muttered something unkind and turned away with a shake of his head. Colton picked up what was left of his beer and followed Gretchen to an empty booth. If Duff hadn't been watching, Colton would've pounded his own fist into his face. What the hell was wrong with him? But more importantly, why was Gretchen suddenly here and wanting to talk to him?

He waited until she was seated before taking the opposite bench facing the stage. After setting her bag on the seat and slipping the coat from her shoulders, she lifted her whiskey in the air. "To cheating, stealing, fighting, and drinking." Then she shot back the whiskey with the ease of a distiller.

Colton stared wide-eyed and open-mouthed. He glanced at the bar and found Duff with the same expression.

"What?" Gretchen said, setting her glass down. "It's an old Irish toast that my grandfather used to say."

"If you're here to propose to me, I accept."

There, finally, the slip of a smile. It lifted the corners of her mouth just enough for him to know it was genuine. But it disappeared quickly, and she straightened in her seat. "I *am* here with a proposal of sorts, to be honest."

Colton slung his arm over the back of the seat. "I'm all ears, darlin'."

"How would you like to be the new face of Carraig Aonair Whiskey?"

His brain screeched to a halt. "Huh?"

"I know this is probably not the way you're accustomed to

being approached about things like this, but my family asked if I would make the initial proposal to you and—"

"Your *family*?" But even as he said it, his brain whirred into action again and started connecting all the floating dots. The CAW 1869. The way she took her shot. The Irish toast. The unexpected visit. The *It's in my blood*.

Holy shit. Colton's spine slumped against the back of the booth. "You're one of *those* Winthrops?"

"It's not something I advertise."

"Why the hell not?"

"Because I'm embarrassed by them."

He let out an incredulous laugh that sounded unhinged. It died as quickly as her smile. "So, let me get this straight." He swiped a hand across his jaw. "I don't hear from you for a year despite my best efforts to get you to talk to me—"

"This has nothing to do with that night."

That night. Jesus. That's all it was to her? "—and suddenly you walk into a bar that almost no one knows I come to and, just like that, ask if I want to, what, endorse your family's company?"

"That's a decent summary, yes."

"Wow."

"I can't give you any details, because you'd have to negotiate that with whatever people normally handle that sort of stuff for you, but—"

"Stop."

Her mouth closed.

"I—" Colton shook his head and dragged both hands over his hair. "What the hell, Gretchen?"

"I'm not sure how to answer that."

Colton leaned forward, arms on the table, and lowered his

voice. "You have to be kidding me. You ignore me for *a year,* and this is what I get from you?"

Her shoulders tensed. "I'd rather not bring our previous entanglement into this."

"Well, sorry, sweetheart, but I'm dragging it front and center. And for fuck's sake . . . *previous entanglement*?"

"How would you prefer I refer to it?"

"How about what it was? A night of amazing sex and the start of something with serious potential?"

She looked at her hands. The only other sign of discomfort was a hard swallow. "I'm sorry," she said after a moment, finally raising her gaze again. "That was a mistake."

"Two minutes ago, I would have disagreed with you."

She had the decency to flush. "I didn't mean to insult you."

"Well, congratulations. You did it without even trying."

"Look." She sucked in a breath. "I'm here because my brother asked me to talk to you and gauge your level of interest."

"That would be zero."

Gretchen bit her lip, and an unwelcome flashback intruded on the conversation. Her standing nearly naked in front of him, chewing her bottom lip, trying to explain why they could never work.

She swallowed. "If you're only saying no because of our . . . that night, can I at least convince you to listen to an official proposal from the company?"

Colton grabbed his beer and sucked down the last warm remnants. God, he hated Budweiser. He set the bottle down harder than he intended. Tense silence throbbed between them as he tried and failed to think of something to say. Un-fucking-believable. Could this day get any worse?

On the stage, J. T. started to play the intro melody to a classic, "River" by Joni Mitchell. "This is my favorite Christmas song," J. T. said before launching into the lyrics.

Gretchen made a disgusted noise. "This is *not* a Christmas song."

"Of course it is," Colton fired back, not because he cared but because he was pissed off and arguing with her seemed like a good idea. "The word *Christmas* is in the first line."

"Just because the word *Christmas* appears in the song doesn't make it a Christmas song. It just happens to take place at Christmas."

"Which makes it a goddamn Christmas song."

Her eyes sparked. "Turning this song into a Christmas song dilutes its message."

"Oh, please, enlighten me."

"The entire song is an apology. It's a wistful homage to the bittersweet loneliness that follows the end of a relationship."

He blinked. That was actually deep, but he'd be damned if he'd show her he was impressed. "Loneliness at *Christmas*," he countered.

She waved her hand. "Don't trivialize it."

"Is there something trivial about Christmas music?"

"Everything about Christmas, or the way we celebrate it at least, is trivial."

Okay, those were fighting words. He leaned into the battle. "I love Christmas. It's my favorite time of year."

"Of course it is."

"Enlighten me again."

She shrugged. "You're happiness and frivolity personified."

He sucked his teeth to cover the sting of those words. "Them's some big words for a dumb hick like me."

"Stop pretending to be insulted. I never insinuated you were dumb or a hick."

"Oh, trust me, honey. I heard your insinuation loud and clear when you ran out of my hotel room like I was some kind of diseased reptile."

Her eyes flashed again, this time with shame. That should've been his cue to shut up, but instead he plowed forward.

"What was the problem? Were you too embarrassed to let people know you'd lowered yourself to sleeping with happiness and frivolity personified? Is the great and powerful Winthrop name too good to be sullied by the likes of a clichéd country bro? Or was this your plan all along? Fuck me and keep it in your pocket until you needed me for something?"

Her face fell, and in the brief second when her mask slipped away, he saw that his words had wounded her. Deeply. He really should've shut up. "Gretchen," he breathed, pinching his eyes shut. "I'm sorry. I didn't mean that."

He opened his eyes at the sound of her sliding out of the booth. "I can see this is going nowhere," she said tightly.

"Wait," he said, reaching for her hand.

She jerked it from his reach and instead grabbed her coat and bag. "I'll tell my brother you're not interested."

Her heels sounded an angry retreat as she stormed away. A cold blast of air chilled the bar as she threw open the door and left.

"Fuck," Colton breathed, once again squeezing his eyes shut. He needed to go after her, but when he opened his eyes to get out, Duff blocked his way.

"You handled that well," Duff said.

Colton glared up at him. "Let me out."

"Best to leave it be at this point."

"How much did you hear?"

Duff dropped into the seat Gretchen had just vacated. "Enough to know you're an asshole."

No point arguing that fact.

Duff crossed his arms. "You know what your problem is?"

"I'm sure you're going to delight in telling me."

"You still don't know the answer to my question."

Colton rolled his eyes. "Not this shit again."

"You're unhappy, Colton."

The use of his real name—not *princess* or *dipshit* or any other derogatory nickname—caught his attention as much as the sharp edge of the words. "Didn't you hear, Duff? I'm happiness personified."

"Happiness is the expectation that weighs you down."

Okay, that was it. He'd had enough bullshit for one day. He slid out of the booth, dug his wallet from his back pocket, and dropped some bills on the table. "Merry Christmas," he grumbled before turning away.

He heard the slow creak of Duff sliding from the booth. "We all wear the chains we forged in life, princess. You need to figure out what yours is made of before it's too late."

CHAPTER FIVE

The problem with having such a close group of buddies is that they were unapologetic about calling you out on your bullshit.

Colton should've known he wouldn't be able to evade questions when he met up with the guys the next morning for breakfast at their regular diner, the Six Strings, but he did his damnedest to try. He immediately lifted the menu to cover his face as soon as he joined Noah, Malcolm, Mack, and Vlad at their table. Three other chairs remained unclaimed, waiting for the rest of the crew.

Vlad plucked the menu from Colton's hands and tossed it on one of the empty seats.

"Hey," Colton grumbled, picking it back up, "I was reading that."

"You get the same thing every time," Vlad said. He leaned close to study Colton's face. "What is wrong with you?"

Colton pushed his friend back by the shoulder. "Nothing's wrong."

"I don't believe you." Vlad pointed. "You're doing that thing."

"What thing?"

"He's right," Malcolm said, studying Colton's face. "You're doing the thing."

"What fucking thing are you talking about?"

"The thing with your right eye," Noah said. He adopted a drunken expression with his right eyebrow arched. "You always do that when you're perturbed about something."

"I do not," Colton said. But he lifted his knife to look at his reflection, and sure enough, his right eyebrow was arched. He dropped his knife. "Fuck off."

Mack nodded appreciatively at Noah. "*Perturbed* is a good word."

"I use good words because I'm a genius."

It was actually true. Noah had a genius IQ. "Well, you're wrong about me," Colton complained, reaching for the carafe of coffee in the center of the table. "There's nothing wrong."

"Did everything go okay with the meeting?"

His stomach soured. "Great. Fine."

"Fine?" Noah repeated.

"Yes."

"That's all we're going to get?"

Colton forced a shrug. "There's nothing else to tell."

"So, they liked the new songs?" Vlad asked.

Luckily, he was saved from answering by the arrival of Gavin, Yan, and Del. They strolled in together, dressed in workout gear again, probably for a training session after breakfast. They sat down and looked at Colton, and then all three of them leaned closer.

"For fuck's sake," Colton grumbled. "Nothing is wrong with me."

"He's doing the eyebrow thing," Del said to the table.

"We know," Noah said, once again mimicking the expression.

Colton fell into a silent sulk when a waitress appeared to take their orders. They'd been coming here for so many years that the entire staff knew them well enough to just ask, "Y'all want the usual?" For Colton, that was ham-and-cheese grits. The Six Strings was the only place that made them the way his mom used to when he was a kid. She'd make a panful every Sunday night, and it was just enough to feed Colton, his sister, and his brother for breakfast before school all week. There were a few years after he'd left home that Colton couldn't stand the thought of eating it again, not because he was sick of it but because he resented it. The memories it evoked. His siblings were too young to know the reasons why their parents had to rely on cheap, filling meals that lasted a long time, but Colton knew. Just like he knew his parents were lying when they said they had to leave their house and move to a small apartment in 1991 because they thought the kids would enjoy living closer to the park.

The waitress left the table, and Colton hoped the guys would move on from berating him.

They did not.

"Out with it, douchebag. What's going on?"

It was pointless to avoid it any longer. Besides, they'd find out sooner or later. His life intersected with Gretchen's in too many ways; it was actually a miracle they hadn't crossed paths until last night. There was no guarantee Gretchen wouldn't mention it to Elena, Liv, or Alexis.

"Fine," Colton said, leaning his elbows on the table. "I saw Gretchen last night."

Mack's eyebrows tugged together as he stirred cream into his coffee. "Gretchen . . . *Winthrop*?"

"Yes, fuck stick. Which other Gretchen would I be talking about?"

Mack and Noah exchanged a glance, probably at Colton's petulant tone. "What do you mean, you saw her?" Noah asked. "Like, for a date?"

Ha. Right. Colton ripped open a packet of sugar for his coffee. "Did you know she was one of the CAW whiskey Winthrops?"

Mack lifted his mug. "Yeah, didn't you?"

"Wait, I didn't know that either," Gavin said. "Are you serious?"

"Doesn't make sense, does it?" Mack said. "She wears secondhand clothes, lives in a tiny apartment, hates expensive gifts."

As Mack talked, Colton felt an unfamiliar surge of jealousy. He hated being reminded that Mack and Gretchen had briefly dated. Which made zero sense and was sexist as hell, to boot. She didn't belong to either of them, yet here Colton was. Seething because Mack knew where Gretchen lived.

"So what happened last night?" Malcolm asked.

"She was sent as an ambassador." His words were even more bitter than his coffee. He reached for more sugar.

"What does that mean?" Noah asked.

Colton leaned back in his chair and spread out his arms. "CAW whiskey wants to sign yours truly to an endorsement deal."

"Holy shit," Del said. "That's fantastic. Congratulations."

The guys all chimed in with *way to go* and *nice job* and *get us some free samples.*

"I told her no."

Silence exploded like a popped balloon.

"Why the hell would you say no?" Yan sputtered after a moment.

"I don't feel like doing it."

Gavin's eyeballs nearly fell out. "You don't feel like a multi-million-dollar endorsement deal for a major global brand?"

"Not right now."

Vlad leaned over and put his hand on Colton's forehead. Colton swatted him away. "What're you doing?"

"Checking for a fever."

"I'm not sick. I just don't want to do it."

"Okay, no." Yan shook his head. "This doesn't make any sense. What aren't you telling us?"

"She hates Christmas." He leveled Mack with a glare. "Did you know *that*?"

"Nope, but that doesn't surprise me."

"You turned down the endorsement deal because Gretchen hates Christmas?" Noah was staring at him as if he'd just sprouted a unicorn horn.

"No."

"Then what does that have to do with anything?"

Shit. He'd talked himself into a trap. He couldn't explain himself without explaining . . . other things. "Forget it," he grumbled.

Fat chance of that. Mack ran a hand across his jaw. "Colton, I swore I'd never ask you this because I never felt like it was any of my business, but . . ." He paused to inhale, and Colton instinctively held his own breath. "What exactly happened between you and Gretchen at my wedding?"

Colton's fingers tightened around his coffee mug. "Nothing."

He must've said it too quickly because Mack let out a slow *Fuuuck*. "You slept with her, didn't you?"

Colton stiffened. "As you said, Mack. That's none of your business."

"That's a yes," Noah said, picking up his phone as if he couldn't stand to even look at Colton anymore.

Colton grabbed the phone and set it back down. "It's nothing."

The silence that followed was of the *we knew it* variety. The accompanying expressions were of the *you're an asshole* kind.

Mack swiped a hand down his face and made an annoyed noise. "Christ, Colton. You could amuse yourself with any woman in the world. Why the hell would you do that to Gretchen?"

Um, wow. That was a whole lot of insult for two tiny sentences. He pointed at Mack. "Okay, first of all, I resent the implication that I *amuse myself* with women on some kind of regular basis. I haven't even been on a date since your wedding."

Every eye widened in surprise.

"Second, why are you so sure I was the one who initiated it with her?"

Mack's eyebrows shot into the stratosphere. "Are you saying it was the other way around?"

"Yes! I was walking her back to her hotel room, but she jumped me in the elevator and the next thing I know—"

He snapped his mouth shut.

"The next thing you know . . . ?" Malcolm prompted him.

"Nothing. Whatever happened between Gretchen and me is one hundred percent private, and I don't want to hear another goddamn word from any of you that might cause her embarrassment. Do you hear me? Not one goddamn word."

Noah poked his tongue in his cheek. "Normally, I would abide by your wishes, but this is Gretchen we're talking about. She's a friend, and I need your word that you didn't do anything to hurt her."

For fuck's sake, how long had his friends held such a low opinion of him? "I didn't hurt her."

"Just tell us what happened," Vlad said.

Colton hesitated. For one thing, he'd promised to keep it a secret. But, also, it was embarrassing as fuck. "I don't know what happened."

"As in, you don't remember or you're confused?" Malcolm asked.

"Of course I remember! I wasn't drunk."

"So?" Mack prompted.

"I don't know," Colton grumbled, staring into his coffee. "We had a great time, or I thought we did. I mean, I *liked* her, you know? But the next morning she ran out like she was . . . like she was embarrassed. I asked if we could see each other again and she said no, and she hasn't talked to me since."

He felt a tremor at the table and looked up to find the guys biting back laughter. If he thought Mack's faulty assumptions were insulting, this was like a kick in the balls. "What the fuck is so funny?"

Noah broke first. He snorted and sent a spray of coffee over the rim of his mug. Malcolm was next, and then Gavin, and within seconds they were all gasping for breath. It took a full minute and a couple of exasperated glares from nearby tables for them to stop laughing.

"I would pay serious money to have seen your face," Noah wheezed.

Del wiped his eyes. "Dude, has that *ever* happened to you?"

"Has what ever happened to me?" Colton scowled.

"Being ghosted by a woman," Gavin said.

He lifted one shoulder. "Of course."

The laughter went up an octave. Apparently he hadn't been convincing.

"So, just to make sure I'm understanding," Malcolm finally said after things had calmed down. "You turned down what would likely be a very lucrative career move because you were mad that she rejected you?"

Colton returned to sulking.

"Wow," Malcolm said, shaking his head. "That's pretty childish, Colton."

That stung. Malcolm was the group's resident Zen master and philosopher, and being scolded by him was like getting in trouble at church.

Their food arrived then, and the guys ate in hungry silence just long enough for Colton to reconsider his shitty life choices over the past twenty-four hours. Malcolm was right. He'd been an asshole last night. If his manager found out that Colton had so blithely turned down a major endorsement deal, he'd start to question a lot more than whether Colton was serious about music anymore.

But that wasn't what was making him so cranky this morning. He hated how he'd treated her last night. He'd replayed his nasty words to her a thousand times in his mind while tossing and turning in bed.

After a few unsatisfactory bites, Colton wadded up his napkin and tossed it on the table next to his plate. His appetite was officially gone. "We gonna pick a book for this month, or what?"

"Yes," Vlad said, nodding so enthusiastically the table shook. "A Christmas romance."

"As long as it has sex in it," Colton grumbled.

Noah held up a fist for him to bump. "Yes. How come so many Christmas romances don't have sex in them?"

"And how come so many are about a woman going back to her hometown and, like, leaving behind a rich fiancé or something?" Colton added. "What's wrong with having a rich, professional fiancé?"

"I think the point is usually that when we go home, we're forced to deal with our past," Malcolm said, adopting his *about to drop some knowledge on your asses* pose. Everyone stilled in anticipation of some learning. "And once we deal with our past, we realize why we ran away in the first place."

The last thing Gretchen wanted to see when she arrived at the office was Addison teetering precariously on a rickety ladder and draping twinkling white lights across the ceiling tiles.

"What are you doing?"

Addison gasped and whipped her head to peer over her shoulder. The ladder rocked beneath her feet. Gretchen dropped her bag and lunged to hold it in place.

"Thank you," Addison said, steadying herself again.

"Since when do I allow Christmas decorations in the office?"

"Since I stopped asking your permission."

"Addison, we go through this every year. This is a serious office dealing with serious issues. Christmas decorations send the wrong message, especially since not all of my clients celebrate Christmas."

"Lights make people happy," Addison argued, securing a section of lights with tape. "Not that you'd recognize happy if it hit you in the face."

She grumbled the last part, but she clearly intended for Gretchen to hear. Gretchen chose to ignore it. "Where the hell did you even find this ladder? It's ancient."

"I borrowed it from the tattoo dudes next door."

"Are they going to pay the workers' comp when you break your neck?"

"You're in an especially chipper mood this morning. What's wrong?"

"Nothing," Gretchen mumbled. Just that last night had been a humiliating disaster, and not only because of Colton's cold words but because she had to figure out a way to tell Evan she'd failed. If she thought there was even a ghost of a chance that Colton might be persuaded, she would endure another round of hostility from him just to avoid Evan's inevitable scorn. But Colton had been as emphatic as a punch when he said he wasn't interested.

"Well, whatever nothing is, don't take it out on me," Addison said. She secured a final segment of lights and started to back down the ladder. "Also, *he* called again, and lucky for you, I promised him you'd call him back today."

Gretchen backed up to make room for her. "You're lucky you're good at your job."

"*You're* lucky I'm good at my job."

That was true. Gretchen had hit the lottery the day Addison applied to be her office manager. Not only was she more capable than ten people, but also for some reason she put up with Gretchen's shit. "You're right. I'm sorry. If I buy you coffee from ToeBeans, will you forgive me?"

"I already forgive you, but I'll accept the offer anyway." She held out her hand, palm up. "Spring for a muffin, too, and I'll even go get it."

"Deal." Gretchen pulled money from her bag and handed it over.

"Tell Alexis I said hi."

Addison grinned and grabbed her coat. "Be back in a half hour."

"A half hour? ToeBeans is one block away."

"But Zoe might be there." She emphasized the point with a suggestive twitch of her eyebrows.

Addison had a crush on Zoe Logan, one of Alexis's employees and her future sister-in-law. It was just one in a dozen ways Gretchen's life intersected with Colton's, because Zoe's brother, Noah, was one of Colton's best friends. It was her own nightmarish game of six degrees of separation, and it was a miracle the two of them hadn't bumped into each other over the past year because of their mutual friends alone.

But those mutual friends were one of the many reasons she'd run out on him the morning after the wedding. If they'd tried to make a relationship out of their night together, their friends would be put in the awkward position of choosing sides if things went sour. And things *would* go sour eventually, because she was a Winthrop and therefore carried the toxic gene of chaos and greed that infected everyone who came in contact with them. Last night was evidence enough of that, wasn't it?

Gretchen carried her stuff into her office and stared at the phone. Addison was right. She needed to call Jorge back and get it over with.

She dialed his number and prayed for his voice mail.

No such luck.

"I hope you are calling with some good news for me," he answered.

"I'm sorry, Jorge—"

"No, don't say that."

"There are hundreds of attorneys around the United States you could call."

"There aren't. You have the exact skills and experience we need."

"I have clients here who need me."

"Do we need to increase our salary offer? I can go to our donors and—"

"No! Money has nothing to do with it."

She could've sworn he actually let out a relieved breath. She understood. It was hard enough to raise money to fund legal services. Any donor would be rightfully pissed to know their money was going to pay for some greedy lawyer.

"Look," he said, his change in tone suggesting a change in tactic. "What about coming out here for Christmas to help us with our annual donation drive? You can meet the staff, review some of our cases. You know you work over Christmas anyway."

Gretchen pressed her fingers to her throbbing temple. How could she say no to that? And it was true. She did work over Christmas. She usually worked *on* Christmas.

"Just give it another couple of weeks to think about it," Jorge pleaded. "Let me send you some information."

"Okay," she agreed. Reluctantly. "Send me what you have."

"You'll think about it some more?"

"Yes. But I should warn you that I highly doubt my answer will change."

"Well, the best present you could give me right now would be to at least give me more time to convince you."

Gretchen ended the call and massaged her forehead, where her light tension headache was starting to throb with the thud of guilt. No more than five minutes passed before her inbox dinged with the sound of an incoming email. Jorge hadn't wasted any time.

G–

Thanks for humoring me. ☺ I hope after you have a chance to review our work and our priorities for next year, you'll do more than that and actually consider my offer. Send me your thoughts, or better yet, let's talk about it in person. We could use the extra set of hands to put together our donation boxes for the refugee center. Leticia would also love to see you, and you won't believe how big the girls have gotten.

Best,

J

Yeah, so reading that only made the guilt worse. Gretchen hadn't seen Jorge or his wife and their twin daughters in at least seven years. She'd been friends with both of them at Georgetown Law and had visited them every summer for a few years after graduation. But then she'd opened her own clinic, and there was never enough time after that.

She'd just opened the attached list of the group's legislative priorities when she heard the front door open. Addison was back early.

"No Zoe, huh?" she called.

"Sorry. Was I supposed to bring her?"

That was *not* Addison's voice. And when she swiveled in her chair, it was most definitely *not* Addison filling up the doorframe.

In the split second that followed, Gretchen's brain had just enough time to chronicle three things. First, it was Colton, and he was carrying two ToeBeans coffees. Second, he wore a bright yellow puffer vest that would've looked ridiculous on most men but so definitely worked on him. And third, he hadn't shaved. Gretchen was never a fan of the scruffy look, but on Colton, it was sexy enough to make her want to strip naked on the spot.

"What—what are you doing here?"

He lifted one of the cups. "Peace offering."

"I don't need a peace offering."

"Well, I do." He walked in and set a cup in front of her. He held her gaze just long enough to make her sweat. "I said some shitty things last night. I'm sorry."

"That's not necessary." Yet she was touched. Like, really touched. Especially since she'd deserved most of what he'd said.

"Not that it's any excuse, but you caught me off guard at the end of a particularly bad day, and I took it out on you."

As far as apologies went, it was as sincere as any she'd heard. And since she wasn't used to sincere apologies from men in her life, she blanked on what to say next. She finally blurted out, "Why did you have a bad day?"

"It's a long story." He sat down in the chair opposite her desk and casually sipped his coffee. "I want to reconsider your offer."

He said it so nonchalantly that she thought she'd misheard him. Her mind blanked again. "My offer?"

"Yes. You know, the one about becoming the face of a whiskey brand that you're so embarrassed about that you don't even like people to know you're part of—"

"I'm not embarrassed by the brand. I'm embarrassed by . . ." Her mouth snapped shut.

"By what?" he prompted.

"Nothing."

He lifted his eyebrow in a way that said they'd be circling back to that. "As I was saying, I gave it some thought last night, and I'd like to start over."

"I'm not going to Belize with you." Oh God, why did she say that? The last thing this conversation needed was a reminder of one of her greatest humiliations.

"How about dinner, then?"

Blank brain struck again. "Dinner?"

"Yeah, it's this thing where two people go out and get something to eat together. It's sometimes referred to as a date."

"You're high."

"I'm totally not."

She scoffed. "I'm *not* going on a date with you."

"Sorry. That's the deal."

"That's extortion!"

"That's one of those big, fancy lawyer words, isn't it?"

A flush of annoyed heat raced up her cheeks. He was goading her on purpose, and it was working. "Stop that. I've never, not once, done or said anything to suggest—"

He cut her off with a grin. "I'm just messing with you."

A noise akin to a growl crawled its way out of her chest. He pretended not to notice as he instead surveyed her tiny office, pausing to read the posters on the walls titled KNOW YOUR RIGHTS and DO YOU QUALIFY FOR DACA? He moved on to the notes tacked to her corkboard.

She crossed her arms. "Are you quite finished?"

"How long you been doing this?"

"Doing what? Practicing immigration law?"

He nodded, eyes now studying the scribbled list of *Don't Forget* on her dry-erase board.

"I've been an attorney for ten years, but I spent the first couple of years of my career as a public defender before moving into immigration law."

"Why the change?"

"Why do you care?"

He leveled his gaze on her. "Humor me."

Gretchen sucked in a breath and crossed her legs. "I got sick of defending clients for petty crimes, only to see them deported with no representation. I realized I could make a bigger difference on this side of the law."

"And are you? Making a difference?"

She waved her hands. "This is ridiculous. I am not going on a date with you."

"You sure about that?"

"One thousand percent."

He shrugged with an exaggerated sigh. "Well, shucks. Then I guess you have to find another handsome face to sell your whiskey."

And just like that, he stood up, set his coffee on her desk, and walked out.

Shock rendered her speechless and inert as she watched him go. But only for a second, because that's all it took for her dignity to rustle up some self-righteousness. Gretchen shot to her feet and stomped after him. "Where the hell are you going?"

He turned around at the other end of the short hallway. The small space looked even more cramped with his tall frame filling it up. "You said no. I'm going home."

"Just like that?"

"Is there anything more to be said? At least I'm actually saying goodbye instead of running scared."

Indignation sparred with a dash of shame, and it made her, as Uncle Jack liked to say, as cross as a raccoon in a trap. She cocked a hip. "Oh, I get it now. This is some kind of revenge, isn't it?"

"Revenge?"

"You're doing this to get back at me for committing the unforgivable sin of walking out on the Great Colton Wheeler. That must've been a serious blow to your ego, but I am not willing to prostitute myself for your self-esteem."

A look of horror crossed his face, as if it hadn't occurred to him she might construe things that way. "Jesus, Gretchen. I'm not demanding that you sleep with me. I want to take you on a date. That's it."

She planted her hands on her hips. "Why?"

"What do you mean, why?"

"I mean, you must have millions of women who would give up a lung for a chance to go out with you—"

He nodded. "I do. Sometimes they even toss their bras at me with their phone numbers written on them."

She tossed up her hands. "Great. Call one of them."

"I don't want to. I want to go out with you."

"Why?"

"Because I like you."

"No one likes me."

Colton winked. "With your cheerful disposition? I find that hard to believe."

"Is that called flirting?" She pressed her hand to her chest. "Be still my beating heart."

Colton laughed, and Gretchen realized with a start that he was enjoying this. His long legs closed the distance between them, and Gretchen had the momentary instinct to back up. But she held her ground, even when he stepped so close that they could have been dancing. Her body reacted as if she'd been struck by lightning. She remembered distinctly what it was like dancing with him . . . and what it led to.

"Let me try this another way," he said, his voice dropping into *who's your daddy* range. "Gretchen, I like you. I thought you liked me. I have no idea what happened last year that made you go running off like that, but I would love to try again. So would you do me the honor of letting me take you out tonight so you can make your best pitch for why I should consider your family's proposal?"

It was the sincerity that cracked her resolve. Her voice came out airy. "*Why?*"

He shrugged. "Why not?"

"Because it's a waste of time."

"For who? You or me?"

"Both of us."

He lifted his eyebrows. "Pick you up tonight at seven?"

Gretchen gulped. "I don't have much choice, do I?"

"Of course, you have a choice."

Sure. A choice between having to tell Evan that she'd lived up to his low expectations of her, or go out with the only man who had the power to make her feel the worst emotion ever . . . vulnerability. It wasn't much of a choice. "Fine," she ground out.

"Awesome." He grinned, stepping back. "I'll pick you up at home."

He gave a gentle tug to a lock of her hair and then turned around. He paused before opening the front door. "Oh," he said, looking over his shoulder, "and be sure to dress warm."

"Why? Where are you taking me?"

"It's a surprise."

"I don't like surprises."

"You'll like this one."

She doubted that very much. "And I hate being cold!"

It was too late. He'd already left.

She chuffed out an *argh* and returned to her office, her concentration ruined. She had clients relying on her, but her fingers suddenly itched to look up cute cold-weather outfits on Pinterest. The only thing that made the personal humiliation tolerable was knowing she got to call Evan and say she was making progress.

So, so pathetic.

CHAPTER SIX

Colton parked his Lincoln SUV across the street from Gretchen's house just before seven that night.

She lived in a stately Victorian that had been subdivided into individual apartments. A wide front porch wrapped around both sides of the house, one wing featuring a collection of worn wicker furniture and the other a large swing. He couldn't picture Gretchen ever using either of them. It would require a willingness to slow down and relax, and she didn't give off a *put your feet up* vibe.

He waited for a couple of slow-moving sedans to pass before crossing. The front door was unlocked and opened into a converted foyer with built-in mailboxes along one wall next to an intercom system. He searched for her apartment number and hit the buzzer. A moment passed before he heard her voice.

She offered no greeting, just a brusque instruction to use the stairs directly in front of him to the top floor. The staircase creaked beneath his footsteps as he followed her instructions. On the top floor, the stairs opened into a long hallway with a single door on the right. He'd just raised his hand to knock when the door opened.

Gretchen stood before him wearing a black turtleneck sweater, jeans that made his mouth water, and a scowl that made him smirk. "How'd you know?"

Her scowl deepened. "Know what?"

"That a woman in jeans and a black turtleneck does things for me."

She turned around and left him standing in the doorway. He walked in to see her heading down a single dark hallway. "Where're you going?"

"To change."

He jogged around in front of her to block her path. "Don't even think about it."

She rolled her eyes. "I have to get my coat and my purse."

She changed direction and instead walked to the small closet by the door to retrieve both, and as she did, he turned around to survey her living space. "You weren't kidding, woman. You do hate Christmas."

"Don't call me *woman*," she grumped, slipping on her coat. "And what was your first clue?"

"No tree?"

"Why would I spend money on something that only I would ever see?"

"Because it would make you happy." Colton sauntered into the small living room, where the only pieces of furniture were a couch, a coffee table, and a small flat-screen TV atop a cheap particle-board table. There was a severity to her apartment, a starkness that struck him as both sad and startling. For a woman who exuded so much energy, she lived in a colorless sea that drained the life out of everything. Her couch was beige. The rug was gray. The cream-colored walls were devoid of any kind of artwork or photos. A circular table to the right of the living room looked like it spent more time as a workspace than a dining space. Stacks of folders and notebooks took up an entire half, and her laptop sat open but asleep on the other half. He wandered closer to the coffee table, which looked close to collapsing under the weight of a stack of nonfiction books about the death of democracy, the rise of global autocracy, and growing income equality in the United States.

She closed the closet door and turned around. "Stop that."

"Stop what?"

"Judging my lack of decorating skills."

"I'm just checking the place out."

"You're trying to psychoanalyze me based on the fact that I don't waste money on cutesy throw pillows and Santa figurines."

"Anyone ever tell you you're paranoid?"

"Anyone ever tell you you're annoying?"

"Just you, darlin'." He winked for good measure. "Ready to go?"

He opened the front door and waited as she stomped out. He chuckled over her shoulder as she locked the door. "Your enthusiasm is overwhelming."

"So is your cologne."

He laughed and reached for her hand. She shoved it deep in her pocket. "No way. We're not holding hands."

"Why not? This is a date."

"It's a hostage situation."

Another laugh burst from his chest, but at the same time, the words needled him with guilt. He followed a step behind as Gretchen stomped down the stairs and into the entryway of the house. Her footsteps were heavy and loud as she descended the porch steps outside. Colton clicked his key fob to unlock his car, and she followed the chirp to the passenger side. He'd hoped to be a gentleman and open her door for her, but she beat him to it. She yanked the handle with all the attitude of a pissed-off teenager and climbed into the seat with equal exasperation. Colton reached for the door to at least close it for her, but she slammed it shut in his face.

Shaking his head, Colton rounded the car to the driver's side. He barely had time to get in before she started griping again. "I can't believe you're making me do this."

His thumb hit the start button. "Let's go have some fun." As he pulled away from the curb, he flipped on the satellite radio and turned the dial to a Christmas station. She immediately turned it off.

"My car, my rules," he said, clicking it back on. And just to rub it in, he turned up the volume, filling the car with the distinctive bebop melody of Mariah Carey's "All I Want for Christmas Is You."

Gretchen groaned and banged her head several times against the seat. "I changed my mind. Let me out. This is torture."

"Come on," he yelled over the music. "How can anyone not like this song?"

"How many times can I tell you? I hate Christmas!"

He pointed. "And by the end of the night, we're going to get to the bottom of that."

Her frustrated *argh* was music to his ears. Who knew it could be so fun to irritate someone? "Want me to sing along?"

"Want me to throw myself from this car?"

Colton barked out yet another laugh and finally acquiesced. He turned the music down and told her to open the glove box. "There's a present in there for you."

She withdrew the wrapped book-shaped package and set it in her lap. "Please tell me you did not give me a romance novel."

"Even better."

She tore the paper to reveal a paperback titled *A Cold Winter's Night*. The cover featured a couple staring into each other's eyes as snow fell around them. She gave him a deadpan look. "It *is* a romance novel."

"It's a *Christmas* romance. The best kind."

"You can't seriously expect me to read this."

"It's your first lesson."

"In what?"

He waggled his eyebrows at her.

She pursed her lips. "I'm sufficiently well-versed in that."

"Don't I know it?" He winked, and she pretended to be annoyed, but he saw a spark of amusement and—dare he hope—carnal interest in her eyes.

"Get your mind out of the gutter," he teased. "It's your first lesson in the magic of Christmas."

She turned the book over in her hands and skimmed the back.

"You're going to love it," he said. "Promise."

Gretchen made a disbelieving noise and laid the book on her lap again. "What's my second lesson going to be?"

"We'll be there in a few minutes."

"Tell me now so I can prepare mentally."

"It's time you began to appreciate the joy of Christmas lights."

Her head whipped in his direction. "Please tell me that doesn't mean what I think it means."

"I'm taking you to the riverfront, darlin'."

Her head once again fell back against her seat. "Please, God. No."

"You're going to love it."

She rolled her head in his direction again and narrowed her eyes. She was probably aiming for annoyed but instead achieved adorable. He damn near swerved into oncoming traffic.

They drove the next several minutes in silence—his content, hers contemptuous. The closer they got to the riverfront, the slower traffic became until people with strollers were passing them. The streets were clogged, the sidewalks nearly impassable. Gretchen pulled her face from the window. "This is even worse than I imagined."

"You got something against crowds?"

"Don't you?"

"If I did, I wouldn't last long in my business."

"You must get swarmed, though."

"Sometimes. Tonight, I'll just give them my *not right now* face if someone comes toward us."

"What's that look like?"

He took his eyes off the road and gave her a tight-lipped smile followed by a crisp, no-nonsense, barely there head shake.

She flinched. "Wow. Even I want to avoid you."

"That's not a very high bar."

She turned her head to hide her grin.

"Ha," he said, peeling one hand off the wheel to point at her. "I saw that. That was a gen-u-ine smile right there."

"It's indigestion."

He eased around the long line of cars waiting to get into the public lot. He'd prepaid for valet parking in a VIP section.

"I can't believe you're doing this to me," she said. "I've spent my entire life in Nashville and have never once been forced to endure Christmas on the Cumberland."

"You're shitting me. You've *never* been?"

"Nope. Not once."

"But even as a kid? Your parents didn't bring you here?"

"This isn't exactly my parents' kind of scene."

"Why?"

"If you knew my parents, you'd understand." Her words carried a sour note of bitterness, but it was the hint of sadness that rang loudest in his ears. He burned with the temptation to press for more information, but he let it drop as he pulled up to the valet stand.

"Hey," he said gently because it seemed appropriate after what she'd just said and not said. "Can you grab the baseball hat and glasses case in the glove box?"

She opened the door once again and pulled out both. "Is this your disguise?"

"Yep."

She laughed for the first time all night. "I was being sarcastic."

"You want to avoid the crowd, right?"

"You could wear a ski mask and people in this town would still recognize you, Colton."

"You'd be surprised." He pulled the cap over his hair and donned the fake, black-rimmed glasses. He checked the rearview mirror and then grinned at her. "How do I look?"

"Ridiculous." She was smiling when she said it, though, and his heart took off on a wild gallop. Gretchen could move mountains with that smile if she wanted to, and he was suddenly jealous of any other man who'd ever seen its brilliance.

He left the car running and got out as an attendant opened

Gretchen's door. Colton showed a screenshot of his receipt and waited as the valet scanned the barcode. "You're all set, Mr. Wheeler."

Gretchen draped the strap of her purse over her head to carry it crossbody. A slight shiver shook her arms as she waited for him to join her on the sidewalk.

"Cold?"

"Freezing," she grumped, pulling a white wool hat from her bag.

"Let me." He reached for it, and in what could only be a Christmas miracle, she didn't argue. Colton tugged the hat over her hair and halfway down her forehead. She shivered again, but if the flash of heat in her eyes could be believed, it had nothing to do with the chill in the air and everything to do with the fact that just being near each other produced a hot blast of memory she couldn't ignore any more than he could.

He held her gaze. "Better?"

She stepped back with a hard swallow. "Let's get this over with."

"Don't sound so glum. This is going to be fun."

"We have different definitions of fun."

"And mine are starting to include aggravating you."

She shot him a sardonic look. "Then you are going to have an absolute blast tonight."

Damn. She could fire a comeback with the aim of a sharpshooter. She was right, though. Tonight was shaping up to be the most fun he'd had in a long time.

He let her lead the way, keeping a steady pace with her quick steps. She walked with the same determined gait as when she'd found him in the bar last night—rankled but resigned, as if she'd just been dared to go through a haunted house and would rather die than let her friends see how nervous she was. The rhythm of her stride reminded him of a drum corps leading the band onto the field. If he stopped walking, he doubted she would even notice.

"We aiming for a six-minute mile here, or what?"

"You have trouble keeping up?" She sounded winded.

"Just wondering what your hurry is." He stretched his hand out to capture hers, tugging her back a step. "Slow down and smell the chestnuts."

"Is that what smells? I thought it was you."

He swung her around, pulled her flush against him, and slipped an arm around her waist. She fit against him even more perfectly than he remembered, and judging by the way her pupils dilated as she gazed up at him, her body remembered it too. He dipped his mouth close to her ear. "You know, sooner or later you're going to have to accept that I was there that night too. You're not fooling me."

He heard her gulp. "Don't flatter yourself. I was bored."

"If that was boredom, I'd love to see you excited."

She sucked in a small breath. The sound sent a signal straight to his groin, and he released her before he embarrassed himself. "Let's get something to eat," he said, reaching again for her hand. This time, she let him take it. Her small fingers folded into his, cold and soft against his guitar-calloused palms. "What sounds good?" His voice was tight.

"What are my options?" So was hers.

"Pretty much anything you can think of." He pointed with his free hand to a long line of food trucks along First Avenue.

"Hot chicken?"

He grimaced. "Okay, anything but that." His tastebuds loved Nashville's staple dish as much as anyone, but his stomach did not.

She grinned up at him. "Does Colton's tummy have trouble with spicy stuff?"

"Colton's tummy doesn't want to ruin the night by spending a half hour in the bathroom."

"I don't think I've ever discussed bodily functions on a first date."

"Second date," he corrected. "And since our actual first date involved a lot more personal stuff than that, I see no reason to hide it from you."

"I'm not sure there's anything more personal than your bathroom habits."

He tipped his head to the sky and groaned. "Can we please stop talking about it now?"

"How about that meat-and-three truck?"

He followed her point to a truck that served another famous Nashville meal, which was as simple as it sounded. A plate of meat—usually meatloaf, brisket, or country ham—and three traditional southern sides. "Deal," he agreed.

Most people paid them no attention as they wound through the slow-moving throng, but a handful saw through his disguise, as usual. He brought out the *keep away* head shake as a surge of protective instincts had him tightening his hold on her hand. Dating as a celebrity was hard enough when he went out with other famous people who were used to the attention. But Gretchen didn't exist in his world, and he suddenly wanted to hide her from it. And from them. The stares from the dozen or so people who obviously recognized him suddenly felt intrusive in a way he hadn't expected.

Sensing his tension, she looked up and then followed his gaze to a wide-eyed group of women who were one sorority shriek away from rushing him for a selfie.

"Don't disappoint the fans on my account, Clark Kent."

"Not tonight," he said, tugging her closer to his side. "Tonight, it's just us."

The line was short at the food truck. He ordered the country ham with mac and cheese, greens, and biscuits. Gretchen ordered the same but with brisket. When he pulled out his wallet, she interjected, "I can pay."

"Don't piss me off."

"Why would it piss you off if I pay for dinner?"

"Because the date was my idea."

"Fine. We'll split it."

He shook his head. "You can buy dessert, how about that?"

Her jaw jutted sideways, and he damn near kissed her. "Fine," she said, shoving the money back in her bag. Colton handed his credit card to the guy at the counter and shrugged at the man's bemused expression.

"But I'm perfectly capable of buying my own dinner," she said as they stepped to the side to wait for their food.

"Quit your bitchin'," he teased. "I'll let you buy me a hot cocoa, too, if it'll make you feel better."

Gretchen planted her hands on her hips. "Did you just tell me to quit my bitching?"

"I did." The urge to kiss her nearly stole his breath this time. The only thing that saved him from doing so was the shout of their order number. After collecting their tray, he lifted his chin toward a table where a group of college-age women were getting ready to leave. They approached, and Colton asked if he and Gretchen could grab their table.

One of the young women looked up and smiled. "Sure—" She stopped short, mouth agape. "Oh. My. God."

Her friends looked up quickly, blinked, and erupted in shrieks.

"Omigod," another one gushed. "Are you Colton Wheeler?"

Colton set down his tray and tipped the brim of his cap. "At your service."

The girls squealed as one again. "Can we get a selfie?" the first one asked.

He glanced at Gretchen, who was smothering a smile badly. "Be my guest."

"Sure thing, ladies," he said, laying on the drawl. The girls crowded around him, and he had to bend his knees to get in the picture.

"Omigod," one of them giggled. "My grandma is going to die. She loves you!"

An unabashedly amused voice piped in. "Then your grandma has good taste, doesn't she, Colton? I'm sure he'd love to sign something for her, too, maybe as a Christmas present."

The girl damn near passed out. "Are you serious?"

"Of course," Colton said. Gretchen grinned cheekily and handed him a pen and piece of paper she'd dug from her purse.

Colton cleared his throat and uncapped the pen. "What's your grandma's name?"

"Jennifer."

Colton scribbled his name on the paper and handed it to the girl. She clutched it to her chest.

"Merry Christmas," he said.

The girls ran off in a fit of giggles. He sat down with a grimace. "I think I just crossed the generational dateline. Her *grandma*?"

Gretchen patted his arm. "Don't sweat it. It happens to the best of men."

"Great. I'm the celebrity equivalent of erectile dysfunction."

Gretchen dipped her chin to hide her face, but not before he saw it. Another real smile. "Admit it," he said, handing her a plate and a packet of utensils.

"Admit what?"

"You like me."

She rolled her eyes and attacked her food with gusto. He chuckled. "Hungry?"

"Starving. I haven't eaten all day."

"Why not?"

"Too busy."

He swallowed a forkful of greens and wiped his mouth. "What's that look like for you?"

She barely glanced up from her brisket. "What does what look like?"

"A busy day."

She lifted a shoulder as she continued to eat. "It would seem boring to you."

"I'll try not to be insulted by that."

She did the eye-roll thing again.

"Try me, Gretchen."

She swallowed a bite and sat back in her chair. "Well, it looks like a lot of research—"

"Of what?"

"Case law, mostly. Relevant precedent, new rulings. Anything to convince a court that deporting a person with children is cruel and inhumane. I also spend a ridiculous amount of time writing briefs, filing extensions for Canadian songwriters who overstayed their visas, and doing my best to make sure the families of my clients awaiting deportation don't starve."

Wow. Professional Gretchen was a sight to behold. A tug low

in his gut told him he was about to embarrass himself again. "You do all of that yourself?"

She resumed eating. "I have three interns who help out, and my assistant, Addison, keeps me organized. This time of year, though, she has to spend most of her time figuring out how we're going to keep the lights on next year."

His eyebrows tugged together as he finished off the mac and cheese. "Why?"

"Our clinic is donor funded. Most of my cases are pro bono because my clients can't pay."

He cocked his head. "But you're a Winthrop."

"Doesn't mean I have access to Winthrop money."

She had no access to Winthrop money, but her family had her doing tasks like asking him to endorse the company? "You'll have to explain that one to me."

"It's a long story." It wasn't so much her tone of voice as her expression that said she had no intention of telling it. He wanted to push, but something told him she'd bolt if he did. He'd made too much progress with her tonight to risk that, so he redirected her attention.

"If you're not going to finish your biscuits, I'll eat them." He pointed his fork toward her plate, but she snatched it out of reach.

"Don't even think about it."

"Well, hurry up. Our night's not over."

"Don't rub it in."

CHAPTER SEVEN

They found a spot to sit on a bench facing the river. The bridge was to their right, the lights casting a colorful reflection on the water. He struck an effortlessly manly pose, his legs extended casually in front of the bench and crossed at the ankles. When he draped an arm around her shoulders, she got light-headed.

A man pushing a cart offering hot cocoa and spiced cider wheeled by. Colton caught his attention and bought them each a hot chocolate.

"I was supposed to buy that," she said as he reclaimed his seat.

He shook his head. "You're welcome."

He relaxed in silence next to her. Every so often, she heard the quiet slurp of him sipping the piping hot cocoa. But mostly she stared at the river, at the gentle kaleidoscope of color atop the soft ripples of the flowing water. On the other side of the bridge, a roaming choir sang carols, and the distance created a haunting echo where they sat.

Children ran and parents chased. Couples kissed and teenagers laughed. Fathers hoisted toddlers on their shoulders, and mothers wiped sticky hands.

She couldn't think of a single time in her life when her parents had done either.

"It's okay to admit it," Colton suddenly said, dipping his mouth close to her ear.

"Admit what?" She made the mistake of looking over at him, bringing her lips within kissing distance of his.

"That it's beautiful."

If Colton kept looking at her like that—like she was a candy cane he wanted to suck on—she was going to play prisoner for real and beg for handcuffs. So she resorted to her default self-defense mechanism. Sarcasm. "Actually, I just keep thinking about how much money is wasted on something like this that could be used for helping the needy pay their electric bills. People freak out over the idea of their tax dollars going toward anything that even looks like welfare, but they have no problem with this."

"This isn't paid for with tax dollars. This entire display is paid for by the downtown development foundation, which is all funded by private donations."

"And imagine how much good those donations could do if they gave that amount of money to something worthy."

"Something like your pro bono immigration clinic?"

"Among a million other important causes."

"Hey." The feel of his finger beneath her chin, turning her face to his, was like an electric shock. She forgot to breathe as he settled his gaze on hers. "Where does that come from?"

"What?"

"That guilt over how fortunate you are."

"It's not guilt. It's empathy. Why should I have so much when so many people have so little? What right do I have to stand here and take in this frivolous beauty when there are people in this very city who have to rely on food banks just to feed their kids?"

"That is guilt. You're directly blaming your own family's wealth for everyone else's lack of it."

"No, I blame a system that allows one family like mine to accumulate so much wealth at the expense of others. That's why I get so annoyed at Christmas. Rich people rush to get in their last-minute charitable donations so they can write it off on their taxes in January, while others are forced to choose between dinner and an empty stocking for their kids. How did the world get so unequal?"

He quirked an eyebrow. "And here I thought we were just going to look at some pretty lights."

She looked at her lap. "Sorry. I'm not exactly a fun person."

"I beg to differ. I'm having the time of my life with you. I had a helluva good time last year too."

She clutched her cup. "I'm not going to sleep with you tonight," she blurted out.

He nearly choked on his cocoa. "Excuse me?"

"That's what you're doing, right? Trying to make me feel special so I'll sleep with you again tonight?"

Colton clicked his teeth as he wiped the corner of his mouth. "Damn, girl. That's a Texas-size chip on your shoulder. You might want to see someone about that. But since you're interested in my after-hours plans, I have to get some sleep. I have a busy day tomorrow." He grinned at her. "Sorry to disappoint you, though."

Heat infused her cheeks. "What does that look like for you?"

"A busy day?" He shrugged. "Meetings and shit."

"What kind of meetings does a country star have?"

"Well, for starters, I have an appointment with my hairstylist, and then I have a facial, and then I need to pick out the next amazing photo of me to sign and send out to all the women who have been begging me for an autograph, and then there's the all-important meeting with my style consultant for some new clothes . . ."

"I can't tell if you're joking or not."

He shook his head. "I am definitely joking. I just have a lot to do tomorrow, so no fear. I have no plans to ravage you this evening."

Chagrined, she sank farther against the hard back of the bench. "Well, good," she said after a moment. "Because we have business to discuss."

"Ah, yes. Business." He sat up straight. "So, convince me."

She narrowed her eyes in confusion. "Convince you?"

"Why should I take an obscene amount of money to pose with some whiskey?"

"I never said anything about it being an obscene amount of money."

"It would have to be for me to consider it."

Her lips twitched with a suppressed smile. "For standing around and having your picture taken?"

He pointed at his cheek. "You want this handsome face, you gotta pay for it."

"Nothing wrong with your ego, is there?"

"It's not ego if it's fact. This here gorgeous face of mine is worth a lot of money."

His swagger worked. Her face lost all traces of her previous tension, and she surrendered to a smile. "Fine. But you'll have to take that up with my brother. I'm just the middleman."

He sucked his teeth. "You're not exactly selling me on it, honey."

She crossed her arms. "Carraig Aonair is one of the most recognizable labels in the global market today. Being chosen as a brand ambassador is one of the most coveted endorsements available to celebrities. Appearing as a representative for us would extend your own brand far beyond anything you've been able to achieve so far."

"I don't know. I'm already pretty damn famous, honey."

"What do you need to hear to convince you?"

"A number."

"A number?"

"Ballpark figure to open negotiations."

An excited spark lit up her eyes. He wished it was because she was as suddenly turned on as he was, but he knew better.

"How much does it need to be?" she asked.

"Thirty million, minimum."

She didn't even blink. "So if they give you an official proposal, you'll consider it?" she asked.

"I'd be an idiot not to. I mean, as you said, it's just standing around having my picture taken, right?"

"Thank you," she breathed.

Something about the way she said it must have pissed him off, because he shot to his feet and held out his hand. "Come on."

"We're done?"

"Sorry. No. I want to dance with you."

"I—I'm not going to dance with you."

"Why not?"

"I'm embarrassed to be seen with you."

He laughed like he'd been doing all night—a heady, familiar

sound that made stars dance before her eyes and her feet feel clumsy. If he *was* annoyed with her, he was suddenly hiding it well. He took her hand and pulled her to her feet. "Well, I'm not embarrassed to be seen with you. You're not only the most beautiful woman here—"

She snorted to cover the flush of swoony heat.

"—you're also the most brilliant. I'd show you off everywhere if you'd let me."

"I'm surprised you're this good at flattery, seeing how women just throw themselves at you."

"It's not flattery if it's true."

She snorted again.

"You keep making that noise. Is there something wrong with your sinuses?"

"It's your hair spray. I'm allergic to it."

His laughter was softer this time, more intimate. It managed to simultaneously call out her bullshit while also seducing her. He brushed her hair from her shoulder. "Come on. One dance. No one will pay us any attention. I promise."

Right. Colton Wheeler couldn't go unnoticed in full camouflage in the middle of a forest. But even if he didn't notice the attention, she felt the weight of every single eyeball on her and heard every whisper that followed them as he tugged her toward the stage.

Every step they took garnered double takes. He paid no attention. Somehow, over the years, he'd obviously learned to ignore the stir he created. But even if he weren't famous, people would've stared at him. He took up space like no one else she'd ever known, as if the air and the ground bent around him in acquiescence to his unnatural beauty.

As they entered the swirl of dancers, he swung to face her, and in one smooth move he wrapped an arm low around her waist and captured her hand with the other. She couldn't have resisted even if she'd wanted to, and damn it all to hell, she didn't want to. Because he smelled good. And he was warm. And he was the perfect height, just as she remembered from Mack and Liv's wedding. Tall enough that she had to look up to see him but not so tall that she couldn't rest her cheek against his shoulder if she wanted.

And she wanted.

"You're tense," he murmured, the deep vibrations of his voice sending tickles of energy and awareness through her body. His hand slid an inch farther down her back, and though she might have been imagining it, he pulled her a fraction closer.

"Have you ever performed here?" she asked, because if she didn't say *something*, she was going to do something completely illogical. Like kiss him.

"Many years ago."

"Before you were big time?"

"Honey, I've always been big time."

"There's that ego again."

"Speaking of which . . ."

"I feel a whine coming on."

He chuckled, sending warm vibrations from his chest to hers. But then he turned his mouth close to her ear, and all traces of teasing vanished. "Let's get back to why you walked out on me that morning."

That's what she was afraid he was going to say. She searched for something vague enough to satisfy him and settled on, "We're not a good fit."

"Oh, I remember us fitting together quite well."

"Fine. The sex was great. I'll give you that."

This time, his laughter sounded brittle. "Gee, thanks."

"Oh, come on." She tilted her head back to look at him. Big mistake. He was gazing down at her in the same way that had made her lose all her senses at the wedding and launch herself at him in an elevator. She gulped. "You can't actually be worried that you're bad at *that*."

"Everyone has insecurities, Gretchen."

"Even big-time Colton Wheeler?"

"Even me." His fingers splayed wider across her back, branding her straight through her coat and sweater.

She covered her reaction with her old standby. Sarcasm. "Maybe you're just not used to being rejected."

"Does it make me an asshole if I say that I'm not?"

"Arrogant, maybe."

"So you *did* have a good time?"

"I assumed it was obvious that I did."

"Then why?"

She bit her lip.

"You have no answer?" he murmured.

"You're you, and I'm me."

"Oh, Gretchen," he quipped in a bad British accent. "What a safe and terrible answer."

"Really? Quoting *A Christmas Carol*? That's a bit on the nose."

He chuckled and tugged her more tightly against him. "It's a classic. I read it every year and have seen every movie version. If you want to learn to love Christmas—"

"I never said I did."

"—then this is your first lesson. Every person you know is represented by a character in that book."

"Which one are you?"

"Nephew Fred, of course. I'm happy and live to make other people happy."

"I suppose you think I'm Scrooge?"

"If the humbug fits."

"Well, you're wrong. Just because I don't read it every year doesn't mean I don't know what it's about. I studied it in college. And it has less to do with Christmas and more to do with an unwillingness to interfere for the greater good. To sacrifice for the sake of others. That's not a Christmas message. Some of the loudest Christians I know wouldn't sacrifice a single manicure to help those less fortunate. They'll pretend to care at Christmas but then spend the rest of the year crossing the street to avoid a homeless person."

"Okay, but you *are* grumpy and hate Christmas."

"Humbug."

He chuckled again. The vibration of it against her chest was becoming hypnotic.

"Just so you know," he murmured, "I haven't been with anyone since that night."

She snorted even as her heart raced. "You've fed me a lot of bullshit, but that's the first outright lie that's ever come out of your mouth."

"Not a lie. You are the last woman I slept with, Gretchen."

She wrenched her face back to his. She aimed for a stony expression but likely failed. She didn't believe, not for one second, that he'd been celibate since Mack and Liv's wedding. And even if she did believe it, she wouldn't be naive enough to think that it had anything to do with her. Still, her heart raced again with a foolish feminine fantasy of having rocked his world so much that he couldn't stand to be with anyone else.

The song faded away, and before she could protest what he'd just said, he stepped away from her. "Thank you," he said.

"For what?"

"The dance." Colton's thumb traced the swell of her bottom lip, and she lost a year off her life.

She backed away from the circle of his arms. "I'll tell my brother to set up a meeting."

Colton followed her with his eyes but didn't move. "I don't want to meet with your brother."

"But you said—"

"I said I'm open to a proposal. But I want to hear it from you." Slowly, deliberately so, he inched as close to her as possible without touching. He hit her with the double-barreled attack of a heavy-lidded gaze and a seductive lick of his lips. Her nipples tightened under her sweater. And then, as if he knew he'd achieved his aim, he smirked and stepped back. "We can plan our next date in the car."

He turned and started walking, leaving her there with her mouth hanging open. "Hold up." She hurried to catch up with him. "I agreed to one date."

"I don't recall putting a number on it. I said, *Go out with me.*"

"That's cheating."

"That's business." He glanced down at her. "And I think some of ours is unfinished, don't you?"

Nervous tension rendered the drive back to her house silent. When he turned the Christmas station back on, she didn't argue, and he didn't comment on her subservience. Every molecule of matter between them vibrated with the weight of two words. *Unfinished business.*

He slowed and stopped in front of her house. "Stay put," he ordered when she reached for her door handle.

"Why?" The word came out a squeak.

"Because I want to be a gentleman and open your door for you."

Oh. She wasn't sure if she was relieved or disappointed. It wasn't as if she'd been hoping he wanted to lean across the console, hook a hand around the back of her neck, and— Her door opened. She jumped and looked up at him. Colton held out his hand to her, and she was too jittery to do anything but accept the help.

As soon as she slid from the car and stood, his eyes dropped to her mouth. She gulped. "So when is our next date?"

"Eager, huh?"

"Eager to get this over with."

"Friday."

"I'll check my schedule, but that should work."

"Got another hot date you might have to cancel?"

"Yeah, a Pap smear."

"An agenda item for our next meeting?"

She had to clear her throat to scrape away the traces of lust. "What?"

"Do I get to kiss you?"

"Do you want to kiss me?" Oh God. Had she actually said that? Where was her pride? Her dignity?

"I think you know the answer to that question."

"Maybe we should table that discussion until I can weigh the pros and cons."

"Let me know how I can help your research."

She summoned her self-respect and stepped aside. "I'll call you when I have a number for you."

"You do that."

She vowed not to look back at him as she strode up the sidewalk, climbed the porch steps, and walked into the house.

A Cold Winter's Night

Simon Rye was late.

Not just a little late. A lot late. Like, almost a half hour late. And if there was anything that set Chelsea Vanderboek's molars to grinding, it was tardiness.

Her entire life was a fine-tuned schedule. It had to be if she hoped to become the youngest ever junior partner at the Hollywood talent agency where she worked. From the moment she'd graduated from college, she'd made every minute count, and this meeting was no exception.

She had exactly two nights to finalize the sale of her family's historic inn in northern Michigan before flying back to California in time for her agency's annual Christmas party where, she hoped, she would get the promotion she'd been working toward.

Unfortunately, an infuriating local ordinance required approval by the Leland Township Historic Preservation Department for the sale of any property that had been held by the same family for more than one hundred years. Something to do with "safeguarding the heritage" of the area, according to the documents she'd been sent by her aunt's probate attorney. It should have been just a formality, until *Simon Rye* got in the way.

Chelsea checked her watch. He was now thirty-six minutes late. Which was thirty-five minutes longer than she'd hoped to spend here. There was a reason she'd vowed to never return. Memories haunted every corner like Jacob Marley clanging his chains at Scrooge's door. She'd instinctively hugged her arms around her torso the instant she walked in to ward off the chill and the sense of doom that clung to every square inch of the place.

She probably would have had to deal with the house eventually, but it shouldn't have been this soon. Her aunt was supposed to have had two more decades of life in her—time to enjoy her golden years and to figure out what to do with the family estate before it ended up in Chelsea's lap—but cancer in all its cruelty had stolen that. And now Chelsea was the sole member of the Vanderboek clan left to rid the world of this haunted, hated house. Fate had a sick sense of humor.

Chelsea stomped to the large bank of windows at the front of the house overlooking the serene, blue, icy waters of Lake Leelanau. The lake was barely visible now, though, hidden behind the veil of snowfall. The flurries that had followed her all the way from the tiny Traverse City airport to the Leelanau Peninsula had become heavy, fat flakes. She reached for the phone in her coat pocket to check the weather forecast but then swore as she remembered that she'd lost service somewhere outside Traverse City.

One more reason why she couldn't wait to get back to Southern California.

If *he* ever bothered to show up.

Finally, the gun of an engine shifting into low gear outside brought her to the front door. She whipped it open just as a black truck roared up the steep incline and parked behind her rental car.

The man who emerged from behind the steering wheel was not what she'd expected. For starters, he was about forty years younger than anyone with the title of historic preservation director ought to be. He was also taller, leaner, and wider—more like one of the beefy locals who worked the docks over in Fishtown.

He wore a heavy, brown Carhartt coat and well-worn winter boots, but it was his easy smile that caught her attention as he strode up the snow-covered brick pathway to the front porch. But Chelsea wouldn't be swayed by a dazzling smile. She worked in Hollywood, for God's sake. Insincere grins were a dime a dozen.

"You're late."

Simon paused at the bottom of the porch steps. "I tried texting you."

Chelsea grabbed her phone and held it up to show the screen. "Did it ever occur to you that I can't get service out here?"

"Nope. Mine works just fine." He stomped his boots on the ground to shake free the clumps of snow. "I suppose you missed the weather alert then too."

"What weather alert?"

He gestured to the falling snow. "Big storm coming. We're supposed to get more than a foot."

"I thought that was supposed to hit south of here."

He shrugged. "You know how Michigan weather is."

"I do. So we'd better work fast, because I need to get this over with."

She spun on her heel and went back into the house, leaving him at the bottom of the steps. His boots were muffled against the blanket of snow that already covered the stairs as he followed her inside.

He shut the door and faced her with that same smile. "How about we start over." He extended his hand. "Simon Rye. I'm sorry I was late, and it is a pleasure to meet you."

She stared at his hand for a split second and then sighed as she accepted the handshake. "Chelsea Vanderboek."

He squeezed her hand longer than was necessary. "I was sorry to hear about your aunt. She was an amazing woman."

An unexpected swell of emotion filled her chest. Chelsea pulled her hand away.

Simon sat down on a bench by the front door and untied his boots. Then he toed them off before he stood.

"That's really not necessary," Chelsea said, unnerved in a strange way by the sight of the man's stocking feet.

Simon lifted an eyebrow. "It absolutely is. I have snow and salt caked on those boots, and the floors in this house are century-old walnut. You should take yours off too. If we have a chance of salvaging them—"

Chelsea held up her hand to silence him. "I already told you that I have no intention of keeping it."

"I know you told me that. I'm here to change your mind."

"No. You're here to sign off on the sale."

"Sorry." He ran a hand over his snow-covered hair, leaving it standing up in spiky layers. "I'm not going to agree to let you sell this landmark property to some greedy Detroit developer who will tear down the house and throw up some cheap condos in its place."

"This is *my* property."

"And this is *my* job."

"Look, Mr. Rye—"

"Simon."

"*Mr. Rye*, I can appreciate your passion for saving historical sites. But the house is mine to sell. What gives you the right to tell me I can't do it?"

"I have no interest in stopping you from selling your family house."

Surprise rendered her speechless for a change.

"What I'm interested in is convincing you to sell to someone who will maintain the property as is."

"Impossible. I already have a buyer lined up."

Simon shrugged. "Then I'm afraid we're at an impasse."

A scraping sound outside brought them both up short. It sounded like a sled on a hill. Simon sucked in a breath. "Please tell me you set the emergency brake when you got out of your car."

"I—"

"*Shit.*"

Simon whipped open the door and raced back outside, still in his socks. He stopped at the top of the porch steps, hands on top of his head, because there was nothing else to do. She ran out and stopped next to him, and together they watched her car slide backward until it collided with his truck.

Chelsea held her breath and prayed that would be the worst of it.

But she already knew how foolish it was.

With a creak, his truck began to slide, too, and then both of them careened over the side of the hill into a deep ditch.

CHAPTER EIGHT

The wait at ToeBeans the next morning was as long as Gretchen's fuse was short. When she arrived just after eight, she could barely squeeze through the door because the line of sleepy-eyed patrons waiting for their morning dose of motivation stretched all the way to the entrance.

Gretchen stifled a yawn behind her hand. There wasn't enough caffeine in the world to make up for how little she'd slept last night. Colton and his almost-kiss were only partly to blame. The rest was that book. Apparently, romances were the *can't eat just one* of literature. One chapter became *just a few more pages* until it was suddenly two a.m. Even when she realized that the main female character bore a striking and insulting resemblance to her, Gretchen couldn't stop reading.

She had way too much to do today to be this tired, not the least of which was emailing Evan to tell him Colton was open to negotiations.

When her phone buzzed in her coat pocket, she pulled it out

and quickly did a double take. It was Evan. "I see you found my cell number," she said in greeting.

"Had to ask my wife for it."

Of course he did.

"Got some news for me?" he asked.

"I met with Colton last night."

He snorted. "I know. I've seen the pictures."

A blast of cold air turned her skin to ice, and it had nothing to do with the door opening behind her. "What pictures?"

"You didn't actually think you could go on a date in public with Colton Wheeler and not have someone post a picture of it on social media, did you?"

She had, actually. She wasn't a social media person and paid zero attention to celebrity gossip sites. Besides, people took pictures of him, asked for selfies with *him*. Why would they bother taking pictures of her?

Gretchen's heart pounded a nervous beat. The last thing she needed was for Evan to think she wasn't taking the task seriously. "It wasn't a date, Evan."

"I don't care what it was," he said. "I just care if it worked. What did he say?"

Another blast of cold air behind her forced her to inch forward as much as possible. "He agreed to hearing a proposal about an endorsement deal, if that's what you mean."

"Great. I'll get a meeting set up and—"

"No."

"No?"

"I mean, he wants me to give it to him." And since that carried all kinds of embarrassing innuendo, she added quickly, "The proposal."

"He wants *you* to deliver it?"

She bristled at the emphasis. "Yes. If you send *me* the proposal, I'll give it to him."

"So you can wrangle another date?"

"It wasn't a date."

He made a *yeah, right* noise. "I'll email you something tomorrow."

"I'll watch for it—"

He hung up. Gretchen pulled the phone away and stared at the screen, jaw clenched. But annoyance at her brother quickly turned to dread. The pictures. She didn't have an Instagram account and only used Twitter to stay on top of various immigrant news stories. So she had to Google it. She typed, "Colton Wheeler Christmas on the Cumberland."

The first result was an older news article about the last time he'd performed at the event. She ignored that and scrolled down until she found it. Or, rather, *them*. A row of thumbnail images from Instagram, Facebook, and Twitter.

She clicked on the first one and was taken to Instagram's page. The picture showed them dancing, and the way Colton was looking down at her couldn't be mistaken for anything other than affection. The caption under the photo read, "What do I have to do to get Colton Wheeler to look at me like this? #Whosthatgirl"

"How many times have I told you?" A playful voice interrupted her.

Gretchen looked up from her screen and quickly shoved the phone in her pocket. Alexis had suddenly appeared next to her in line. She wore an apron covered with red-and-green cat paws all over it. With her hair in a high bun and a twinkling Christmas light necklace around her neck, she looked like one of the residents of Whoville. Anyone else would've looked unhinged, but it actually worked for Alexis.

"Friends don't wait in line," Gretchen said. "I know, but I feel bad cutting in front of all these people."

"Follow me." Alexis tugged Gretchen out of line. "You have a lot of explaining to do."

Shit. That could only mean one thing. Alexis had seen the pictures too. But even if she hadn't, of course she would know that she'd gone out with Colton last night. The book club guys and their partners were a tight-knit family, and everyone knew everything about one another. So she probably should not have been surprised that when she followed Alexis into the kitchen, she found Mack's wife, Liv, in there too. Liv and Alexis were best friends, and even though Gretchen had briefly dated Mack before he met Liv, Gretchen had formed a friendship with her too.

"Look who just walked in," Alexis said.

Liv practically lunged at her, grabbed her hand, and dragged her to the nearest chair. "Omigod, we were just talking about you!"

Gretchen smirked. "I never would have guessed."

"You have to tell us everything."

"About?"

"Don't play dumb."

She wasn't playing dumb. She was just dragging out the inevitable.

"Give her some space," Alexis said.

"I am giving her space," Liv whined. "I just really want to hear the story directly from Who's That Girl."

"It *wasn't* a date."

"Who are you trying to convince? Us or yourself?"

"Here, try this." Alexis handed Gretchen a plate with a muffin fresh from the oven. "Orange cranberry with a simple glaze."

Gretchen took a bite and groaned. "Fuck, that's good."

"Right? It's like Christmas on a plate."

"Don't say that," Liv said quickly. "She might spit it out. She makes Scrooge look like one of Santa's elves."

Why was everyone giving her shit lately about her attitude about Christmas? She took another bite and set the plate down. "What do you want to know?"

Liv's eyes danced with mischief. "Let's start with why we had to find out from Instagram that Colton attended Christmas on the Cumberland last night with a woman who looked remarkably like you."

As quickly and as vaguely as she could, Gretchen told them about the endorsement proposal and how Colton said he'd agree to consider it if she went out with him. "So there. It wasn't a date. It was strictly professional."

Liv smirked. "The way he's looking at you in that picture is the farthest from professional as a man can get."

"Trick of the lighting."

"Is it true that you slept with him after my wedding and totally ditched him afterward?"

Alexis gasped. "*Liv!*"

Heat licked the sides of Gretchen's face. "How—how did you hear about that?"

Alexis immediately held up her hand. "You don't have to talk about it. We shouldn't have pried."

Gretchen could count on one hand the number of real, true friends she'd had in her life. Friendship required the one thing she'd never developed—a faith that someone you'd put your trust in wasn't going to turn around and stab you in the back with it. But she felt so guilty about Alexis's discomfort that Gretchen raced to reassure her. "You weren't prying. It's just . . . Colton promised he wouldn't say anything."

Liv's eyes went as wide as the muffin plate. "Tell us everything!"

Gretchen scowled. "I'm not going to give you details."

"I don't think Liv was asking about the sex," Alexis laughed.

"Hell, yes, I was," Liv said. "I'm dying to know what he's like in bed."

"Liv, that's not fair. We'd be mad if the guys shared our intimate details. We need to respect their privacy, as well."

Liv stuck out her lip in a pout. "Fine. I don't need details about how he is in bed. But I do need to know everything else."

There was no getting out of this. Gretchen crossed her arms and exhaled with an annoyed huff. "We had an amazing night and—"

Liv sucked in enough air to seal a compression bag.

"—and then . . ." Gretchen paused. She wasn't ready to admit to anyone that she'd jumped out of bed and raced out like the room was on fire. "And then all of a sudden he's talking about going away to Belize on his private jet."

All of that was true but left a lot of pertinent information out.

Gretchen prepared herself for a *what the hell is wrong with you* speech. Instead, Alexis nodded knowingly. "That was absolutely the wrong thing for him to do, wasn't it?"

Gretchen blinked. "I—yes."

"I understand why you handed him his ass."

"So do I," Liv said, polishing off her muffin.

Gretchen looked from one to the other. "You do?"

Liv shrugged. "Look, it's the same type of shit that made you dump Mack, right? He tried to impress you with a thousand-dollar cupcake."

Gretchen groaned. "Can we not talk about that, please?"

Though she had long ago lost any awkwardness around Liv over the fact that she'd briefly dated the man Liv was now married to, the one thing that remained an embarrassing memory between them was what happened the night she'd dumped Mack. It was the same night he'd met Liv.

"The point is," Alexis said calmly, "anyone who truly knows you knows that you have no patience for ostentation."

"Yes."

"You're a very deliberate person, a serious person," Alexis continued. "Colton thinks the entire world is one big dance party."

"Yes, thank you."

"You hate Christmas. He's basically Santa Claus."

"Exactly."

Liv snorted. "Which is why you're perfect for each other."

"Right. Wait, what?"

Alexis peeled away from the counter. "Opposites attract."

"We're not just opposites. We're, like, from different planets. He spends his days with a *private plane*, and I spend mine with people who can barely buy groceries."

"You care about the same things inside," Alexis said. "That's what matters."

"Yep. You're exactly what he needs, and vice versa."

"I do *not* need Colton Wheeler. He's—he's . . ."

Alexis lifted her eyebrows as Gretchen searched for all the insults that used to come so easily to her.

"He's annoying," she finally said. "And arrogant. And . . ."

Her brain unwittingly filled in the blanks. Generous. Kind. Funny. Devastatingly gorgeous.

"Trust me," she finally answered. "We're not compatible."

Liv scrunched up her face. "Bummer. You're so perfect for each other."

Gretchen snorted. "Right."

"I'm serious," Liv said. "You've got that whole opposites-attract, grumpy-one-falls-for-the-sunshiny-one thing going on."

"Mack has you reading romance novels, too, doesn't he?"

"You should try them. They can be very inventive." Liv wiggled her eyebrows for effect. But then she tugged them together. "Wait. *Too*? Is Colton trying to convert you?"

"Leave her alone," Alexis chided.

"I need to get to the office," Gretchen said, shaking her head.

Alexis glanced at her phone, blinked a couple of times, and then looked up at Gretchen with a sheepish expression. "So, I need you to believe me when I say I did not plan this."

She gulped. "Plan what?"

The kitchen door swung open and a dark-haired Adonis strode in like he owned the place. He wore a flannel shirt and a pair of jeans, and this time his vest was red. He carried two Christmas wreaths, one in each hand, that matched his green eyes. Eyes that were staring at her now in a way that suggested he'd been standing outside the door and heard everything they'd said.

He grinned. "Well, isn't this convenient?"

No, it was not convenient. It was a nightmare. Another nightmare.

"What are you doing here?" Gretchen demanded. "Were you eavesdropping on us?"

He winked. "Nope, but now I'm super curious." Colton then

turned his gaze to Alexis and Liv. "Ladies, good to see you this morning. Y'all are looking gorgeous, as always."

"Colton," Alexis said, smiling nervously. "What brings you by?"

"Well, I was going to ask your opinion on these here Christmas wreaths, but seeing how the person I was going to give them to is standing right here, I could just ask her instead."

Alexis didn't even bother trying to hide her smile. "I see."

Liv lifted her eyebrows at Gretchen. "Well, which one is better?"

"They both suck."

Liv cackled. "This is why I love you. You're even grouchier than I am."

"It's part of her charm," Colton said. He raised the wreaths higher for Gretchen to consider. "One's for your office and one is for home."

"I don't like Christmas decorations at work."

"Probably this one then," he said, thrusting forward the one of eucalyptus leaves. "It doesn't scream Christmas. Just holiday."

He stared at her expectantly, waiting for her to take it from his hands. Sighing, she finally reached for it. The scent of the eucalyptus leaves reminded her of a day spa, which, admittedly, was not unpleasant. Of course, the last time she'd spent any time at a day spa was for Evan's wife's bachelorette party, and that had been entirely unpleasant. She was the only bridesmaid who had not been a member of Anna's college sorority, and they'd all treated her like a bug stuck to a corkboard. An oddity to poke and grimace at.

"I have to get back to work," Gretchen said.

"What about your coffee?" Alexis asked.

Dammit.

"I'll make them fast." Alexis raced back out the kitchen door.

"I have to get going too," Liv said. She paused on the way out to grin at Gretchen and punch Colton on the arm. "Be good, you two."

As soon as she was gone, Colton leaned down teasingly. "You were talking about me, weren't you?"

"No."

"Liar. I know when I walk into a conversation about me and—"

"You told the guys that we slept together after the wedding."

He sputtered for a moment. "No, I didn't."

"Then how did Alexis and Liv know?"

Colton winced.

"How could you do that?" Gretchen shoved the wreath at him. He caught it with his free hand against his chest.

"It's not like I just blurted it out," he said. "They figured it out."

"You could've denied it."

"I tried. They read the truth all over my face. Those guys know me well enough to know when I'm lying. And trust me, it's as annoying as it sounds."

Alexis returned carrying two to-go cups of coffee bearing the ToeBeans logo, one for her and one for Addison. "Thank you," Gretchen said, accepting them. "Put it on my tab?"

Alexis winked. "I know where to find you."

Without looking at Colton, Gretchen lifted both cups toward the door to use her forearms to push it open. But then a hand holding a wreath reached around her. "Let me," Colton said.

He opened the swinging door and held it open with his butt so Gretchen could walk through.

Unfortunately, he followed.

"I'll walk with you."

"Not necessary." Gretchen kept her gaze to the floor to avoid any cell phones that might capture them together again. In this lighting and at this close distance, the images of her would likely be much clearer.

"Yes, it is," Colton said. "I have to hang this wreath for you, and we have to plan our next date."

As they approached the door, she quickened her step so he wouldn't open it for her again. Turning, she used her backside and walked backward. Once outside, she turned again and let the door shut in his face.

A moment later, she heard the door open again and his footsteps behind her. "You're mad."

"Just late for work." Her breath puffed around her face in the cold.

"Gretchen, hold up." When she kept walking, he snagged the sleeve of her coat with a pinkie finger. Then he circled around in front of her, forcing her to stop. "I swear I didn't tell them. I would never betray you like that."

She believed him, and that made her grumpier. "There are pictures of us on social media."

"I know. I'm sorry."

"My brother saw them."

"Is that a problem?"

"It is if he thinks I'm not taking this endorsement proposal seriously but just using it as an excuse to get in your pants."

A carnal flash of awareness turned his eyes a darker shade of green. Gretchen swallowed an *argh* and walked around him. "I have to get to work."

Unfortunately, he followed.

When they reached her office, she looped a finger around the handle to tug it open.

Unfortunately, he followed her again.

Addison was fussing with another string of lights when they walked in. She glanced over her shoulder and then did a double take at Colton. "Oh my God, are you . . . ?"

Colton tipped his head. "Colton Wheeler. Pleased to meet you."

"Holy shit," Addison breathed.

Gretchen handed Addison her coffee. "He's not all that. Trust me."

Colton set the wreaths on the receptionist's counter and shook Addison's hand. She looked at it afterward as if she'd just touched God.

Colton then walked to Gretchen's side again, tugged on a lock of her hair, and gave her a look that turned her knees to pudding. "Pick you up at seven on Friday?"

At her silence, he tilted his head in a puppy-dog way, and somewhere, angels began to sing. Dammit. With a growl, she whipped around and began to stomp toward her office.

"Hey," he called behind her. "Why does Santa have three gardens?"

"Please don't tell me—"

"So he can ho ho ho."

Gretchen shook her head and looked at the ground. *Don't laugh. Don't laugh.* She chanted it in her head, but it was no use. She laughed.

"Ha," he said triumphantly behind her. "My work here is done. See you Friday."

Gretchen escaped into her office, set her coffee down as she sat, and immediately lowered her forehead to her desk. Mere seconds went by before Addison came in.

"Holy shit, what the hell was that, Gretchen?"

"The Ghost of Christmas Past."

"Are you seriously going out with him Friday? How did this happen?" Her voice rose an octave with each subsequent question until she hit a crescendo with, "Tell me what's going on!"

"Nothing is going on. My family wants him to be our new brand ambassador."

"But he's picking you up Friday night."

"For a business meeting."

"Whatever that was out there between you two, it wasn't business. That was foreplay."

"Go back to work," Gretchen ordered, turning on her computer. It would be five minutes before it properly booted up. She couldn't afford a new one, though.

"Come on! Can you honestly say you're not at all, even just a tiny bit, starstruck by him? I mean, it's *Colton Wheeler*."

Gretchen logged in to her computer. "You going to do any actual work today, or . . . ?"

"I knew it," Addison said. "You like to play the ice queen, but not even you can be immune to someone like that."

She shut the door behind her, leaving Gretchen alone with a single thought.

That was the whole problem.

She wasn't immune to him. She was as susceptible to his infection as a dog to fleas.

But nothing had changed in the year since she'd scurried out of his hotel room. They were no better suited now than before. There was one reason and one reason only why she was going through with this: to secure her family's blessing to join the foundation board.

The sooner this little charade ended, the better.

It was never a good sign when Vlad cracked his knuckles.

But that's how he greeted Colton an hour later when Colton walked into the fitness center for Silver Sneakers. He was the last one to arrive and almost missed Vlad's glare because standing behind him were two more guys Colton had not invited to class—Vlad's hockey coach and some dude he'd never seen before.

He dropped his duffel bag and pointed. "What the hell are they doing here? Has Mrs. Porth seen them?"

Vlad's eyes narrowed menacingly. "Forget them. We've seen the pictures."

"And we've talked to the girls," Noah added in a voice that Colton had only heard one other time, and that was when they raced two hours down the freeway in Colton's car so Noah could get to Alexis before she underwent surgery, only for Colton to let it slip later that he had access to an actual helicopter.

He'd been intimidating then. He was terrifying now. The shit was clearly about to hit the fan. "Are Gavin, Del, and Yan not coming today, or . . . ?"

"Shut up and tell us what's going on," Mack said.

"Okay, look—"

"Are you seriously blackmailing her into going out with you?" That was Malcolm, whose voice rarely rose above a calming baritone but was rising toward Vienna boys' choir.

"It's not blackmail."

"You gave her an ultimatum," Noah said, staring at Colton as if he'd just sprouted a third eye. "Go out with you or go back to her family and tell them she couldn't even get you to listen to a proposal."

"I gave her a *choice*. Not an ultimatum."

"Same fucking thing in this case," Mack said. "When one option is clearly worse than another, that's an ultimatum."

"And don't get excited that she decided you were the least awful of the two," Noah added. "That's not saying much."

Malcolm pinched the bridge of his nose. "Just when I think one of you dipshits has reached the pinnacle of douchebaggery, someone still manages to eclipse it."

Vlad's coach and the other dude inched closer then. "So, uh, thanks for letting us in the class," the other dude said.

"I didn't invite you," Colton griped.

"I did," Vlad said.

"Did you ask Mrs. Porth?"

"Yes, I emailed her last night to ask."

"You emailed her? Since when do you have her email address?" This was his class. He was the one who discovered it. His friends were going rogue.

"Stop changing the subject," Mack barked. "You have about three seconds to explain your intentions with Gretchen before I call Mrs. Porth over here to make you do push-ups."

Colton gulped and darted his eyes to the front, where Mrs. Porth was thankfully distracted.

"Just tell me this isn't about soothing your ego," Mack said.

Mack might as well have punched him. "You know, I wish I'd known you guys had such a shitty opinion of me."

"It's not about you, brother. It's about her. You two live in vastly different worlds. Gretchen is a private person, and although she grew up with a famous family, she has chosen not to live that life. So even if your intentions are pure—"

"They are."

"—they can have real, unintended consequences for her."

Colton thought about her reaction to the photos this morning. "I know," he admitted, squeezing the back of his neck. "But I'm serious about this. She's amazing, okay? Smart and funny and successful and dedicated and, I mean, what kind of person walks away from a fortune like her family's to help people? I'm not even sure I'm good enough for her."

The guys blinked in silence for a moment.

"Damn," Malcolm finally said.

Colton kicked the toe of his sneakers against the floor. "What?"

"You really *do* like her, don't you?" That was Mack again.

Colton pinned him with a glare. "Yes, I really like her."

"Then you've gotten off on the wrong foot," Noah said. "You don't blackmail a woman—"

"It's not blackmail."

Noah held up his hands. "Whatever you want to call it, it's a bad way to start. And I don't know if we can help you."

"I didn't say I want your help."

A round of skeptical snorts greeted his words. Mrs. Porth chose that moment to announce that class would begin in two minutes. Colton made the mistake of meeting her gaze and damn near pissed himself.

"Hey," Mack said, laying out his mat next to Colton's.

Colton glowered. "What?"

"I'm sorry I upset you."

Colton started stretching his triceps. "You hurt my feelings."

Mack patted his back. "I'm sorry. Hug?"

"No." Colton kicked the floor again.

"Come on, brother. Give me a hug."

Colton gave in and let Mack wrap his arms around him. A second after that, Colton embraced him back. They did a couple of back-pounding reassurances before stepping away from each other.

"Okay, good," Noah said, approaching them again. "Everyone make up over here?"

Colton nodded, strangely emotional. He didn't like fighting with his friends.

"So when is your next date?" That was Vlad.

"Friday. I'm going to bring her to my house to decorate my Christmas tree."

"Is that a euphemism?" Mack asked.

"What? No."

Mack snorted. "Well, then, it's a shitty idea."

Noah swatted him. "Hey, come on, Mack. You guys just made up."

"It's still a terrible idea," Mack said.

"I didn't ask your opinion." Colton pouted.

"Well, you're getting it."

Malcolm cleared his throat to ward off another spat. "So, just so we're clear here, not only are you basically forcing her to go out with you, you're also making her do Christmas stuff even though she told you she hates the holiday?"

"I want to change her mind about it."

Malcolm breathed in a lungful of steadying oxygen and let it out with a sigh. "Colton, I feel like I speak for the group when I say that when she hands you your ass, don't come running to us. You're on your own with this one."

"Gee, thanks."

A beefy hand landed on his shoulder. "My friend, I love you like a brother," Vlad said.

Colton patted his hand. "Thanks, man. I love you too—"

"But I am predicting a disaster."

Colton barely had time to process that nut punch before Malcolm turned his gaze squarely on him. "And remember, Colton. No one hates Christmas. They hate their *own* Christmases. If you hope to start something with Gretchen, don't fuck it up by confusing the two."

CHAPTER NINE

This isn't a date.

For the past two days, Gretchen had chanted those words in her head enough times to actually come close to believing them. And when her faith in the words began to wane, she buried herself in work or went on a punishing run. But now here she was, trying on a third possible outfit with just ten minutes left until he was supposed to pick her up. Either it was more complicated picking out clothes for a nondate than an actual one, or her brain was officially calling bullshit on her attempt to pretend she wasn't nervous about seeing him again.

This was ridiculous. And humiliating.

But who was she kidding? Gretchen didn't dig out her skintight leather leggings that showed off her toned runner's legs for just anyone. She didn't accessorize for a business meeting. And she sure as hell didn't curl her damn hair for a nondate.

Pa-the-tic.

The buzz of the intercom sent her heart into a frantic zigzag.

He was here. Shutting her bedroom door—mainly so he wouldn't see the mess she'd made of discarded outfits—she hurried down the hallway and pressed the button to let him in. Moments later, his footsteps grew louder as he climbed the stairs. She opened the door just as he was raising his hand to knock.

"Where's the wreath I gave you— Wow." He stopped and planted his hands on either side of the doorframe. Then he dragged his eyes down her body and back up again. "If you dressed up for me, it worked. I'm yours."

Warmth spread over her skin as if she'd just sunk into a bubble bath. It quickly scalded like spilled tea. What was she thinking, dressing like this? Now *he* would know she considered this a date. And since that was worse than admitting it to herself, she covered her embarrassment the only way she knew how. She scowled. "Nothing else was clean. Don't read anything into it."

"I already did." He stepped inside and swung the door shut behind him. "As I was saying before you damn near killed me in those pants . . . Where's the wreath I gave you?"

She pointed to the coffee table, where it sat atop a pile of books she had vowed to someday put on a shelf but probably never would.

"Want me to hang it for you?"

"No." She retrieved her coat from the back of the couch. As she reached for the belt to tie around her waist, he gripped her hands.

"Let me do it," he said, his voice like melted caramel.

Probably she should have swatted him away. Probably she should have backed away from his reach.

Probably.

But she didn't.

Colton took his time tugging the belt into a knot, somehow managing to also reel her closer to him with every twist of the fabric. When he was done, he moved his hands to her hips and closed the remaining minuscule distance between their bodies to a mere inch. The heat of his fingers soaked through her coat and her clothes, but it was nothing compared to the scorch of awareness when he dipped his mouth close to hers. "You give any more thought to that unresolved agenda item?"

Yep. A lot. Pretty much nonstop. "Nope."

"Too bad," he murmured, his lips hovering over hers. "Because I'd love to hear your thoughts on the matter."

Her common sense finally slapped her weakening willpower. "I think we have other pressing issues to discuss first."

She walked to the small dining table adjacent to the living room to retrieve the manila envelope with the information Evan had put together. She turned back around and held it out. "Here. A formal proposal."

"Great. I look forward to your thoughts on this too." He rolled the envelope and wrapped both hands around it. "Ready to go?"

"Do I get to find out where we're going this time?"

"You sure you don't want to be surprised?"

"One hundred percent sure."

"We . . ."—he dragged the word out—"are going to decorate my Christmas tree."

"Please tell me that's a euphemism."

Colton waggled his eyebrows. "It can be."

Gretchen rolled her lips in to hold back the smile threatening to ruin her aloof act. When that didn't work, she turned away and pretended to be looking for something.

Behind her, the door opened. "Stop stalling."

"I'm not stalling. I'm looking for my purse."

"You're trying to hide that smile from me."

She plucked her purse from the dining room chair and turned around, mustering the darkest scowl her features would allow.

"Sorry. You're still adorable," he said. "Let's go."

He waited in the hallway for her while she shut and locked her door. "Not that I'm ungrateful for this experience—"

"Yes, you are."

"But can I ask if there's going to be food provided at any point this evening?"

He leaned in, one hand propped on the doorframe behind her. "I'm going to force-feed you sugar plums and gingerbread cookies."

"I need meat."

"Oh, I can definitely give you that."

She rolled her eyes and ducked under his arm. "You know what I mean."

"Yes," he said, trudging behind her. "I plan to feed you, and meat will be provided. I have a ham in the oven."

She was halfway down the stairs but stopped and wrenched her head over her shoulder. "You have a *ham* in the oven?"

"You say that like it's a bad thing."

She continued on the stairs. "I'm just confused about the fact that you know how to cook one. Or anything, for that matter."

"I'm a grown-ass man. Of course I know how to cook. And ham is the superior Christmas meat, as far as I'm concerned."

"But you could afford an entire fleet of personal chefs."

"Indeed, I could. But imagine how disappointed you'd be in me if I admitted to using one."

They reached his car, and she let him open the door for her this time. The coy smile decorating his lips suggested he was *this close* to pointing it out, but the quiet politeness as he helped her in said he wasn't going to chance her wrath. Smart man.

After he shut the door, he jogged around to his side, and she used the moment to study him. He wore what she was quickly coming to think of as his uniform—a T-shirt under a long shirt atop a pair of well-loved jeans, and his red vest.

He grinned at her when he got in. "Do I meet with your approval?"

"No. Those clothes look terrible on you."

His laughter bounced off the windshield and echoed throughout the car. "You should know, honey, that I'd rather be insulted by you than be fawned over by anyone else."

Before starting the car, he tossed the rolled-up envelope in the back seat. She twisted around to look at where it landed on the floor. "What the hell?"

"We'll look at it later." He started the car. "So, I could torture you again with some holiday tunes or—"

"Whatever *or* is, let's do that." She clicked her seat belt in place.

"Or we could talk about the book."

She might have growled. "Is there a third option?"

"Sure." He pulled onto the road. "You could finally tell me why you walked out on me that morning."

And there it was. The question she dreaded more than any other. And though she knew a conversation about it likely couldn't be avoided forever, she was going to do her damnedest to try. "The book. Definitely the book."

"So you *did* start reading." He flipped his blinker at the stop sign, stopped for an oncoming car, and then hung a right. "What do you think so far?"

"I think I'm supposed to see myself in Chelsea, and I resent that."

"Interesting."

"Like that wasn't your intention."

He shrugged but kept his eyes on the road.

"Come on, seriously? You just happen to give me a book about a woman who hates Christmas, avoids her family, and has a career she deeply cares about?"

"That could describe any number of women, especially those who are characters in Christmas romance novels."

"Well, I'm not her."

"Noted. Anything else?"

It was a trap. If she admitted that the book had kept her awake long past her bedtime twice this week, she'd never hear the end of it. On the other hand, she was actually curious about a few things. "Fine," she huffed, mostly to herself. Then she twisted in her seat to look at him. "Why does this Simon guy care so much about what she does with her own house?"

"You'll find out. Just keep reading."

"But he's kind of pissing me off right now. If I don't find out soon why he's so obsessed with this, I'm going to have a hard time understanding why she'd fall for him."

"Because it's a sunshiny one–grumpy one trope."

"A what now?"

He turned again onto Shelby Avenue. "It's a classic romance trope. One character is all happiness and joy, and the other is stern and grumpy, and the only person who can ever make the grumpy one smile is the sunshine one, and the only person who can make the sunshine one look deep within himself is the grumpy one."

That sounded way too close to what Liv had said about her and Colton being a perfect match. Gretchen narrowed her eyes. "Is this a conspiracy?"

He barked out a laugh and glanced at her. "A conspiracy?"

"Yeah. You and Liv and Alexis . . . you're all in on this, aren't you?"

"In on what? Making you read a romance novel?"

"That and trying to get me to love Christmas and—"

"You're cute when you're paranoid."

This time she for sure growled. "Stop being the sunshiny one."

His quiet chuckle sent an infuriating tickle through her belly. "How far is it to your house?" she griped.

"I live south of Brentwood, so about twenty minutes."

"Do you live near Vlad and Elena?"

"Sort of. They're in a subdivision near me, but, uh, my house is a little more tucked away."

Gretchen had been around rich people her entire life and knew when they were purposely trying to two-step around the appearance of lavishness. Her parents were masters of the dance and liked to refer to their estate with its sixteen bedrooms, full-size ballroom, and indoor pool as "the shack." Because the uber rich cosplaying at poverty was just so hilarious.

And just as she suspected, "tucked away" was a quaint way to describe the location of Colton's house. The zip code might have said Brentwood, but he lived in a lush, secluded area where mansions were shrouded from public view by acres of trees. After punching in the code to a wrought iron security gate, he drove up a private road lined with historic streetlamps and mature deciduous trees that were probably breathtaking in fall but were now stripped of their leaves for the winter.

A quarter mile later, the house came into view. Made of gray stone with a peaked white roof, it rose high above the grounds on a soft, rolling bluff and was divided into two wings with a wide covered porch in the center. A grand stone staircase descended to the circular driveway in the front.

He'd already been busy putting up decorations. A wreath the size of a kiddie pool was affixed to the peaked gable above the porch. Garland adorned with red bows and white lights ran the length of the stone balustrade along the porch and down the long staircase. And in the middle of the circular drive was a two-story pine tree encircled with more lights.

Colton was uncharacteristically quiet as he turned off the car. "It's probably a bit much for your standards."

"It's beautiful," she said, hoping her sincerity came through.

"It's a lot more than I ever had growing up, that's for sure." He sucked in a quick breath and let it out with a laugh that sounded fake. "Anyway . . . ready to decorate?"

"If I say no, will you take me home?"

The injection of sarcasm brought back his swagger. "Nope. Nice try, though."

He met her on the passenger side and reached for her hand. They climbed the stairs to the porch together, and as he punched in another security code to unlock the front door, he looked over his shoulder at her. "Are you allergic to cats?"

"Um, no. Why?"

Colton stepped aside to let her go in first. Gretchen didn't have time to pay attention to the interior of the house because all her focus was on the apparent answer to her question sitting in the middle of the foyer. It had the body of a cat but was big enough to consume a corgi.

"Colton, I don't want to alarm you, but there's a mountain lion in here."

Colton laughed and swung the door shut behind her. "That's Pickle."

"Yeah, well, Pickle has a human face and is about to call her lawyer."

Colton bent to scoop the fluffy beast into his arms. Pickle meowed and rubbed her face against Colton's chin. "She loves me."

"She's *immense.*"

"Purebred Maine coon. They get pretty big."

Gretchen tentatively reached her hand out to give Pickle a scratch behind the ears. She was rewarded with a warm purr.

"That's my girl," Colton crooned before setting Pickle back on the floor. The cat immediately meowed in protest and wound herself through Colton's legs.

"I can take your coat," he said, holding out his hand.

She slid it from her shoulders and waited as he hung it up in the entryway closet, taking the moment to cast her gaze around the place. For such a big house on the outside, it felt small on the inside.

No. Not small. Cozy.

Colton's house was warm and welcoming. Everything her parents' house was not and had never been.

"Something to drink?"

His voice yanked her out of her silent observation. He'd shoved his hands in his pockets, and his posture seemed insecure, just like in the car, as if he really was afraid of her censure.

"Sure. Thank you."

"Kitchen's this way. Follow me."

Pickle trotted ahead of them both, her fluffy tail held high as if she knew something special awaited her. She wasn't wrong. As soon as they entered the vast kitchen, Colton walked directly to a low cabinet and pulled out a box of treats. He gave it a shake,

Pickle meowed, and then Colton poured a small handful onto the floor.

After returning the treats to the cabinet, he focused on Gretchen again. "Wine? Beer? CAW 1869?"

A smile coaxed itself past her defenses. "You know the answer to that."

As Colton got their drinks, she studied the kitchen again. Though large and outfitted with the kind of high-end appliances that would put Wolfgang Puck to shame, it was also surprisingly intimate. A place where she could easily imagine a boisterous, loving family singing "Happy Birthday" around a cake.

The kitchen opened up to a sitting area with a fireplace, and a set of French doors led to a balcony overlooking the backyard. Without asking, she opened the door and walked out into the cool night. Below was a courtyard and a large pool. More trees lined the back of the property, a natural privacy shield for the house.

He returned with two glasses of whiskey. After handing one to her, he held up his glass. "To cheating and . . . what was the rest?"

"Stealing, fighting, and drinking."

He clinked their glasses together, and she resumed her staring.

"I know, I know. Just say it."

"Say what?"

"That it's an obscene amount of money to spend on a house when so many people like your clients can barely afford to feed their kids—"

"I was *not* thinking that."

"—but this isn't just for me. I wanted a big space for my whole family to enjoy. Like they're on vacation when they're here. My parents come and stay several times a year, and it's awesome at Christmas. The kids run around and—"

She set her hand on his arm. "Colton, you don't have to explain anything to me. You're a huge success. I've never said that people shouldn't enjoy the rewards of their hard work."

"But I can feel the judgment radiating off you."

He said it in a teasing tone, but his words stung anyway. Is that truly what he thought of her? Is that what she projected to the world?

Good God. Was she really Ebenezer Scrooge?

Now it was her turn to be insecure. "We gonna decorate this tree or not?"

"Look at you," he said, teasing once again. "Getting in the spirit."

"More like getting it over with."

He winked. "That's my grumpy girl."

When the tickle returned to her belly, she knew that maintaining her vow that tonight was not a date was hopeless.

CHAPTER TEN

"I've never actually done this before."

"Never done what?" Colton looked up from the floor where he'd been opening boxes of new lights and plugging them together, end to end.

Gretchen was perched on the edge of the couch, fingers wrapped around her glass. "Decorated a Christmas tree."

He glanced up again and huffed out a laugh. "Right."

"I'm not kidding."

His hands went still of their own accord, and he raised his gaze again, this time slowly. She didn't look like she was messing with him. But this was even more absurd and unbelievable than the fact that she'd never been to Christmas on the Cumberland, and a helluva lot sadder. "*Why?*"

"I've never gotten a tree for myself, and our house growing up was part of the whiskey trail holiday tour, so my mother always hired professional Christmas decorators. We usually had more than ten trees in our house, and the decorators did it all."

"But you must've had a private tree, like just for the family?"

She shook her head.

"So, let me make sure I've got this straight." He moved the bundle of lights off his lap and then rubbed his hand over his hair a couple of times. "You never had, like, a family decorating night? No fighting with your siblings over who got to put the star on top?"

"Nope."

"No sneaking candy canes off the tree when your parents weren't looking?"

"Nope."

"No teasing your mother when she got all teary-eyed when she pulled out the paper ornaments you made in kindergarten?"

"Is there a 'none of the above' box I can check on this conversation? Because I guarantee, whatever you think of, the answer is the same."

"But . . . she kept them, though, right? Your handmade ornaments?"

"I have no idea." She sipped her drink again. Her fingernails were nearly white from the tense grip she held on her glass.

The emotion that tightened his chest was a cross between anger and sympathy. "So, how did you decide which tree to put your presents under?"

"We didn't."

"You didn't give each other presents?" His voice had taken on a falsetto that would've made Freddie Mercury proud.

"Yes, but we didn't put them under a tree. My mom said it looked cluttered, and my dad was always worried that one of the tourists would steal them, so they would just bring them all out Christmas morning."

"I—" He blinked several times. "I'm speechless."

Her lips twitched into a tight smirk. "Christmas miracles *do* happen."

"So—"

She looked at the ceiling with a groan.

"—you never knew that amazing feeling of watching the pile of presents grow under the tree in the days leading up to Christmas and constantly checking the tags to see which ones were for you?"

"I usually already knew what I was getting, so . . ." She shrugged. The gesture was probably meant to convey nonchalance, but her clipped tone and tense jaw sent the opposite message.

A voice in the back of his mind—which sounded remarkably like Malcolm—warned him to change the subject but, Jesus, every answer she gave just opened up a new line of questions. "Why did you always know what you were getting?"

"For as long as I could remember, I would give them a list, and they would buy everything."

He was officially dumbfounded. "You're shitting me."

"Why would I lie about that?"

"I don't think you're lying. I just can't believe it. The best part about Christmas as a kid is ripping open the presents and finding the thing you wanted most but your parents had been telling you for weeks you weren't getting."

She cocked another smirk. "We have very different families."

The anger and sympathy converged into a seething ball of resentment on behalf of the child she once was. What kind of parents denied their kids the most basic holiday traditions for the sake of something as frivolous as a holiday house tour?

"Don't look at me like that."

"Like what?"

"Like I was some kind of neglected child. I grew up in a mansion with more money than most people could ever even imagine."

"There are a lot of forms of neglect."

"Not decorating a Christmas tree isn't one of them."

The conversation had taken all of five minutes, but it was as if she'd read her entire autobiography aloud to him. No wonder she hated Christmas. There was never any magic in it for her. She challenged his prolonged silence with a raised eyebrow. He had to clear his throat to find the right tone of voice. "Well, then, I guess I have the privilege of being your first."

She rolled her eyes, but his joke worked. Her brittle smirk became her pretending-to-be-annoyed-but-actually-amused smile. He was starting to live for that smile.

He stood up from the floor. "So, you gonna help me or just sit there all night admiring my ass in these jeans?"

"There's that ego again."

"Because I'm actually fine with either."

She stood up and set her glass on the coffee table in front of the couch. "Tell me what to do."

He lowered his voice. "Honey, I'm going to replay those words all night long in my dreams."

She did the eye-roll, annoyed-but-not-really thing again. "Do we start with lights or ornaments?"

"Lights, *duh*."

"I told you. I'm a virgin here."

"You're not going to make this easy on me, are you?"

"Nope."

He made a low, growly noise and picked up the lights he'd discarded on the floor. "Here," he said, handing one end to her. Then he pointed to the other side of the tree. "You stand there, and I'll start wrapping these around."

"Geez, and you think I'm the grumpy one?" She walked to where he'd indicated, stretching out the connected string of lights as she went.

He wasn't grumpy. He was one innuendo away from popping a goddamn boner. Which made him feel like the lowest rung of humanity, considering the stuff she'd just admitted about her childhood.

It took only a handful of minutes to get most of the lights up, but he had to drag over a ladder that he'd brought in earlier to reach the highest peak of the tree.

When he was done, she playfully shoved his shoulder. "Let's go, Colton. Pop my Christmas cherry so we can eat."

He groaned and stumbled backward, hand over his chest. "Are you actively trying to kill me?"

"If that's what it takes to get the meat, then yes."

"Okay, that's it." He grabbed her hand and began to tug her toward the hallway.

She stumbled and let out a surprised laugh. "Where are we going?"

"I have something to show you in my bedroom."

She laughed—like, really laughed, loud and hearty—and pulled back on her hand. He didn't let go but instead looped around and used the leverage to pull her against him. She gently collided with his chest and gazed up at him in a way that made the world turn faster and slower all at once, like spinning out on a snowy road. The scenery sped by in a blur but somehow his senses noted every color, every object, every sound and smell, until he was left with nothing but the certainty that something big was about to happen. And it was either going to end in relief or disaster.

If he'd learned anything from reading romance novels, it was that a painful confession led to vulnerability, and that vulnerability always came with a cost. She was vulnerable. If he took advantage of the situation, the cost might be more than he could stand.

"Do you remember the first time we kissed?" His voice was strained, like sandpaper against rock.

So was hers. "Yes."

"I'd been wanting to do it all night. I was desperate for you." He let his thumb drift from her chin to her bottom lip. Another tremor shook her body. "I wish it hadn't happened like that."

Her eyes asked *why*, but she didn't voice the question. Maybe she trusted her voice even less than he did his.

Colton slid his hand up her back until his fingers met the depths of her thick hair. "We deserved something soft for our first kiss. Something slow." Her breathing hitched as he used the pad of his thumb to massage the top of her neck. "We deserved to know each other better. To take our time."

He lowered his mouth atop hers, hovering a breath away in a silent query for permission.

"Colton," she breathed.

His fingers spread wide across her back. "Yeah?"

She curled her fingers into his shirt, rose on tiptoe, and kissed him.

The blood in his veins became roaring rivers. She opened beneath him, welcoming the tangle of his tongue with hers, and just like that, a sun rose between them. Hot and fiery and bright. He leaned into it, turned toward it like the first graze of warmth on his face after a long winter.

He burned to go deeper, farther. To lay her down flat and touch every part of her. But he didn't because he wanted to take his time.

He wanted the simple beauty of teasing her lips with his, the hazy joy of learning her mouth differently this time. He wanted to let the taste of her linger on his tongue, explore all her flavors, and savor each one. He wanted to start again.

Her hand found a home against the center of his chest, and even through his clothes, she branded him. Colton moved one hand to lace their fingers together atop his heart.

She'd said they made no sense, but they did. They were a shared memory. A promise of something good. They were single-syllable truths in a conspiracy-theory world. They were heat and touch and faith and joy. They were a kite in the sky. A storm on the sea.

She was the sand, and he was a wave.

She was a song.

He was its voice.

Holy shit.

Holy shit.

Colton lifted his mouth from hers, reluctantly, desperately. "Fuck, Gretchen." He lowered his brow to hers. "I'm sorry."

She blinked, and confusion turned her sultry voice to a squeak. "Wh-what's wrong?"

"You have to go."

See, *this* was the problem with kissing Colton Wheeler. He turned her brains to scrambled eggs.

Gretchen's cognitive functions froze somewhere between the caress of his fingers against hers and the moment when his lips touched hers, which is why she was having a hard time keeping up now with the sudden cessation of her latest cliff-jump into mistake canyon. "Go *where*?"

"I'm sorry," he breathed, and it sounded sincere. "Fuck, you have no idea how sorry." He dropped his mouth once again onto hers in a quick, efficient kiss. "But I have to get to my piano."

"Your piano?" Yeah, her brains were definitely poached, because she couldn't even remember what a piano was at that moment.

"I have a song in my head."

A song. So, he wasn't freaking out. He wasn't backward crawling like a frightened hermit crab because she, like, had bad breath or something. He'd just been struck by some kind of creative inspiration lightning. The relief to both her ego and libido took over her common sense again. "Wait . . . you want me to *leave*?"

"I can't explain it. Fuck." He dragged his hands through his hair. "I just, I could tell you to wait here, but I don't know how long this is going to take, and I *have* to get this song out of my head."

Maybe she should've been offended, but the passion on his face drowned out every other emotion. He was transformed. Like a Holy Spirit had possessed his soul. "Right. No, I understand. I will, um, call an Uber or something."

He was already distracted by whatever melody was playing in his head. He stared at her for a moment as if he hadn't heard her. But then, "Wait. No. An Uber will have to wait for the gate. Just take my car."

He dug into his pocket for the key fob and handed it to her.

She folded it into her palm. "Is this what it's always like when you get a song idea?"

"No," he breathed, shaking his head. "I mean, not in a long time." He gripped her shoulders then and planted a toe-curling kiss on her lips. "I think you're my muse."

In the short annals of her dating history, that line was definitely going to the top of her *How to Make Gretchen Melt* list.

"I swear to God, I will make this up to you," he said, still holding her shoulders.

"There's nothing to make up. Go do your thing."

"The gate will open when you approach it." Once more, he bent and kissed her.

Then he turned on his heel and strode toward the hallway with a gait she recognized. Not because it was his, but because it was *hers*. He moved with the purpose and determination that she felt every time she got a new case.

He stopped suddenly, turned around, and jogged back to her.

"Drive careful," he said. "These roads get really dark, and the deer dart out before you can see them."

"Worried about your car?" she teased.

"Worried about you."

Colton pressed his fingers to his lips and turned around for the final time. His quick footsteps faded as he disappeared into a wing of the house she hadn't explored. She opened her hand and looked at the key fob he'd given her. Loaning her his car was perhaps as intimate as their kiss. A person didn't just loan their car to anyone. Because it insinuated something intangible. Something she'd had precious little of from the people closest to her.

Trust.

And not as in, *I trust you won't wreck my car.*

More like, *I trust that you won't wreck me.*

And that's what scared her. He could give her a hundred romance novels to read and change her mind about Christmas, but one thing wouldn't change.

She was a Winthrop. And eventually, they wrecked everything in their paths.

CHAPTER ELEVEN

Colton heard voices. Faraway voices.

"I think he's dead."

"Poke him with a stick or something. See if he moves."

"What if he doesn't? Do we have to call someone? Because I really need to get these presents wrapped today."

Colton peeled open one eye and found the whole crew—Malcolm, Mack, Noah, Vlad, Gavin, Yan, and Del—all staring down at him as if conducting an autopsy. Each wore apprehensive expressions and blinking reindeer antlers.

"Jesus, you look like roadkill," Mack said. "You sick or something?"

"What are you doing here?" His voice was like sandpaper.

Vlad held up a roll of wrapping paper. "Wrapping party, remember?"

Fuck. Colton had, in fact, *not* remembered. He sat up, stifling a yawn. "What time is it?"

"It's eleven o'clock, fuck stick," Noah said. "That's what time you told us to come over." His hand dove into one of the bags he carried, and he pulled out another set of antlers. "We got some for you too."

"How'd you get in?" Colton groaned and pressed the heels of his hands into his eye sockets.

"You gave me a key and the security code," Vlad said.

"That was for emergencies."

"This *is* an emergency," Vlad said. "Elena wants presents wrapped early to see if they'll all fit in my Santa sack, and if they don't then we have to figure out something else."

Mack snorted. "Santa sack."

Noah backed away from the couch and cast a gaze around the room, taking in the chaos left over from last night. Scraps of paper were all over the floor by the piano bench, some crumpled. Four empty bottles of water were lined up along the rim of the piano. Leaning against the legs, two of his guitars.

"Rough night?" Noah asked.

"I was up late writing." Which felt like the world's biggest understatement. He'd been possessed last night. As soon as Gretchen left, he'd sat down at his piano, and the songs had poured out of him. He didn't stop until he passed out on the couch sometime before dawn. He hadn't been that inspired in years. It was as if some great dam in his mind had been cleared of debris and the river of words began to flow again. Which was so shitty of a metaphor that he'd be ashamed to use it in a song, but still . . . it fit.

Noah patted his shoulder. "You wrote another new song? That's great, brother."

"Three," Colton corrected.

"*Three?*" The guys said it together in a harmonized *holy shit* pitch.

"You wrote three songs *last night*?" Yan said, apparently just to clarify.

"That must be some kind of record," Vlad said, plopping down on the opposite end of the couch. His reindeer antlers jostled back and forth with the movement. "Will you play them for us?"

"No."

Vlad pouted. "Why not?"

"Because they're just first drafts."

"That's never stopped you before," Noah pointed out.

True. But this was different. For the first time in his life, he was well and truly terrified that people wouldn't like his songs. And not even just because of what happened with the label, but because these new songs were a total departure from what he'd written before. They were the most honest things he'd ever written.

Colton stood, stretched his arms over his head, and stifled another yawn. "I'm going to go take a shower. Help yourselves to the kitchen."

The sound of a stampede followed him as he jogged upstairs. When he came back down twenty minutes later, he found them all gathered around the kitchen table with plates loaded with ham, potatoes, and squash—all the things he was supposed to serve Gretchen last night.

Mack grinned, fork halfway to his mouth. "Damn, dude. You had a whole-ass meal in the fridge."

"I made it for Gretchen last night, but we didn't get a chance to eat it." He'd belatedly remembered to put the food in the fridge an hour after Gretchen left.

Malcolm coughed and recovered. "Okay, there is so much about what you just said that requires further explanation."

"Yeah, starting with why the hell you made Gretchen a *ham*?" Gavin laughed.

"Because ham is the superior Christmas meat!" God, why did everyone have some kind of vendetta against ham?

"Dude, chill," Mack said. "We're just trying to get details."

Colton dragged his hands over his wet hair. "Fine. Gretchen came over last night to decorate my Christmas tree—"

"Is that a euphemism?" Del interrupted.

"No."

Malcolm shushed everyone's laughter with a single look. They settled down as if scolded by the teacher. "Please continue, Colton."

"We literally decorated my Christmas tree, or, I mean, we started to. And we were going to eat afterward but we got interrupted."

"By what?" Yan asked.

The most amazing kiss of my life. "A song in my head."

"You wrote the songs with her here?" Noah said.

"But you won't play them for *us*?" Vlad added.

"No, I didn't write them with her here. I . . ." he winced. They were going to lose their shit over this. "I sort of told her to go."

"You . . . told her . . . to go." Malcolm repeated the words as if they'd never been strung together in that order before.

"It's just that I knew I needed to get the song down, and I couldn't do that with her here, so . . . I let her drive my car home."

Vlad set down his plate and started cracking his knuckles.

"Okay, before you go off," Colton said, holding up his hands to protect himself from the coming verbal attack, "she wasn't pissed or anything when she left."

Conversation ceased suddenly as Pickle exited the mudroom and the location of her litter box. Trailing her was a smell to wake the dead. It spread throughout the kitchen like a dark storm cloud until it blanketed everyone and everything.

Noah covered his nose and mouth with his hand and mumbled beneath it, "Fuck, dude. What the hell are you feeding that thing?"

"Fancy Feline," Colton grumped. "And who are you to talk anyway? Your girlfriend's cat is a menace to humanity."

"But he's not rotting from the inside out."

Malcolm gagged. "You gotta switch her to something organic."

"No cat should produce a smell like that," Mack said, grimacing at his now-forgotten food. "You need to take her to the vet or something."

Colton didn't have time for this shit. "I thought you guys were here to wrap presents."

"Yes," Vlad said, shoving one last bite of ham in his mouth. "We must wrap."

As the guys scattered, Colton grabbed the bags of gifts he'd bought for the guys' kids and met them all back in the living room. He found them all seated on the floor near the Christmas tree, and the room already looked like an explosion inside Santa's warehouse. Wrapping paper and bows overflowed from craft store bags next to each man, and towering piles of unwrapped presents filled the center of the room. Clothes and baby dolls and stuffed animals and purses.

Colton chose a puppy-themed paper from the pile in the center of the room and rolled it out between his splayed legs. Then he pulled his first present from the bag—a toy guitar that played songs with a push of a button.

"Please tell me that's not coming to my house," Yan said.

Colton grinned. "To Oscar, love Uncle Colton." Oscar was Yan's three-year-old son with his wife, Soledad.

Yan groaned. "Someday I'm going to get you back for all the loud things you have given my kids."

"My wife had to hide that mini drum set you got Grady last year," Del said of his two-year-old son. He and his wife, Nessa, also had a six-year-old girl named Josephine, or Jo Jo for short.

"It's my job to promote music education," Colton said, plopping a red bow on top of the gift.

"What the hell did you get my kids this year?" Gavin asked. He and his wife, Thea, had twin girls.

Colton pulled two ukuleles from a bag. Gavin groaned. "Thanks."

"Bring the girls to my house," Colton said. "I'll teach them how to play."

"Can I leave the ukuleles there too?"

"Nope." He wrapped them in the same puppy-dog paper as the toy guitar.

Noah suddenly gaped at Gavin. "What the hell are you doing?"

Gavin's eyebrows tugged together. "Wrapping."

"Have you *never* wrapped a present before?"

Gavin looked down at the crumpled red-and-green monstrosity in front of him. "What's wrong with it?"

"Way too much paper," Colton said, mostly because he was grateful that the spotlight was now shining on someone else.

"And you just, like, wrapped that blanket without putting it in a box," Del added, aghast. "It's all floppy and ugly."

"It's *wrapped*," Gavin snapped. "Who cares what it looks like?"

It was as if someone had just torn the exit door off an airplane. All the air was sucked from the room. Papers flew. Packages fell. Yan actually screamed.

"A well-wrapped present is an expression of love," Malcolm said. "Please tell me you take a little more care with your wife's gifts."

"I usually put everything in gift bags."

Yan shook his head, mumbled something that sounded unkind, and started to stand. "I am leaving."

Noah grabbed his arm and tugged him back down. "I'm sure he didn't mean it," Noah said, looking at Gavin. "Right? You don't actually just toss everything in gift bags like they never mattered at all."

Gavin scowled but started over on his package anyway.

Soon, Pickle joined the group and promptly settled on top of Mack's unrolled paper. Mack reeled back as if she had something contagious.

"What're you getting Gretchen for Christmas?" Del suddenly asked.

"I don't even know. I'm not even sure if we'll still be dating then." And wasn't *that* a cat turd of a thought?

"So you *are* dating?" Noah asked. "Like, for real? Or are you still pretending this is just some business negotiation?"

Colton scowled, mostly because he didn't know the answer to the question.

"Have you kissed?" Yan asked breathlessly.

"Fuck off. I'm not going to kiss and tell. We're allowed some privacy, aren't we?"

Yan stuck out his lip. "You're no fun."

"But you *have* kissed." Vlad looked at Colton sideways. "I mean, you obviously kissed before and did other stuff." Vlad's face flamed, and he shut up.

"You're obviously falling for her," Noah said.

Heat rose on Colton's neck, and he shrugged half-heartedly to cover it. He knew how he felt, but he couldn't say how Gretchen felt. All he knew for sure was that everything had changed last night. Not just because of how she kissed him but because of everything she'd revealed about her life growing up. Malcolm was right. There was a difference between hating Christmas and simply hating your own experiences with it.

"Do your teeth tingle when you're around her?" Gavin asked.

"What?"

"Thea used to make my teeth feel funny." Gavin tapped his top teeth with his finger. "Like there was just electricity racing through my body whenever I thought about her."

Colton fought a smile. "She makes me feel like I can't breathe normal."

Mack laughed. "I still can't breathe around Liv sometimes."

"It's a wonder I haven't passed out yet around Alexis," Noah said.

"What else?" Del asked, clapping his hands. "This is the good stuff. The romantic stuff."

"Is she the reason you were so inspired to write last night?" Malcolm asked.

"I don't know. But I think they're the best songs I've ever written." Colton's mouth went dry at the admission.

"In what way?" Mack prodded.

"They're honest, serious. Like I'm telling stories I was too afraid to tell before."

A reverent silence descended on the group.

"Damn," Malcolm said. "This is the real thing, isn't it?"

Colton's stomach clenched. "It is for me. I'm not sure about her."

"What makes you think that?" Mack asked.

"She still won't tell me why she ditched me last year. I've asked her twice, and she either dodges the question or gives me some vague non-answer."

"Maybe you're just not used to having to work for it," Mack said.

"What the hell does that mean?"

Mack shrugged. "You're a celebrity. When was the last time you had to worry that someone didn't want to go out with you?"

The pointed accuracy was a sharp stick in his side, especially since she'd all but accused him of the very same thing. But then she'd kissed him last night as if she couldn't help herself. He shook his head. "It's more than that. She likes me, but it's as if she doesn't *want* to like me."

Noah clapped his hands. "Oh, I *love* this trope."

Colton glowered. "It's not a trope. It's my life."

"Noah is right," Malcolm said. "This is a classic storyline. One character resists their attraction to the other for some unknown reason. But there's always a reason. You just have to dig into her—"

The group spoke in unison. "Backstory."

"It never fails, brother," Malcolm said. "Backstory is everything."

The guys were right, as always. Colton had gotten a small glimpse into her past at his house, but it wasn't enough. "I think she had a pretty messed-up childhood. She'd never even decorated a Christmas tree until last night."

"*Ever?*" Noah's stunned tone of voice matched everyone else's expressions.

"How is that possible?" Del asked.

"I think her parents had some pretty shallow priorities."

Malcolm pointed emphatically. "That's where your answer lies. You find out more about *that*, and you'll find out why she's holding back with you."

"Easier said than done. She's a closed book."

"Then keep trying to crack it open," Mack said.

"And don't give up," Malcolm added. "I suspect she's used to people who do."

Just before noon, Addison poked her head in Gretchen's office. "Got a minute?"

"Sure," Gretchen said, swiveling in her chair. "Come in." Addison had been unusually quiet all morning, and the tentative way she walked in, her hands nervously twisted against her stomach as she sat down, didn't exactly ease Gretchen's mind.

Addison glanced at the computer. "I can come back if you're in the middle of something."

"Okay, now I'm worried. You're never concerned about interrupting me."

Even Addison's laugh was missing its normal gaiety. "True. This is just sort of embarrassing."

"Embarrassing as in you've been arrested for streaking naked down Broadway, or embarrassing like—"

"We need more people."

Gretchen crossed her legs under her desk. "More clients?"

"Ha, no." This time, Addison's laugh contained no joy. "We can barely keep up now."

"So you mean we need more people working here."

"I've been wanting to talk to you about this for a while now, but I know how busy and stressed out you are, so I've just been biting my tongue, but I can't anymore. I'm sorry."

"How long is a while?"

"Since last year."

Annoyance flared her nostrils, but Gretchen forced herself to breathe through it. "Okay. We're going to circle back to that, but what made you decide to speak up now?"

"I've applied for a new job."

Betrayal and fear mixed in her mouth to form a sour taste. "Where?"

She named a major law firm in Memphis—the kind with plush carpet and shiny elevators and zero honor. "Seriously? Addison, you would hate it there."

Addison responded with silence.

Gretchen blinked. "Do you hate it *here*?"

"Not yet."

"But you hate it enough to send out résumés, apparently."

"I sent out résumés because I know you're considering that job in D.C."

"I'm *not* considering that job." Gretchen rolled her lips in and out. "What can I do to get you to stay?"

"Hire more help."

"Addison, you know how tight our budget is."

"Which I don't understand. You're, like, an honest-to-God heiress."

"I don't get anything until my parents die."

Addison winced. "I'm sorry. I just mean, you must have money."

"I've already dumped most of the money my grandfather left me into the clinic, and the rest is our emergency fund." And it would be a cold day in Hell before she asked her parents for financial help. Any money from them would come with an *I told you so* tax that she would never be able to pay off. If she couldn't make a success of her work on her own, they'd spend the rest of their lives smugly reminding her that she should have gone into the family business.

"This *is* an emergency," Addison said, leaning forward. "We're all overworked. Which we don't mind because we believe in what we do here. But—"

"But what?"

"I didn't seriously think about leaving until that email you sent out yesterday."

"What email?"

"The one about working Christmas Eve."

"I send out a weekly overview every week. I didn't even realize which day Christmas Eve was."

"Exactly!" Addison bit her lip, as if losing her nerve. But then she sucked in a deep breath and sat up straighter. "Unlike you, we have lives outside our work. We would like to enjoy them."

It was the *unlike you* part that stiffened Gretchen's spine. "Excuse me, but I have a life outside work too."

Addison's eyebrow rose so high it nearly blended into her hairline. "You didn't even know what day Christmas Eve was."

"It was an oversight," Gretchen said. "And I do have a social life. I even went out with Colton again last night."

Addison's face went blank for a moment, but then she suddenly lit up. "Are you serious?"

Gretchen sighed. "The point is—"

"No, no. We're not just going to ignore that little revelation. Are you guys actually dating?"

"Five seconds ago, you were threatening to quit. Now you want me to talk about my love life?"

"With Colton Wheeler? Yes. I want every detail."

"Are you going to tell me about you and Zoe?"

"I'm going out with her again tonight. Your turn."

"Keep this up, and I just might fire you."

"Have you slept with him?"

"I am not answering that."

"Oh. My. God. You've had sex with Colton Wheeler." Addison did a little dance in her chair.

"Can we please get back to the issue at hand? Why didn't you tell me earlier that you felt this way?"

Addison sobered once again. "I didn't want to seem ungrateful or lazy."

"You're neither of those things. You're the heart of this office, but obviously I've been relying on you for way too much."

"So you'll think about it? Hiring more people?"

"I'll figure it out." She had no idea *how* she would figure it out, but she couldn't afford to lose Addison. "And I'm *not* considering the job in D.C."

Addison shut the office door as she left, leaving Gretchen alone with a distracted mind and a heavy sense of foreboding. She truly hadn't thought about the fact that Christmas Eve was next week when she sent out the weekly schedule. It bothered her that Addison had been holding all that in for so long. Was she *that* unapproachable? Did her staff really see her as some kind of . . .

Oh, shit. She really was Ebenezer Scrooge, and it had nothing to do with how much she hated Christmas.

Gretchen stared at the ceiling, counted to ten, and then stood up. She opened her door and walked out into the lobby. "Addison—" The words faded at the sight of a well-dressed woman walking in the front door.

She wore a long winter-white coat, clutched a limp pair of baby-soft leather gloves in her right hand, and bore a striking resemblance to her mother. But that was impossible. Her mother had never been to her office before. As far as Gretchen knew, her mother didn't even know where the office was located.

"There you are, darling," the woman said with a smile.

Wow, she even sounded like her mother.

The woman breezed across the small waiting area, her velvet scarf and heeled boots looking as out of place as a giraffe in a petting zoo. Gretchen braced for the impact of her stiff embrace. "I was just in the neighborhood and thought I would stop by to see you."

Gretchen caught Addison's eye. They exchanged a shocked gaze, the tension from a few moments ago replaced with shared confusion. Gretchen cleared her throat. "In the neighborhood? Are you lost?"

"There's a first time for everything, isn't there?" Her mother cast a purposeful gaze around her surroundings. "So this is where you work."

"This is the law office that I own, yes."

"It's smaller than I imagined."

"My clients don't really care about the size of my office."

"Right. Well—" She beamed at Addison, turning on the artificially whitened socialite smile that had charmed everyone from President Bush—the second one—to Little Richard, which was a really long story. "I'm Diane Winthrop, Gretchen's mother."

Addison extended her hand over the reception desk. "Nice to meet you."

"Seriously, Mom. What are you doing here?"

"Goodness. It's nice to see you too."

"I'm sorry. You just really, *really* surprised me."

"That was my plan." Diane smiled. "Have you eaten? I thought maybe we could get some lunch at that little cafe you're always talking about."

Gretchen wanted to stick a finger in her ear and shake it around to make sure her hearing still worked. "You want to have lunch at ToeBeans?"

"Yes, that's the one. What do you say?"

"I don't understand. What's going on?"

"For heaven's sake, Gretchen. Can't a mother take her daughter to lunch?"

"Sure. But you've never, not once, come to my office and suggested lunch at a place where you have to order from the counter. So forgive me for being a little suspicious."

"Yes, well, as I said, there's a first time for everything." It wasn't so much what she said as the way she said it that caught Gretchen off guard. Her mother's eyes shifted sideways, and she moved her gloves from one hand to the other. Twice. As if she was nervous.

Gretchen turned to Addison at the reception desk. "How does my afternoon look?"

Addison cleared her throat and clicked the mouse a couple of times. "You have appointments at two-thirty and four."

"See? Plenty of time," her mother said.

"I'll get your purse," Addison offered. While she walked back to Gretchen's office, Gretchen slipped into her own coat and gloves. Addison returned a moment later and handed Gretchen her bag. "You want anything from ToeBeans?" Gretchen asked her.

"No, thanks."

Gretchen followed her mom outside onto the sidewalk. They walked in silence for a block before her mother said, "This is a cute neighborhood."

Gretchen stopped short. "Okay. Who are you and what have you done with my mother?"

"What do you mean?"

"A cute neighborhood? Do you not see the tattoo parlor? The art gallery with the nude sculpture in the window?"

"Of course I see them."

"That is not your idea of cute."

"I'm trying to make conversation. Now, come on, I'm cold."

Gretchen started walking again. The theme to the *Twilight Zone* played softly in her head. "Yes, it's a cute neighborhood," she finally said. "I love it here."

"And your apartment is close by, right?"

"Just a couple of minutes away."

"Well, you'll have to show me that too."

"My apartment?"

"Yes."

"Mom, seriously. What is going on? Are you dying or something?"

To her utter surprise, her mother barked out an uncharacteristic laugh. "No."

"Dad? Is Dad dying?"

"No! Gretchen, for God's sake."

"The business is going under, and you're here to tell me that you're about to go full *Schitt's Creek*."

Her mother laughed again and shook her head. "Are you truly that cynical?"

"You've met me, right?"

"I just wanted to come see where you work and live."

"After seven years?"

"It hasn't been that long, has it?"

Yes. Seven years. That's how long Gretchen had lived and worked in this neighborhood, and neither one of her parents had ever come to see it. "Well, this is it. Where I work and live." Gretchen pointed to the café on the corner. "And that's ToeBeans."

The cafe was even busier at lunch than in the morning. A line of people waiting to order stretched to the doorway, and another cluster of a half-dozen people waited by the counter for their to-go food. Nearly every table was full. If she could pull it off, Gretchen would try to film her mother's reaction to—gasp—having to wait for so long to be served.

But then Alexis spotted them, and she marched over in mock annoyance. Today she wore a Christmas scarf braided through her long hair. "How many times do I have to tell you?"

"I know. Friends don't wait." Gretchen smiled. "Um, this is my mom, Diane."

"So nice to meet you." Alexis beamed. Sincerity oozed from her voice because Alexis did everything with sincerity and generosity. "Grab a table, and I'll be over in a minute to take your order."

Gretchen didn't bother arguing this time because her mother had already thanked Alexis profusely and was heading toward a table by the window.

"This is charming," Diane said, lowering daintily into one of the hard-backed wooden chairs.

"Alexis has worked really hard."

The small bistro table was only big enough for the two of them. A vase with a small arrangement of holly and berries was in the center. Wedged between the salt and pepper grinders were two thin menus.

"What do you recommend?" her mother asked.

"Everything is good here, but I like the chicken salad sandwich and the cream of asparagus soup."

"Well, that's what I'll get too."

The *Twilight Zone* theme played louder. "Don't you want to know what's in it?"

"If you like it, I'm sure I will too."

Something was definitely going on. Her mother practically demanded a list of ingredients for everything she ordered because Lord knows there would be hidden calories just waiting to attach themselves to her slim, Pilates-toned hips.

"The sandwich has mayonnaise in it," Gretchen said.

"Sounds wonderful."

"And I'm pretty sure the soup is loaded with butter."

Her mother wasn't paying attention. Her eyes were looking around the café, studying people in silence. Gretchen's lawyerly instincts kicked in, and she decided to use her mother's distraction to her advantage. People often revealed as much in their quiet moments as they did when they spoke, and her mother was leaking like a sieve. The gloves were once again wrapped tightly in her fingers. A pink flush highlighted her natural cheekbones, partly from the chill outside but also, Gretchen sensed, from discomfort.

"Mom."

Diane looked at her, smile returning. "Hmm?"

"What's going on?"

"I really did want to visit you at work and have lunch with you."

"If I say that I believe you, will you tell me the rest?"

Her mother shoved her gloves in her purse, and Gretchen wished suddenly that she hadn't pushed matters. She wished it could have truly just been a mother's desire to see her daughter, but things were never that simple in her family.

Diane pulled in a long breath and let it out. "Your father has decided to retire."

No, nothing was ever simple with her family. "That's great. I mean, it's definitely time. He's seventy-five."

"I've been after him for almost ten years," Diane said.

"You or Dad could have told me this over the phone, though."

"This seemed more fun."

Alexis came over and took their order, pausing for a few minutes to trade niceties with Diane before sauntering off again.

"So, this is the real reason you came to see me today."

"It was a convenient excuse for doing what I've wanted to do many times."

"But never did."

"You've never asked me to, Gretchen."

"I didn't know a daughter had to beg her mother to come see her."

"Don't be so dramatic."

And there it was. She was too dramatic. Too hysterical. Too chaotic. Too unreliable. Too *much*. A low buzz in her ears began to drown out the hum of the café. There was only one reason her mother would take the extraordinary step of physically visiting Gretchen to share this news. Because there was another shoe to drop. "What aren't you telling me?"

To her mother's credit, she met Gretchen's gaze head-on for once. "I thought you should know that Evan is going to take over as CEO."

A sense of weightlessness turned her stomach upside down. "Why not Uncle Jack?"

"Jack is almost seventy, honey. It doesn't make sense."

"But Evan is a narcissist. He won't make decisions that are best for the company, only for himself. You know that."

Her mother reached across the table and covered Gretchen's hand with her own. "I know you two have your differences."

"*Differences?* Is that how you see it?" Gretchen pulled her hand away. "It's a lot more than that, and the fact that you showed up here out of the blue to break it to me that he's going to be CEO tells me that you know it."

"You were children, honey. All siblings fight. But you're both grown now, and look how he offered you a spot on the foundation board."

"Which he only did so I would talk to Colton."

"Speaking of Mr. Wheeler." Her mother's face brightened at the convenient change of subject. Another painful conversation averted. "How are things going on that front?"

Gretchen tried to hide her disappointment that this was all her mother wanted. Business. It was the only blood that bound her family together. "I gave him an official proposal. He's considering it."

"How come you never told me that you had a relationship with him?"

"We don't," Gretchen said quickly. "Have a relationship, I mean. We just have some mutual friends." And a bad habit of kissing like the answer to life's deepest questions could be found in each other's arms.

Jesus. Even she was starting to sound like a country singer.

"I'm not as oblivious as you seem to think," her mother said. "I don't need to see pictures of you and Colton Wheeler dancing by the river to know there's something going on. I can see it in your face."

"I've never said you were oblivious, Mom. Just . . . disinterested."

"Well, I'm not." She smiled. "Why not bring him out to the Homestead? Show him around the tasting room and the offices. Bring him by the shack. Let him see the family he'd be joining."

"He wouldn't be joining a family. He'd be joining a corporation." Of course, for the Winthrops, those were one and the same. And Colton was too good for both.

"Well, bring him out anyway. We'd all love to meet him."

"I'll think about it."

A lull in the conversation turned what was already an awkward moment into a torturous one. Diane looked one way and Gretchen the other, anything to avoid looking at each other. It had always been like this with her mom. Or, at least, it had been for as long as Gretchen could remember. Usually, she was grateful for her mother's aversion to all things confrontational. Keeping their conversations superficial ensured that Gretchen wouldn't have to be reminded how small of a priority she was on her parents' agendas. But today, frustration screamed too loudly to ignore. Colton's interrogation last night about her family's lack of Christmas traditions had exposed a deep well of resentment that she thought had long dried out, but he'd dropped a bucket into it and apparently found one last drop of rancid water.

"Did I ever make you handmade ornaments for Christmas?"

Her mother's brows tugged together. "What do you mean?"

"Like at school. Paper Christmas trees or my handprint in glitter on a scrap of paper."

"I'm sure you did when you were little."

"Did you keep them?"

Her mother's shrug was noncommittal. "They're probably in storage somewhere."

Right. Storage somewhere. "How come we never had a family Christmas tree?"

"What are you talking about? We had a dozen Christmas trees."

"But not one that was just ours. Private."

"Honey, where are these questions coming from?"

"Forget it," Gretchen said. "It's nothing."

Alexis returned with their food just in time, because her mother's face said she was gearing up for another *stop being so dramatic* speech.

"Everything look okay?" Alexis asked, but the way she said it, with her eyes pinched at the corners and her gaze squarely on Gretchen, said she wasn't inquiring about the food.

"We're good," Gretchen answered.

"Glad to hear it. You'll let me know if you need anything?" She squeezed Gretchen's shoulder before she walked away.

"She's certainly colorful, isn't she? Very bohemian."

"Alexis is one of the kindest human beings on the planet."

"I wasn't suggesting otherwise." Her mother's lips thinned as she snapped a napkin onto her lap. "Really, Gretchen. You always read the worst into everything I say and do."

Of course. It was Gretchen's misunderstanding that was the real problem. Her overreactions. Her dramatics.

Can't you just ignore him?

Not now, Gretchen. We're busy.

He's just teasing you. Don't be so sensitive.

She'd heard it all. Any excuse to ignore the truth about Evan because facing it would create a scandal. And Lord knew, there was nothing worse than that.

Her mother was right about one thing, though. Colton did

need to know what he was getting into if he was seriously going to consider the endorsement. He needed to see the whole ugly truth. So when the interminably long lunch finally ended and she returned to the office, Gretchen texted him.

Tomorrow night. Seven p.m. It's my turn for a surprise.

A Cold Winter's Night

Simon Rye had met more than his fair share of stubborn people in his life.

As director of the historical commission for one of Michigan's ritziest zip codes, he'd done battle with everyone from greedy home-builders to cranky widows. But Chelsea Vanderboek was quickly rising to claim the number one spot on his list of *People He'd Like to Throttle.*

Not just because she'd sent his truck careening into a deep ditch during a snowstorm. And not even just because she was intent on selling one of the region's most prized historic properties.

But at this moment, it was mainly because he'd made her some goddamned hot chocolate and she was eyeing it as if he'd poisoned it.

"What is this?" She squinted at the steaming mug.

"Cocoa."

"Where did you find it?"

"If you don't want it, just say so. I just thought you could use something to thaw that ice block around your heart."

"I'd thaw a lot quicker if I knew how we were going to get out of here." She took the cup anyway and settled back into the chair where she'd been sitting and stewing for an hour. She took a sip and gave him a side-eye. "Thank you."

"You're welcome."

He took the chair on the other side of the fireplace. The heat from the fire was just enough to keep them from seeing their breath.

"Why are you so determined to sell this place?"

"Because there's no one left in my family to run it."

"You could run it."

The noise that emerged from her was half snort and 100 percent *Are you joking?*

"I'm serious," he said, curling his hands around his mug, hoping some of the warmth from the hot cocoa would defrost the room. "A place like this is a gift. How can you just throw it away?"

"It's not a gift. It's a curse."

He studied her face in the firelight. Gone was the hard-edged annoyance from before, replaced by a softer and far more devastating emotion. Loneliness.

Sadness oozed off her like melting snow.

"What happened?"

She looked over quickly. "What?"

"What made you hate this place so much?"

"Nothing."

"No one hates a house the way you hate this one without a reason. And that reason is usually not the house itself but what happened inside it."

She stiffened. "Have you heard anything yet?"

He'd left a message with every person he could think of to pull their cars out. The answer had been the same every time. It wasn't going to happen for a while. "Sorry. I don't think we're getting out tonight."

A howl of wind seeped through the peeling weather stripping around the windows. If he wasn't mistaken, she tensed as if afraid. "What are we going to do?"

"The only thing we can do. Settle in and try not to kill each other."

"Settle in? What the hell does that mean?"

Simon kicked his legs out in front of the chair and settled his mug on his stomach. "It means get cozy and accept reality that we're going to be here for a while."

"I can't—I can't stay here."

He rolled his head to look at her. Her fingers gripped her mug so hard that it trembled, and her chest rose and fell with rapid breaths.

"Chelsea."

Her head whipped in his direction. "What?"

"You okay?"

The mug shook in her hand again. Jesus, was she afraid of *him*? Is that what was going on? She was afraid of being stuck in the house alone with a man she didn't know? It would make sense, but still, Simon sensed something else was going on.

"Would you feel more comfortable if I stayed in a separate part of the house?"

"No," she said quickly. Too quickly. "You don't have to go anywhere else."

Simon set his cup down and stood up. She watched him approach her chair and held his gaze as he crouched in front of her. "I promise you're safe, Chelsea. I'm not going anywhere if you don't want me to."

The relief in her eyes was as shocking as the way it affected him. He didn't want to throttle her anymore. He wanted to hug her. And come hell or high water, he was going to get to the bottom of why she hated this house.

CHAPTER TWELVE

"Not gonna lie. I've had a lot of fantasies about taking you out on a dark country road."

Colton peeled his eyes from the windshield to grin at Gretchen in the passenger seat. She'd picked him up at home in his own car with the joke, "Get in, loser. We're going to meet my dysfunctional family."

"It's coming up," she said, pointing to a small sign in the distance that said TASTING ROOM.

He turned into the parking lot of what looked like a historic farmhouse. He instinctively reached for the glove box to get his hat and fake glasses, but she was already holding them and passed over both with a smile. As they got out, she explained that the farmhouse and barn were mostly original but had been updated throughout the decades. A wraparound porch was decorated for Christmas in a rustic, homespun way. Rocking chairs and blankets. Real evergreen garland and old-fashioned lights. He started toward the porch and what appeared to be the front door, but she tugged at his elbow.

"This way."

He followed her around to the side of the house, where she punched in a security code to a side door. From there, they entered what appeared to have been, at one time, a mudroom of sorts. The kind where a man might kick off his winter boots and wash up over a basin of water before going in for supper. The room had clearly undergone updates over the years—steel door and security system included—but it was too small and rough-hewn to have been anything other than the real deal. The walls were made of cold, gray stone, and the ceiling was low enough that Colton could've flattened his palms on it if he stood on tiptoes.

Colton glanced down at her. "Did someone actually live here?"

"Of course. This was my great-great-great-great-grandfather's house." She gestured with a tilt of her head. "Follow me."

He followed her into a separate room, equally small and rustic, where a gray-haired security guard in a black uniform sat behind a tall, skinny desk. Gretchen waved. "Hey, Charlie."

The guard brightened. "Miss Gretchen. Haven't seen you in a month of Sundays. What brings you by?"

"Just showing a friend around."

She looked at Colton with eyebrows raised, as if asking permission to introduce him. Colton nodded and reached over the desk to shake the man's hand. "Colton Wheeler. Nice to meet you."

If Charlie recognized Colton's face or name, he showed no sign of it. "Welcome to the Homestead."

"Charlie, you've been here how many years?" Gretchen asked, smiling warmly.

"It'll be thirty-three years in April."

Colton nudged her with his elbow. "Almost as long as you."

Charlie's smile spread into a broad grin. "Want me to tell your friend here about the time when you were four and came running in here to hide so you could eat the candy bar you'd stolen from the kitchen?"

"Absolutely not," Gretchen said.

Colton crossed his arms. "Absolutely yes."

"She was a tiny little thing. Bare feet and pigtails flopping around. I let her hide behind my desk and eat that whole candy bar."

Gretchen shrugged. "The punchline of the joke, though, is that no one knew or even cared that I had the candy."

"A rebel without a cause at four years old," Charlie mused.

"I was a bit of a handful."

"You were the joy of this place." Charlie beamed. "Wish we saw more of you."

After bidding him goodbye, Gretchen led Colton down a short, cramped hallway where the low din of hushed conversations greeted him and grew louder with each step. They entered what had clearly been a simple living room at one time but was now a gallery of sorts. The walls were lined with sepia-toned photos in carefully mismatched frames. A dozen or so people moved slowly to study each photo as they sipped samples of the whiskey.

No one paid them any attention as Gretchen brought him to a photo of a man in a black suit sitting at a table, his left hand wrapped around a plain brown bottle.

"The family patriarch." Gretchen was standing close enough for their arms to brush. "Cornelius Donley. He came over just after the Civil War."

"Donley, not Winthrop?"

"My great-grandfather only had daughters, and men didn't leave their companies to women in the 1930s, so he left it to his oldest daughter's husband, Samuel Winthrop. It's been passed down through Winthrop men ever since."

"Seems kind of sexist."

"It is." She pointed to another photo—this one of an image that appeared to be the inspiration for the company logo—a lighthouse on a rocky shoal. "Do you know what it means? The name of the company?"

He shook his head.

"It means 'lone rock.' The lighthouse is a real place. People started calling it Ireland's Teardrop because it was the last thing people would see as they left Ireland for America to escape the famine."

"Did Cornelius come over during the famine?"

"No, it was over by the time he came, but his family never recovered from it. After his parents died, he packed up his siblings and sold everything they had to pay for the trip over. He had one thing of value left to his name, a whiskey recipe."

As she spoke, she moved down the line of photos, but he kept his eyes on her. She came alive talking about the company, the ancestry. And though her tone sparked with the same passion as when she talked about her work, her eyes shone with a softer emotion. This mattered just as much to her, but in a different way. For someone who actively hid her connection with her family, she sure had a great deal of affection for it. Or its history, at least.

"They tried New York for a few years but couldn't make it work, so he headed south and started selling jars of the original recipe along the road leading out of Nashville. After a few years, he built up a strong customer base who started to call it Donley's Dare because it packed such a punch. They created the Carraig Aonair label later in the 1920s."

He knew that much, at least. The company now featured three distinct labels—the original Donley's Dare label, Carraig Aonair, and CAW 1869, the limited edition.

"Some of the old Confederates wanted to run him out on rails," she continued.

"Because he was Irish?"

"Because he hired freedmen." She pointed to another set of photos showing a dozen or so black men interspersed with twenty or so whites in a barn surrounded by large barrels. "The original distillery where this picture was taken was burned down by a group of white men who didn't approve."

"You're shitting me. Like, the KKK?"

"Pretty much, yeah, but I don't know if they called themselves that. It took him a year to rebuild, and he hired all the same people back."

The pride in her voice matched the glow in her eyes, both so discordant with the cold detachment she displayed when talking about her parents and her youth that it was as if she'd had two separate childhoods. It was on the tip of his tongue to point that out, but now wasn't the time. Not with other people around who could overhear, and not when he couldn't be sure she wouldn't just shut down on him. Instead, he settled for, "That's an amazing history, Gretchen."

A deep voice resonated behind them. "Indeed it is."

Gretchen's face lit up as she turned around. "And this is Uncle Jack."

A wide-shouldered man with a thick head of hair that was maybe a year from fully gray stood a few feet away, smiling at

Gretchen with a warmth that would have revealed the familial connection even if Gretchen hadn't called him "uncle." He wore a black polo shirt with the Carraig Aonair logo stitched on the sleeve and looked like a man who would be just as comfortable breaking up a bar fight as serving the booze.

"Charlie buzzed me and said you were here," he said, opening his arms.

Gretchen walked into his embrace, and Colton was struck again with the disharmony of the easy warmth she showed here and the image she'd painted of what it was like for her growing up. "I wanted to show Colton around," she said, squeezing her uncle around the torso.

After a quick kiss on her cheek, Jack let her go and turned his attention on Colton with a decidedly colder stare. Colton knew when he was being sized up, even when the other person was trying to be discreet. Jack made no secret of it. He gazed with narrowed eyes and a stern thinness to his lips. "So, you're Colton Wheeler?"

Colton offered his hand. "Pleasure to meet you."

"Jack Winthrop." He gave Colton's hand a hard pump. "I hear you're thinking of putting your face to the company."

Colton shoved his hands in the pockets of his jeans. "Considering it."

"I figured he should know what he's getting into before he makes a decision," Gretchen said.

"And?" Jack prompted.

Colton winked at Gretchen. "I like what I see so far."

"I'm sure you do," Jack said flatly.

Gretchen cleared her throat. "Jack is my dad's younger brother. He runs the distillery and tasting room, and my father takes care of the boring side of things."

"Where does Evan fit in?" Colton asked.

Gretchen and Jack shared an eye-roll. But then Gretchen jabbed her finger in Jack's chest. "Speaking of which, you and I need to talk."

"Your mother told you, huh?"

"He can't be CEO, Jack. You have to block it."

Jack shrugged and stuck his hands under his armpits. "They have more voting shares on the board together than I will alone. Not sure there's much I can do."

Gretchen sucked in a breath that said *Time to change the subject.* "So," she exhaled. "Are my parents home? I was going to take Colton up to the house."

"I don't think so. They had some fancy Christmas party to go to downtown."

"You didn't want to go?"

"It was black-tie. The only time you're gonna see me in a tux is when you get married." Jack emphasized the point with a lifted eyebrow in Colton's direction.

"Yikes," Gretchen said. "On that note, we'll get out of your hair."

"You should take him to see your treehouse before you go."

"Treehouse?" Colton grinned.

Gretchen groaned. "I can't believe you just said that."

"I built it for her when she was ten or eleven. Little Gretchy wanted a place to read in the woods."

"Little Gretchy wanted a place to hide from Evan." She gave Colton a pointed look. "And no, we're not going to see it."

"Oh, I think we are."

"Thanks, Jack," she sighed.

With a laugh, he hugged her again. "Anytime."

As Jack left, Gretchen turned on him. "We are absolutely not going to my treehouse."

Colton stepped closer than was probably advisable in public. Lowering his mouth to her ear was probably even worse. "Compromise?" he murmured.

"Maybe," she whispered. "What did you have in mind?"

"Little Gretchy's bedroom."

Colton had seen his fair share of impressive houses in his time—fuck, he'd once performed in an actual palace in Belgium—but Gretchen's family home was the most immense, lavish private residence he'd ever seen. It was three stories of white limestone with columns and arches and massive stone verandas. As in plural. Three tiers of verandas spanned the center wing of the house.

As in, this was straight out of the goddamn Gilded Age.

And to think he'd worried about how his house would look to her. He lived in a cottage compared to this.

"No way," he said, slowing his car at the end of the long, paved private road so he wouldn't gape too long and veer straight into the opulent fountain in the center of the wide circular drive. "There's no way you grew up here."

"It's obscene, isn't it?"

"It's a *hotel.*"

"With a ballroom and everything."

He stopped in front of the main entrance; he had a hard time calling it the front door because—how pedestrian. He leaned across the console to gape some more. "You *grew up here*?"

"I'm starting to think we shouldn't go in."

"No chance of that." He tossed his hat and glasses into the back seat, threw open his door, and then met her on the passenger side. He had to tilt his head all the way back to see the red terra-cotta roof.

"We don't usually go in this way," Gretchen said. "The family, I mean. This is basically the public entrance."

"The public entrance," he repeated, disbelieving. "Your house has a public entrance."

"For the Christmas tours and other things. There's not much my parents do on the first floor except entertain."

"So it's basically the White House."

"That's actually a pretty apt description."

He followed her up the twenty limestone steps to the first covered veranda, which led to the double-doored *public entrance,* and was half surprised when a butler with a silver tray didn't greet them as they stepped inside.

There was no entryway. No foyer. No coat closet or decorative table with a little bowl for the car keys or a corner for discarded shoes. Instead, the public entrance opened directly into a square ballroom that stretched all three stories high. Surrounding it on three sides were balconies overlooking the room from upper floors.

Colton didn't know where to look first. The marble floor. The three hallways that branched off from the main room to parts unknown. Or the six Christmas trees that circled the entire hall, each barricaded by red velvet ropes.

She had *ropes* in her house.

"What the fuck do you even call a room like this?"

He didn't realize he'd asked the question out loud until she answered. "My parents call it the Great Hall. It's modeled after the Breakers."

"The Breakers?"

"One of the Vanderbilt mansions on Rhode Island."

So it really was Gilded Age shit.

"Trust me," Gretchen said, shame dragging her voice down, "I know how it looks. My mom wanted a place to host huge parties and meetings. The first floor is all for show."

"Do they?"

"Do they what?"

"Host huge parties and shit?"

Gretchen laughed, and this time there was nothing but bitterness in the sound. "Only about six times a year. They're having one next week, actually. The annual foundation gala."

Gretchen wandered to the center of the room, her shoes squeaking on the floor like sneakers on a basketball court. "Back that way is the commercial kitchen," she said, pointing limply to the hallway directly opposite the public entrance. She shifted to indicate a second hallway. "Over there is a library and a formal music room for, like, performances." She gestured to the final hallway. "And over that way is, actually, I don't know."

"You don't know?"

"It was designed to be guest quarters. I think they intended for my grandmother to move in here after grandpa died, but she died shortly after him, so . . ." She shrugged. "I don't really know what my parents are using it for now."

He blinked, stunned into silence. "But, where, I mean . . ." He spun in the room, looking up and down and everywhere at once. "Where do you *live*?"

"Family rooms are on the second and third floors."

"How do you even get there?" He couldn't see a single staircase anywhere.

She pointed again toward the kitchen area. "There's a private staircase back there. We use a back entrance because it leads to that staircase."

"Gretchen, I'm going to try to say this as delicately as possible, but *What the fuck?*"

She laughed, and it legitimately echoed. "I know," she said, a little sigh following the words. "Trust me. I know."

He raked a hand over his hair. "Look, I'm not trying to second-guess your choices or anything . . ."

She shoved her hands in her coat pockets. "It's never a good sign when you start a question that way."

"Why do you live in that apartment when you could be living *here*?"

Her response was another bitter laugh. "You haven't met my parents."

"True, but you could live here and never see them."

This time she didn't respond at all. Because maybe that was the problem. This was a house designed to show off to strangers, not for snuggling your loved ones. It was meant to impress, to intimidate, to create awe and envy.

This wasn't a house.

It was a fucking museum.

And she'd been a little girl here.

A little girl who was closer to an uncle and a security guard than her own parents. A little girl who grew up to be a woman who preferred living in a single-bedroom apartment with a creaky radiator than within all this opulence.

Looking at her now, a tiny speck of fire in the center of a cold, soulless room, a flush of an emotion he couldn't identify filled his chest and scrambled his senses and turned his voice to sandpaper. "Show me your room."

CHAPTER THIRTEEN

If there was one thing Gretchen hated, it was pity, and it was radiating off Colton in waves.

"You're doing it again," she snapped, spinning on her heel.

He followed closely behind, his footsteps a quiet thud on the hard, shiny floor. "Doing what?"

"Looking at me like I'm some kind of poor little rich girl."

She wouldn't have brought him here if she'd known he'd end up looking at her like she needed a hug or something. She didn't. She'd had everything she needed growing up here. Food. Shelter. Clothes. Education.

"I didn't say anything," he said, still following her down the long hallway toward the back staircase.

"You didn't have to. I can see it in your eyes."

Colton's hand snagged her elbow and tugged her to a stop. He circled around in front of her. "The only thing you should see in my eyes is that I think you're one of the bravest, smartest, and most impressive women I've ever met."

Her heart flipped over. Sarcasm rose to the occasion. "Then you need to get out more. There's nothing particularly brave or impressive about me."

He quirked a smile. "But smart?"

"I'll own that one. I'm incredibly smart."

He gave her elbow a squeeze as he inched closer. "Your confidence is the sexiest thing about you."

She smirked, mostly to cover the shiver of awareness, and brushed past them. "This way, Clark Kent."

The back staircase was private but no less absurd than the rest of the house. It was twenty steps to the first landing, which was big enough for an entire sitting area that no one in her memory had ever used, and then continued for twenty more steps to the second floor of the house. The stairs opened into the hallway that overlooked the Great Hall, but that too was just for show, a place to show off paintings of the family and other artwork her parents had purchased just because they could.

"This way." She gestured for him to follow her to the right. At the corner were a set of double doors that opened into the private rooms. He followed her into the foyer and paused again to look around, settling his gaze inexplicably on the coat closet.

"So you do have one," he said.

"A closet?"

"I couldn't figure out where you hung stuff up when you got home."

She let him wander for a few minutes, trying to imagine it all through his eyes. This part of the house—the residence, as her parents called it—was softer but no less lavish than the first floor. The family living room could've fit three of her entire apartments in it. The family kitchen was the same size as Colton's but probably got used a lot less than his. She couldn't ever remember seeing her parents cook.

"Where's your room?" he asked after a moment of exploring.

Hers was the farthest down a window-lined hallway that overlooked the back of the house. At least it was too dark outside to see that with any clarity. If Colton thought the inside of the house was over-the-top, she'd wilt from shame when he saw the financial atrocities her family had committed outside for the sake of relaxation.

She stopped in front of her bedroom door. "I'm not sure I'm ready for this."

"Maybe you should let me go in first." He gently pushed her aside and then mockingly did some shoulder rolls and a couple of boxing jabs as if warming up for a fight. Then he tugged down on his coat. "Okay. I'm ready. I'm going in."

He dramatically turned the knob, pushed open the door, and sailed through. He stopped instantly. "Oh. My. God."

"It's a nightmare, isn't it?"

Colton laughed incredulously. "This is the least Gretchen thing I've ever seen."

Pink walls. Pink canopy bed. Pink comforter. She sighed and walked in after him. "I was a late addition to the family, and since they'd only had boys before, they went a little overboard."

He spun in the center of the room. "Gretchen, the whole house is overboard. *This* is a bona fide crime."

"Now you understand why I wanted a tree house in the woods."

"Honey, I'm starting to understand *a lot* of things about you tonight."

Which is why she couldn't wait to leave. And in that, she felt another unwelcome kinship with Chelsea Vanderboek. This house was as haunting as the one in the book. "Okay. You've seen Little Gretchy's room. Let's go."

"Not so fast. I've got a lot of research to do in here. This is like an archaeological site."

"With nothing but embarrassing details of my past to dig up. Let's go." She tried again to drag him toward the door, but he pulled some kind of gentle self-defense twirl, and she ended up plastered against his chest. She fell into him with a gasp, and then every breath of oxygen escaped on an exhale at the feel of his body against hers. Her left arm was wrapped behind her, her fingers entwined with his.

She was, quite literally, his hostage.

"So . . ." His voice deepened into a sexy murmur. "Tell me about all your lonely nights in this room, Little Gretchy. How did you satisfy your rebellious goth soul?"

Her heart was chanting *Lock me up*, but her mouth blurted out, "I wasn't goth."

He lifted an eyebrow. "Emo?"

"More like just a loner."

His voice deepened even further. "And are you sure we're *alone* right now?"

"Yes," she whispered.

And just like that, he pulled another swift move, scooped her up in his arms, and started toward the bed with her.

"What are you doing?" she laughed.

"I have more exploring to do."

He had to duck his head to avoid smashing his face into the canopy frame as he deposited her on the mattress with an ungraceful toss. She bounced and protested with an *oof*, but in reality, she was near to self-combusting because, holy shit, she was apparently into being swept off her feet. She barely had time to scoot back before he crawled onto the bed with her. His hands and knees pressed into the mattress on either side of her, blocking her in beneath him and his hungry gaze.

Eyes that had drooped with pity just a little while ago were now wild with a ravenous need. For her.

A canyon beckoned in those eyes. She teetered on the edge of it, feeling that tug of fear and anticipation, not because she was afraid of falling but because she was afraid she'd jump. She'd made that leap before, fallen hard down into the valley of his arms, his kiss, his desire. She would've leaped again the other night if they hadn't been interrupted by creative inspiration. And now, her feet were on the precipice again. Longing and desire became the oxygen in her lungs, the blood in her veins.

"What are you doing?" she whispered again.

"Wondering where to start." He bent his elbows and burrowed his face into the curve of her neck with a deep inhale. "This might be a good place."

Yes. That was an excellent place. His lips brushed the tender skin of her throat. Once. Twice. Then the flick of his tongue against the racing pulse point that gave away what he was doing to her.

"How about over here?" he rasped, dragging his mouth to the other side of her throat, to a spot just below her earlobe. "What secrets might I uncover here?"

The very, very dirty kind.

He nibbled with his lips, a slow crawl along her jaw, a torturous pursuit that left her panting. Her skin was on fire beneath the layers of coat and clothes between them, and if her heart pounded any harder or faster, they were going to have to dial 911.

"Or maybe here," he murmured, his voice hot against her skin as he lowered his lips to the tip of her collarbone.

Gretchen curled her fingers into fists against the comforter. Eyes squeezed shut, she tilted her head to give him more room to keep exploring, keep digging. By the time he found the exposed curve of breasts in the open *V* of her shirt, she was trembling. And when he bent to lick the valley between them, she gasped out loud.

"Colton."

"Patience," he whispered, blowing on the skin he'd just kissed.

"That's not one of my virtues."

"I'll make it worth the wait."

"Promises, promises."

"I promise," he said, moving a half inch to the left. "To explore." Another kiss. "Every inch of you." He pulled her shirt aside, and a primal need had her arching upward, her nipple in search of his mouth, but all she got was another gentle puff of air as he blew on her.

Then his mouth landed on hers, and the decision became moot. He jumped, and she jumped with him. Gretchen wove her fingers in his thick hair and opened wide for his kiss. When he lowered fully on top of her, she spread her knees to welcome the hot, heavy pressure of him between her thighs.

"Hurry up," she rasped. She meant for it to sound sarcastic. It came out desperate.

"This is my exploration, remember? I'm gonna do it my way."

With agonizing slowness, he fumbled with each button, exposing more and more of her skin as he inched downward. And finally, when the last button was open, he slid her shirt wide open, rose on his elbows, and gazed down at her. His nostrils flared as he gazed at her bra, black lace over taut nipples that begged for his touch.

"Take this off," he ordered.

Yes, sir. She wiggled to sit up, reached behind her, and unhooked her bra. And then his hands replaced hers, sliding both her shirt and the black lace from her body before tossing them both somewhere. With a gentle push, he sent her onto her back once again, and his exploration began anew. His palms rolled atop her nipples. Gretchen arched into him, seeking and finding. He played with her, toyed with her, flicking his thumb over the taut nubs, rolling them between his fingers.

"Colton," she moaned, covering his hands with hers, "either put your mouth on those or stop before you kill me."

"So demanding," he chuckled. But finally, he gave her what her body craved. His tongue flicked her nipple, followed quickly by a nip of his teeth. Every nerve ending in her body sparked to life.

"Colton." Her voice came out a tortured groan. She gripped his head and directed his lips to her right nipple. She wanted it hard. He gave it soft. The tip of his tongue traced her, licked her, teased her. Her body acted on its own, arching into him again, and he moved to the other nipple, tormenting her again with his restraint when all she wanted from him was rabid.

She couldn't wait a second longer. If they were going to do this, they were going to do this *now.* She grabbed the hem of his shirt and tugged it from his jeans, and after that it became a scramble of frantic disrobing every bit as hurried and clumsy as when they'd stumbled into his hotel room after Mack and Liv's wedding. What *was* this between them? What force of nature made one body, one person, crave another long past the point of desire until it was something simpler, something urgent, something *primal*?

Colton rose on his knees and lifted his T-shirt over his head. Then he grabbed her hands and brought them to his stomach. She scratched the coarse hair that covered the lean outline of abs. God, she remembered this, what his skin felt like.

His eyes fluttered shut. "God, Gretchen," he rasped. "You have no idea how often I dream about you touching me."

He fumbled with the button of his jeans. Hands shaking, she did the same with hers. He swore twice as his fingers slipped from his zipper, but finally he freed himself. His erection strained, and all she could do was stare. She wanted him so bad. She wanted him now.

Gretchen lifted her hips and shimmied her pants down, and, fuck, as she did, his hand came around his erection and he began to stroke himself lightly.

"Only you," he rasped. "You're the only person who does this to me."

Gretchen tried to free one leg from her jeans. Just one leg. That's all she needed to get out. His hand worked himself as he gazed at her breasts. It was the single most erotic thing she'd ever seen.

A sound made them both freeze.

He blinked. "What was that?"

And then they heard it again. A door closing. Followed by footsteps. And then a voice. "Hello?"

"You have to be kidding me," Colton growled.

Her fucking parents were home.

And *this* was the problem with getting naked with Colton Wheeler. If kisses scrambled her senses, letting him touch her boobs made her lose her entire goddamn mind. She'd been one pant leg away from having sex with him in her childhood bedroom.

Colton uttered a quiet *Fuck* as he reached for his shirt where it was draped off the end of the mattress, nearly invisible amid the disheveled pink frothiness of the comforter. He lost his balance, though, and tumbled to the floor, barely missing a collision with the corner of the end table. He dropped three more consecutive F-bombs and scrambled onto all fours.

Gretchen threw him his shirt and sat up, hands over her breasts. "Where's my bra?"

He pulled the shirt over his head. "I don't know."

"You took it off me! Where'd you put it?"

"I don't know. I was a little distracted by your boobs." He winked suddenly. "Which are spectacular, by the way."

Growling, Gretchen scanned the area around the bed.

"Here it is," Colton said. He crawled to where both her shirt and bra were snagged on a branch of the Christmas tree.

Outside, her parents' voices grew louder as they entered the living area.

"I don't know whose car that is," her father snapped.

"Should we call the police?" her mother asked.

"It's a Porsche, Diane."

As if that automatically ruled out any criminality. Even when they thought they were being robbed, her parents managed to be snobs.

"Got it," Colton whispered, crawling back. Gretchen grabbed her clothes from him as he rose on his knees to zip his jeans. He winced as it dragged over his still-massive erection.

Gretchen shimmied into her bra and swore under her breath as her fingers slipped from the clasp. It took two tries before it finally caught. The footsteps approached the hallway leading to her bedroom just as Gretchen began rebuttoning her shirt. Shit. *Shit*.

Colton stood quickly, running his hands through his hair to smooth it back down. Gretchen pointed at his crotch, eyes wide.

He looked down, swore again, and started breathing slowly in and out.

"What are you doing?" she hissed.

"Picturing the lunch lady at my high school. It's not working."

"Oh my God," Gretchen groaned. "This is my nightmare."

Her mother's voice rang out, just feet from her bedroom door. "Hello? Evan, is that you? Did you get a new car?"

Gretchen hopped up from the bed, ran her fingers through her hair, and cleared her throat to answer her mother. But before she could, her mom rounded the corner from the hallway just then and stopped short in the open doorway of her bedroom. "Oh. Gretchen, my goodness. What a surprise."

Gretchen waved. "Hi, Mom."

CHAPTER FOURTEEN

Her mom's eyes glanced to Colton and then back to Gretchen again, seeing everything and missing nothing.

Perfect.

Of all the times for her mother to finally pay attention.

Her father appeared then and stopped the same way her mother did. His eyes darted from Gretchen to Colton to the state of her bed. Each movement of his eyes brought a new level of understanding of what had apparently been going on before they walked in, followed by confusion over *why* it had been happening.

"Mom. Dad," Gretchen said. More like gulped. "Hey. This is, um—"

"I know who he is," her father said.

Colton stepped forward, all swagger and aw-shucks smiles. He extended his hand to her father first. "Nice to meet you, Mr. Winthrop."

Colton then turned his superstar attention to her mother and offered a handshake to her as well. "You have a gorgeous house, ma'am," he said, laying the drawl on extra heavy and sealing it with his signature wink.

"Thank you." Her mother preened.

"Might I also say that if Gretchen hadn't told me you were her mother, I'd swear you two were sisters."

Gretchen mentally gagged. Especially when her mother blushed and began to fiddle with her necklace. The surefire fastest way to her mother's heart was to tell her that all the money spent on facials and luxury skincare was working. Her mother approached aging like a toddler fighting a nap—kicking and screaming and crying that she wasn't ready yet.

"I understand your house is part of the Christmas home tour," Colton said.

"Yes, I just love to decorate—"

"What are you two doing here?" her father interjected.

Her mother's lips thinned into an annoyed line at the interruption. "This is her home, Frasier. She can come over whenever she wants."

Gretchen cleared her throat against the acid rising from her stomach. "We were— I mean, I was showing Colton around the Homestead. Like you suggested."

Her father's left eyebrow rose an inch, a gesture that managed to both shame and amuse her. Shame because she was thirty-five and had just been busted by her parents. Amusement because, well, same. She'd shocked her parents a lot over the years, but never for this.

"Yeah, Gretchen has been very diligent in trying to talk me into this endorsement deal." Colton slung an arm around Gretchen's shoulder, and her life flashed before her eyes. She was going to punch him in the dick as soon as they were alone.

"Gretchen is nothing if not *diligent.*" Once again, her father's tone said more than his words. She was a diligent pain in the family's ass, he meant.

Gretchen shrugged Colton's arm off her. "We really should go."

"But we just got home," her mother said. "Can't you stay for a little while to chat? Evan and Blake are on their way up too."

Oh, yeah. No. They were definitely not staying for that. "I'm sure you're ready to settle down for the night after your, um, thing."

"Nonsense," her father said. "In fact, I could use a drink to settle in. Colton, get you anything?"

"Hell, yeah. Jack and Coke?"

Actual flames burst from her father's eyes.

"Just kidding," Colton laughed. "Coupla fingers of the CAW would hit the spot just right."

Her father nodded crisply and walked away without even asking Gretchen if she wanted anything.

"Well, isn't this so nice?" Her mother touched her necklace again, and the fact that they were still standing in Gretchen's bedroom became a neon sign of awkwardness. "You know what? Let me go hang up my coat, and I'll see if I can scrounge up some crudités for us."

"We really can't stay long, Mom."

"Nonsense." Her mother waved a dismissive hand and followed her father's path to a quick retreat. No doubt because they knew Gretchen and Colton needed another few minutes to get themselves together.

Gretchen whipped around on Colton and slugged him in the arm.

"Ow," Colton whined, rubbing the spot on his upper bicep. "Damn, girl. What was that for?"

"Are you kidding me? I do not want to stay and have a drink with my parents and my brothers. Especially not after . . ." She waved her hand toward the bedroom and then to his crotch.

He jerked his eyebrows suggestively. "After they almost busted us exploring?"

"Oh my God," Gretchen moaned. "They knew, didn't they?"

He snorted.

Gretchen groaned.

Colton closed the small distance between them and lowered his voice further. "We're adults, Gretchen. There's no shame."

"On my childhood bed?!"

"Okay, that part is a bit embarrassing at our age."

"And why did you have to flirt with my mom?"

"I was trying to defuse the situation." He did the suggestive eyebrow thing again. "Not a woman in the world can resist the ol' Colton charm, amirite?"

"I'm going to set you on fire."

Colton barked out a laugh, hearty and loud. Then he gripped her hips and tugged her closer still. "God, I love this side of you."

"The violent side?"

"The riled-up side. Makes me want to lie and say I didn't vote in the last election just so you'll get mad and do dirty things to me." He bent his lips to her ear. An involuntary shudder went through her. "And honey . . . you've already set me on fire."

"Oh my God." Gretchen planted her hands on his chest and shoved him backward. He stumbled twice, laughing.

She spun around and stomped toward the hallway. The lush carpeting absorbed her footsteps but not the sound of Colton chuckling as he followed. How could he find any of this funny? She shot a murderous look over her shoulder, but all she got in return was a cheeky grin.

Things got worse when they exited the hallway at the same time that Evan, Blake, and their wives—Anna and Kayla—walked in. They all wore evening attire and matching expressions of *What's she doing here?* She'd been getting that look her entire life.

"Gretchen," Evan said blankly. "Wasn't expecting to see you here."

"Nice to see you too."

Evan seemed to remember that he was supposed to be luring Colton to the company, so he quickly flashed his smarmy smile. "Mr. Wheeler. We meet at last."

Colton strode forward with the confidence and cockiness he normally saved for the stage. "Call me Colton," he said, offering his hand once again.

Her brothers maintained a look of boredom as they shook his hand—because, really, they were just too high-class to be excited to meet a bona fide superstar. Like, how pedestrian. But Anna and Kayla were another story. They swooned like the village women in *Beauty and the Beast* the minute Colton turned that megawatt smile their way.

"I must say," Colton drawled, "y'all look amazing. Guess Gretchen missed the family invitation."

The pointed comment was met with nervous twittering from Anna and Kayla and an awkward foot shuffle from Blake. Evan, however, didn't even blink. "I assume the Porsche Cayenne out front is yours?"

"Guilty," Colton said.

"Gretchen would never spend money on something so luxurious."

Colton rejoined her side. "That's because she's a better person than you and me. Got her priorities straight."

Blake shrugged out of his overcoat. "Which she likes to remind us of every chance she gets."

Oh, goodie. Colton was really getting a front-row seat to the family shit show tonight. The shadows that always surrounded her around her family began to crowd in, and she wanted to shrink into them. The shadows were safe. No one to nitpick her. No one to disappoint. No one to measure up to and fall short.

"As she should." Colton bumped her playfully with his hip. "She certainly makes me think about things differently."

"Is that right? What has she tried to make you feel guilty for?" Blake continued. "Climate change? Income inequality?"

Colton laughed insincerely. "Nah. Just the clueless superiority of the superrich."

"Why don't we sit," Evan suggested, hanging up his and Anna's coats. "Get you a drink, Colton?"

"Your father's already taking care of it, thanks."

They studied each other silently for a moment, like two boxers in the ring, circling and sizing each other up. Gretchen so rarely had anyone on her side in this particular prizefight other than Uncle Jack, but Colton was making it clear that he was most definitely in her corner. As the others made their way to the living room, Colton hung back and shot her a quick, private wink. Not like the flirtatious one he'd laid on her mother, but a softer one. An intimate one. One that said, *We're in this together.*

Her brothers each chose a seat on the couches next to their wives, leaving the love seat and a pair of wingback chairs as Gretchen and Colton's only options. Colton chose the love seat, and as soon as Gretchen sat down next to him, he draped his arm across the back of her cushion. She couldn't have relaxed even if someone slipped her a Valium. Not with her brothers staring at her with familiar smirks. Not with Anna and Kayla going googly-eyed at Colton. And especially not when her parents walked back in and her mother's eyes lit up at the cozy scene on the love seat.

She carried a small tray of hors d'oeuvres and three empty glasses. Her father followed, clutching a bottle in one hand and his own glass in the other.

Gretchen gasped when she saw what he carried. "You opened one of the old Donleys?"

"I figured that Colton should get the full effect if he's going to join the family," her father said. An awkward pause descended on the room before he added, "The business family, that is."

"One of the Donleys?" Colton asked.

"It was produced with the wrong label," Evan explained. His voice was smooth, but his smile was tight. "They're a big collector's item. We have one case left."

"We've only opened two bottles before," her father added.

"Then I'm honored," Colton said.

As her mother poured, her father handed out the whiskey. Only to the men, of course. Colton alone seemed to notice. "Did you ladies want some?"

Anna and Kayla's eyes grew soft and dreamy. Evan and Blake's grew hard and threatened.

"No, thank you," Gretchen said, curling her lips in to hide her smile.

"Well, all right, then." Colton lifted his glass. "What're we drinkin' to?"

"To business," her father said.

Evan raised his glass. "To making a deal."

Colton raised his glass higher. "To diligent daughters."

Gretchen had to roll her lips in again to keep from laughing. Next to her, Colton took a drink and sucked in an appreciative hiss. "Wow."

Her father tipped his glass toward Colton. "That's what a fifty-year-old whiskey tastes like."

Evan downed his in a single shot and reached for the bottle. Anna gently grabbed his knee. With a disgruntled look, Evan sat back down.

Anna attempted to cover the uncomfortable moment with a bright smile. "So, you guys knew each other before all of this, right?"

She and Colton spoke at the same time.

"Not really."

"We sure did."

The awkwardness grew heavy until Colton laughed and nudged her with his elbow. "Come on now, Gretchen. You don't have to protect my ego."

Oh God. Gretchen held her breath and braced for bullshit.

"Gretchy here is the only girl who ever broke my heart."

Her sisters-in-law sucked in enough air to rival a Hoover Deluxe.

Gretchen coughed. "He's messing with you guys."

Colton adopted his aw-shucks accent. "Sadly, I'm not. We met at a friend's wedding last year and then she never returned my calls."

"And here I thought you were just acquaintances," Evan said.

Before anyone could respond, Colton kicked it up a notch. "Y'all must be proud of Gretchen."

"Oh, we are," her mother gushed. "So proud."

Gretchen looked sharply at her mother. Her parents had never, not once, said they were proud of her.

"Absolutely," Evan said. Gretchen's head whipped so fast in the other direction that she heard a popping noise. "She does important work."

What the hell was going on? Actually, she knew the answer to that. They were trying to impress Colton so he would sign the endorsement deal. She'd be furious if it weren't clear that Colton could see right through them.

Blake snickered. "Yes, Gretchen is very devoted to her little cause."

"How could you not be?" Colton said. "It takes an incredible person to walk away from everything to help people who have nothing."

Blake snorted. "In Gretchen's case, it was more like *running* away, but—"

"Blake." Her mother's sharp tone split the air and stunned the room into silence. Her mother never raised her voice, and certainly never at her brothers. To do so in front of an outsider was akin to blasphemy.

"So," her father said, swirling his whiskey with deceptive nonchalance, "just what did Gretchen show you tonight before we interrupted?"

Colton tensed, the muscles of his arm around her shoulder growing stiff and heavy.

"I took him to the gallery in the tasting room," Gretchen said quickly.

Colton's fingers gripped his glass so tightly she feared he'd break it. "Your company has quite a history."

"Indeed it does," her father said. "Our family has a legacy that goes back generations. Did you know it takes a minimum of twelve years to make a batch of whiskey?"

Colton's fingers brushed her shoulder. "I did not."

"The bottles on the shelf today were put in barrels back when you signed your first record deal."

"No kidding."

"And the bottles on the shelf back then had been started when Gretchen was still in elementary school."

"Impressive."

"We don't ask just anybody to put their face to our family's brand. We care very deeply about a person's values."

"In that case, I'm honored to be considered."

"But you haven't signed a deal yet," Evan jumped in. "Why is that?"

Her mother interrupted. "Evan, Frasier, please. Can we not talk about business right now?"

Colton smiled. "It's okay, Mrs. Winthrop—"

"Please call me Diane."

He nodded. "Diane. It's okay. A man has to be careful who he associates with, right?" Colton set his glass on the coffee table and leaned forward, elbows on his knees. "I'm careful too. Every person on my team is carefully vetted to make sure we're all in it for the same reason, creatively and financially."

"What kind of team does a country music star have?" Blake asked the question with a practiced condescension that sparked an almost PTSD response in her. That tone had mocked her for her entire life.

Colton threw it back in their faces. "Well, let's see. I have my manager, my agent, my rights attorney, an entertainment attorney, the touring company, a publicist, and a marketing manager. All in all, I employ roughly a hundred people if you count the sound guys, my photographer, and the two women who clean my house."

Gretchen openly gaped as he spoke. Because gone was the good ol' boy drawl, and in its place was a confident businessman. It was every bit as sexy and intoxicating as the man who'd tossed her on the bed.

"I don't invite just anyone into my life," Colton added. "They have to be someone I trust. They have to be someone special."

He was talking about her. If the words alone weren't clear enough, the way he looked at her was. And everyone in the room knew it.

"We really need to go." Gretchen stood up. She couldn't do this anymore. And she wasn't talking about the discomfort of being around her family. If she didn't get him alone soon, she was going to drag him back to her pink bedroom.

Colton took his time unfolding from the love seat. He picked up his glass and casually shot back the remaining whiskey. This time, he didn't hiss.

He lifted the now-empty glass in her father's direction. "Thanks for the drink."

"I'll walk you out," Evan said, standing.

"No need," Colton said. "I'm sure Gretchen knows the way."

Gretchen made it all the way to the car before she threw herself at him. He'd just opened her door and turned around to let her in, and she did it again, just like in the elevator. She threw her arms around his neck and smashed her lips onto his.

And just like in the elevator, he immediately took charge, backing her against the cold exterior of the car. They kissed and clawed at each other and moaned into each other's mouths until the need to breathe finally brought them apart.

An entire conversation passed between them in silent, heavy gazes. He cupped her jaw and pressed his forehead to hers.

"Your place or mine?"

CHAPTER FIFTEEN

His was closer.

But it was still more than twenty minutes away, and that was too long. "Can't you drive any faster?" Gretchen whined. She crossed her legs, but nothing eased the throbbing ache.

"Geez, you're bossy when you're horny." His tone was teasing, but he was white-knuckling the steering wheel, and there was just enough light from the dashboard to illuminate the unmistakable proof of his own urgency behind the zipper of his jeans. He was dying too.

"Just drive," she said, banging her head against the seat.

By the time he careened to a stop in front of his house, she was ready to straddle his lap right there in the car. Even taking the time to go inside was too much. For him, too, apparently, because when he shut off the car, he leaned across the console, palmed the back of her head, and brought her mouth to his. It wasn't until the windows fogged up that they finally wrenched apart again. He was sweating and shaking when he ordered her to get out of the car.

His hands trembled as he unlocked the front door, and when

he tossed his keys onto the table by the closet, he missed. They clanged to the floor, and that's where they stayed. Because he was busy driving her crazy again. He kicked the door shut, dragged her against him, and backed her toward the stairs.

"Wait," he breathed at the bottom step. Then he bent and scooped her up in his arms.

"What are you doing?" she panted.

"Carrying you to bed. It's supposed to be romantic." He grunted, though, through the first three stairs.

"It won't be romantic if you fall down and I have to spend the rest of my life as the woman who killed Colton Wheeler."

"But what a way to go out, amirite?" He made it one more step. "Okay, you're right. This is dangerous."

He set her down and instead began backing her up the stairs, pausing to kiss and paw and swear at the buttons on her blouse. She stumbled on the top step and went down on her butt.

"This is far enough," Colton said, bending his body over hers with another breath-stealing kiss. His knees rested on the top stair between her splayed legs, and he grabbed one ankle to spread her wider beneath him. She clung to him with greedy hands, tangling her fingers in his hair so she could force him closer, closer, until all their best parts collided in a grinding, desperate pursuit of pleasure.

Oh, God, he was so hard against her, so hard and hot. The expanse of his back flexed beneath the fabric of his shirt, and the biceps bracketing her head strained and popped with every dip and dive of his mouth into hers. Suddenly, one of his knees slipped from the stair, sending his full weight down on top of her. With an *oomph* and a muttered curse, he regained his balance but rose from her. "I'm too old for this," he panted with a nod to the end of the hallway.

"We're the same age," she protested.

"And we're both going to regret it if we pull a goddamn muscle while trying to fuck on the stairs."

"We're not *that* old."

He stood fully and stripped off his fleece. He tossed it without paying attention to where it went. "Let's go, woman."

"And you think *I'm* bossy when horny?"

"Bedroom. Now."

She rolled onto all fours, intending to scramble to her feet. But then he let out a reverent breath behind her. "I will give you anything you want if you'll do that in bed."

She smiled over her shoulder. "Anything?"

"Yes. Anything."

She wiggled her butt. "I want a ham sandwich when we're done."

"You can have the entire goddamn pig. Now, move it."

So apparently she was also a sucker for being bossed around. Her legs were weak, her knees wobbly, but she found the strength to stand again. She turned around, planted her hands on her hips, and bit her lip. "Tell me what to do."

His nostrils flared. "Go to the bed and remove everything but your panties."

Gretchen covered her ears, backing up. "Do not call them panties."

"What the fuck else should I call them?" He advanced toward her, backing her toward the bedroom.

"I don't know. Undies or something. I hate the word *panties*."

"Whatever the hell you call them. Take off everything but those."

"Why not those?"

"Because I said so, dammit."

Oh, yes. She remembered suddenly that he swore when he was turned on. He'd done it that night after the wedding too. When she kissed him in the elevator, he whispered a reverent *Fuck* before backing her against the mirrored wall and turning her into a hussy. Knowing she could do that to him—turn this easygoing charmer into a groaning, swearing, desperate dom—was enough to make her womb clench.

They reached the bedroom, and he kissed her again as he maneuvered her toward the bed. When her legs hit the mattress, his hands cupped her ass and squeezed, lifting her higher against his erection. She ground against him until a ragged exhale shook free from his throat.

"Clothes," he panted, stepping away and pointing. Then he turned around and made a beeline for his attached bathroom.

"Where are you going?" She lifted her blouse over her head because it was easier than trying to undo all the buttons.

"To get things we need."

"What the heck do we need?" Her jeans got caught on her ankles, and she had to kick them twice.

"Condoms, for starters."

"Yeah, but what else?" Her bra joined the blouse on the floor, and her nipples puckered in the air. The need to be touched was so strong, so overpowering, that she did it herself.

"I don't know, dammit. Just the condoms. I'm a little frazzled, okay?"

Oh, how she liked him frazzled. She pinched her nipples harder.

He returned from the bathroom, saw her touching herself, and stumbled to a rough stop. His mouth dropped open.

She tugged on her nipples. "I got impatient."

Colton dragged a hand along his jaw, swallowed hard, cleared his throat. "Keep doing that."

She twirled them between her fingers. "This?"

His nod was more a tremor, an uncontrolled jerk. Gretchen did it again and, oh shit, she was turning herself on. Or maybe it was the way he watched. She moaned slightly and tilted her head back.

"Don't stop," he ordered. "Don't you fucking stop."

He tossed the box of condoms on the bed and then dropped to his knees in front of her, and now she understood why he wanted her to keep her panties—undies—on. So he could torture her. He gripped her hips and tugged her toward his mouth. He started with his lips, brushing a gentle kiss atop her belly button. And then he switched to tongue, licking a slow path along the thin elastic top that stood between his touch and her pleasure. Then came the teeth. He bit the elastic, gave it a tug, and let it snap back.

"Just do it," she moaned.

"Do what?" The words vibrated against her skin, teasing and tickling her.

"Touch me, dammit." At this point, she wasn't above begging. She'd bark like a dog if that's what it would take for him to put that tongue to work on her. Just thinking about it made another moan emerge.

He hooked his fingers into the stretchy silk and began to drag it. Inch by inch. Kissing her exposed skin as he moved down, down, down. And then finally, oh God, finally, she was bare to him. She kicked her undies free from her legs and sucked in a breath as he leaned forward to place gentle, barely there kisses atop her throbbing center. Just enough pressure to drive her crazy but not enough to satisfy.

He paused in between each kiss to torture her another way. With dirty little directives. "Spread your legs."

She obeyed and was rewarded with the slide of his finger inside her.

"Pinch your nipples for me." She looked down to find him gazing up at her from beneath heavy lids. She did as ordered and earned the flick of his tongue.

"Colton," she moaned.

"Hmmm?" He hummed the word against her labia.

"Shut up and make me come."

He laughed in a raspy wheeze, dug his fingers into her hips, and finally dove in with the vigor she needed. He parted her with fingers and tongue, found her clit like the master excavator that he was, and sent her clear to space.

Maybe she should've felt sheepish about how quickly the tension built, how hard she gripped his hair, or how vigorously she pumped her hips against his mouth. But there was no time for anything other than to throw her head back and cry out with the shock of her orgasm.

If she hadn't been near the bed, she would've collapsed to the floor. Instead, she fell back onto the mattress. He never let her go. His hands slid down her body and gripped her hips and pulled her forward to his mouth again to coax every last tremor from her body. It didn't seem possible that she could have anything left in her, but when he began to suck, she arched her back again and let go with another cry.

As she returned to herself, she was peripherally aware of the sound of fabric and skin, the soft whoosh as he shed his clothes, and then the dip of the mattress next to her. Her eyes fluttered open as she rolled her head and found him propped up on one elbow, gazing down at her with a tender smile.

Sweetness was her undoing. She could meet him toe to toe when he flirted and charmed and teased. But when he looked at her like this, with his heart in his eyes, she was as disarmed as a cornered rabbit. She'd fled from him like one before, and it took all her willpower to not let the same fear kick in now.

He dipped his head and brushed his lips across hers. "Do you need anything?" he murmured.

She rolled toward him. "Just you."

Colton slid his hand over the curve of her hip and around to her stomach until his fingers met hers. Between their bodies, the urgent press of his erection was the only reminder that she alone had found release. Because even though he sucked in a sharp breath as she shifted closer, he made no move to roll her over or seek the same pleasure for himself that he'd just given her.

"Tell me what to do," she whispered, trailing a finger along the length of him.

His eyes darkened, but still he didn't move. "Just let me look at you for a minute."

"I get shy when I'm looked at too long."

"Well, you better get used to it, because I could lie here and look at you forever." He ran his knuckles across her cheek. "I can't believe you're actually here."

He was going to be the death of her if he kept being so damn nice. She closed her fingers around him and began to pump up and down, slowly, circling his tip with her thumb. He shuddered and closed his eyes, and finally his restraint snapped. He rolled her onto her back and covered her mouth with his. They kissed in a tangle of arms and legs until his breathing grew ragged and rough, his movements shaky and frantic. He rose quickly, sheathed himself in a condom, and returned to her arms.

He entered her slowly and then quickly, adjusting and readjusting, remembering and reacquainting, until they moved in sync, giving and taking, whispering incoherently, panting feverishly. She lifted her legs to take him in farther, and the tension built again. Pulsing and searching. Faster and faster. He pressed his forehead to hers, begged her to come.

And once again, she obeyed. With a muffled cry, the dam broke again. She stiffened as the waves crashed again and again. When he withdrew from her suddenly, she grabbed for him, protesting.

But he wasn't done with her yet. "Roll over," he whispered.

She could've orgasmed again from his voice alone. Gretchen did as he asked, lifting her butt in the air. Colton pressed against her, his hands rubbing and squeezing her butt cheeks. Then he reached between her legs, toyed with her some more. She couldn't help herself. She moved her hips in time with his fingers. "Please," she moaned.

He buried himself inside her again with a hard thrust and a guttural oath. "Fuck, Gretchen."

She didn't know if it was an exclamation or a command, but she was going with the latter. She moved against him, taking him deeper, harder. And when he grabbed her hips, his fingers digging into her skin to hold her steady against his thrusts, she was gone. She came in a sudden burst of white-hot waves, and he swore again and joined her over the cliff. His body spasmed and stiffened behind hers before he collapsed on her back, panting into her neck. Her legs gave way, and together they flattened against the mattress. She had to turn her head to keep from suffocating, but the feel of him atop her, spent and weak and sweaty, was worth the struggle.

Time floated. It could have been thirty seconds or five minutes. Her eyes had just drifted shut when she felt his breath hot against her cheek. "You are all of my dreams come true."

Dammit. He was going to kill her.

Colton rose from her back and kissed a line down her spine and up again. Finally, he nuzzled his nose against her neck. "I'll be right back."

She watched him through heavy lids as he padded to the bathroom. A moment later, he returned, knelt by the bed, and brushed the hair from her forehead. "You still want that ham sandwich?"

She rose on her elbows. "Feed me."

"By the way," Gretchen said ten minutes later as she watched him slather a piece of sourdough with mustard. "You can say it. I know you want to."

He looked up and licked the knife. "I don't like your family very much."

"Now you know why I don't live there."

Colton layered ham onto the bread. "They always treat you like that?"

"My whole life."

"I'm sorry. You deserve better." He put half of the sandwich on a plate and slid it toward her, keeping the other half for himself. "You can tell me more, if you want, but I'm not going to push you to talk about something until you're ready."

She would probably never be ready, but he deserved to know the full truth about her if they were going to keep doing . . . whatever this was. "I was a bit of a handful as a teenager."

He chomped out a massive bite and spoke around it. "Everyone is a handful as a teenager."

"I was worse than most. I ran away a lot."

"Like, literally ran away, or like, packed a backpack with some granola bars and a teddy bear and walked up the road before coming home?"

"I made it all the way to Michigan once."

He coughed and set down his sandwich. "*What?!* How? How old were you?"

"Sixteen. I had just gotten my driver's license. Blake was home for Christmas, and I took his car. He was so pissed. They reported the car stolen the next morning when they discovered it was gone."

Colton crossed his arms over his bare chest. "Wait . . . they woke up one morning to find both you and the car gone, and they only reported the car?"

"It would've been too much of a scandal to report me missing."

"Jesus, Gretchen."

"It made sense, actually. People are more likely to remember seeing a red Corvette than some random girl."

"Is that how they justify it, or how you do?"

She toyed with her sandwich. "Anyway . . . my point was, I used to act out a lot and did some stuff that they resented me for, and that only got worse when I dared to not go into the family business."

Colton abandoned his sandwich and slid over to stand in front of her where she leaned against the counter. He planted his hands on either side of her on the counter, barricading her within his shirtless embrace. "None of what you just told me justifies even a tiny bit the way they treat you."

"I know. Years of therapy made me realize I acted out *because* they treated me like shit. I'm used to it at this point."

"You shouldn't be."

His kind scrutiny made her squirm. She looked at the floor. "I don't think my family has ever had anyone shove their bullshit back in their faces like you did tonight. Especially not for me."

Colton placed a finger under her chin and lifted her face. "I'm available to do so whenever you need me."

"You'll have plenty of opportunities if you take this endorsement."

"You don't think I ruined my chance of that tonight?"

"I doubt it. They look at you and see dollar signs. They'll put up with anything if it makes them richer."

"Good. Because I officially want it now."

"You do?"

"Yeah." He kissed her swiftly and backed up. "Just to piss them off."

Somehow, she managed to laugh, but it died quickly. Colton wasn't vindictive. He lived to make people happy. But a few dates with her, and he was already absorbing her family's toxicity. The best thing she could do for him would be to rip off the tentacles before they injected their poison any further.

But when he looked at her as he was now—with desire and kindness—it was hard to remember why this was a bad idea.

"You're killing me in that shirt, you know," he said, dragging his eyes up and down her body. She'd thrown on his discarded T-shirt before coming downstairs. He wore just a pair of basketball shorts.

"Maybe you should take it off me," she suggested.

"What about your sandwich?" He was already reaching for her, though.

"I'll eat later."

"Does that mean I get to eat you now?" Colton slipped the shirt from her shoulders, hoisted her naked body in his arms, and deposited her on the counter.

"You know what I'd love to do with you this weekend?"

"Stay in bed and have sex all day?"

"That too. I was thinking we should go to Vlad and Elena's party."

"You . . . you want me to go to that party with you?"

"Hell, yeah."

Her heart did a triple axel. Going to a party together with their friends was couples shit. It was like announcing to the world that this thing between them wasn't about business and never had been. Like announcing to herself that every time she chanted *This isn't a date* in her head, she was lying to herself.

Worse, it would be like walking straight up to Liv and saying the words she most loved to hear: *You were right. We're good together.*

It's not that she didn't know it before.

She did. And that's what scared her.

He lifted the corner of his mouth in a knowing grin. "You know you want to say yes. Just say it."

She said yes.

She never got back to the sandwich.

A Cold Winter's Night

The house was quiet when Chelsea awoke.

Not the normal kind of quiet, but the kind where she knew instinctively that Simon wasn't in the house. At some point over the past three days, she'd become accustomed to his presence in big and little ways—the sound his feet made on the stairs, the way he breathed when he was lost in a book, the way he looked at her when he thought she wasn't aware.

The roads were supposed to reopen sometime today. There was no reason to stay.

The thought brought a dull thud to her chest.

She stared at the ceiling and tried to convince herself it was for the best that this thing was ending. But she couldn't think of all the reasons that would have come so easily a few days ago.

Finally, she rose and headed for the bathroom to take a shower. Thank God the water still worked. But just before stripping out of her clothes, she heard something out back. She stood on tiptoe to peer out the high bathroom window . . . and gasped.

Simon stood at the edge of the property wrapping lights around a small pine tree. He was decorating a tree.

Chelsea grabbed her coat and threw on the old winter boots she'd found in her aunt's bedroom closet. By the time she got outside, he was nearly done. At the sound of the back door, he paused and turned to look at her.

"What are you doing?"

"It's Christmas Eve. I figured we should have a tree."

"You got up pretty early."

"I couldn't sleep."

"Why?"

He started toward her across the lawn, his feet shin-deep in the snow. His eyes never wavered from hers and sent her heart into a rapid pattern behind her breastbone. Simon stopped at the bottom of the porch steps and looked up at her with an expression that could have melted the ice.

"Because I want to spend Christmas with you," he said.

"The tow truck is coming today." It was officially the saddest sentence she'd ever said.

"Doesn't mean we have to leave yet."

Chelsea's feet began to move toward him, drawn by a gravity she didn't understand. She stopped on the lowest step, which brought her eye to eye with him. "You don't want to leave?"

"I don't want *you* to leave."

She could barely hear her own voice over the pounding of her heart. "But you don't even like me."

His features pinched in remorse. "Is that what you think?"

"What else should I think?" Somehow, they'd inched closer to each other. Close enough that she could make out the mixture of hues in his growing beard. Reds and coppers and light browns.

"The truth is," he said, reaching for her hand, "I'm falling for you."

CHAPTER SIXTEEN

"Is he messing with her just to get her to sell that house?"

Colton had no idea what Gretchen was talking about when she climbed into the front seat of his car Saturday night.

"Is who messing with who?" he said, starting the car.

"The book. *A Cold Winter's Night.*"

"You're still reading, huh?"

"I'm getting nervous. You're sure this is going to turn out?"

Colton picked up her hand from where it rested on the console between them and kissed her knuckles. "I promise. It's a romance novel. A happy ending is the only requirement."

"But this is impossible. She lives in California. He lives in Michigan. She still wants to sell that house and he still wants her to keep it."

"Have faith."

"I don't know. I don't see why he would fall for her. She's so grumpy all the time."

"Weird how that can happen, isn't it?"

She tried to pull her hand away with a disgruntled noise, but he held fast and pulled it back to his lips. "The sunshiny one always falls for the grumpy one, honey. It's science."

Vlad's house was bright with Christmas lights when they pulled into his driveway.

"Are they going to make a big deal out of this?"

Colton's hand was poised to knock on Vlad's front door when Gretchen spoke. She stood next to him on the stoop in her practical black coat and the same turtleneck sweater she'd worn on their first date, but it was the way she gnawed at her bottom lip that caught his attention.

"A big deal?"

"Like shriek and yell, *Oh my God, they're here*, and pat you on the back and say, *It's about fuckin' time*, and all that stuff?"

"Well, it *is* about fuckin' time," Colton said, bending to kiss her upturned lips. "But no, they're not going to make a big deal out of it."

"Are you sure?"

"Why? You still embarrassed to be seen with me?"

"I have a reputation to uphold."

The door flew open, and a frazzled Noah glowered from across the threshold. His hair stood on end as if he'd been trying to yank it out, and red fuzz clung to the front of his navy sweater vest. He wore a flannel shirt under it and was officially the only man alive who could wear an outfit like that and not resemble a Teddy Graham.

"Where have you been?" Noah grumbled.

Colton stepped to the side to let Gretchen go in first. Noah offered her a tight smile. "Hey, Gretchen, good to see you."

"You too," she said, shrugging out of her coat. "Are we late?"

Noah turned back to Colton. "You were supposed to be here a half hour ago."

"We got delayed." And this time, it *was* a euphemism. An energetic, quick one that Colton would've been happy to continue all night long.

"Well, we need you," Noah said, shutting the door.

"What's wrong?" Colton set down the bag of wrapped toys and his guitar case so he could take off his coat.

"Vlad is nervous."

"Tell him I'll be there in a minute."

Noah stomped to the stairs and raced up them two at a time.

"What's Vlad nervous about?" Gretchen asked.

"It's a surprise."

"I hate surprises."

"I know, but this one is great." Colton pressed his lips to hers again and then—

"Oh my God!" A joyous shriek brought them apart. Gretchen whipped around as if they'd just been busted again by her parents. At the end of the hallway stood Liv, a glass in one hand and a bottle of wine in the other. On her face was a grin so wide that her cheeks appeared to strain in protest. Then, as if in a slow-motion scene from a horror movie, Liv turned around and yelled, "They're here!"

An excited cheer erupted from the kitchen. Gretchen skewered him with a look that would've wilted any other man but made him want to haul her into an empty room and beg for mercy. But there wasn't time for even a quick apology kiss because Liv was now racing toward them. She'd shifted both the glass and wine to one hand, freeing up the other to grab Gretchen's arm and start to tug.

"Come with me," Liv ordered. She gave Colton a saccharine smile. "We'll take care of her. Don't worry."

Gretchen looked back at him over her shoulder and mouthed *Help me*. He was absolutely going to pay for this later.

He couldn't wait.

"Are you coming or what?" Noah yelled from upstairs.

Grabbing the bag of toys, Colton took the stairs two at a time and hung a left turn toward Vlad's bedroom. He found the guys in various stages of exasperated collapse around the room. Mack was flat on his back on the bed, arms spread-eagled, a blank stare in his eyes. Malcolm was slouched in a chair by the window, absently stroking his beard and muttering under his breath. Gavin and Del were playing catch with what appeared to be a balled-up pair of socks. Yan had apparently just given up. He sat on the floor, back against Vlad's dresser, scrolling on his phone.

Colton dropped the bag and startled them all.

"It's about fucking time you got here," Mack griped, sitting up.

"Sorry. Where's Vlad?"

Yan jerked a thumb over his shoulder. "Still in his closet. He won't come out."

"Why?"

"He says the suit doesn't fit right."

"Of course it doesn't fit right. He has—"

"Hockey butt." The guys finished his sentence in unison. Hockey players often struggled to find pants that fit over their unusually muscular thighs and butts *and* a trim waist. He and the guys had become intimately familiar with Vlad's backside last year as they'd helped him following his injury.

Colton walked to the closet door and knocked. "Hey, buddy. It's Colton. You okay in there?"

A muffled sound was the only answer.

Colton leaned closer. "Come on, brother. Open up. Let me see it."

A moment passed before the door handle finally turned from

inside. Then Vlad walked out in full Santa gear—red pants, red coat, red hat, bushy white beard. But his downcast eyes and defeated slump were as far from jolly as a man could get.

Colton put his hand under Vlad's chin and lifted his face. "Look at me, man. What's the problem?"

Vlad tugged on the coat. "It doesn't fit."

Colton stepped back, tilted his head, and studied Vlad for what he hoped was an appropriate amount of time to be convincing. Then he nodded. "I understand the problem. You bought it extra big to go over your—"

"Hockey butt," the guys said again.

"—but that makes the jacket too loose. Right?"

Vlad nodded glumly. "I already have a pillow shoved in here. If I put another one, it will fall out and the kids will be scarred for life."

"You do need another pillow," Colton said. "What if we duct tape them all together around you?"

"That is an excellent idea," Mack said dramatically, rising from the bed. "I will go find some."

He ran out like a teenager who'd just been given a reprieve from doing the dishes.

"Noah, hand me another pillow," Colton said.

Noah picked one up from the bed and threw it. It smashed Colton in the face before falling to the ground, and Vlad smiled for the first time beneath the bushy white beard.

"Let's get this coat off you," Colton said. Vlad spread his arms out so Colton could work the buttons. The red velvet fell open, revealing an undershirt stretched to the breaking point from the pillow underneath.

"See? If we put another one around the back, that will fill out the coat perfectly," Colton reassured him.

Vlad looked unconvinced. "The kids are going to know I'm not real."

"No, they won't."

"What if they recognize my voice?"

Colton shrugged. "Tell them that people from the North Pole always have an accent."

Mack returned with the duct tape. He tossed it, and Colton let it hit him in the chest for Vlad's benefit. Bending to pick it up, he glanced back at Mack. "Did you see Gretchen down there?"

"Yep." Mack grinned and jerked his eyebrows.

"She okay?"

"Why wouldn't she be?"

"She was nervous about tonight."

"She's fine. Roman is feeding her cheese."

"*Cheese Man* is here?" That was bad news. Roman ran an underground black market for cheese, which, frankly, Colton hadn't even known there was a demand for until he and Vlad discovered the place and became addicted. And though they'd all become friends with Roman over the past year, they had not, as of yet, formally invited him into book club. No one quite trusted him, not only because his background was a mystery, but because he also possessed an innate charisma that turned all their wives and girlfriends into melted puddles of lust the minute he walked into a room.

"Don't worry," Mack said, seeing Colton's reaction.

"If he gives her the gruyere, I'm in trouble."

"Okay, I *know* that was a euphemism," Noah said.

Colton growled. "Shut up and come help me."

Noah wandered over with a reluctant *why me* drag to his feet. Colton told him to hold the extra pillow in place across Vlad's back while he wrapped the duct tape around him.

"So, things are good, yes?" Vlad asked, holding his arms up. "With you and Gretchen?"

Heat blazed across Colton's cheeks, and Vlad gave a hearty belly laugh. "That's my boy. I am so happy for you, brother."

Noah peeked around from behind. "Are your teeth tingling?"

"Everything is tingling." Colton peeled off the end of the tape and stuck it to the center of Vlad's undershirt. Then he stretched out a long section and handed the roll to Noah. "Let's wrap it around a couple of times."

He realized the guys were all staring at him expectantly, but he shook his head. "I told you guys. I'm not going to kiss and tell."

"So there *is* kissing to tell about?" Yan said, his hands now clutched to his heart.

"I'm not answering that."

An *awww* rose up from the group, and the razzing was officially on. Yan ran over and ruffled his hair. Gavin hugged him from behind as Del slugged him on the shoulder.

"Look at you, blushing and shit," Mack said, standing aside with arms crossed.

"So does this mean you got things settled with her?" Gavin said, dropping his hug.

"We've made some progress." Colton continued wrapping duct tape around Vlad.

"Which is a non-answer," Malcolm said. "You haven't actually asked her yet, have you?"

Colton feigned ignorance. "Asked her what?"

"To be your girlfriend, slapnuts." That was from Del.

"How do you ask someone to be your girlfriend at my age?"

"You've had girlfriends before, right?" Del snorted.

"Yeah, but things moved naturally. There was never a conversation necessary about whether we were an actual couple or just having some temporary fun."

"Well, this one is different." Gavin shrugged.

Yeah, no shit. Yes, they'd shared an incredible night of unmatched passion, but he'd also learned some things that made him more—not less—certain of what she wanted.

"Talk to us, man," Mack said.

"I met her parents last night."

Another simultaneous exclamation went up in the room, but Colton paused in his duct-taping to hold up his hands. "It wasn't like that." He quickly filled them in about what happened, leaving out the part about her parents nearly walking in on them half-naked in her bedroom. He'd save that memory for himself.

He looked directly at Mack. "Did you know her family treats her like shit?"

"No." Mack blinked. "What do you mean?"

"I thought they were just superficial assholes with the whole Christmas shit. But it's worse than that. They treat her like an outcast. Like she's some kind of traitor for not going into the family business. They actually call her career her *little cause*. Can you believe that? They don't see how amazing it is, what she does. They don't see how amazing *she* is."

As he ranted, the guys' eyebrows rose farther and farther up their foreheads.

"Her brother couldn't wait to fill me in on all the mistakes she apparently made as a kid. Her father is an overbearing asshole. I swear, I wanted to punch him right in the face. I've never felt so, so—" He searched for the right word, and Noah found it for him.

"Protective."

Colton released his pent-up breath. "Yeah. I wanted to literally pick her up and carry her out of there. I've never felt like that before."

"Like you'd tear the world apart for her?" Gavin asked.

He nodded.

"Like you'd light things on fire for her," Del said.

"Yes."

Mack winced and patted him on the shoulder. "Sorry, dude."

"For what?"

"You've got it bad. It only gets more intense from here."

Colton paused, not sure if he should share the next part, but he also wanted the guys' perspective. "She, uh, she used to run away a lot."

Malcolm's eyebrows drew together. "Run away?"

"She once stole her brother's car and made it all the way to Michigan."

"Fuck," Mack whispered, sitting down on the bed.

"I don't blame her," Colton said, ripping off the end of the duct tape. "I'd want to run as far away from them as possible."

"Yet she's still in Nashville," Malcolm mused. "She could've moved anywhere she wanted, but she stayed here."

A female voice called up the stairs. "Are you guys coming down or what?"

Vlad's eyes got wide. "We gotta move. Elena likes to keep things on schedule."

Colton nodded. "Let's get you finished here."

Vlad lowered his arms and stood still as Colton went down the row of black buttons of the coat and then refastened the belt. He stepped back and nodded. "Perfect. Go look."

Vlad patted his midsection and walked to a full-length mirror. "Yes. Much better."

"Good. Now, let's hear it," Colton said. "We know you've been practicing."

Vlad turned around, put his hands on his stomach, and bellowed out a perfect "Ho ho ho."

The guys clapped and cheered, so Vlad did it again.

"You got this, man," Noah said. "You're going to be great."

"Okay, so let's review the plan," Colton said. "Yan will stay up here to help put all the presents in Vlad's sack—"

"Vlad's sack," Mack snorted. Del smacked him on the back of the head.

"And the rest of us will go downstairs and round up the kids," Colton finished.

"How do I know when to come down?" Vlad asked.

"When you hear me playing 'Santa Claus Is Coming to Town.'"

Colton started for the door, but Mack grabbed his arm. "Hold up."

Colton spun back around. "What?"

"You can't go down like that." Mack reached up and messed around with his hair.

Colton swatted his hand away. "What are you doing?"

"Fixing you up."

"You made it worse," Noah said. He came over then and rubbed his hand over Colton's hair. He winced. "Okay, *I* made it worse."

Colton ducked down to see his reflection in the glass of a picture frame on the wall. His hair stood on end in front as if he'd stuck a fork in an outlet. "What the fuck?"

"Don't worry about it," Noah said. "She's not going to leave you for Cheese Man because of your hair."

"She might." Malcolm winced. "Someone get him a comb."

Yan whipped one out of his back pocket. Everyone grew silent and stared at him. Yan shrugged. "You never know when you will have a hair emergency."

"I didn't have a hair emergency until you dumb fucks started messing with it." Colton took the comb, ducked down again, and started straightening his hair to something a little less *just went sky-diving.*

"Good enough," Mack said, grabbing the comb from his hands.

Noah gave him a thumbs-up. "You look good."

"You're gorgeous, brother," Gavin said, patting his shoulder.

"Go impress your girl," Del said.

"Look, you guys can't make a big deal out of us being together, okay? Just be cool."

"When are we ever not cool?" Mack asked.

"Every fucking day since I've known you." Colton turned once again to leave, but again, he was stopped. This time by Malcolm.

"She's here for a reason, Colton."

"At the party?"

"In Nashville."

Frustration laced his voice with impatience. "What's your point?"

"That maybe she doesn't want to run away. Maybe she just wishes someone would ask her to stay."

CHAPTER SEVENTEEN

"Hypnotic, isn't it?"

Gretchen barely heard Liv's voice. She was in a trance. A cheese coma. All thanks to the man standing on the other side of the island in Vlad's kitchen. They said his name was Roman, and he was the elusive Cheese Man she'd heard so much about. But the moniker was wholly inadequate for the leather-clad seducer standing before her. He was the God of Gouda, the Prince of Provolone, the Captain of Curd.

And right now, he was holding a slice of Havarti close to her lips. An invisible force propelled her forward in her chair, lips parted.

"I promise," Roman murmured in a voice that turned her insides to the consistency of fondue, "that you will never know such pleasure as this."

"Down, boy," Liv said sarcastically. "Don't you know she's officially off the market?"

The Havarti hit a dry spot in Gretchen's throat, and she nearly choked. From the moment Liv dragged her in with a shriek that could've interfered with air traffic control, Gretchen had been doing everything possible to avoid questions about her and Colton. Secrecy about her private life was a habit at this point. It was hard to open up to people when you'd been on guard your entire life to ensure that no one ever got to know the real you.

She choked again, this time on self-awareness.

Food. She obviously needed more food.

Roman gave her a slow, heavy-lidded wink before turning his attention to the only other unmarried woman in the room—Michelle, one of Vlad's neighbors. And judging by the look that passed between them, hot enough to melt mozzarella, she'd dipped her bread in his Raclette before.

Suddenly, twin girls with swinging pigtails and chocolate smears across their faces raced into the room and circled the island with high-pitched shrieks. Gavin's wife, Thea, pressed her fingers to her temples. "Where are the guys? I asked Gavin to watch them."

"I don't know," said Nessa, Del's wife. She shifted her two-year-old son from one hip to the next. "What are they even doing up there?"

"Wait," Gretchen said, looking around. "I'm not the only one who doesn't know what the surprise is?"

"What surprise?" asked Tracy, Malcolm's wife. She cradled a small baby bump beneath her red sweater.

"I know what it is," Elena crooned.

Liv reached down with both arms and caught her nieces, one in each arm. "Go back in the living room," she told them. "I'll sneak you some more candy later."

As the girls ran off, Thea gave her sister a withering look. "Thanks."

Liv ignored her, plopped down in the empty seat next to Gretchen's, and leaned her elbows on the counter. Her pointed look said that the reprieve from girl talk was about to end.

Gretchen sighed and cradled her glass of wine. "Okay," she said. "Fire away."

The questions began all at once. How many times had they gone out? Were they officially dating, or were they still pretending it was some kind of business deal? Whose idea was it to come to the party together? Were they going to spend Christmas together?

"Whoa, let her breathe," Alexis said. Then she squeezed Gretchen's shoulder. "Sorry. We're all just really happy for you. Both of you."

"Thank you." Alexis's sincerity sparked a wave of guilt, and Gretchen felt she owed them an explanation. "It's just that this is all really new."

"Not for him, it isn't," Liv said. "He's been pining for you for over a year."

Gretchen would've argued the point if Colton's words weren't still fresh in her mind. *You're the last person I was with . . . I can't believe you're actually here.* Gretchen was still struggling to believe it too. Or maybe she didn't want to believe it.

Maybe she was afraid to.

And wow, okay, there was another unwelcome observation.

She must have winced or something because Alexis squeezed her arm again and changed the subject. "So, Thea. What're you getting the twins for Christmas?"

Gretchen shot Alexis a grateful smile as Thea launched into a lament about some hard-to-get doll the girls wanted. "We can't find them anywhere," Thea said, sipping her wine. "Sold out online.

Sold out in stores. I hate to disappoint them, but I'm running out of time."

Nessa made a sympathetic noise. "Del asked for the new PlayStation. Can't find it anywhere."

"I managed to get the last one before they sold out online," Liv said. "Mack's going to scream like a little girl when he opens it."

Nessa laughed. "You realize that means the boys will be at your house every night, right?"

Liv groaned. "Never mind. I'm sending it back."

The women all suddenly shut up.

"Why do I feel like we're being talked about, boys?"

Gretchen turned in her chair to find Mack, Malcolm, Del, Gavin, and Noah strolling into the kitchen. Bringing up the rear was Colton. A weird fluttering tickled her insides from her stomach to her chest at the sight of him. But it was Mack who approached her.

Heat once again rose on her neck. Her fling with him had been brief, barely a blip on the relationship radar. But she'd dumped him on a sidewalk outside a restaurant the same night he'd met Liv, and if she'd known then that she would eventually become friends with Liv and some of these other women, she would've been a bit more delicate with her words that night. Even with Mack and Liv now married, she still squirmed around him.

Mack bent down to brush his lips across her cheek. "Good to see you, Gretchen," he said. Then, he straightened and turned toward Colton with a grin that spelled trouble. "Let us know if he does anything we need to kick his ass for."

"Hey," Colton said in mock offense. "Whose side are you on?"

The guys all spoke in unison. "Hers."

Colton came to stand by her chair then, and everyone made an obvious display of *not* watching their interaction. He dropped his voice low enough that only she could hear him. "Ready for the surprise?"

"I thought Roman was my surprise."

His eyes flashed deliciously. "If you're trying to make me jealous, it's working."

"The Great Colton Wheeler, jealous?"

He lowered his mouth close to hers, and for a moment, she forgot she was supposed to be uncomfortable with such open displays of affection. "I'm jealous of every man who has ever looked at you," he said. And then he sealed the words with a quick kiss before returning to his full height.

He looked at his friends then. "Boys, we ready?"

"Ready for what?" Thea asked.

Gavin kissed her. "You'll see."

Confused, they all watched the men file back out toward the living room.

A moment later, the sound of a guitar from the living room stopped all conversation. And then Colton's unmistakable voice rang out with the opening lyrics to "Santa Claus Is Coming to Town."

The kids began to laugh and clap and sing along, and Colton responded like a true performer—by bellowing the song louder and with comical gusto.

"I guess this must be the surprise?" Thea asked, picking up her wine.

Laughing, the other women peeled away from the counter one by one to head toward the living room to see what was going on, but a strange panic rendered Gretchen paralyzed in her seat. She could convince herself to remain detached from the charming

Colton, the tender Colton, the flirty Colton. But she didn't know if she could handle *this* Colton. The musician. The performer. The one who was so passionate about writing a song that he'd sent her home in his car.

"You coming?"

She blinked out of her thoughts to find Alexis watching her with a concerned tilt to her head. Alexis always saw too much. "Yes," Gretchen said quickly. She grabbed her wine and slipped from her chair.

The living room was a short walk from the kitchen. She lagged behind Alexis and hung back as each woman found her man and stood in cute little couplets as they watched their children circle Colton, laughing and squealing and wiggling to the goofy song. He put his all into it too. He might as well have been performing at the Opry instead of for an audience of toddlers and tikes.

Gretchen couldn't tear her gaze from his fingers. They stroked each string with sensual competency, like the familiarity of a lover's hands on a body he'd caressed a thousand times. Melody soared from his expert touch, coaxed and fluttered with experience and tenderness. Every story she'd ever read about him said he was a self-taught musician, but how was it possible for someone to master a skill like that without training? And he was, truly, a master. The song became something new under his tutelage. Something better. Something uniquely his.

And despite her effort to hide in the back, to remain invisible, he found her with his eyes, and she became the audience. An audience of one. Without breaking his stride or missing a single beat, he winked at her.

"Where's Vlad?" Alexis suddenly asked, looking around the room.

A loud "Ho ho ho" from the hallway was the answer.

The children whipped around, and every adult in the room tried to hide smiles behind their drinks as Vlad sauntered in from the hallway wearing a Santa suit. His face was obscured by a fluffy fake beard, and over his shoulder was a huge red bag with the corners of several gifts poking out the top.

He stopped in the middle of the room with his hands on his squishy pillow belly and let out another boisterous "Ho ho ho."

Colton ended the song with dramatic flair. Vlad took a seat by the Christmas tree and opened his bag. As the children sat in front of him, some on their knees, some wiggling on their butts, another observation made the room tilt in her vision. The reason she felt uncomfortable, the reason she'd always hugged the periphery of this group of friends despite the many ways they'd always welcomed her, the reason she'd raced out of Colton's hotel room the night after the wedding, was because this wasn't just a group of friends.

This was a family.

It didn't matter that they weren't related. They were a family in every other way. The kind of family that teased one another and hugged one another and gave one another gifts and snuggled one another's children. The kind of family that celebrated Christmas together.

The kind of family she'd never been part of and had no idea how to be part of now.

Colton, though. He wasn't just part of them. He *was* them. A harmonious chroma in their vibrant palette. She was, and had always been, the unused lime green forgotten in the box. You might use it eventually, but the color would ruin the rest of the picture.

A choking sensation clutched her throat, and the heat in the room became oppressive. Wine wasn't going to cut it. She needed water. As quietly as she could, she slipped from the room and back into the kitchen. She dumped out her wine, refilled the goblet with water from the faucet, and gulped several long swallows.

"Was my singing that bad?"

She whipped back around. Colton had followed her.

"Terrible," she said quickly. And because her attempt at a teasing tone was an octave lower than convincing, she forced a smile. "I had to wash away the lingering taste of it." She lifted her glass as if he needed proof.

He crossed the kitchen and didn't stop until the toes of his shoes touched hers. She bit her lip and stared at his chest. "That was really cute," she said. "You're really good with the kids."

"Gretchen."

She glanced up.

He hooked his arm around her waist and tugged her toward him. His hand on her back was warm, reassuring. "I know that face."

"What face?"

"The one that says you're about to grab your shoes and run out on me again."

Her cheeks heated. "You're never going to let me live that down, are you?"

"Just tell me why you're making it again."

"I'm no good at this, Colton." She spoke to the floor.

He ducked his head down to catch her eye. "At what?"

"This." She gestured toward the living room, where the children were still shrieking with glee as they received presents from Santa Vlad.

"Christmas?" He smiled again. "I know. But we're working on that."

"No, I mean, I'm not good at this." She put her hand in the center of his chest.

He immediately covered her hand with his own. "You're good for *me*."

Oh, wow. Okay. He was rewriting her entire notebook. She sputtered against her racing heart before shaking her head. "I'm not, though. I'm a Winthrop. You've met my family. You see how they are."

"And you're not one of them."

"But I am. The only reason I agreed to talk to you is because my brother offered me a spot on the family foundation board." Shame brought a sour taste to her mouth, and she braced for his scorn.

Instead, he simply squeezed her hand. "So?"

"So that should tell you I'm no better than them!"

"Well, if that's your criteria, then I'm no better than them either, because the only reason I said I'd consider the endorsement is to get you to go out with me."

"I know. And this is our third date."

He jerked his eyebrows suggestively. "Four, if you count last night. Which I do."

She pulled her hand free from his. "Are you going to sign an endorsement deal or not?"

"I don't know. I think I need more time to research it. Many, many more dates like last night, I think." His light, teasing tone was starting to grate.

"I'm being serious, Colton."

"So am I."

"We can't be *this*"—She gestured between their bodies—"if you endorse the company. Especially when I join the foundation board. It would be unethical. There are rules against that sort of thing."

"And joining the foundation board is important to you?"

"Yes, but—"

"And that's already a sure thing?"

"Basically, yes, but—"

Colton shrugged. "Then, no, I'm not going to sign the deal."

"Colton, you can't just—"

"Yes, I can."

"This deal is a huge opportunity. You have to know that."

"You're more important."

Her thoughts screeched to a halt, along with her heart. How did he do that? How did he say all the right but wrong things? "You can't make major life or career decisions because of me."

"Why not?"

"Because we haven't been dating long enough!"

"We've been dating long enough for me to know that if I have to choose between you and the endorsement deal, that's a no-brainer."

"I'm not worth giving up thirty million dollars, Colton."

His jaw clenched hard enough to make a muscle pop. He removed his hand from her back and stepped away from her, leaving a cold, empty void between them. It was the angriest she'd ever seen him, which was saying a lot because he'd been downright furious the night she ambushed him at Old Joe's. "I'm going to pretend you didn't just say that."

"Colton—"

"Because *that*?" He cut her off with a point. "That sounded exactly like your family."

"I just think you need to be realistic."

"Realistic." He spat out the word like it tasted bad. Then he rolled his lips in and out, nostrils flared, before finally reaching some sort of conclusion. She held on to the edge of the counter behind her for support, bracing herself for what was to come. Here it was. The moment when he finally came to his senses and realized he should have just let her pick up her shoes and run again.

But when he finally spoke, there was no anger in his voice. No condemnation. Just resignation. "Am I wasting my time with you?"

"Wh-what?"

"Just tell me now, Gretchen. Because it stung when you ran out on me before, but this time might hurt for a long, long time. So just tell me before I let myself fall for you more than I already have."

Her knees wobbled. She tried to talk but couldn't. The lump in her throat made even breathing impossible.

He stepped closer again. "Tell me if I'm the only one here that thinks we have something good and real."

"You're not," she whispered. "But—"

He pressed a finger to her lips. "No buts. I know this is what you do. You're afraid of getting too involved because you don't trust people easily, so you either look for reasons to run away or try to provoke someone into pushing you away."

That . . . that wasn't true. Was it?

"But I'm not them, Gretchen. I'm not like your family. You don't have to prove anything to me. I'm in. All the way. So what do I need to do here? Do I need to slip you a note in study hall to ask you to be my girlfriend?"

Against all odds, a laugh worked its way past the chaos in her chest and the lump in her throat.

He tilted his head, the expression in his eyes a mix of innocence and naughtiness. "Can I take that as a yes?"

"I—yes?" She didn't mean to voice it as a question, but her voice had to squeeze through a clogged pipe of jumbled emotion.

"Good enough." Colton nodded. And then he kissed her. Not one of those sweet, gentle kisses from when they'd first arrived. It was a *get a room* kind of kiss. A *bend her backward against the counter* kind of kiss. A *please don't let anyone walk in right now* kiss.

No such luck.

Mack's voice intruded. "Christ, it's about fucking time."

"Oh my God." Gretchen wrenched away from Colton and turned around against the counter. "Can you please shove me into the garbage disposal?"

Colton hugged her from behind and chuckled against the top of her head. "Welcome to the family."

A surge of footsteps and laughter followed Mack into the kitchen. No one paid them any attention. No one except Mack, who slipped a surreptitious wink in their direction before planting a loud kiss on his wife's mouth. Around them, children ran and glasses clinked and Vlad bellowed "Ho ho ho" again and Cheese Man fed Michelle, and they were just there. Leaning against the counter. Part of it.

Part of the family.

"Hey." Colton nudged her with his elbow.

She looked up at him, warmth spreading through her belly at the look in his eyes.

"I just have one more question," he said.

"What's that?"

"Your place or mine?"

CHAPTER EIGHTEEN

Now this was how Colton liked to wake up.

Naked, warm, and pressed against a woman who'd blown his fucking mind but who was an absolute mess when she slept.

In romance novels, characters always woke up gazing longingly at each other, the rising sun casting a warm glow upon their features and sending a rainbow of color into their shiny hair.

Gretchen was none of those things.

Her face was smooshed into the pillow at an awkward angle, sending one cheek into a contorted puff above her parted lips. Her hair was no adorable mop of bedhead. It was a tangled fright, some of it twisted atop her head on the pillow and some draped across her forehead. A dark smear of mascara gave her face a gothic shadow. He couldn't be sure, but there might also be a spot of drool on the pillow next to her mouth.

And he still wanted to roll her over, cover that sensual mouth with his own, and thread his fingers into that tangled mess of hair as he woke her up and nudged her legs apart. But today was Monday, and that meant they couldn't spend another day in bed like yesterday. They'd chosen his place after the party on Saturday, and she was still here.

As quietly as he could, he slipped from bed and padded to the bathroom to answer nature's call. He winced at the flush of the toilet and the splash of water in the sink as he washed his hands, afraid the sounds would wake her up. But when he emerged, she was still sound asleep. Still in that same messy position.

When Gretchen slept, she slept hard.

Colton pulled on a pair of sweatpants, quickly brushed his teeth, and then tiptoed downstairs to start some coffee. As it brewed, he filled Pickle's bowl and checked the neglected messages on his phone. He hadn't looked at it once since they'd stumbled to his bedroom late Saturday night.

Two messages were from his mom reminding him that their plane would land at seven tomorrow night and to make sure—this was emphasized with several emojis—that Gretchen was there so the family could meet her.

There were several from the guys giving him good-natured shit for finally having the balls to make it official with Gretchen.

And then there was one from his manager sent just a few minutes ago. Listened to the new stuff. Call me. Anxiety made his armpits prickle with unease.

Best to get this over with now.

Buck answered immediately in a breathless tone that said he was on the treadmill. The man conducted business twenty-four hours a day and was even known to take a call on the toilet. "I'm not sure if I should be pissed at you right now or kiss you."

Colton's stomach rolled over. "How about you just tell me what you thought?"

The whir of the treadmill picked up a notch. "I think it's the best stuff you've written in years."

"Don't bullshit me, Buck."

"No bullshit. I fucking cried, man."

And now Colton wanted to. Relief made his knees weak.

"You've tapped into something here, Colton. I don't know how you did it but keep doing it. Let me know when you're ready to send stuff over to Archie."

"Give me a few more days," he said, an idea taking hold. "I want to tweak a few things."

"Got it." The treadmill whirred faster. "Seriously, though, man. What happened?"

Colton looked at the ceiling. "I found my muse."

Who was awake by the time he returned upstairs. The bed was empty, and the bathroom door was closed. Colton set two coffee mugs on the nightstand and crawled back into bed. A moment later, the bathroom door opened. She walked out wearing one of his shirts—the one he'd discarded Saturday night. It hung to her thighs and draped loosely across the swell of her breasts.

She literally made his mouth water.

"Morning, sunshine," he teased. "Coffee?"

She made an unintelligible noise that might have been *thank you* but could have easily been *humbug*. But even grumpy and disheveled, she made his heart race.

"What time is it?"

"Time for you to come back to bed for a few minutes."

She set down her coffee and let him draw her onto his lap. She immediately hunched up and leaned into his chest, her head on his shoulder. A warm *mmm* emerged from her chest as he rubbed his hands up and down her back. "You're going to put me back to sleep," she murmured.

"So call in sick."

"My clients can't call in sick."

He kissed her temple. "Your devotion to your work is one of the sexiest things about you, so I suppose I should let you go."

She sat up and gazed down at him. "And I need to go talk to Evan."

Right. To tell him that Colton was going to pass on the endorsement. "Let me do it."

"No, it needs to be me."

Colton brushed the hair from her shoulders. "Want me to at least go with you?"

"Probably best if I do it alone."

He disagreed but didn't voice it. "How do you think he's going to react?"

"Oh, I'm sure he'll just shrug and say it's no big deal and thank me profusely for helping him out."

Gretchen reached out her hand toward her coffee. Colton passed it to her and watched, amused, as she cradled it, breathing it in like the steam from a nebulizer. After taking a first sip, a scant flash of alertness brightened her eyes.

His phone buzzed on the nightstand. She glanced at it and smiled. "It's a text from your mom."

He groaned dramatically and reached for the phone. He hammered out a quick response. Sorry. Been busy. Seven tomorrow. Got it.

She immediately responded. And Gretchen will be there?

He turned the screen around for her to read.

Her face went slack and soft. "You told your mother about me?"

"Of course. I even sent her a link about you and your legal clinic." He set the phone aside and sat up straighter to wrap his arms around her. "So what do you say? Come to my house tomorrow night and meet my family?"

She peeled one hand off her mug and ran it up and down his fuzzy cheek. "Yes."

"That's becoming my favorite word from you." He dipped his head and caught her bottom lip between both of his. With a gentle tug, he invited her to open up for a kiss, and when she responded with a little sigh, he realized he could do this forever. Kiss and cuddle lazily in bed with her.

She tucked her head against his shoulder and released a contented sigh. "What are you doing today?"

"Trying to save my career." Oh, shit. He hadn't meant to say that, but it just came out in the blissful haze of her kiss.

She sat up, eyebrows pulled together. "What do you mean?"

"Nothing." He leaned toward her mouth, hoping to distract her again, but she pulled just out of his reach with a pointed lift of her eyebrows.

He collapsed against the headboard. "I suppose I have to tell you sooner or later, seeing how you're officially my girlfriend."

Her cheeks turned a pretty shade of pink. God, she was killing him. How could she look at him like that and not expect him to immediately roll her over?

He scratched his stubbled jaw. "Things, uh, haven't been going great for me career-wise."

"What are you talking about?"

"My last album wasn't very well received, and my label doesn't like the new stuff I wrote over the past year. They've given me until the start of the year to work with a songwriter or lose my contract."

"*What?!*" Her spine went rigid, and sparks brought a laser focus to her tired eyes. "Those bastards. Can they do that to you?"

Her indignation was as much a turn-on as the shy blush. "They can."

"That's bullshit," Gretchen spat. "You have to call their bluff."

"What if they're not bluffing?" Voicing the question that had plagued him for weeks eased the sharpness of it, but not by much.

"Another label will snatch you up immediately, that's what."

"What if they don't? What would you think of me?"

Gretchen went rigid atop him. Her jaw clenched and her hands gripped the coffee mug as if she were afraid she might throw it at him. Goddamn, she was hot.

And angry. She was very, very angry.

"Are you asking me what I think you're asking me?"

He lifted one shoulder.

"Are you *serious*?"

"Everyone has insecurities, Gretchen," he said, repeating what he'd told her on their first date.

"Yeah, well, remember the other night when you got mad because I said I wasn't worth losing thirty million dollars? Now it's my turn. If you say something like that again, I'm going to start pulling out pubic hairs."

"This tendency of yours to immediately threaten violence is interesting. You might want to talk to someone about it."

"The first time I went to therapy, I wanted to punch my counselor."

"That's my girl." He slid his hands up her bare thighs. "What's your answer, though?"

"Do you actually think I wouldn't want to be with you anymore if you weren't the Great Colton Wheeler?"

"You've never known me as anything else."

"That's not true. The person who sings for children and loves Christmas lights and cooks a ham and buys a house so his whole family can enjoy it isn't the Great Colton Wheeler. It's just you. And that's the person I care about."

It wasn't until relief surged through him that he realized how much he needed to hear her say that. Relief instantly became desire. Hot and potent and urgent. She must have sensed the change in him—not that it was easy to ignore, seeing how it was pressing insistently against her inner thigh—because she planted one hand in the middle of his chest to hold him off.

"What did you mean about trying to save your career *today*?"

"I have a songwriter in mind to try. Someone I think will understand my vision." If he could track the kid down, that is. Duff would have J. T.'s number, probably. And if he didn't, he'd find another way to get in touch with the kid.

"Don't let the label bully you," she said. "It's *your* music."

Okay, yeah. He couldn't wait another minute. Colton took the mug from her hands and set it back on the nightstand. "Take that shirt off," he rasped.

"No. I'm still mad at you."

"I like mad sex." His hands crept beneath the hem of the shirt. "I like mad *you*."

Her breathing caught as he palmed her breasts. "Well, I'm . . . I'm pretty mad."

"Good. We just had our first official argument, and now we

can have our first official makeup sex." He tugged on her nipples. "Shirt. Now."

She whipped it off.

He rolled her over.

And got down to official business.

CHAPTER NINETEEN

"Did you have an appointment with him? I don't see you on his schedule."

Gretchen's smile felt brittle as she stood on the opposite side of Sarah's desk late Monday afternoon. "I'm his sister and a member of the Winthrop family. That should be sufficient."

"You know how busy he is this time of year."

When Gretchen didn't respond, Sarah rose with a pointed sigh at the impertinence. "I'll let him know you're here."

As she waited for Sarah's return, an image on top of the woman's desk caught Gretchen's eye. It was a conceptual design for what appeared to be a new whiskey, simply called Rock. Gretchen picked up the drawing and realized it wasn't for a whiskey but for a hard cider.

"What are you doing?" Sarah marched up from behind and snatched the drawing from Gretchen's hands. "That is proprietary and confidential."

"It was open on your desk," Gretchen said.

"That doesn't give you the right to—"

"That's enough, Sarah," came a calm but stern voice behind her. Uncle Jack had emerged from his own rarely used office.

The secretary's face burned red, and Gretchen regretted the confrontation. She didn't want to get anyone in trouble. It wasn't Sarah's fault if her head had been filled with ugly things about Gretchen.

"It's my fault," Gretchen said, facing Jack. "I was reading something off her desk. It was inappropriate."

"You're allowed to read anything you want in this building," Jack said, still glaring at Sarah to drive the point home.

Gretchen walked into his quick embrace. "What are you doing up here?"

He squeezed her and then let her go. "Sometimes I have to sign my name to shit."

"So, since when are we in the hard cider business?" Gretchen asked.

A muscle jumped along Jack's jaw. "We aren't."

"So what is that?" She gestured behind her toward Sarah's desk.

"Just Evan refusing to take no for an answer."

The door to Evan's office opened, and he poked his head out. "I only have a few minutes, Gretchen."

The urge to fire back with something equally terse flared but fizzled immediately. Fighting with Evan was as pointless as arguing with Sarah. They were going to think what they wanted about her no matter what she said or did, and she didn't particularly care what they thought today. She glanced back at Jack. "Want to join us?"

He shrugged jovially because nothing amused him more than annoying Evan. "Why not?"

Jack followed her into Evan's office and immediately crossed to the wet bar. Evan watched with lips pursed as Jack helped himself to a bottle of sparkling water and some ice cubes. They clinked in the glass as Jack poured.

"What's this about?" Evan asked brusquely. He lifted his own ever-present glass of whiskey to his lips as he leaned against his desk.

"Little early for that, isn't it?" Jack said, eyebrows lifted as he sat down next to Gretchen in front of Evan's desk. She laid her hand on Jack's arm to shush him. No point in poking the bear.

"I need to talk to you about Colton," she said.

Evan's face lifted. "And?"

"I'm sorry. He's not interested."

Evan's eyes flashed. "Maybe you didn't push hard enough."

"I did what I could."

Evan rose to his full height, jaw clenched. "I never should have trusted you with something this important. You've wasted my time. I'll talk to him myself."

One part of her brain told her to ignore the bait, to walk out now that she'd done what she came to do. But that part of her was a weak opponent against the one that refused to back down from a fight with her brothers.

"It was a lost cause from the beginning, Evan. He was never going to do it, whether the offer came from you or me."

Evan made an ugly noise. "Or maybe this is something a lot more personal."

Walk away. Walk away. Walk away. The drumbeat in her brain was almost loud enough to obey, but it was the whisper in the background urging her to stand her ground, to fight back, that she listened to. But this time, it didn't feel like a mistake. It felt like a choice.

"Is that supposed to mean something?"

"It was pretty obvious the other night, but I refused to believe even you could be that stupid." He lifted his hands in mock surprise. "But as always, Gretchen, you rise to the occasion."

"If you're asking me if Colton and I are dating, the answer is yes."

"Is that what you're doing with him? Dating? Because I got the impression it was something a lot less wholesome."

Jack's face darkened. "Watch it, Evan. That is your sister you're talking to, and you will show her some respect."

Evan tilted his head, challenging Jack in a way she'd never seen him do. "Or what? What exactly are you going to do? I'm going to outrank you soon."

"Out*rank* me?"

"I am the next CEO. With my say-so, I can have security up here in five seconds to haul you out of my office."

Jack's hands clenched at his side. "And with my say-so, I can change your inheritance in your grandfather's will."

Evan's face paled. Jack had played the one card he held, and it happened to be the only card that truly mattered to Evan. His future inheritance. Evan downed his whiskey and rounded his desk. "I've got another meeting in about thirty seconds. You know your way out."

Gretchen rose and waited for Jack to do the same. Jack leveled an icy stare at Evan before standing.

Outside the office, Gretchen pulled Evan's door shut. "That went about as well as I expected."

"I should've planted my fist in his face for what he said to you."

"I would've done it myself, but he'd probably just retaliate by blocking all of my projects after I join the board."

"I have to find a way to block him from becoming CEO. As soon as he takes over, he's going to launch that cider, and he's going to ruin this company."

Gretchen realized Sarah was watching them suspiciously from her desk. "We should go."

Jack followed her to the elevator and hit the down button. "I'm sorry," he said after a moment.

"For what?"

Jack gestured with a tilt of his head back toward the offices. "For him. For the way he has always treated you."

"It's not your fault. Evan is who he is."

The elevator arrived, and Jack followed her inside with a sly look. She hit the button for the ground floor. "Why are you staring at me like that?" she asked, looking over at him.

He shrugged, softly smiling. "Nothing. It's just nice to see you like this."

"Like what?"

"Relaxed." His grin widened. "I take it that it's serious with you and Colton?"

Gretchen lowered her face to hide her expression.

Jack laughed. "You going to bring him to the gala?"

"Not sure that's a great idea after what just happened up there."

Jack nudged her with his elbow. "Come on. Think how much it will annoy Evan."

A quiet hum of conversation greeted them as the elevator doors opened on the ground floor. The lobby was a steady buzz of activity. A tour group huddled by the front doors, eyes wide as they gazed at the clever mixture of rustic memorabilia and opulent decor. Others meandered among the displays.

"What about the job in D.C.?" Jack asked suddenly.

Gretchen blinked. She hadn't even thought about it in days. "It's not the right fit."

"Something here fits better, huh?"

Her cheeks got hot. Jack laughed and looped his arm around her shoulder for a warm half hug. "I like him, honey. For you. And that's saying something."

"It's weird. We don't really make much sense."

"Falling in love rarely does."

The word was as much a jolt as the cold blast of air when they walked outside. "I didn't say *love*."

Jack lifted an eyebrow. "I know more than you think I do."

"How? You haven't been on a date in twenty years." She punched his arm playfully.

"*Ten* years. And it doesn't matter because I know *you*. It's about damn time you found someone worthy of you."

A twinge of insecurity tiptoed into her consciousness and waved its arms about for attention. "What if I'm not worthy of him?"

Jack circled in front of her on the sidewalk. "Look at me."

His mouth was set in a firm line, his gaze penetrating and paternalistic. "That's Evan talking right there. And your parents. And Blake. You've been chasing their approval your entire life. It is long past time for you to realize that you're never going to get it."

"Ouch." She laughed and folded her arms across her chest to cover up the sting of his words.

"The problem is with *them*, Gretchen. Not you. Somehow you emerged from their shallow, fucked-up priorities with more drive, more purpose, more generosity than Evan or Blake or your parents could muster in a hundred lifetimes. And deep down, they know it.

They've known since the day you were born that you were different. Better. They look at you and see how far they've strayed from the legacy of Cornelius Donley. And your refusal to join the business or to follow in their footsteps is like holding a giant mirror in front of their faces. They hate what they see in their own reflection. And they hate that you make them look at it."

Jack gently poked a finger into her shoulder. "You. You are the true standard-bearer of Cornelius's legacy. So I don't ever, *ever* want to hear you question your worthiness again. There is no person on this Earth more worthy of love than you. And anyone who has ever made you doubt that doesn't deserve a single second of your attention."

He ended his monologue with open arms. She walked into them and hugged him around the waist. "Thank you, Jack."

He squeezed her tightly. "You don't have to go to D.C. or Michigan or even that damn tree house to run away from this family, Gretchen. You just have to stop wishing that people who will never appreciate you will someday wake up and beg you to stay. And if Colton is the person I think he is, then the only place you need to run to is him."

The salty sting of tears made her blink rapidly. "He is," she said, voice thick as she stepped from Jack's embrace. "The person you think he is."

Jack cocked a smile. "Then what are you waiting for? Start running, honey. And don't you dare look back."

J. T. Tucker was about to puke all over his scuffed-up Converse shoes.

Colton almost felt sorry for him when the kid walked into Old Joe's that afternoon, pausing just inside the doorway to let his eyes adjust to the darkness. J. T. carried his guitar in a soft-sided case slung over one shoulder and all his anxieties in a gnawed lower lip.

Colton could sympathize. If he'd been invited to meet with Brad Paisley when he was eighteen, he'd have been too nervous to speak a single word, much less sing.

Duff opened a bottle of Bud in front of Colton. "Go easy on the kid. He still thinks you're something special."

"Go easy on *me*. Where's the good shit?"

"I told you. That's only for people I like." He smiled when he said it, though.

Colton slid from his barstool and lifted a hand. J. T.'s eyes were as round as a banjo as he shuffled closer, as if he was about to be granted his wildest wish. Sometimes, Colton could barely remember what that was like—to be at the beginning of it all, nothing but talent and a guitar and big-assed dream.

The kid practically gulped as he held out his hand. "Mr. Wheeler?"

"Colton," he corrected, shaking J. T.'s hand. A lot of people called him "Mr. Wheeler," but that coming from the mouth of someone who had a nervous habit of picking at the scab of a still-healing zit on his chin made him feel as if he actually belonged in Silver Sneakers. "Thanks for coming to meet with me."

J. T. showed the first signs of life. He snorted. "Are you kidding? Thanks for even knowing I exist."

"I heard you in here a couple of weeks ago."

"I know. I saw you. I almost shit my pants." He blinked. "Sorry, I mean—"

Colton chuckled. "Don't worry. Takes a lot more than some foul language to upset me."

"Right. Sorry."

Colton motioned toward the empty booths with his beer. "Let's have a seat."

J. T. set his guitar case on the floor before sliding into the booth. When it careened sideways and banged on the floor, he nearly jumped clear out of his seat. Poor kid was about to burst a blood vessel. Colton decided to take mercy on him. "No need to be nervous. I called you, remember?"

"Right. Sorry." His fingernails found the scab.

"You're an incredible talent, J. T."

J. T.'s eyes nearly fell out of their sockets. "You—you think so?"

"I do. Don't you agree?"

He shrugged, clearly unsure how to respond.

"First piece of advice," Colton said, leaning his arms on the table. "Own your gift. Believe in it. This town is full of people who are going to do everything in their power to make you doubt yourself and tell you you're not good enough. Shitting on other people's dreams is practically its own industry in this city. Don't make that easier by agreeing with them."

J. T.'s head nodded up and down in rapid tremors. "Okay."

Colton drummed his fingers on the table. "Good. So do you want to know why I called?"

"Yes." The word came out a squeak.

"I'd like to work with you."

J. T. turned gray. And then green.

Colton puffed out a laugh. "You okay?"

"You—you want to work with me?"

"I do. I'd like to collaborate with you. I have some new stuff that I'm going to be taking to my label, and they've asked me to work with a songwriter on some other stuff I already submitted. I'd like that to be you."

J. T. damn near fainted. Colton tried not to laugh. "Put your head down for a minute."

"I—I'm okay."

He didn't look it. Colton caught Duff's amused eye and motioned for some water. Duff rolled his eyes but brought it over anyway. He was smiling when he left the table.

"Drink it," Colton said, sliding the glass across the table. J. T.'s hands shook as he gulped it down.

"Here's the thing, though," Colton said as the kid recovered. "I need you to think about this before agreeing to anything."

"What's there to think about?"

"A lot, actually. You're going to have a lot of opportunities. Don't just grab the first one that comes along unless it aligns with the vision you have for your career."

J. T. nodded, but it was clear by the empty look in his eyes that he didn't quite understand.

"It's okay if you're not sure what that vision is yet."

"Did you know?"

Colton kicked back. "At eighteen? Sure. I wanted it all. Stardom. Adoring fans. Girls screaming my name. A mansion in Nashville. Enough money to light it on fire and not even miss it."

"And you got it all."

"I did. But there's a price to it as well. Don't let anyone force you into something you're not ready for yet."

J. T. bit his lip. "My dad said I'd better get a manager soon or I'll miss my shot."

"A good manager who recognizes talent won't get sick of waiting."

"But my dad said—"

"Who wants this, J. T.? You or your dad?"

"I do. But, I mean, he wants it for me too."

"But he doesn't have to do the work. He doesn't have to pour his heart out into a song and then hear people trash it. He doesn't have to spend months on the road touring. He doesn't have to carry the burden of knowing that other people's lives depend on your success. It's your life and your music. Don't let anyone else craft an image for you just because they think it will sell. Sooner or later, that image will start to feel like a costume that you just don't want to wear anymore. You gotta do what makes *you* happy."

A snarky *pft* from the general direction of the bar told him that Duff was listening to every word.

Colton sat back against the booth. "So after all that . . . would you like to work with me?"

J. T.'s mouth spread into such a goofy, earnest grin that Colton had to hide his own behind his disgusting beer. "Is that a yes?"

"Yes." The kid let out a whoop. "I can't believe this. Holy shit."

Colton felt like Santa Claus, like he'd just delivered the season's most sought-after toy that had been sold out for a month. A lightness he hadn't felt in a long time about his career spread through his chest.

"Go get set up," he said, rubbing his hand over the spot in his chest that suddenly felt warm. "I'm in the mood for a jam session."

"You—you want to play with me right now?"

"Why not? Let's see what we can do."

J. T. tripped over his own guitar as he awkwardly slid from the booth. He'd barely vacated his seat before Duff claimed it. The old man plunked a bottle of CAW 1869 and a sort-of clean glass in front of Colton.

Colton poured a short shot and tipped the glass in Duff's direction. "I knew you liked me."

On the stage behind them, J. T. strummed a few warm-up chords and paused to tune the strings.

"That was a nice speech you gave him." Duff smirked. "You believe any of it?"

"Aren't you sick of psychoanalyzing me yet?"

"Aren't you sick of avoiding my questions yet?"

"Come on, man. I'm on top of the world. Shit's finally going my way."

"So I guess you found what you were looking for."

"I did." Colton spread his hands out wide and adopted his bad British accent again, this time to quote the Ghost of Christmas Past. "'Would you so soon put out the light I give?'"

Duff poured a shot for himself. "That quote doesn't mean what you think it means."

Jesus, not this again. Why did everyone think they knew the meaning of *A Christmas Carol* better than he did? But he took the bait anyway. "Fine. What does it mean?"

"That your journey ain't complete until you're willing to stare into the glare of your own past."

CHAPTER TWENTY

Gretchen couldn't remember the last time she'd been this nervous.

The next night, Colton met her on the front porch when she pulled up to his house. He wore those sexy jeans again and a T-shirt, and two thoughts came to her mind. First, he was too damn good-looking. Second, coming home to him was too damn appealing.

He left the doorway and met her halfway up the porch stairs. "Okay, so I should warn you."

"Uh-oh."

He dropped a kiss on her upturned face. "My family is really, really eager to meet you."

"Are they going to scream *Oh my God, she's here!* and all that stuff again?"

"I guarantee it."

Colton reached for her hand, and she folded her fingers into his and let him lead her inside. He swung the door shut, kissed her again, and—

"Oh my God! She's here!"

Colton laughed against her lips. High-pitched shrieks blended with childish giggles and the pitter-patter of feet all headed their way.

"Where is she?" The question came from a tone of voice that had *Mom* written all over it.

"Don't scare her, Mom, geez." That came from a younger woman's voice.

Gretchen clutched her hands in front of her and then let them drop and then clutched them again. *Breathe.* She could do this. Colton placed his hand on her back and led her into the living room just as his family emerged from the kitchen.

Colton smiled at her as if nothing were amiss. "This is Gretchen," he said, beaming at her as if he really were proud to show her off.

Gretchen lifted her hand in a wave and then mentally used the same hand to smack herself. Who the hell waves?

Without warning, Colton's mother threw her arms around Gretchen's neck. "Oh my gosh, I am so excited to meet you."

"Let her breathe, Mary," Colton's father scolded playfully.

His mother let go, stepping back with a laugh. "Sorry. I'm just so happy you could come tonight."

"Kyle Wheeler," Colton's father said, holding out his hand.

His grip was strong, his hand massive. If she hadn't already known he'd once been a football coach, she would've guessed it by now.

"This is my sister, Jordan," Colton said, motioning to a petite brunette with the same deep dimples as her brother. Next to her was a youngish man with glasses and a slouchy wool beanie, the kind the hipsters wore around the East Side neighborhood. "And her husband, Danny. And these are their kids, Daphne, Phoebe, and Gabe."

Gretchen filed the names away in her mind as everyone greeted her.

"My brother, Cooper, won't get in until tomorrow," Colton added, as she tried to keep up.

"Finish taking those suitcases upstairs," Mary said to no one in particular. "Gretchen, come keep me company in the kitchen while the men do some heavy lifting."

Colton gave her that special wink of his before grabbing a suitcase in each hand and rolling them toward the stairs. His father and brother-in-law followed, and soon they were trudging up the stairs and bitching playfully about how much the women had packed.

"Kids, go finish hanging the candy canes on the tree," Jordan told her children. They ran off with another one of those squeals. Jordan tipped her head back and let out a long breath. "They are never going to sleep tonight." She looked at Gretchen then. "Welcome to the circus."

"How was your flight?" Gretchen asked, following Jordan and Mary into the kitchen.

"Long. Traveling with kids is like opening a bag full of squirrels on a plane."

Mary made a *psh* noise. "Oh, they were fine. Kids are supposed to be excited at Christmastime." She gestured for Gretchen to sit at the island. Exactly the same spot where a few days ago Colton had done very naughty things to her. She gulped.

Mary returned to a cutting board where carrots, potatoes, and celery had already been chopped into bite-size pieces. "I'm making beef stew. It's Colton's favorite. I always make it the night we get here."

"Can I— Do you want some help?" Gretchen asked.

"Nope. Just take a seat." She barely paused to take a breath. "So tell us about your legal clinic. Colton has told us some, but I want to know more. He says you're working on some pretty big cases right now."

"Yes. Well, big for me. Most people probably wouldn't pay much attention to them." She hoped her cynicism didn't come through in her voice.

"It's barbaric, what they're doing," Mary said, her voice for the first time conveying anything other than congeniality. "Taking children from their parents. Deporting people who've been here all their lives. It's not right."

"Sometimes I feel like I'm fighting a losing battle, though. Every time one case is resolved, two more land in my lap."

Mary looked up from the cutting board. There was a glint in her eye that looked so much like Colton that Gretchen actually sucked in a breath. "Colton's got a thing for smart girls. I can see why he's so smitten with you."

Gretchen's cheeks blazed with heat, and Mary laughed. "I'm sorry. I'm embarrassing you."

Colton bounded back into the room. "You're embarrassing my girl?"

"I was just about to tell Gretchen how she's the only woman you've told us about in years."

"Oh, man. Don't do that. She'll get all flustered and lawyerly and pretend she doesn't care."

Mary laughed again. Colton stopped next to Gretchen's chair

and did the unthinkable. He dropped his head to hers and plopped a hard, purposeful kiss on her mouth.

Oh God. His mother and sister didn't even blink, though.

"Colton tells us your family owns the CAW whiskey company," Mary said, scooping handfuls of vegetables into a pot.

"She's about to join the charitable foundation board," Colton said, popping a carrot in his mouth. His mother playfully swatted at him.

"CAW is Kyle's favorite whiskey. He almost died when Colton told us you were connected to the family."

"Really? I could, I mean, if you're interested, I could take you guys on a tour of the tasting room and distillery, if you want."

"Kyle would *love* that."

Colton's father walked in then, a hand on his lower back. "What the hell did you pack, Mary?"

"You know exactly what I packed. In fact, you can start putting some of it under the tree."

"Yeah, old man, and get a fire going while you're at it." Colton punched his dad on the arm.

"Get a fire going," Kyle grumbled. "You mean turn on your fancy gas fireplace with the remote control?"

Jordan snorted. "You really want to leave him alone in this big house with matches?"

Mary looked at Gretchen with a mischievous expression. "Colton once burned down the high school chemistry lab."

Colton held up his hands. "Okay, first of all, *burned down* is a gross exaggeration."

"The biology teacher had to come running in like Rambo with a fire extinguisher before throwing himself out the window," Jordan said.

"Second of all, I didn't start a fire. I just failed to properly turn off my Bunsen burner."

Jordan snorted again. "Which ignited the lab station and burned an entire corner of the room before the fire department got there."

Colton looked down at Gretchen. "Get ready for a lot of this. They live to give me shit about stuff."

"That's convenient, because so do I." Gretchen grinned.

Jordan barked out a laugh. "I'm definitely going to like you."

Colton made a face at her, and Jordan made one back.

"Kyle, the kids are fighting," Mary called, back to chopping veggies.

"Tell them they're grounded," Kyle yelled back from the living room. That sent the children into hysterics over the idea of their mom and uncle being grounded.

"Who's ready for some Christmas carols?" Colton suddenly said, voice raised loudly enough for the kids to hear.

The kids let out more excited yells.

Colton grabbed her hand to pull her along. Gretchen looked at Mary. "I should help your mom with dinner."

"Absolutely not," Mary said. "Go have some fun."

Colton kept hold of her hand until they entered the living room, at which point he dropped dramatically to the floor and let the kids crawl all over him. After a long minute of wrestling with several near-misses between the coffee table and his head, he finally raised himself onto all fours and let the youngest climb on his back as if he were riding a horse.

Jordan laughed and made a joke about being careful with Colton because he was an old man now, and from beneath the pile of children, Colton raised his hand and secretly flipped her off.

This. This is what a family was supposed to be like. Happy and affectionate and playful and—a lump formed in her throat.

"Uncle Colton, I've been practicing my ukulele," Daphne, the oldest child, said. "Can I show you?"

"I'm countin' on it." He got the girl settled with the ukulele across her lap. "Show me what you got."

Daphne's tiny fingers splayed competently across the strings as she strummed out a tune in fits and starts. It took a moment for Gretchen to realize she was playing "Jingle Bells." Colton reached around her and fit his fingers on either side of hers. He struck another chord that harmonized perfectly. And then, in a voice that seemed to come straight from heaven itself, he began to sing with her.

He wasn't trying to impress. Wasn't putting on a show. He was just singing a Christmas song with his niece, but the effect was complete and immediate. When she stumbled, he paused to quickly help her, and then picked right back up where they'd left off.

Gretchen was so transfixed by it—by him—that she barely registered when Mary came to stand next to her.

"She's been practicing so hard to show him what she can do," Mary said quietly.

"He's so good with her."

"With all of them. They all just adore him."

"They must think it's pretty cool to have a famous rock star as an uncle."

"I don't think they are actually old enough to understand that he is famous. He's just Uncle Colton to them."

Just Uncle Colton.

The lump grew. He was just a man. A good, decent man who—

for some unknown reason—wanted her. With all her flaws. All her insecurities.

"He's been lonely," Mary said quietly. Gretchen looked over sharply to find Mary gazing at her with knowing eyes. "I think maybe you have too."

"Wh-what?"

"Being famous isn't what people think it is. The more famous he got, the more isolated he got. People all over the world claim to love him, but they really just want to own him. I think maybe you know a little something about that."

Gretchen didn't need to ask for clarification to know that Colton had obviously told his family the truth about hers.

Mary's eyes glistened suddenly. "I haven't seen him this happy in a long time."

Three hours later, after dinner had been eaten and more carols sung, Jordan sent the kids around the room for goodnight hugs. When they opened their arms to her, Gretchen automatically bent to let them hug her.

The damn lump returned. She cleared her throat. "I really should go. I have an appeal hearing in Memphis tomorrow, so . . ."

Kyle smiled. "I suppose we've held you hostage long enough."

"It has been wonderful meeting all of you. Thank you for dinner and . . . everything."

"You'll be here on Christmas Day, right?"

The spotlight of Mary's question burned hot and bright on Gretchen's face. "Um, I—"

"I'll talk to her about it," Colton said smoothly, sliding up next to her. His hand found a spot on her back. "I'll walk you out."

"You don't need to."

"But I'm gonna."

As soon as they were outside, Gretchen laughed. "They're going to talk about me as soon as I'm gone, aren't they?"

"I'm sure they already are."

She crossed her arms and faced him next to the driver's side of her car. "They're great, Colton. Really. You're very lucky."

"I know." He leaned then, propping one hand against the hood of her car so he could lower his face toward hers. "But not just because of them." His other hand cupped the back of her neck. Before she had time to react, just like inside, he kissed her.

When he pulled back, she felt dizzy. "Do you think they'd mind if I borrow you tomorrow night?"

"You don't have to borrow me. You already own me."

Sweet heaven, the man had a way with words. "It's the foundation gala tomorrow night. I want you to come with me."

"Does it involve you in a fancy dress and me glaring at your asshole brothers?"

"Yes to both."

"Then I can't wait." He kissed her lightly. Then not so lightly. They were both panting by the time he pulled back again. "Spend the night here Christmas Eve," he said gruffly.

"With your family?"

He winked, understanding her meaning. "I'll try to behave."

"But you have traditions and—"

"And I want you to be part of them." He straightened and lifted the hair from her shoulder. "It's time someone showed you what Christmas morning should be like."

When she didn't answer, he grinned. "Say yes. You know you want to."

The way he could see right through her. "Yes."

"Text me when you get home," he said, stepping back.

"Worried about the dark again?"

"Worried about you."

In that moment, the final puzzle piece fell into place. He wasn't *Colton Wheeler* to her either. He was just Colton. The man who made her swoon and melt. The man who made her want to know what Christmas morning could be like.

The man who now held every single piece of her heart.

CHAPTER TWENTY-ONE

"I changed my mind. We're staying in tonight."

Colton lost all sense of time and place when Gretchen walked out of her bedroom the next night. She'd chosen a form-fitting, black velvet gown that dipped low in front to reveal two creamy mounds of flesh that required further inspection.

"Too late," she said, draping a black wrap around her shoulders that blocked his view of her breasts. He was both annoyed and relieved. He would crash the car if he caught a glimpse of them while driving.

She actually allowed him to open her car door this time. "You're sure your family isn't mad that I'm taking you away tonight?"

He leaned down for a quick kiss. "I'm sure. You can do no wrong in their opinion."

"Give 'em time. They don't know me yet."

"Well, I know you. And every minute makes me want you more, so . . ."

She squinted her eyes at him in the dark. "You're after something. What is it?"

"Just that we leave early enough tonight that I have time to take full advantage of that dress."

"Trust me," she said, settling into her seat. "We will stay only as long as necessary for them to announce my position on the board."

When they arrived at her parents' house, she directed him to park around the back so they could use the family entrance, which not only afforded some privacy but saved time as well. The line of cars waiting for a valet attendant at the front was a half-hour deep. The fact that they could actually fit that many people in their house was still difficult to get his mind around.

"Do me a favor," he said, tucking her arm in the crook of his elbow as they entered the long hallway toward the Great Hall.

"What's that?"

"Point out all the convenient dark closets I can drag you into."

"There's always my pink bedroom again."

He growled. "Don't tempt me."

The party was in full swing when they made their way to the hall. The room that had been mostly empty a week ago was now packed with tall cocktail tables, waiters with trays of food and drinks, and people. Lots of people. The last time he'd seen this many women in evening gowns was when he'd won his third-straight Artist of the Year Award. A live string quartet had set up on one of the balconies overlooking the room but could barely be heard above the rise and fall of conversation.

"You want something to drink?" he asked, leaning down to be heard.

"Not yet," she said, a hand pressed to her stomach. "I haven't eaten much."

Their appearance had gone mostly unnoticed at first, but whispers eventually started to spread and with them, craning necks. Gretchen's fingers tightened around his elbow. "I'm usually pretty anonymous at this thing," she said. "I don't know how you get used to everyone staring all the time."

"You learn to ignore it." He covered her fingers with his hand. "But let me know if it becomes too much. I'm more than happy to find one of those dark closets."

"Let's just mingle and get this over with."

He switched his hand to the small of her back and stayed close as she led him through the room. He alternated between his normal smile and his keep-away face, depending on how she reacted to particular people. She tensed when the click-clack of high heels announced the approach of her sisters-in-law, two other women clickity-clacking behind them.

"Oh, God," she groaned quietly. "Here we go."

"Anything I should know?"

"Those are Anna's friends from college. They hate me."

Enough said. Colton wrapped his arm fully around her, letting his fingers curl possessively over the curve of her waist.

"Gretchen," Anna crooned. "We've been waiting for you."

Gretchen snorted.

Anna blinked and turned her attention to Colton. "I'm so glad you could make it."

"Wouldn't miss it," he said.

"Can I introduce you to a couple of my friends?" Anna stepped aside before he could respond. "These are my dearest friends, Shanna and Renee. They're such huge fans of yours."

The two women fawned over him with *oohs* and *aahs* and gushed about how they'd been to three of his concerts. Not once did they even look at Gretchen.

"Can we get a picture with you?" one of them asked. He couldn't remember which one was which. She'd already gotten out her phone and was coming to stand beside him, completely blocking Gretchen.

His blood pressure spiked. "Sorry, ladies. Not tonight."

Their faces went blank as if it was the first time they'd ever been denied something they wanted.

Colton gazed down at Gretchen. "Tonight, I'm just here to support my girl."

"Oh," one of them said. She finally realized Gretchen was there. "I— Are you guys actually *dating*?"

"We are."

Gretchen said it with a smile. He didn't know how she managed it. He wanted to break something. Instead, he laid heavy on the drawl, making sure to hold her gaze as he spoke. "Finally. I had to chase this woman for over a year to convince her to give me a chance."

The blank expressions returned.

How had Gretchen put up with this kind of dismissal her entire life? Colton dipped his head. "Ladies, if you'll excuse us? I need to show her off some more."

He squeezed Gretchen's waist and led her away.

"I think I want one of those dark closets now," she said, her voice breathless.

He knew the feeling. He was officially on fire. "Your bedroom," he said. "And this time we're locking the fucking door."

"There you are, Gretchen." Her mother's voice ruined everything.

They turned in unison to find her approaching in clipped, tense steps, her expression drawn tight. She wore a long red gown, looking as regal as a queen.

Diane forced a pleasant smile when she saw Colton, but it clearly took some effort.

"Colton, would you mind if I steal my daughter for a moment?"

"Actually, Mom, we were just about to—"

"I need to talk to you." Diane's expression changed again as she spotted something—or someone—over Gretchen's shoulder. Colton glanced that way to find Jack, Frasier, and Blake in a huddle. Even if their tense postures hadn't given away that something was amiss, their facial expressions did the trick. The men had enough simmering rage in their eyes to contribute to global warming.

Diane gripped Gretchen's arm. "This will just take a second, honey. Please."

"Go ahead," Colton said. "I can find a way to amuse myself."

He squeezed her hand, and as she trailed her mother through the crowd, he snagged a glass of champagne from a passing waiter.

"Colton. You made it."

It was Evan's voice this time. Colton turned around in time to see the man sauntering his way with just enough of a drag to his feet to suggest he'd had a little too much of the signature product already. Maybe that was what had the rest of the family so upset, but when Colton looked around for backup, he was on his own.

Evan approached with his hand extended. "Good of you to come," he said. His grip was stronger than necessary, as if he was trying too hard. Whether he meant it to intimidate or to cover up the slur of his words remained to be seen.

"I'm here for Gretchen," Colton said carefully.

"Well, I'm glad I got you alone."

"Yeah? Why's that?" Colton sipped his champagne for no other reason than to give himself some time to measure Evan's intentions. He didn't trust this asshole any farther than he could throw him.

"Well, you know, I figured maybe a little man-to-man might be in order."

"This about the endorsement?"

Evan pointed. It was unsteady. "See, that's what I like about you. You get right to the point."

"Let's keep that trend going, shall we?"

"Fair enough. I was surprised when Gretchen told me you'd passed on our proposal."

"It wasn't the right fit."

Evan snorted with ugly meaning. "And Gretchen is?"

Colton nearly cracked a tooth. "Excuse me?"

Evan held up his hands, palms out. "All I'm saying is that just doesn't make sense to me. You and her."

"Really? Makes perfect sense to me."

"I mean, you walked away from how much money? Thirty million minimum for her?"

The look on Colton's face must have deterred Evan from continuing. He laughed again and shrugged. "Opposites attract, I guess, right?"

Colton searched the crowd for her and found her all the way on the other side of the room, standing with her back to him. Her mother was gesturing for Jack and Frasier's attention, but it was Gretchen's posture that grabbed his attention. Her spine was rigid, the exposed muscles of her back popping as if she were engaging every single one to remain upright. Against her thighs, she held her hands in tight fists.

"What's going on?" he asked, facing Evan again.

"I think they're just delivering the news."

"What news?"

"Gretchen was hoping to get a spot on the foundation board, but, uh, well, we voted to go another way." The blood drained from Colton's head, leaving him light-headed as Evan continued. "We're announcing the new member tonight, and my parents thought we should give her a heads-up."

"You unbelievable sonofabitch," Colton breathed.

He shoved his champagne at Evan and skirted the edge of the crowd to get to her. As he neared the group, her voice rang out, hollow and tinny. "You can't be serious."

"Honey, I promise you," Diane was saying in a beseeching voice. "We tried to intervene. We know how much this meant to you."

"Bullshit," Jack barked. "Evan orchestrated this entire thing. That little prick is a vindictive piece of shit."

Frasier drew up tall. "That little prick is my son."

"Yeah, some father you turned out to be. Letting your son bully your daughter their entire lives?"

Colton inserted himself into the group and planted his body between Gretchen and the rest of them. Her face had drained of all color. Colton tried to tuck her against his side, but she stood stiffly, unbending.

Colton glared at Frasier. "What the hell is wrong with you people? You call this a family?"

Diane's eyes darted nervously around them at the curious stares directed their way. "We need to take this someplace private."

"Yes, because God forbid anyone find out the truth about us," Gretchen snapped.

Jack pointed at Frasier. "Five minutes. The back office. And bring Evan. This isn't over."

The family scattered, but Colton held Gretchen back. He searched her face. "Do you want to leave?"

A spark ignited in her eyes. "No. Not until I hear it from Evan himself."

"He's drunk."

"What else is new?" She gathered the skirt of her dress in one hand to keep from tripping on it as she stormed through the crowd after her parents. Colton had no choice but to follow. He'd never punched another human being in his entire life—except for the occasional scrap between him and his brother when they were kids—but it was going to take superhuman strength tonight to keep his record clean. He'd never met a man more in need of an uppercut to the jaw than Evan fucking Winthrop.

The *back office* that Jack referenced was yet another palatial absurdity. Like a library from *Downton Abbey.* Any minute, a butler was going to walk in and bow with a demure *your ladyship.*

Jack and Diane hovered by the door as Gretchen stormed inside. Jack stepped in front of her with what he probably thought was a reassuring look. "We'll overturn the decision. I have sway on the foundation board."

"You have no more sway than I do," Diane snapped. "You're just as close to being pushed to the side as I am."

Jack clenched his jaw. "I have more power than you think around here."

"Then why the hell have you never used it?" Diane blurted out the question with a rage that suggested she'd been holding that one in a long time.

But before Jack could answer, Frasier and Evan chose that moment to join the party.

"You sonofabitch," Jack seethed. "How could you do that to her?"

Evan crossed to the wet bar behind the massive desk on the other side of the room. He grabbed a crystal decanter and started pouring. "We did what was best for the foundation."

Jack pointed. "That is not a decision you get to make on your own."

"Look, we know how unreliable she is," Evan said, replacing the stopper on the decanter. "She thought she could join the board knowing full well that she's planning on moving."

Her mother whirled around to face Gretchen again. "What is he talking about? Where are you going?"

"She's taking some new job in D.C." Evan took another long drink.

Colton circled in front of Gretchen. "What's he talking about?"

"Ha," Evan snorted. "She didn't even tell her boyfriend. I told you she wasn't worth the trouble, man."

"I got an offer from a college friend to go work for his nonprofit, but I am *not* taking it." She turned on Evan. "But you and I both know this has nothing to do with that."

"She had one task. I asked her to do *one thing*. And what did she do? Did she prove that she could be counted on? Nope. She started fucking him instead."

Colton growled. "Insult her one more time, Evan, and I am going to shove that entire glass down your fucking throat."

Evan rolled his eyes again. "You don't actually expect any of us to believe this little thing between you is real, do you?"

Her mother stared with disgust at Evan, as if seeing her son for the first time. "Evan, what is *wrong* with you?"

"I guess I can't blame you, on the one hand," Evan said. "You get access to the Winthrop name and money without actually having to do anything." He shrugged. "Although now that I think about it, you could've gotten the money without the hassle of dealing with Gretchen. No piece of ass can be worth that."

What happened next was outside Colton's control, outside his consciousness. He watched, detached, as if someone else were in charge of his body as he stormed across the room, grabbed Evan by the lapel of his jacket, and slammed a fist in his face.

Evan careened backward and fell on his ass, blood spurting from his nose. Glass broke. Whiskey spilled. Chaos ensued.

Jack grabbed Colton around the chest and hauled him back just as Diane raced forward to check on her son. Frasier crouched down on the other side of him and helped him sit. Evan held a hand to his nose and bellowed that he was going to sue.

Colton's hand began to throb as the adrenaline crashed.

He turned around.

And that's when he realized.

Gretchen was gone.

CHAPTER TWENTY-TWO

She stole Blake's car.

It had been completely unintentional, which is what made it so perfect. She'd grabbed the first set of keys she found by the back entrance, beeped the key fob until she found the right one, and climbed in. It wasn't until she'd been driving aimlessly for a half hour that she realized which family member the car belonged to.

Even then, she kept driving. She went down dark country roads and onto the freeway. She took exits she didn't recognize. Sat in a McDonald's parking lot. Bought a slushy at a gas station. Stared at the lights over the river.

On the passenger seat, her phone buzzed incessantly with texts and phone calls and voice mails. Colton. Her mother. Jack. Colton. Blake's wife. Which was weird. Probably she wanted the car back. Colton again. Jack again. Her mother again.

She ignored everyone.

An hour passed.

And then another.

The road beckoned. The urge to run until the pain was gone was the navigation system in her mind. But when she began to drive again, it seemed to steer itself here, back to the place where she'd started. Down the same dark country road.

Somehow, she'd unconsciously known she would end up here.

Somehow, she'd known he would too.

The moonlight above was just enough to guide her to the path to her tree house, but she would've known the way even without it. She emerged into a clearing and paused to stare at Jack sitting alone on the swing, his hands hanging onto the rope and his eyes staring at the ground. The ends of his bow tie hung loosely around his neck, the top button of his shirt opened to the cold.

The crunch of her heels on the stick-strewn ground brought him to his feet with a surprised but then relieved breath. It puffed around his face in a misty cloud.

"Jesus, Gretchen. Where the hell have you been? I've been going out of my mind. Everyone has. Colton's out driving around looking for you."

"I needed to think." She hugged her torso and shivered. "How did you find me?"

He winced.

Of course. "Blake reported the car stolen?"

"He called the vehicle assistance service and asked them to locate it."

"How clever."

"He's not mad, Gretchen. He's as worried as everyone else."

She tried to roll her eyes, but another shiver raced through her instead.

Jack scowled. "Where's your coat?"

"In the car."

"Here . . ." He took off his tuxedo coat and set it around her shoulders. It chased away some of the night chill but did nothing to thaw the block of ice in her chest. He studied her face for a moment, opened his mouth to say something, and then apparently thought better of it. He backed up. "I need to let everyone know you're all right."

As he turned away with this phone, she hobbled on her heels to the tree. With a fingernail, she picked at the chipped edge of one of the old boards that Jack had nailed to the trunk so she could climb as a child.

Behind her, his voice was muffled as he spoke into his phone. "I found her . . . Blake can give you directions . . . I don't know . . . Okay, I'll tell her."

His footsteps drew near again. "Colton is on his way here to get you. He's a good man. I didn't think there could ever be anyone good enough for you, but he is."

Flick. She chipped off another sliver of wood. "That's a very *dad* thing to say."

"I'm sure your father feels the same."

"We both know that's not true." Flick. Another sliver gone.

"It's too cold out here," Jack said. "We should wait for Colton in the car."

"All the times I used to hide out here, did you know what I used to wish for?" Flick. A stubborn chip of wood clung to the edge. "I had this crazy fantasy that maybe I would find out someday that you were my real dad."

He let out a breath. "Gretchen . . ."

"I almost convinced myself of it too. There's the age difference between my brothers and me, you know? So I built this whole story in my head that my mother was a stranger or some woman who died or something and you decided that maybe I would be better off being raised by *them*. Stupid, huh? But it was better than believing that my parents just simply didn't give a shit that their son was actively abusing their daughter."

"What are you talking about?"

"Remember when I broke my arm?"

His breath became a shudder. "Are you saying—"

"It was Evan. I was too scared of him to tell anyone the truth."

"Shit, Gretchen . . ." His voice was a tightrope, wobbly beneath the weight of regret.

"He used to lock me out of the house at night."

"What?!"

"I was so naive. Every time, I thought we really were just going to play a game. I spent an entire night outside once when I was nine."

"Why didn't you tell anyone?"

"I tried. No one believed me." She flicked her fingernail against the stubborn sliver of wood, and this time it broke free and stabbed her skin. With a muttered curse, she resorted to slapping the board with the palm of her hand. "No one ever believed me!"

"I'm sorry," Jack croaked. "I'm so sorry."

She sucked in a sniffle and turned around. "You were right, though, what you said yesterday. All those times I ran away, I didn't really want to. Every time I was just desperate for someone to notice I was gone and to care enough to beg me to come home."

"*I* cared enough. I always came for you."

"I know. And I'm sorry, but I was so disappointed every time to see you walk in. So that last time, I thought, maybe I just need to do something really crazy, you know? Maybe if I go far enough, maybe if I really fuck up, maybe if I take Blake's car and go all the way to Michigan, maybe this time they would care enough to come themselves. My *parents*. But they didn't. They sent you."

The crunch of tires announced Colton's arrival. A car door opened and slammed. The snap of Colton's footsteps—hurried and urgent—grew louder. "Gretchen?"

He burst from the path with a near skid on the damp, cold grass. When he saw her, Colton jogged toward her, opened his arms, and let out a relieved breath when she walked into them. His chest was warm, his voice soothing. "I was worried."

"I'm sorry."

He framed her face with his hands and tilted it back so he could see her. "Are you okay?"

"Fine."

He stepped back and dragged his hands over his hair. "You can't do that, Gretchen. You can't just take off."

"It's what I do. You said so yourself, remember?"

He spared a single glance for Jack. "I'm taking her home."

Gretchen slipped Jack's coat off her shoulders. "This is his."

Colton took it from her and handed it unceremoniously to Jack. Then his hand was on her back and steering her back to the path.

Jack tried to follow. "Gretchen . . ."

Colton stopped and whipped around. With a single point and a glare, he ended Jack's pursuit. "Jack, I think you're a good person, the only good person in this whole fucking family besides Gretchen. But right now, I don't want to hear a single goddamn word from any of you."

They left him standing there in the halo of the moonlight, his coat hanging limply from his fingers, an apology hanging uselessly on his lips.

Colton guided her over the knotted roots and the jagged sticks, the path now alight from his headlights. His car was still running. She let him open her door and help her inside. She even let him help her with her seat belt. And when he was done, he paused to cup her face once again before kissing her sweetly.

"Let's go home," he said.

They didn't speak during the drive, but he kept one hand wrapped around hers on the console between them, even when he stopped at his gate to punch in the security code. He didn't let go until they were parked in front of his house.

Through the front windows, the Christmas tree glowed with welcome, but the rest of the house appeared dark. "I don't want to wake the kids up," she said when he opened her door.

"We won't." He took her hand to help her from the car. "And even if we do, they'll go back to sleep."

The front door opened as they walked up the porch. His mother stepped out, a robe wrapped around her body and a worried glaze in her eyes. "I've been stress baking," she said, an attempt at humor that fell flat from the catch in her voice.

"I'm sorry," Gretchen said. "I didn't mean to worry anyone."

"Nonsense." His mother pulled her into an embrace. She smelled like vanilla and chocolate.

Colton followed them inside, softly shutting the door behind them. Gretchen glanced back at him, and he just smiled as his mother led her toward the kitchen. "I'll be right there."

His mother's arm was tight around her shoulders. "I have cookies fresh from the oven. It doesn't solve anything, but it certainly doesn't hurt either."

Gretchen managed a soft laugh for her benefit.

"Are you hungry for anything else? I can heat up some stew or—"

"I'm okay. But thank you. I'm sorry I kept you awake. I didn't mean to worry anyone."

The look on her face was a cross between offended and sympathetic. "Of course I waited up." She filled a plate with chocolate chip cookies, still so warm that a spiral of steam wafted up. "Sit," she said, nodding at one of the island stools. "I'll get you some milk."

Gretchen had no appetite for anything, but she sat anyway. She smiled in thanks when Mary set a glass of milk in front of her. Colton walked up behind her and set his hands on her shoulders. "You're still cold," he said, sliding his hands down to her bare arms.

"Are you hungry, honey?" Mary asked him. "I can make something for you too."

"No, thanks. I just want to get her to bed."

"Good idea. You both must be exhausted."

Colton bent and kissed the top of her head as he squeezed her arms. "Ready?"

Embarrassment flooded her limbs to have him discuss their sleeping arrangements so openly with his mother. Which was dumb. They were adults. But it was so foreign—this unconditional acceptance as part of the family.

Gretchen stood up. His mom hugged her once again. "I'll make a big breakfast in the morning. Everything will look better after some sleep."

Colton's hand settled on her back and led her away. The upstairs was dark and silent, but Gretchen wondered if his sister, dad, and brother were all lying awake and listening.

Colton flipped on the overhead lights in his bedroom before quietly shutting the door.

"I don't suppose you have an extra toothbrush?"

Colton untucked his shirt. "I'll set it out for you. Do you want a T-shirt or anything to sleep in?"

"Sure."

He dropped a kiss on her lips. "Top drawer of my dresser. Grab whichever one you want. I'll be right out."

He walked into the bathroom. When the door clicked quietly, she went to the dresser and grabbed the first thing on top—a gray Legends T-shirt. Feet aching, she kicked off her heels and fumbled with the zipper on the side of her dress. She never wanted to wear this thing again. If she didn't hate the idea of wasting something that could be donated, she might even consider tossing it in the fireplace and watching it burn.

It pooled at her feet as she unclipped her strapless bra, leaving her in just her panties as he walked out of the bathroom.

Colton let out a reverent breath behind her. "It's probably the wrong time to say this, but you could bring me to my knees right now."

She turned around and found him staring at her with unmasked desire. He'd removed his shirt in the bathroom, and all she could think was, *Same.* "I don't think there's ever a wrong time to say something like that."

"There is. You need to sleep tonight." He closed the distance between them. The T-shirt she'd chosen was on top of the dresser. He picked it up. "Arms up."

She obeyed and he threaded it over her head. She wiggled into it until it draped over her body. He kissed her briefly again. "I set everything out for you in there."

Not just a toothbrush, she discovered. But anything else she might need. A clean washcloth. A towel. Facial cleanser and moisturizer. Which she desperately needed. She stared with a grimace at the mess of her reflection in the mirror. Mascara streaks darkened the area under her eyes. Her long-stay lipstick had faded into a dry pink. Her updo had shifted atop her head into a loose, frizzy bun.

And somehow, Colton still found her sexy.

He deserved better than this mess. And she didn't mean how she looked right now. He deserved better than the destructive cyclone she and her family created every time they breathed.

She brushed her teeth and washed her face and then answered nature's call. When she finally emerged, she found him already in bed, one arm hooked under his head and the covers up to his waist.

He rolled his head to smile at her. "Ready for bed?"

"You should've told me I looked like Medusa."

"You look beautiful." He followed her with his eyes as she walked to the other side of the bed. "You're giving me heart palpitations in that T-shirt."

He was trying to lighten the mood by flirting with her, but it had the opposite effect on her. By the time she slid beneath the covers, her heart was fully in her throat. He rolled toward her and caressed her cheek, but when his fingers met the tears, he rose up on one elbow.

"Tell your parents I'm sorry about all this tonight. All of this is so embarrassing and humiliating and—"

"And none of your fault."

"But your parents are such good people. They deserve better than that . . . So do you."

His hand stilled on her face. "Better than what?"

"Than this." She waved her hands around. "Me and my sordid, toxic family."

"You're exhausted, Gretchen. You need to sleep."

He lifted his hand to brush the hair from her face, but she caught his fingers in hers. His knuckles were purple and red and swollen. "Does it hurt?"

"Not anymore."

"How was Evan when you left?"

"Does it make me a bad person if I say I don't really give a shit?"

Did it make him a bad person? No. But it made him *not him*. "You hit my brother tonight, Colton. You. Who has never gotten in a fight in your entire life."

"And I'd do it again."

"That's what scares me. That wasn't you tonight. But this is what happens when you get involved with me. My family stains everything."

His jaw hardened. "If you're about to say what I think you are, just stop."

"I have to say it." She rose on an elbow. "*I'm bad for you.*"

Colton suddenly rolled away from her and rose from bed. He towered over her, hands on his hips. "Let me make one thing very clear to you, because it obviously isn't."

She gulped at the gravity in his tone and his eyes.

"I am in love with you."

Her mouth fell open. She snapped it shut for fear her heart would leap clean out of it.

"I am in love with you," he said again, "and I would give up any amount of money for you. I would protect you a million times if necessary. All those horrible things your brother said, none of it was true. None of it. All I want to do is prove that to you. That you are worthy of love."

He returned to bed and covered her body with his. "Just let me in, Gretchen. Let me show you how I feel."

So she did.

She let him show her what love was like. She let his hands and his mouth and his body teach her what it meant to be cherished.

They were quiet, swallowing each other's moans with their mouths, muffling their passion with faces pressed into necks.

They fell asleep in a tangle of exhausted limbs and hearts.

And woke up when the phone rang.

CHAPTER TWENTY-THREE

There were very few reasons why his manager would call in the wee hours of the morning, none of them good.

Colton ground at his eyes, fumbled for his phone, and answered sleepily. "Jesus, Buck, What's—"

"Did you get in a fight with Evan Winthrop last night?"

Shit. Colton glanced at Gretchen, who was miraculously still asleep. "How did you hear about that?"

"There's a video."

Colton slid out of bed as quietly as he could and padded to the bathroom to speak in private. "It's a long story," he said, closing the door and turning on the light.

"Well, start practicing your right to remain silent about it."

Adrenaline turned his muscles to Jell-O. "What's going on?"

"The cops are on their way to your house. Winthrop is pressing charges."

"That sonofabitch." Colton clenched the phone so hard it was a wonder the thing didn't break.

"I called Desiree, and she's on her way to your house too." Desiree Childs was one of the attorneys that Buck kept on retainer. Colton had never dreamed he'd ever need her services, though. She specialized in criminal law.

"With any luck, we'll beat the cops there," Buck said. "Do not say *anything* until we get there. We'll deal with this, I promise."

The roar of blood in his ears nearly drowned out Buck's last reassuring words. Colton ended the call and yanked the faucet on. Hands shaking, he splashed water on his face, the sting of cold like a slap of reality. He'd never even had a goddamn detention in school. Now he was being arrested for assault. By tomorrow morning, the news would be all over celebrity gossip sites, his mug shot circulating faster than a joint at a Jimmy Buffett concert.

Colton sucked in several deep breaths. He had to be calm when he told Gretchen. But when he walked out of the bathroom, she was already sitting up in bed, staring in anguish at her own phone. She met his gaze, and the pain he saw in her eyes made him momentarily forget that he was the one about to get in trouble.

"Colton, I'm sorry. I'm so sorry."

"This isn't your fault." He went to his dresser. "We need to get dressed. The cops are on the way here."

She scrambled out of bed, and he handed her a pair of his sweatpants and some socks. He slipped into a pair of jeans and a T-shirt. "I'll be right back. I need to go wake up my parents."

"Colton—" Her voice shook.

He gripped her face and kissed her. Hard. "It's going to be okay."

But he wasn't sure if he believed his own words. He left the room, and before he could even knock on the door of the guest room where his parents were sleeping, the door opened. His father was there, a worried crease along his forehead. "There's a video of the fight."

"I know. The cops are on their way here."

"You're being *arrested*?"

"It looks that way." His voice conveyed greater calm than he felt. His mother appeared in the doorway next. "I need you to take care of Gretchen," he said. "She's freaking out like this is her fault."

"I'll get dressed," his father said, moving back into the room. "If they take you in, I'm following."

Another door opened, and his brother walked out. "What's going on?"

And then a third door opened, and this time his sister walked out, sleepy, her arms crossed over her torso. "What's wrong?"

"Don't let the kids wake up," Colton said quietly. "I don't want them to see this."

"See what?" His sister's voice rose, so Colton took her elbow and pulled her away from the room. As he explained to Jordan and Cooper what was happening, her eyes widened and filled with tears as his brother's became enraged.

"It's going to be okay," Colton said. "But I don't want the kids to see me being put in a cop car in handcuffs."

His sister nodded and then hugged him. Colton squeezed her tightly, briefly, and then turned to jog down the stairs. He'd just reached the front door when he got an alert from the front gate.

He typed in the code, walked onto the front porch, and waited for the cavalry.

Gretchen suddenly appeared at his side. "Go back inside," he said quietly, not daring to look at her.

"I'm not leaving you. They need to hear what really happened."

"Look at me." He finally dared to meet her eyes. They shimmered with angry, guilty tears. "This is not your fault. I made my own choices, and I would do it a million times again to protect you."

Two police cruisers drove up the driveway with the words WILLIAMSON COUNTY SHERIFF emblazoned on the sides. Colton's heart stopped and sputtered as the doors opened and uniformed deputies stepped out.

One took charge. "Colton Wheeler?"

"Yes."

"We have a warrant for your arrest on the charge of felony assault."

"Jesus," his father whispered. Colton hadn't even heard the old man come out.

Without looking at him, Colton said, "Dad, take Gretchen inside."

"No," Gretchen argued.

"Please, Gretchen. This is humiliating enough. I can't stand for you to see this."

"I'll take her," his mom said. Again, he hadn't even been aware of her presence. "Let's go, honey."

"Don't come back out," he ordered. "Promise me."

"Colton . . ."

He looked down at her and attempted to smile. "It'll be okay. I'm big-time Colton Wheeler, remember?"

Her expression didn't change. But she finally nodded, and with a shuddered breath, she let his mom walk her back inside. The click of the front door was the last thing he heard before two more cars sped up the driveway. The cops reacted with tense stances and hands on their weapons.

"It's my manager and my attorney," Colton said, his voice shaking.

Buck and Desiree left their cars running as they got out. "Let me see the warrant," Desiree demanded.

Buck jogged to where Colton stood. "I'll meet with Archie, and we'll get started on a statement."

"What's it going to say?"

"That we look forward to the dismissal of these ridiculous charges."

"There's a video, Buck."

"Which never tells the whole story."

The attorney finished reviewing the warrant and handed it back to the police officer. The officer stepped forward, an apologetic look on his face. "Sir, can you please turn around and place your hands on the door?"

"Oh my God," his father whispered, lacing his fingers atop his head.

"It's okay, Dad." Colton obeyed the officer, flattening his palms against the front door. The only silver lining of the moment was that his mom, sister, and Gretchen couldn't see it.

The officer came up behind him. "I'm going to search you now, sir. Are you carrying any weapons?"

"No."

"Is there anything sharp in your pockets that I need to be aware of?"

"No."

The officer quickly patted him down. Apparently satisfied, he stepped back and said, "I'm going to read you your rights now, sir."

That brought another expletive from his father's mouth.

"Please put your hands behind your back, sir," the police officer said, after advising him he had the right to remain silent.

Colton couldn't pretend to be brave after that, not when he

heard the cold click of handcuffs and felt them tighten around his wrists. His knees shook, and his breath caught in his throat. "I'm sorry you had to see this, Dad," he said, voice tight.

"Where are you taking him?" Desiree asked.

"He'll be booked at the Williamson County Jail."

"Can he post bond?" his father asked.

"That'll be up to the court."

"We'll be right behind you," Desiree said.

"Me too," his father added.

The officer put one hand on his shoulder and the other atop his shackled wrists. With a nudge, he led Colton down the porch steps and toward the waiting cruiser.

"I'm going to place my hand on your head now, sir, as I place you in the back of the car."

He'd seen it done a million times on TV shows and movies. Nothing, though, could have prepared him for the feeling of being placed on the hard back seat of a police car, his hands wedged painfully behind him. The officer clicked a seat belt around him and then asked him with discordant politeness if he was comfortable.

"I'm fine," Colton said.

The officer nodded, backed up, and shut the door.

The last thing Colton saw before the cops pulled away was Gretchen in the window, silhouetted against the Christmas tree, watching it all.

Gretchen stood at the window until the last taillights disappeared. Somewhere behind her, chaos had taken over the house. Colton's brother, whom she hadn't even met yet, was raging in the kitchen. Mary was trying to calm him down to no avail.

A hand touched her arm. "Honey."

Gretchen jumped. Mary had joined her at the window.

"Come to the kitchen," Mary said. "I'll make us some coffee. I doubt either of us are going back to sleep after this anyway."

Gretchen should be the one making coffee. She should be the one doing the reassuring and the comforting. She was the reason everyone was awake. The reason Colton had just been dragged away in handcuffs.

"They won't keep him," Mary said, perhaps more to herself than Gretchen. "We'll post bail as soon as we can, and he'll be back in a few hours."

Gretchen finally faced her. "I'm sorry."

"Don't say that. None of this is your fault."

Gretchen sidestepped her and walked away from the window. "I—I need to go."

"No, you don't."

"I have to do something."

"There's nothing either of us can do."

A cell phone blared. Gretchen recognized a split second later that it was hers. She'd shoved it in the pocket of the sweatpants Colton had given her to wear. She dug it out with trembling hands. It was Elena.

Mary patted her arm. "I'll go make that coffee."

Gretchen answered as she sat stiffly on the couch. "Hi," she said by way of a greeting.

"What's going on?" Elena asked urgently. "*Nashville Scene* is reporting that Colton was just arrested."

"How do they already know? It just happened."

"It's *true*?" Elena's voice shook, as if she and Vlad had been hoping that the report was incorrect. She said something to Vlad in the background. Even if Gretchen didn't understand a word of it—Elena and Vlad always spoke Russian with each other—the deep urgency of Vlad's voice told her how worried he was.

"What happened?" Elena asked, returning to the phone.

"I'm sure you've seen the video."

"It doesn't even look like Colton. I've never seen him like that."

"He was . . ." Gretchen's voice broke. "He was standing up for me. It's my fault."

"No, it's not. Where are you right now?"

"His house."

"Stay there," Elena said. "We'll come over."

"Don't. His whole family is here. I don't want to disturb them any more than they've already been."

"We're his family too."

Her phone vibrated against her cheek with an incoming text. "I have to go. I'll try to call later, okay?"

She hung up over Elena's protest and checked her notifications. The text was from Liv. What's going on? Mack and I are freaking out. Do you need us?

Another text came in. This time from Alexis. Are you okay? Do you want Noah and I to come over?

We're his family too.

Yes, they were. They were as much Colton's family as his parents and his sister and his nieces and nephews. One big happy functional supportive family.

And no matter what Colton said, she was screwing it up.

They could tell her a million times that this wasn't her fault, but none of this would have happened if she hadn't gone to see him in that dive bar and invited him into the chaos that was her family. If she hadn't given in to temptation all those months ago at Mack and Liv's wedding.

His reputation. His career. This arrest would forever be an asterisk next to his name. Soon, she had no doubt, his mug shot would be made public. It would be plastered all over the media and retweeted a million times, and she could practically write the headlines in her mind.

Soft footsteps on the carpet wrenched her from her thoughts. Jordan walked in carrying a sleepy Phoebe, her little hand rubbing her eyes.

"I tried to get her back to sleep, but . . ." Jordan's voice was as fragile as her smile was brittle.

"I'm sorry."

"Where's my mom?"

"In the kitchen making coffee."

Jordan padded away, and Gretchen heard her and Mary's soft voices gently coaxing Phoebe to go back to sleep. In all her life, she'd never heard that kind of tenderness in her own family. Her own mother was too worried about getting something on her clothes to rock her grandkids. She'd never once seen her mother in a robe, fussing over a tray of warm cookies.

Gretchen spied her purse on the table by the front door. She had no shoes, but she wouldn't need them. Not where she was going.

She grabbed her purse and Colton's keys from where he'd left them.

And walked out the front door.

CHAPTER TWENTY-FOUR

This time, she knew exactly where she was going.

Down that dark country road.

On the horizon, a pink sunrise peeked above the tree line, turning gold fields lavender. Mist hovered above the ground, ghostly and haunting.

She passed the dark tasting room, its parking lot empty. She passed the road to the tree house, past the entrance to Evan's house. And when she finally came to the main house still ablaze with lights, she was unsurprised to find that once again, she was the only one not here. Evan's car was there. Jack's car was there. Blake's car was there. Another family meeting without her.

The sound of raised voices greeted her when she walked into the residence, but they quickly quieted at the approaching thud of her footsteps. Her father thundered out of his office, ready to chew out whichever lowly servant so rudely interrupted them. He still looked as fresh as ever, his tuxedo showing no signs of crease or wrinkle.

Even his bow tie was still tightly knotted beneath his chin. It was as if nothing had happened.

He stopped short when he saw her, eyes growing wide before he reeled in his reaction. "Gretchen," he said, loudly enough to be sure everyone else heard him. He then looked her up and down. "Good Lord, what are you wearing? Where are your shoes?"

"Where's Evan?"

Jack walked into the vestibule. He also still wore his tuxedo, but his looked like he'd just come back from a hard hike. His pants were dirty, his shirt wrinkled and untucked. His eyes were rimmed with dark circles as if he hadn't slept in days, even though she'd only left him five hours ago. He hurried toward her. "How's Colton?"

"Great. He's probably being fingerprinted as we speak. I'm sure it's a very enjoyable experience."

"We'll get this worked out," Jack said. "I promise."

"Forgive me if I don't have a lot of faith in any promises from this family."

She stormed past both men, yanking her arm out of Jack's reach when he tried to stop her. She found Evan kicked back on the wide leather sofa in the den, feet resting on the ottoman. He, too, still wore last night's clothes. Blood dotted his shirt, his bow tie long gone. Above his eye, a butterfly bandage held together the broken skin where Colton's fist had split it open. Purple bruising darkened his eye socket, and in his hand, an empty whiskey glass tipped precariously toward his wife's lap. Anna silently clutched an ice pack, her evening gown wet where it had leaked.

Blake and his wife hovered nervously behind the couch.

Evan eyed Gretchen coolly. "Nice outfit. Did you get mugged or something?"

"Where's Mom?"

"She took a Valium and passed out an hour ago."

Of course. Because why should her mother have to deal with this? Why should she have to feel anything?

"I need to talk to you alone," Gretchen finally said.

Jack and Frasier had followed her in. "I don't think that's a good idea," Frasier said now.

"It's amazing how little I care about what you think right now."

"For God's sake, Gretchen, grow up," he snapped back. "This is no time for dramatics."

Dramatics.

Hysterics.

Radical tendencies.

The insults that had once so sharply sliced through her now so easily bounced off her. It was hard to hurt someone who'd gone numb. Impossible to pierce skin that had thickened into hard scar tissue. "I need to speak to Evan alone," she repeated.

Evan sighed melodramatically and nodded to the door. "It's fine. I'm sure this won't take long."

"Gretchen, are you sure?" Jack asked quietly.

"Go. All of you."

With reluctance, Anna rose from the couch, still clutching the ice pack. She met Gretchen's eyes as she walked past, a strange and unfamiliar apology in her gaze. When they'd finally all left, their departure confirmed by the click of the door, Evan stood. "Whatever it is you have to say, I don't give a shit. Your boyfriend brought this on himself."

"I need you to drop the charges."

Evan carried his empty glass to the wet bar and began to refill it. "Sorry. He nearly broke my nose."

"I need you to drop the charges," Gretchen repeated.

"You can say it a million times, but it won't make a difference.

And even if I wanted to let this go—which I don't—it's out of my hands. There's a video clearly showing him attacking me unprovoked." He drank deeply from his glass.

"Drop. The. Charges."

Evan shook his head, disgusted. "I think we're done here."

"You know what I can't figure out about that video? Why was it posted online instead of being turned over to the police first?"

Evan shrugged. "You'd have to ask the person who leaked it."

"But that's the other funny thing about the video. It came from our security cameras."

Another shrug. "So?"

"There are only a handful of people in the entire world who would've had access to the security system at that time, and none of them would have had time to do it."

"Obviously someone did."

"Someone who wasn't there," she said. "Someone like Sarah."

He stilled, the glass halfway to his mouth.

"Sarah . . . who is so oddly devoted to you and so similarly resentful of me."

"What's your fucking point, Gretchen?"

"Drop the charges."

He gestured toward the door with his glass. "Get the fuck out of here."

"I will relinquish all claim over any and all inheritance from Dad's will. It's all yours. Just drop the charges. Please."

That got his attention. "Are we negotiating? Is that what this is?"

"No. It's me giving up. You win, Evan. At long last, you win. This has always been about money with you, so fine. Take it. So just tell me what it will take, and I'll do it. You can have whatever you want or think you're entitled to. Just leave Colton out of it."

He didn't hesitate. "Relinquish your inheritance and transfer all of your company stock to me."

She'd known it would come to this, that the only thing he responded to was money, but disappointment still managed to worm its way beneath the cold rock that had once been her heart. "Once you call the DA, it's all yours. I'll sign whatever document you want."

Evan finished his drink and immediately began to pour more. She waited as he replaced the cap on the whiskey and turned back around. He was dragging things out for effect, as he always did. After a long drink, he leaned against the wet bar. "I want one more thing."

"What?"

"The job in D.C." He took another drink. "I want you to take it. And never come back."

"Don't worry," she said, coldness seeping into her tone. "You get that one for free. Because I never want to see any of you ever again."

His smile was triumphant as he tipped his glass to her. "Nice doing business with you."

Robotic steps took her to the door. Her fingers encircled the handle, but she gave him one more look. "Does Anna know?"

"About what?"

"Sarah."

His jaw clenched.

Gretchen shook her head with sadness for a woman who'd only ever shown her civilized disdain. "She deserves better than you."

Five minutes later, she drove home. And cried herself to sleep.

CHAPTER TWENTY-FIVE

Colton was arraigned at ten a.m.

By then, news of his arrest had gone national. Reporters from every state and local news outlet, as well as a handful of Nashville gossip sites, filled the small courtroom. Overflow cameras packed the jury box, their lenses pointed at the defense table to document every humiliating moment of the downfall of Nashville's golden boy.

And when Colton was brought in wearing a jail jumpsuit, the click of cameras sounded like distant fireworks.

His attorney waited for him at the defense table. The clerk called the case number and read his name and the charges into the record, and then the judge asked him directly if he understood the charges against him.

Colton repeated the words his attorney had told him to say. "I do, your honor."

There was more procedural stuff. A date was set for the preliminary hearing where he would officially enter a plea. The judge announced a thirty-thousand-dollar bond. And then it was over. Court officers led him out of the courtroom to the holding cell where five other defendants awaited their turn. In all, it took ten minutes from start to finish, but an entire lifetime had passed. From this point on, his career would be marred by the images of this short hearing. His unshaven face. His bruised knuckles. The orange jail suit.

An hour later, he posted bail, changed back into his clothes, and walked out the front door of the courthouse into a throng of reporters. His attorney and a beefy man Colton had never seen elbowed through them, ignored all shouted questions, and ushered him into the back seat of a black SUV.

The beefy guy took the wheel, and his attorney climbed into the passenger seat.

"Where's my dad?"

"I sent him home as soon as the hearing ended," Desiree said. "Buck wants you to go home and get some rest, and we'll reconvene tonight."

"I need my phone."

Desiree handed it back in a plastic bag that also held his wallet. The battery on his phone was in the red, the screen a stack of unread notifications, mostly about texts from his friends. Only one was from Gretchen. A two-word text that read, I'm sorry.

He called her number. When she didn't pick up, he texted. Stop apologizing. I'm on my way home.

No response.

Colton called his mother next. She answered breathlessly. "Are you okay? Is it over? Where are you?"

"On my way home."

"Thank God."

"Can you put Gretchen on the phone? She's not answering."

His mother paused.

"Mom."

"She's not here."

The world skidded to a stop in his brain. "Where'd she go?"

"I don't know. I've been trying to call her, but she's not answering me either. I didn't even know she'd left. I was in the kitchen, and when I came out she was just gone."

His phone chimed with a warning about the battery. "Mom, I'll call you back."

"Honey, I'm sorry."

"It's okay." He ended the call and leaned forward between the front seats. "We need to turn around."

Desiree looked back. "Why?"

"I need to pick up Gretchen."

"Colton, I highly advise you against going out in public right now. The best thing you can do is go home, hunker down for a few days, and let the team handle this."

"Turn around, or I'm jumping out at the next light."

The beefy driver looked uncertainly at the attorney, who finally sighed and said, "Do it."

Colton rattled off the address to Gretchen's house. If she wasn't there, he'd go to her office next. And if she wasn't there, he'd go back to the place where this entire nightmare started and finish the job until her fucking family told him where she was.

The driver pulled a U-turn at the next light, ignored the honk of an annoyed motorist trying to turn right, and sped through the intersection. With the last ounce of power in his phone, Colton tried to call her again.

Still no answer.

The SUV had barely stopped before Colton leaped from the back seat and jogged up the front walk to her house. He pressed the intercom button and leaned into the microphone. "Let me in, Gretchen."

No response.

"My car is here, Gretchen. That means you're here."

Silence.

"Dammit, Gretchen. I know what you're doing, and I am not letting you run away again."

The intercom finally crackled with her voice. "Can you please stop yelling?"

"Let me in, and I'll think about it."

He heard the lock release on the stairs to her apartment. He burst through the door and took the stairs two at a time. By the time he reached the top, he was winded and sweaty. Long, hurried steps took him to the end of the hallway, where her door remained shut.

He pounded on it with the palm of his hand, sending the wreath he'd given her crashing to the floor. The door flew open, and she stood before him still wearing his sweatpants and T-shirt. His too-big socks had stretched out and hung off her toes like two floppy flippers. Her hair was piled atop her head in a messy bun, and her face bore the streaks of tears. "You shouldn't be here."

"Let me in."

"No."

He wrapped his arms around her and lifted her from the floor. She protested with a fist on his shoulder. He kicked the door shut behind him and set her down. She hit him again in the middle of his chest. "What kind of brutish bullshit was that?"

"The *I just got out of jail* kind." He stormed toward her tiny kitchen.

She followed with quick, padded footsteps. "What are you doing?"

"I'm starving."

He opened her fridge, perused the sad, meager contents, and settled on a single wrapped piece of string cheese. He ripped open the plastic and bit into it like a banana. Three angry bites, and he'd devoured the whole thing.

She crossed her arms. "There. You've eaten. Now go."

"Not without you."

Colton tried to draw her close, but she stepped away, her hands covering her face. "Stop, Colton, *please*."

"For God's sake." He jerked his hands through his hair and laced his fingers on top of his head. "I understand what you're doing, because it's what you do, but dammit, *I* can't do this right now. I'm exhausted. I'm still hungry. I am in desperate need of a shower because I was forced to sit for two hours next to a sweaty hipster named Jacob—spelled Jacob but pronounced *Jah-cobe*, which he told me no fewer than four times—and there are about a thousand reporters foaming at the mouth to get to me. All I want is to go home, crawl into bed *with you*, and sleep for about ten hours. So, please. Get whatever you need because there's a car waiting for us outside."

"No. I'm breaking up with you."

He snorted. "No, you're not."

"I'm leaving Nashville."

"No, you're not."

"I'm taking the job in D.C."

"No, you're not." He hastened to where she stood with her arms crossed and her lips thin. He traced them with his thumb. "And I'm not letting you break up with me."

"That's not how this works. If I want to break up with you, then we're broken up."

He quirked an eyebrow and gazed down at her pouty, upturned face. "Wow. Kick a man when he's down, why don't you? I was just arraigned on assault charges for you, and now you're dumping me?"

He meant it as a joke. She didn't take it as one. She unfurled her arms, only to toss her hands in the air. "I'm dumping you *because* you were just arraigned on assault charges for me!"

"I'm the one who hit him, Gretchen. You didn't ask me to. I did this all on my own."

"Because of me."

At his growled *argh*, she stomped to her small kitchen table and spun around her laptop. "Look at this." She pointed to an article on the screen detailing his arrest with his mug shot front and center. "This is going to follow you forever."

"You're a real comfort, you know that?" He winked to let her know he was, once again, kidding.

But once again, she didn't get the joke. "I am poison to you, Colton."

He tipped his head to the ceiling and ground the heels of his hands into his tired eyes. "We're really doing this right now?"

"The sunshiny one doesn't fall for the grumpy one. The grumpy one corrupts the sunshiny one. That's what I've done to you."

Her words and the tremor in her voice brought his gaze back to hers. He didn't like what he saw there—sad resignation and dogged determination.

"You asked why I ran away from you after the wedding. It wasn't because I didn't want you. It was because I did want you. I fell for you, too, that night. But I knew even then that someone like you deserves better than someone like me and my particular brand of chaos. Trust me, you're better off without me."

"Your particular brand of chaos has made me happier than I've been in a long, long time, so maybe let me be the judge of whether I'll be better off without it."

"You'll get over it. Think of the songs you'll write. The best albums are based on heartbreak."

The first real tug of fear settled in his gut. "Are you . . . are you really doing this? This isn't just some more of your bullshit?"

She stormed to the front door and pulled it open. "Just go, Colton. Please."

"Dammit, I love you!"

She sucked in a breath, and for one second, he thought maybe she was going to drop the whole act. But then she dipped her face to the ground. "And there are a million women who would die to help you move on."

"I can't fucking believe this, Gretchen."

"The longer you stand here, the harder this gets. *Please*."

"Oh, I'm sorry. Am I not making it easy enough for you to kick me in the balls?"

"You're the one who's making this hard."

He took in the scene, detail by detail. Her white-knuckled grip on the door handle. Her quivering bottom lip. The shifty eyes desperate to avoid meeting his gaze.

He should've seen it coming. The choked, tearful confession in the middle of the night. The desperate way she clung to him when they made love. The forlorn, distant look on her face in the window as he was hauled away.

He should've known. A cornered rabbit always ran. "You're a coward, you know that?"

"What?" The word came out in a shocked quiver.

"You're not doing this for me. You're doing it for you." The words were jagged shards, but he couldn't stop spitting them at her. "You're using this as an excuse to do what you were always going to do . . . run when you started to feel something worth fighting for. Because despite this tough act you put on, you're just a scared little girl hiding in that damn tree house wishing someone would come find you and take you home. But it's not going to be me this time, Gretchen. I'm done trying to convince you to stay."

He was panting by the time he was done. Panting and shaking and ready to spew the meager contents of his stomach onto her floor.

"See," she finally sniffed, "I was right. The old Colton would never raise his voice like that."

"Yeah, well, the old Colton had never had his heart ripped from his fucking chest."

Tears quivered on her lashes, swollen dams of sorrow ready to burst, and despite everything, he still wanted to drag her into his arms. Why was she doing this to them? To him? He tried one last pathetic time. "I love you."

"I'm sorry. I never should have let it get this far."

And that's when it hit him. She hadn't said it back. Not just now and not in the wee hours of the morning. It hurt not because he feared that she didn't feel the same but because he knew she did. She just wouldn't admit it. She'd rather tear him to shreds than let herself be vulnerable.

The adrenaline from being arrested and charged and paraded in front of the press fizzled into hollowed-out numbness. His feet were heavy as he forced himself to walk to the doorway and stand next to her.

"I was wrong before," he said. "You're not a coward. You're selfish. So you know what? I'm sorry too. Sorry I wasted my time."

Her fingers clenched the edge of the doorframe. When she spoke, her voice was robotic, detached. "Merry Christmas, Colton."

He stomped out and didn't look back.

CHAPTER TWENTY-SIX

By five p.m., it was done.

Gretchen had forced Evan to put the call on speaker phone and listened as he explained to the district attorney that he no longer wished to press charges. He'd been drinking, he said. There was a misunderstanding. He was as much to blame as Colton. The security tape didn't show the entire incident, and, unfortunately, the company's system had already erased the original video, so whatever evidence existed was now gone.

The DA pushed back. Said it would look bad if he let a country star off the hook without so much as a hearing. That he'd be accused of giving preferential treatment to celebrities. To which Evan, in his casually sinister way, reminded the man how happy the Winthrop family had been to so generously support his previous campaign.

And that was that.

It was done.

Now, all that was left was for Gretchen to sign the two-page document that Evan slid across the desk. "Need a pen?"

"No." She leaned forward in the chair where she sat, brought the document onto her lap, and skimmed the key points. Just as she'd promised, the document stated that she hereby relinquished all inheritance from Frasier James Winthrop and that all of her shares in the company were transferred to Evan William Winthrop.

Gretchen pulled a pen from the purse at her feet. Then, in bold, sweeping letters, she gave up more than seventy million dollars.

A small price to pay for the man she loved.

She slid the document back across the desk, gathered her purse, and stood. "I'll have a copy sent to your office," Evan said, as if this were just another business deal to him. And, frankly, it was. If not for his swollen, purple eye and the bandage over his eyebrow, there'd be no reason to suspect this was anything more than a normal day. All he cared about was winning. Winning at all costs. Defeating the person who stood between him and what he thought he was entitled to.

"May I make one more request?" Gretchen asked, pulling her purse strap over her shoulder. Her teeth nearly cracked under the clenched pressure of having to beg him like Bob fucking Cratchit for another piece of coal on the fire.

"Of course."

He actually fucking smiled when he said it. Gretchen tried to match his tone, even though her internal organs were boiling in rage. "I would like my legal clinic to remain open here in Nashville. I'm going to offer the job to my assistant. She'll need to hire a new attorney, perhaps two or three. I'm going to encourage her to submit a grant application to the foundation to help make that possible. Please don't block its consideration."

"You understand that just submitting the application does not guarantee that it will be approved."

Oh, he was reveling in this moment. Treating her as if she had no idea how the foundation worked. Like the undeserving outsider that she was.

"I understand," she said.

Evan stood and rounded his desk. He extended his hand as if to shake hers, and the absurdity of it brought a bubble of laughter from her throat. She shook her head. "Fuck you, Evan."

The door crashed open. Gretchen whipped around. Evan let out a startled blasphemy as Uncle Jack stormed into the room.

"What the fuck is going on here?"

"Nothing that concerns you, Jack," Evan said.

"Everything in this entire building concerns me, Evan." Jack looked directly at Gretchen. His eyes were bloodshot and ringed with dark circles. "I saw your car. What's going on?"

"Just finishing up some business," Evan said before Gretchen could respond.

"What kind of business?"

Evan had crept back around the desk to pick up the contract, presumably to hide it from Jack's view.

"What is that?" Jack demanded, swooping toward Evan like a hawk to prey.

Dispassionately, Evan shrugged and handed the document to Jack. "I suppose you'll find out soon enough."

Gretchen inched toward the door while Jack's back was turned. But he was a fast reader, and it didn't take a deep dive into the words to understand what she'd done. She'd barely made it outside Evan's office before Jack whipped around again and stormed after her.

He held the contract in his clenched fist. "What the hell is this, Gretchen? Did you really sign this?"

Sarah was at her desk, watching them over the rim of her

glasses, her lips pursed, her expression sour. Gretchen searched her heart for the ill will Sarah had engendered, but all Gretchen could muster was sympathy for the woman. She'd sold her soul to a man who would never repay her loyalty. When it inevitably came out that she and Evan were having an affair, he wouldn't protect her. She would find herself in the same place Gretchen now stood—forgotten, pushed aside, defeated.

"We struck a deal," Gretchen told Jack. She plucked the contract from his fingers, walked with a calmness she didn't feel to Sarah's desk, and handed the rumpled papers to her. "Please give this back to Evan, and make sure a copy is sent to me."

Jack followed at her heels, shouting questions. "You made a deal to give up your inheritance? Your future shares in the company? Why the hell would you agree to this?"

She ignored him, as well as the startled stares of other staffers who'd poked their heads out of offices to see what all the commotion was about. Gretchen made it to the elevators and hit the button for the ground floor.

"Gretchen, what are you doing?" Jack demanded.

"I'm leaving." The door slid open with a quiet ding.

Jack followed her inside. "Where are you going? Why would you sign that document?"

The doors slid shut, locking them in temporary privacy. "Because I had to," she said, facing him directly for the first time. "He wouldn't drop the charges against Colton unless I did."

Jack stumbled back a step. "You can't be serious."

"I'm not going to let Colton suffer because of me and our family."

"That is blackmail, Gretchen. Why would you—"

The elevator came to a stop. Jack jammed his finger into the close-door button to hold it shut.

"Let me out, Jack. I have a plane to catch."

"A plane to where?"

"D.C." Not that she'd warned Jorge or anything that she was coming. But he had invited her out to help, so . . .

Jack made an indecipherable noise. Gretchen gripped his wrist and pulled his hand away from the button. As the doors opened, she walked out, head held high but her heart breaking.

"Does Colton know about this?" He followed her out, still clinging to her heels as they entered the soaring lobby. At her non-response, he swore under his breath, took hold of her elbow, and tugged her to stop.

All around them, company employees scurried about with happy steps, eager to get started on their last day of work before the corporate offices closed for the holiday. Some carried trays and containers of homemade goodies for their departments' holiday potlucks, where they'd reveal their Secret Santa gifts and compete in Ugly Sweater contests. Today was the day they'd wish one another Merry Christmas and joke about seeing one another next year.

And today was the day that Gretchen, once and for all, would leave it all behind.

Jack searched her face. His expression fell. "You should have told him. He loves you. He—"

"Which is why I'm not telling him. Because he would've done something heroic and stupid like plead guilty just to beat Evan at his own game."

"That should be his decision," Jack said.

Something snapped inside her. A rubber band that until now, until those words, had securely bundled all the frustration and anger churning inside her. "What the hell would anyone from this family know about that?"

Her raised voice eclipsed the chipper chatter around them. The employees stopped their happy scurrying to stare, mouths open, eyes wide, Christmas celebrations momentarily forgotten because a Winthrop family drama was playing out in the middle of the lobby.

"I learned from the best, didn't I? How to strike a deal that plays God with other people's lives? Deals that take away all their choices? Isn't that the real Winthrop legacy? Using each other, hurting each other, ignoring the pain it all causes just to avoid a scandal?" She threw her arms out wide. "Well, here I am. The scandal of all scandals. The woman who ruined Colton Wheeler."

People were now also whispering to one another. Jack looked around as if surprised to discover they had an audience. The elevators opened again behind them, and her father walked out. Her mother was right behind him, literally clutching her pearls, her heels making a frantic click-clack on the shiny floor.

Someone must have called them. Alerted them to the shameful Christmas pageant being performed in full view of the loyal congregation.

"For heaven's sake," Frasier hissed as he neared. "What the hell is going on?" He glanced at the gathered crowd and barked an order no one would dare disobey. "Get to work. Now." The ranks scattered like good little soldiers. "We need to take it someplace private," he continued.

"No need. I'm leaving."

"Where are you going?" her mother asked.

"Go ask Evan. He'll be happy to fill you in."

"Honey, please," her mother whispered. "I know you're upset. We can talk about this."

Gretchen swore she wouldn't cry. Wouldn't show any emotion

at all. But a tear found its way to the corner of her eye and then dripped down her cheek. Gretchen swiped it away. "I needed you to talk about it when I was nine, Mom. You wouldn't listen then, and he broke my arm."

The color drained from her mother's face.

"I needed to talk to you about it when I was ten, when I was eleven, when I was twelve. All my life, I've tried to talk to you, and you refused to listen. You refused to see him for what he really was and what he was doing to me."

"I didn't know," her mother whispered.

"Yes, you did. But you made excuses. You justified it. Anything to protect the image of the family, right? Because how would it look if anyone outside the family found out that you'd birthed an abusive psychopath? It scared you more to deal with his bullying than to face how it was affecting me."

"Honey, please. I'm begging you . . ."

"And I am begging you to leave me alone."

Gretchen stepped back, away from the memories and the pain. Away from the betrayal, the lies.

She looked at Jack and rested her hand against his grizzled cheek, rough with whiskers and fatigue. "Goodbye, Uncle Jack."

He tried to follow her to the door. She heard his steps. But they stopped halfway.

It was as if he knew it was useless.

Because this time, she was running away for good.

CHAPTER TWENTY-SEVEN

Colton heard voices. Faraway voices.

Again.

"I think he's dead."

"Poke him with a stick or something."

For fuck's sake. Colton grabbed the nearest pillow and threw it over his head. It was immediately yanked away, and he found himself squinting into a canopy of faces. Malcolm, Mack, Noah, and Vlad all stared down at him as if conducting an autopsy.

"You look like roadkill," Mack said.

He felt like it too. He'd cracked open a bottle of rotgut as soon as he got home from Gretchen's and, after assuring his parents he was fine, collapsed in bed to do what people always did after getting dumped by their girlfriend and charged with assault.

He drowned his sorrows.

He allowed himself to get just inebriated enough to almost forget that the last time he'd been under these covers, Gretchen had been next to him. The sting of betrayal was as sharp tonight as it had been this morning. He needed her. He loved her. But apparently it only went one way. Because the minute he was at his lowest, she was going to pull her disappearing act again.

"Where's my family?" His mouth was wicked dry, and when he tried to sit up, the room swam. He fell back again with a groan.

"Downstairs," Noah said.

Malcolm patted his gut. "Your mom made us a huge dinner."

Colton's stomach pitched at the thought of food. "How long have you been here?"

"About an hour."

"An *hour*? What time is it?"

Vlad looked at his watch. "Almost six."

At least he hadn't slept through his meeting. Buck was supposed to come over sometime tonight with Desiree, his publicist, and whoever else was necessary when one's career was swirling down the drain. Colton had avoided social media and the news all day on Buck's advice, but he didn't need to see the coverage to know it was there and that it was probably bad. The downside of avoiding the reality of his career troubles was that it gave him far too much time to ruminate about his broken heart.

"Other than eating my mother's food, what are you doing here?"

"What do you think?" Vlad said. "You're in crisis. We're here to help."

Colton sat up again, carefully. "Unless you can get that asshole to drop the charges, there's not much you guys can do."

"We're not here about *that*, dipshit," Mack snorted.

Colton looked at each of their faces as a sunrise of understanding pushed through the hangover clouds in his brain. Their presence had nothing to do with saving his career and everything to do with *her*. They were going to try to pull some book club shenanigans. "No. No way. Absolutely not."

"Yep," Noah said. "So get up, take a shower, shave your ugly face, and brush your goddamn teeth because your breath could wilt flowers."

Colton threw the covers off his lap. "Forget it. Gretchen dumped me, and that's all there is to it."

Malcolm shook his head. "All there is to it? When has that *ever* been the case?"

Colton stood, but a wave of nausea had him leaning against the nightstand. The guys all backed up several steps to get out of the kill zone in case he spewed.

A few deep breaths later, Colton straightened. "Remember when you guys were all like, *Don't hurt her, asshole*, and I was like, *What if she hurts me?*, and you guys were all like, *Ha, like that would ever happen*? Remember that?" He extended his middle finger and waved it back and forth to cover the lot of them. "Yeah. Fuck you."

Mack rolled his eyes. "Stop being so dramatic. It's a speed bump."

"I told her I loved her, and she threw me out and said she's moving to D.C. That's more than a speed bump."

"So? Stop her," Mack said.

"I don't have time to stop her. I have to figure out how to save my reputation and my career. And why the fuck should I try to stop her? She dumped me when I needed her, so don't get any big ideas about planning some kind of grand gesture. If anyone needs to be grand-gestured, it's me." He jabbed his finger into his chest for emphasis.

The guys acted as if he hadn't spoken. "Liv, Alexis, and Elena have all been trying to reach her," Mack said, "but her phone keeps going to voice mail."

"She probably turned it off. That's what she does when she runs away from home. You're wasting your time."

His father's voice suddenly called up the stairs. "Is Colton alive?"

"Barely," Mack yelled back.

"Tell him to get down here. Now."

Great. Now what? He looked at the guys, but they all just shrugged as if they had no idea what was going on. He wasn't sure if he trusted them. Colton forced one foot in front of another until he was confident that he could actually walk. "What's wrong?" he asked, stopping at the top of the stairs.

His parents stood side by side looking up at him. "He won't take no for an answer and is threatening to stay out there all night if necessary," his father said.

He sighed. "A reporter?"

"No," his mother said in a stage whisper. "*Jack.*"

"Gretchen's uncle?" Vlad asked. The guys had all followed him from his bedroom.

Colton started down the stairs, gripping the railing just in case. "What does he want?"

"He just keeps saying it's urgent."

At the front door, Colton pressed the button to the intercom for the gate. "What do you want?"

"I need to talk to you."

"Not without my attorney present."

"Luckily, she's right behind me."

A horn blared to prove his point. Colton swore and hit the button to unlock the gate. Then he threw open the front door and stormed outside. A car sped up the driveway that he recognized as Jack's.

Colton met him on the sidewalk as soon as he jumped out. "Why the hell aren't you answering your phone?" Jack demanded.

"It's dead. What the fuck do you want?"

Another car suddenly roared up the driveway. Desiree was behind the wheel, and Buck sat in the passenger seat with a steely glare. They, too, jumped out of the car and ran up the sidewalk.

"Why the hell aren't you answering your phone?" Buck demanded.

"It's dead," came a chorus of voices behind him.

"You can't do that," Desiree said, pointing angrily. "Not when all hell is breaking loose. We have to be able to reach you."

"No shit," Jack grumbled.

"Will someone please tell me what is going on? Why are you here? I thought we weren't meeting until later." He pointed at Jack. "And I have no fucking idea why you're here."

Desiree, Buck, and Jack spoke at the same time. "He's going to drop the charges."

It was as if someone had lifted a blanket from a bird cage. There was a split second of sudden silence before the squawking began again. His parents and siblings raced down the porch steps.

"He *what*?" his mother gasped.

"When did this happen?" his father barked.

"How is that even possible?" his brother said.

Colton didn't need to ask. Because the answer was in Jack's eyes. Colton advanced, gripped the man's shirt, and fisted it in his clenched fingers. "What did Gretchen do?"

He was going to be sick. He sat with his head in his hands, elbows on the granite island in the kitchen. Everyone was gathered around him in various stages of stunned *what the fuck*.

"Why didn't you stop her?" Colton asked.

"I tried!" Jack said.

Colton lifted his face. "You could have shredded that contract. You could have burned it. For fuck's sake, you could have tied her to a goddamn chair to keep her from leaving!"

Jack scoffed. "Do you even know Gretchen?"

His mother rested a soothing hand on Colton's shoulder. "I don't understand. Isn't this basically blackmail? How is that even legal?"

Desiree folded her arms over her chest. "It's not."

"Legal or not," Buck said, "it's done. He's dropping the charges, and I can't for the life of me figure out why you're upset about it, Colton."

"Because she gave up everything for me!" He shot to his feet and started to pace.

"I seriously doubt anything she signed would stand up in court," his father said. "How can Evan have any control over their father's will? If Frasier wants to leave the money to her, some stupid sham contract isn't going to change that."

"And it's not like Evan would be able to fight it if he did," her mother added. "Not without revealing that he blackmailed her."

"It doesn't matter if this is legal or if Evan can hold her to it," Colton snapped. "The point is that she signed that document to protect me. And I . . . I should have seen it. She knew just what to say so I would believe that she was just simply breaking up with me, and I was too wrapped up in my own feelings to realize what she was going through too."

"It's not your fault that you underestimated how manipulative Evan is," Jack said.

"He's more than manipulative," Noah said, his face an unfamiliar mask of stone. "He's *evil*. He's, like, Ebenezer-Scrooge evil."

Colton blinked at Noah in a daze as a memory intruded. Holding Gretchen in his arms. Dancing. Arguing about *A Christmas Carol.*

"Every person you know is represented by a character in that book."

"Which one are you?"

"Nephew Fred, of course. I'm happy and live to make other people happy."

"I suppose you think I'm Scrooge?"

Oh God. Colton sank back into his chair and dropped his forehead into his hands. He'd read the book a hundred times and seen the various movie adaptations just as many, but he'd never truly understood it. Not even when she called him out for it during their date . . . *It has less to do with Christmas and more to do with an unwillingness to interfere for the greater good. To sacrifice for the sake of others.*

She was right. Scrooge was selfish and scared, only willing to change for his own benefit and only when threatened with a cold, lonely death.

But Gretchen? She was fearless. Ready to sacrifice herself for the greater good. Steadfast and loyal, unwilling to be swayed from her values, even when she'd spent her life being ignored, mocked, and rejected for them.

No, Gretchen was nothing like Scrooge.

She was Fred.

So what did that make him? How many times had Colton told himself that he'd built this house, this wealth, this career for his family? To make their lives easier after years of struggle and hardships? It was all a lie. Everything he'd ever done had been out of fear. The fear of ever again having to be that kid who pretended he hadn't overheard his mother crying and his father promising that he'd find another job, that they'd buy another house one day. The kid who'd secretly eaten less so his siblings wouldn't have to go to bed hungry.

Shame thickened his voice as he finally looked up at his friends again. "I called her a coward. I said she was selfish."

The guys emitted a collective moan. "Please tell me that's not true," Mack said, pinching his nose. Noah got a hard look on his face and started to leave. Vlad grabbed him and hauled him back.

"I told her she was just using the situation as an excuse to do what she was always going to do . . . run away."

"I swear, it never ceases to amaze me how badly we can screw up even after all this time reading the manuals." Malcolm sighed.

Colton looked at Jack. "When is her plane leaving?"

"I don't know. She only said that she was afraid she was going to be late."

"I have to stop her. I have to talk to her." He stood again, intending to dash out the door if necessary.

His father held him back with a hand to the chest. "Son, slow down. You can't just go running off when you don't even know where she is. She has to come home at some point. When she gets home, apologize to her."

"It's going to take more than an apology. She deserves more than that."

Vlad grinned. "She deserves a grand gesture."

Colton looked his friends in the eye, one by one, and nodded. Yes. A grand gesture. A big one.

He faced the room again. "I could plead guilty."

Okay, so, the response wasn't quite what he'd expected.

"Are you *insane*?" his father hollered.

"That solves nothing, Colton," Desiree said. "Not to mention that it would open you up to a civil lawsuit as well."

"I'm serious. I could hold a press conference right now and announce that I'm guilty, I did it, and then they would have no choice but to let the charges stand, and then there is no reason for Gretchen to do this."

Jack suddenly laughed.

Colton shot him a glare. "What the hell is so funny?"

"The fact that she predicted you would do that exact thing. That's why she didn't tell you about this. She didn't want you to play hero."

"He's not going to play the hero." Buck pointed directly at Colton. "You are *not* pleading guilty."

"But you could threaten to."

Once again, silence descended as every head swiveled to Vlad, who'd quietly voiced the idea.

"What do you mean?"

"Beat Evan at his own game," Vlad explained. "Tell him you're going to plead guilty and tell the entire world that he was blackmailing Gretchen unless he rips up that contract."

Jack advanced on quick steps. "Even if Evan isn't receptive to it, Frasier and Diane will be. They'll do anything to avoid public scandal and humiliation. Especially now."

Colton stood. "It might work."

"Uh, no, it won't," Buck said. "It only works if Colton is serious about following through with pleading guilty, which he's not. Because, as we've established, that would be batshit fucking insane unless he's willing to risk his entire career for her."

Colton spoke without hesitation. "I don't give a shit about my career right now."

Buck's face shed its color.

Colton gripped the man's shoulders. "You asked me if I still wanted to do this, and the answer is no. Not without her. So if doing this thing risks my career, so be it. It's a risk I'm willing to take if it means getting her back."

He met his mother's eyes. "I'm sorry," he said. "I know this affects you too. But I can't lose her."

She smiled and approached him. "Colton, you have spent far too much time worrying about us. It's not your job to protect us. It never was."

"I know."

"No, you don't. You think we don't know why you've done all this? Why you've worked so hard, why you think you have to be the happy one in the room all the time?"

Shit. She was venturing into *glare of your own past* territory. And she was doing it in front of everyone.

"I said some awful things to her. What if she won't forgive me?"

"She will. Because she sees the real you. The one you think you have to hide from the world. The one you think no one could possibly love if you showed it to them."

"Damn." Malcolm whistled behind them. "Is that true, Colton? Do you really feel that way?"

He gulped and ignored his friends. If he looked at them, he would cry. He didn't have time to cry right now.

His mom patted his chest. "You deserve to be happy, Colton. For *you*. So do whatever you have to do. Go get Gretchen and bring her back."

CHAPTER TWENTY-EIGHT

Colton showered quickly and walked out to find all the guys waiting for him in his bedroom.

"What's the plan?" Mack asked.

"First, Jack and I are going to deal with Evan. Then we're going to bring her back." Colton pointed at Vlad. "I need you to call my pilot to get the plane ready."

Vlad nodded.

"The rest of you, meet us at the airport in two hours. Bring the girls too."

"You want all of us to go?" Noah asked.

"Gretchen needs to see that her entire family wants her to come home. And you are all her family."

"I will bring my Santa suit," Vlad said.

"Um, why?" Noah asked cautiously.

"Because this is a Christmas grand gesture. There must be a Santa suit."

Colton couldn't really argue with that logic. He opened his dresser drawers and pulled out jeans and a T-shirt. Then he dropped the towel around his waist and bent over to pull on some boxers.

"Gah, warn a man!" Noah clapped his hands over his eyes.

"Not your best angle, brother," Mack said.

"That is no one's best angle," Malcolm mused.

"Colton, let's go," Jack called up the stairs.

He threaded the T-shirt over his head and hopped into his jeans, buttoning them as he left the room. He spun back around with a curse and grabbed a pair of socks.

"Colton!"

"I'm coming," he called, jogging down the stairs, the guys right behind him.

Desiree and Buck flanked the front door wearing matching expressions of *This is such a bad idea*. "You should let me come with you," Desiree said.

"I thought attorneys couldn't be party to anything illegal."

Desiree pressed her hands to her ears. "I didn't hear that."

Colton dropped to his butt on the bottom stair to pull on his socks and shoes. When he stood, his mom handed him his fleece coat and a hat. "Your hair is wet. You'll catch a cold."

He kissed her head. "Thanks, Mom." He turned his attention to Noah. "Have Alexis call Addison and get whatever information she can."

"I will," Noah said.

He turned to Buck next. "I'm sorry, Buck. I know I'm putting you in a tough position."

"No, you're not. My job as your manager is to make sure you're happy, not just in your career but in your life. I haven't done a good enough job of that lately."

"What are you going to tell Archie?"

"What I should have said before. To go fuck himself."

It would be a miracle if Colton made it through the next few minutes without decorating Evan Winthrop's face with another black eye. When he and Jack burst through the door to the man's office—his secretary Sarah protesting loudly behind them—Evan leaped to his feet with all the bluster of a comic book villain.

"What is the meaning of this? What the hell are you doing here?"

Colton strode in with a grin. "Just thought I'd stop by for a drink. Got any Johnny Walker?"

"Get the hell out of my office. Sarah!"

The woman ran in, hands twisting and lips pursed. "I tried to stop them," she said.

"Don't worry," Jack said smoothly. "This won't take long."

Evan puffed out his chest but nodded crisply at Sarah. "If we're not done in five minutes, call security."

Sarah hesitated but stepped out of the office, pulling the door shut with her. Jack claimed one of the leather club chairs facing Evan's desk, his demeanor relaxed. But beneath the nonchalance, a simmering rage radiated off him that even Evan was smart enough not to ignore.

"What do you want?" Evan barked, returning to his chair.

"Time to eliminate the middleman," Colton said, matching Jack's deceptively easygoing tone. "So let's just get straight to the heart of the matter. Thirty million."

Evan chuffed. "You can't be serious. You think we'd still consider giving you a penny to endorse us after this?" Evan pointed at his swollen purple eye.

Colton had to flex his fingers just to keep from giving him another one. "I'm not here about the endorsement."

"Then what the fuck is the money for?"

"My silence," Jack blurted out.

Colton blinked. This was . . . not the plan. They were supposed to demand the money in exchange for Colton not holding a press conference and, well, all the shit they'd discussed at the house. And then the money was going to go straight into helping Gretchen expand her clinic.

Evan scoffed again. "Silence about what?"

Colton wanted to lean over and ask the same question.

"About this." Jack pulled a folded piece of paper from his coat pocket and then tossed it on the desk. Colton would've side-eyed Jack if that wouldn't clue Evan in to the fact that Colton had no idea what was going on.

Evan swiped up the piece of paper. "What the fuck is this?"

Same, dude. Same.

"Read it," Jack ordered.

Evan uncreased the paper, and the man's face morphed from obstinate insolence to a queasy shade of dread.

"I'm guessing Anna doesn't know?" Jack said, his voice chillingly quiet.

Know what?!

"This is blackmail," Evan growled. "I will call the fucking police. I will sue your ass."

Jack managed to sound bored in his response. "Ever heard of

the Streisand effect? Not sure you want to do that. And anyway . . . blackmail is what you did to Gretchen. *This* is a negotiation."

"What do you want?" Evan's jaw clenched so tightly that Colton could've sworn he heard a tooth crack.

"Several things." Jack leaned forward with his elbows on his knees, as casual as a man discussing the score of last night's hockey game. "First, you give us that piece of shit contract you made Gretchen sign this morning so we can burn it. She retains all her inheritance and shares, and she gets a spot on the foundation board."

Evan's nostrils flared.

"Second, that thirty million dollars? Gretchen's clinic is going to receive an amazing anonymous donation that will allow her to start an endowment and expand."

Evan's face turned to stone. "What else?"

Colton gulped. What else, indeed?

"You step down as CEO of Carraig Aonair."

Evan leaped to his feet. "Fuck you."

Jack waved off the dramatic display. "You can claim whatever cock-and-bull excuse you want. Illness. Time with family, which, obviously, you need right now. I don't care. But you're done with this company."

"And if I don't?"

Jack looked at Colton for the first time and lifted his eyebrows.

Oh. Right. He leaned forward. "If you don't, I call a press conference right now and tell the world everything. How you blackmailed your sister. How you erased the security video. How I did, in fact, beat the shit out of you because you're a sack of shit."

"That makes no fucking sense. You'd just be admitting to charges that are about to be dropped."

"Of course it doesn't make sense to you," Colton said. "Because you have no idea what it means to sacrifice for someone you love. That's the difference between you and Gretchen."

Evan rounded the desk with a sneer as ugly as his soul. "She talked you into this, didn't she? I can't fucking believe it. You of all people. How the fuck did she get her hooks into you?"

Colton's fist connected with Evan's jaw in a dull thud that sent Evan reeling backward. He tried to catch himself with one hand, but it slipped on the polished surface of his desk. Instead, he careened sideways and crashed to the floor, bringing with him a crystal decanter and an expensive-looking lamp.

The door flew open, and Sarah ran in. "Evan!"

Colton casually picked up Evan's untouched whiskey and shot it back. The burn brought a satisfying rasp to his voice. "He'll live," he said. Then, looking down at Evan on the floor. "You have until five o'clock tomorrow to start the money transfer or—"

"What is this?" Sarah had spoken quietly from the other side of the desk. In her hand was the paper that Jack had given Evan.

Evan scrambled to stand. "Give me that."

"What is this?" Sarah demanded, louder now.

"It's none of your business." Evan lunged for the paper.

Sarah backed up, eyes filling with tears. "None of my business? How many women are you sleeping with?"

Colton blinked. Jack did a double take. "Wait . . . are—are *you* sleeping with him too?"

"You said you were going to leave your wife for me," Sarah whispered.

Blood dripped from the corner of Evan's eye, and his chest shook with spiteful gulps of air. "Get out. All of you."

"You lying bastard. You used me." Sarah turned her back on

him. "He asked me to leak the video of the fight. And Gretchen's paperwork for the board seat? He made me delete it. He never even sent it to the board."

"Get out!" Evan bellowed.

All he accomplished, though, was to bring Frasier and Diane storming into the room. "What the hell is going on now?" Frasier boomed. When he saw Colton, his face hardened. "How dare you come here?"

"Don't worry. We were just leaving."

Jack reached out his hand to Evan. "The contract?"

Diane curled her fingers around her pearls. "What contract? What is going on?"

Sarah marched over to Diane and thrust the paper at her. "I quit. That's what's going on."

As Sarah stormed out, Diane skimmed the paper and then looked up at Evan, her face contorted. "Evan, what is this? What have you done?"

Colton was tempted to peer over Diane's shoulder because he, too, still had no idea what Evan had done. Evan marched to his desk, pulled out a two-paged stapled document, and tossed it at Jack. "Here. Take it. And get the fuck out."

Jack folded the contract and shoved it in his pocket. "Let's go, Colton. Evan is going to need some privacy to tell his parents about his decision to step down."

Frasier became belligerent. "What the hell is he talking about? Step down from what?"

"Wait," Colton said. He got in Evan's face. "You want to know what I see in her? Everything you're not. Everything you could never be. Kind. And smart. And compassionate. And if we never see you again, it will be too soon."

. . .

Even in the nation's capital, the fight to protect immigrants was a lonely, low-paying endeavor.

The offices of the Refugee Resettlement Foundation in D.C. were as unimpressive as hers back home. Aging cubicles held computers that were about five years out of date, and the only view from the conference room window was of the entrance to a Metro stop and a Five Guys with a sign proclaiming it as President Obama's favorite burger joint.

But the office bustled with energy when she walked in just after seven o'clock. More than twenty people of all ages were busy sorting donations into marked tubs for distribution to newly arrived refugees from Afghanistan. Some people donated luxury gifts like purses and iPods, but most people had donated the basic necessities that families needed to start over. Bedding. Socks. Toiletries. School supplies. And all had to be carefully itemized to make sure they went to the right people.

Deep in the middle of it all was Jorge, bent over a single box and checking things off on a clipboard.

"Can I help you?" A youngish woman in an RRF T-shirt greeted Gretchen at the door. "Are you here to volunteer?"

"I am." Exhaustion stole the volume from her voice. She cleared her throat. "Jorge invited me."

At the sound of his name, Jorge glanced up and smiled. "Gretchen, you're here."

She tried to smile. "Surprise."

Jorge spoke to a man beside him and handed over the clipboard. He had to dodge several boxes as he made his way to her. "Yes," he said. "Surprise."

His tone and expression suggested he was not, however, surprised. Jorge gave her a quick hug and then backed away.

She slung her heavy bag over her shoulder—she hadn't even checked into her hotel yet—and shoved her hands in the pockets of her jeans. "So . . . put me to work."

"Why don't we chat first?" He gestured for her to follow him through the crowded room. "My office is this way."

Gretchen stepped over a box overflowing with baby clothes. Her heart clenched. She couldn't imagine how hard it would be to be forced to flee your home country with a baby. "Are you sure? It looks like there's a lot to do."

"We have plenty of help. Come on in." Jorge led her into a small office that obviously doubled as a storage room for donations that had already been catalogued. He shut the door, and Gretchen walked to the window overlooking the front of the building.

"Is that true?" Gretchen asked, pointing at the sign about Obama.

"Doubt it. I've been in this building for a long time, and I never once saw Obama go there." He sat down at his desk and motioned for her to take the chair opposite him.

"I'm sorry to give you such short notice," she said.

"I'm not going to complain. I had given up on you."

They traded the normal pleasantries. His twin girls had started middle school this year and asked for new phones for Christmas, and his wife was working for the Smithsonian now and would love to see her soon. Gretchen shared nothing of her own life. What would she say? The truth was too mortifying. Even if Jorge had been a friend for a long time, he was still about to become her boss. What kind of impression would it make to admit she was only here because her brother was essentially blackmailing her, and she was nursing a broken heart that might never heal?

But Jorge wasn't stupid, and she saw a probing glint in his eyes as he leaned forward. "So, you're here about the job."

"Yes."

"What changed your mind?"

"I reviewed everything you sent me, and I think you're right. It's a good fit."

"Just like that?"

"You know me. When I make a decision, I don't like to waste time."

He studied her skeptically. "Well, I'm not going to lie. Our work can be frustrating. Sometimes I feel like we're talking to ourselves, and the only time anyone actually pays attention to us is during election years. And just when we think we've got a shot at getting an audience on the Hill for some of our legislative priorities . . ." He paused to shrug. "Well, immigration reform makes for a great stump speech, but I've yet to meet a politician who is willing to risk reelection to do the right thing."

"You sound like you're trying to talk me out of the job."

"I just want to make sure you're fully aware of how different your daily life will be on this side of the immigration effort. We don't work directly with clients the way you do now. We work as a clearinghouse to connect clients with attorneys around the nation, but our primary function is to draft legislation and raise awareness."

"I understand."

"I realize it might take you a while to shut things down in Nashville—"

"My paralegal and office manager are going to take over for now until we can hire a new lead attorney. I can start immediately."

He raised his eyebrows. "That fast, huh?"

"No reason to wait. We're entering a new election year, and as you said, that's when things get really busy. I'm actually thinking I might come in tomorrow to review a few things and—"

"Gretchen, tomorrow is Christmas Eve."

"I know. I like working Christmas. There are no distractions. Obviously, I don't expect you to work too."

Jorge ran a hand down his cheek and spoke carefully. "You know how badly I want you to work here."

His abrupt interruption made the hair on the back of her neck stand erect. "I know."

"Tell me what's really going on."

She swallowed. "Nothing. I reconsidered, and I think this is a good job for me."

"Do you remember how we first met?"

She blinked at the change in subject. Of course she remembered, but why he was bringing it up now was a mystery. They had both stayed behind at Georgetown for Christmas break—Jorge because he couldn't afford an international flight home, and she because she wasn't exactly welcome at home. But she'd lied to him when he asked why she was staying. She told him she didn't have any family to go home to. It was sort of true. Even then, her family had felt like strangers.

"Imagine my surprise when I discovered who you really were," Jorge said now.

"I'm not following the segue here."

"I got a call about an hour ago from your assistant."

"Addison?" She shifted uncomfortably in her chair. "What did she say?"

The look he gave her was a humiliating blend of pitying and pointed. He knew the truth. Gretchen stood quickly. "I'm not here because of what happened with Colton. I *want* this job, Jorge. This is important work. I got my bachelor's degree in public policy before getting my J.D. You said it yourself that my qualifications are perfect, and—"

"I didn't like you at first, you know."

"Wh-what?"

Jorge leaned back in his chair. "I thought you were spoiled. Ungrateful for what you had. Driven more by some kind of self-indulgent martyrdom than any real dedication to people."

His words were a punch to the gut. "Wow. Thanks. How long have you been holding that in?"

"But then I realized you were just simply the loneliest person I'd ever met. I think maybe you still are."

Jorge might as well have read directly from *A Christmas Carol*. *There he sat alone. Quite alone in the world, I do believe.*

Colton would have laughed at the irony.

Jorge smiled sadly and stood with a weary slowness. Panic clutched her heart. She swallowed and tried again. "Jorge, please."

"If you still want this job in a month, it's yours. But our clients deserve someone who's here because she wants to be, not because she's avoiding something else."

"That's not fair," she protested weakly.

"Go home, Gretchen. Whatever you're looking for, you're not going to find it here."

She was too stunned, too humiliated to respond. He left his office door open when he walked out, leaving her alone with heated cheeks and a pounding heart. Finally, though, she picked up her bag and tried to summon some semblance of dignity when she walked out.

She had no idea where to go, couldn't see the destination. She took the Metro, lugging her heavy bag down the long, dark escalator into the bowels of the capital city. She used to be terrified of these escalators, so long that from the top you could barely see the bottom.

What an apt metaphor for her life.

A train arrived just as she stepped up to the track, its speed sending a whirl of hot, foul air into her face. The car was nearly empty when she walked on. Just one other person sat at the opposite end, a man in an Air Force uniform. She chose a seat near one of the doors and tucked her suitcase against her legs.

The doors closed, and the train took off, slowly at first, and then it hit top speed. She hadn't even checked which way it was going. It had been so many years since she'd last used the Metro that she couldn't remember which line she even needed to take to get to her hotel.

You're just a scared little girl hiding in that damn tree house wishing someone would come find you and take you home . . .

Colton had called her a coward, and he was right. She could have stayed and fought Evan. She could have stood by Colton's side and let the chips fall where they might. But she didn't. Despite all her talk about not caring anymore about what her family thought, about being immune to Evan's name-calling and gaslighting, she'd still let them win. She'd done exactly what everyone expected of her.

She'd run.

And she'd ruined the best thing that had ever happened to her.

Her body flushed where she sat as her heart raced and her mind whirred. What had she done? And how the hell was she going to undo it?

Jorge was right.

She had to go home.

CHAPTER TWENTY-NINE

The flight to D.C. would take eighty minutes, but it took less than two for adrenaline to give way to panic.

"How do you know she'll be there?" Even though Colton sat across from Jack on his Gulfstream, he had to raise his voice to be heard over the roar of the engine.

Vlad, Mack, and Noah were settled into the rest of the seats with Elena, Liv, and Alexis. The rest of the guys opted to stay behind.

"Addison said that was the hotel she booked."

"How does she know?"

"She has access to Gretchen's credit card accounts."

Colton groaned. If Gretchen found out they'd tracked her down by invading her financial privacy, she'd never forgive him. And at that thought, panic became full-blown fear. There were a lot of things she might not forgive him for. Christ, the things he'd said to her. He pressed the heels of his hands against his eyes and tipped his head back to hold back tears.

"Thank you for loving her so much," Jack said.

"I don't deserve to."

"Of course you do. You might be the only man who does, in my opinion."

"You don't understand. All the things I said to her . . ." His stomach clenched. "She's lived her entire life being rejected and mocked and yelled at by people who are supposed to love her, and what did I do? The same fucking thing. I accused her of pushing people away before they could hurt her, and then I just let her do it to me. Why would she ever trust me again?"

"Because you love her enough to say you're sorry," Jack said. "Not many people in her life have ever done that."

That was hardly reassuring.

The rest of the flight was a painful, slow torture. When the plane finally touched down with a light bump and a hard brake, Colton was out of his seat before it was even safe. He'd arranged for cars to be waiting for them outside the hangar. Jack and Colton got in the first one, along with Mack and Liv.

The rest of the crew divided themselves up in the other two cars. When they pulled away, Colton turned off airplane mode on his phone. No messages from her. No missed calls. No voice mails.

Colton rubbed his sweaty hands on his jeans. "How are we going to get her to come down to the lobby if she's not even answering her phone?"

"I don't know," Jack said.

"There's no way they'll give us her room number."

"Probably not."

The caravan of SUVs merged onto the freeway toward Georgetown. A hand rested on his shoulder from the back seat. Mack. "Breathe, Colton. We're going to find her."

That wasn't what worried him.

What worried him was how she would react when they did.

"You want me to do what?"

The clerk at the front desk of the hotel looked like she was one second away from hitting the security button.

"I need you to check if there is a woman named Gretchen Winthrop staying here, and if so, please call her to come down."

"Um, I can't do that."

"Don't you know who this is?" Vlad asked, elbowing up to the counter. His Santa hat slipped down to his eyebrows. He shoved it back up.

The clerk shook her head.

"This is Colton Wheeler," Vlad said. "Biggest country music star in the whole world."

Colton winced. "That's kind of an exaggeration."

"Just because you haven't put out a new album in two years doesn't mean you're not still the biggest."

"Listen. I could really use your help." Colton leaned on the counter and tried his wink on the girl. It had no effect. He stood. "I'm desperate here. The woman I love thinks she has to leave me to protect my career because I beat up her piece-of-shit brother and—"

The girl's eyes registered recognition. "Wait. I do know you. Weren't you just arrested for getting in a drunken brawl or something?"

"I wasn't drunk."

"And I think, technically, you can't call it a brawl because it was just two people," Vlad said. "Doesn't it require more people to be a brawl?"

For fuck's sake. Colton shoved Vlad behind him. "Yes, that's me. I'm him."

"Why is he dressed like Santa Claus?"

"It's a long story. Please, can you check if she's here?"

The clerk looked around, probably for her boss or security. "I don't know. I could get in a lot of trouble for this."

"Please," Colton begged. "I have no way of knowing what room she's in, and I know you can't tell me that."

"Why can't you call her?"

"Because she . . . she won't answer my call."

The clerk shook her head. "Uh, yeah, no, I'm not getting involved in this. You could be a stalker or something."

"A stalker with an entourage?"

She reached for the phone. "I'm going to call security."

"Wait. Wait. Don't do that. Give me a minute to explain. Her brother was blackmailing her to stay away from me, and I need to win her back because she hates Christmas, and I—"

"Sir, are you still drunk?"

"I wasn't drunk." He bent and banged his forehead on the counter.

"Colton." Jack tugged on his elbow.

Colton shrugged him off and raised his head again. "Listen, I know this is weird—"

"Colton!"

"What?!" he growled.

Jack was pointing. Colton followed the direction of his point and froze.

Gretchen.

Standing with her back to him with a massive bag slung over her shoulder. She hovered in the doorway to the hotel bar as if she couldn't decide whether to go in. His mind flashed back to the night when she'd wandered into Old Joe's and marched toward him, determined and proud. And just like then, his breath left his body in a whoosh. She was here.

She was *here*.

And he couldn't move a damn muscle.

Vlad jumped up and down. "Gretch—"

Colton clamped his hand over Vlad's mouth. "Wait."

"For what?" Mack squawked. "We just flew two hours—"

"It was more like ninety minutes," Noah said. Alexis clamped a hand over *his* mouth.

"—and drove like maniacs to find her. And there she is. What the hell are you waiting for?"

"A grand gesture," Colton said.

"This *is* the grand gesture," Noah said. "Isn't it?"

"Not like this," Colton said, as much to himself as everyone else. It wasn't a grand gesture if the recipient would die of embarrassment over it. And Gretchen would. If he did what the Bros normally did—run and make a spectacle of themselves—it would backfire. She didn't want spectacle.

She wanted something soft. Something slow.

Colton spied the hotel gift shop on the other side of the lobby. "New plan," he said. "I need a hat and some glasses."

CHAPTER THIRTY

Gretchen sat alone at the bar and twirled the straw in her water. If she gritted her teeth any harder, she was going to bust a molar.

No flights.

How was it possible that there were *no flights* available until tomorrow morning? Yeah, okay, it was Christmastime, and that meant everything was booked, but for God's sake. Didn't they know? This was an emergency. She had to get home now. It was hard to carry out a grand gesture for the man you loved when you couldn't even get out of the damn city.

The bartender, a young guy with a goatee, stepped in front of her and set down a glass of whiskey. "From an admirer."

Gretchen inwardly groaned. Of all the times to get hit on. "Can you tell him thanks but no thanks?"

"Listen, I don't normally do this because it's fucking creepy, and for all I know, this guy could be a stalker—"

"Um, yeah, now I'm *really* not going to drink that."

"But he told me to tell you that it's the good stuff."

Every muscle in her body jumped at once. "What did you say?"

"Does that mean something to you?"

Yes. It meant everything. She just didn't understand how. How did he know where to find her? She wanted to turn around and look for him, but she couldn't. Not with her insides suddenly shaking and tears stinging the back of her eyelids.

The bartender shrugged at her reaction. "Anyway, I'm also supposed to say, 'To cheating, stealing, fighting, and drinking.' Whatever that means."

Her stomach turned to Jell-O as her heart rose in her throat. "Where is he?"

The guy pointed over her shoulder. "It's the dude who looks like Clark Kent in the corner."

Laughter bubbled up as if someone had uncorked a bottle of sparkling water in her throat.

"Aaand now he's headed this way." The bartender lowered his voice. "Do you want me to ward him off? I can get rid of him."

She shook her head. "No, thank you." She'd already made that mistake.

The bartender lifted his gaze over her shoulder before looking back at her. "If you need help, I'll be at the end of the bar."

He walked away, and her neck tickled with awareness at the man now standing behind her.

"Can I sit?"

His voice. It sent shivers down her spine and lifted the hair on her arms. She nodded and held her breath as the empty chair next to her slid back from the bar, its steel-tipped legs scraping quietly on the industrial carpet. She didn't dare look at him as he sat, but in her peripheral vision, she saw the bright yellow of his puffer vest.

Her fingers shook as she wrapped them around the glass of whiskey. "What brings you by?"

Colton chuckled quietly at the question. It was exactly what he'd asked her when she'd found him at Old Joe's. "I was hoping to talk to you."

"Yeah? Well, here I am, honey." When Colton had said it at Old Joe's, he'd been cocky, confident. He'd spread his arms out wide. But when Gretchen said it now, it came out shaky, watery. She kept her arms tucked close to her torso. Because if she reached for him, if she touched him, the dam would break. She'd be a puddle on the floor.

Beside her, Colton leaned his elbows on the bar. "I'm here with a proposal of sorts," he said, repeating, again, part of that first conversation.

"I'm all ears."

"How would you like to come home with me and let me spend the rest of our lives earning your forgiveness?"

Joy swelled in her chest. She finally looked at him and— "Where did you get those glasses?"

"What?"

"Can you even see? Those are prescription."

He sighed and whipped the thick black frames from his face. "They're readers. The hotel store didn't have a lot of options."

"Well, I mean, it's a pretty lame disguise."

"Well, excuse me if I didn't have time to properly plan this. I was a little bit frantic when I found out what you did." He glowered then. "Which, by the way, what the hell were you thinking, Gretchen? Why would you sign that bullshit contract?"

"It was the only way Evan would drop the charges."

"So you just decided to give up everything to protect me?"

Another one of their conversations came to mind, this one just two nights ago. It felt like a lifetime. "I would give up any amount of money for you. I would protect you a million times if necessary."

The Adam's apple in his throat rose and fell as he swallowed. "Why?"

"Because I love you."

"I was hoping you'd say that." He lifted a hand and draped it around the back of her neck so he could pull her closer. The brim of his hat collided with her forehead. With a curse, he whipped it off.

She laughed. "I think you're becoming the grumpy one."

"What if I am? Can you love the grumpy side of me?"

"I love every side of you."

This time nothing stood in the way as he once again pulled her closer. Forehead to forehead, they spoke through touch. His thumb caressed her neck. Her hand found his cheek.

"I'm sorry," he whispered after a moment, his voice rough.

"So am I."

"The things I said to you . . ." His voice cracked, and so did her heart.

"I needed to hear them."

"No, you didn't. Because none of it was true."

The sound of his sorrow brought a tremble to her lip. "It was, though. You were right. I ran away because I was scared—"

He didn't let her finish. He covered her lips with his and kissed her so softly, so sweetly, that a whimper emerged from her throat. She leaned into him. Breathed him in. Memorized every sound, every touch.

Until a voice intruded. "Christ, it's about fucking time."

Gretchen's eyes flew open. "Seriously?"

Colton laughed quietly and then turned in his chair just enough so she could see around him. Her eyes widened. How . . . how had she not even noticed them? Mack and Liv. Noah and Alexis. Elena and Vlad. In a Santa suit. Standing apart was Jack.

Colton slid his hand down her back. "Your family is here to bring you home, Gretchen."

She bit her lip. "Did you bring your private jet?"

"Yes, and don't complain about the cost because—"

She kissed him.

Again.

And this time it was deep and passionate, and the applause she heard could have just as easily been in her own mind as from their friends.

They finally parted only when someone cleared their throat.

"Let's go home," Colton whispered against her lips.

She stood and held out her hand. "Your place or mine?"

EPILOGUE

One year later

Now this was how Colton Wheeler liked to wake up.

A quiet Christmas morning. A warm, cozy bed. And the woman he loved more than he'd ever thought possible draped across his chest.

Naked.

"You're right," Gretchen panted. Moments earlier, she'd been atop him and driving him to delirium with her hushed moans. He'd done his best to be quiet with his parents just up the hall, but he'd lost all sense of time and space at the end.

Colton trailed his fingertips up her spine and chuckled when she shivered. "Right about what?"

"Christmas sex is better."

Colton wrapped his arms around her and rolled them both over. "Engaged sex is even better."

Gretchen smiled sleepily and lifted her left hand. The emerald engagement ring he'd given her last night was a half-size too big, but she insisted on wearing it. *After* he promised that it hadn't cost too much.

They'd already decided they would have a small wedding. Just their closest friends and family. Whether that included her parents had yet to be decided. In the past year, they'd been seeing a counselor to establish some boundaries with Diane and Frasier that her parents were not happy about. But Gretchen was, which was all that mattered to Colton. Even if it took the rest of their lives, he would never stop trying to undo the damage her family had inflicted on her. Even now, all these months later, his blood pressure spiked when he thought about what Evan had done to her. If Gretchen eventually chose to reestablish a relationship with him, Colton would support her. But they weren't there yet.

Colton pressed his lips to her throat. "I'm going to miss you so much."

"The tour doesn't start until March."

"I'm already dreading it." The label had loved the new music he'd cowritten with J. T. The album had been released just a week ago, and the first single had instantly hit number one. That meant a stadium tour. He'd missed performing, but the thought of only seeing Gretchen a few times every month was torture.

The sound of giggling in the hallway outside brought a laugh from her and a groan from him. He'd hoped they'd have another hour or so to celebrate privately before his nieces and nephews awoke to see what Santa Claus brought in the night. But it was Gretchen who shooed him out of bed.

"Come on," she coaxed. "We don't want to miss the kids opening their stockings."

She was almost as giddy as they were.

What a difference a year made.

They were the last to go downstairs. The aroma of cinnamon rolls drew them to the kitchen, where his mother had likely been awake for an hour or more.

His brother snorted when they walked in. “Look who finally woke up.”

“Oh, we’ve been awake for a while,” Gretchen said, grinning. Colton winked at her and then found his mother watching them both with an emotional smile.

“Let me see the ring again,” she said, wiping her hands on a dish towel.

As his mother fussed over Gretchen, Colton leaned against the counter and stifled a yawn behind his hand. His brother handed him a cup of coffee and matched his pose.

“Been awake for a while, huh?” Cooper teased.

“Mind your own business.”

Cooper huffed out a laugh over his mug.

“Hey,” his sister called from the other room. “If you guys don’t hurry up, my kids are going to go feral.”

Gretchen walked toward him. Colton set down his mug and opened his arms for her. She snuggled against his chest and sighed. “Merry Christmas,” she said.

Colton kissed her head, his throat too thick for words.

In all his life, he’d never known a moment as perfect as this.

ACKNOWLEDGMENTS

Every time I finish a book, I am overwhelmed with gratitude that I get to do this for a living and even more so that I have such a strong support network of people who make it possible. So, as always, I must first thank my family. I truly could not do this without my parents, my husband, and my daughter.

Writing a book set in the world of country music required a great deal of research. So special thanks to Lauren Laffer, staff writer at SoundsLikeNashville.com, and to Richard Cohen of Mick Artist Management, for walking me through the business and creative side of the music industry. You both spent a gracious amount of time answering my questions, and I am grateful for your expertise. On a similar note, I want to give a big shout-out to the city of Clarksville, TN, which hosts a *real* Christmas on the Cumberland festival!

To my VIP reader Erin Harlow: Thank you for coming up with the name Carraig Aonair for the Winthrop whiskey company. It was a perfect fit in so many ways! Thank you for being part of my reading community!

Major thanks to my writing friends—Meika Usher, Christina Mitchell, Alyssa Alexander, Victoria Solomon, Kelly Ohlert, Tamara Lush, Thien-Kim Lam, Erin King, Elizabeth Cole, G.G. Andrews, Deborah Wilde, Jennifer Seay, Amanda Gale, and Jessica Arden. I am grateful that our writing pursuits brought us together. I can't imagine navigating this industry without your humor and support.

Finally, thank you to my agent, Tara Gelsomino, and my editor, Kristine Swartz. Both of you have helped me become a better writer with your patience, understanding, creativity, and enthusiasm.

Photo by Lauren Perry of Perrywinkle Photography

Lyssa Kay Adams read her first romance novel at a very young age when she swiped one from her grandmother's stash. After a long journalism career in which she had to write too many sad endings, she decided to return to the stories that guaranteed a happy ever after. Once described as "funny, adorable, and a wee bit heart-breaking," Lyssa's books feature women who always get the last word, men who aren't afraid to cry, and animals. Lots of animals. Lyssa writes full-time from her home in Michigan, where she lives with her sportswriter husband, her wickedly funny daughter, and a spoiled Maltese who likes to be rocked to sleep like a baby. When she's not writing, she's cooking or driving her daughter around from one sporting event to the next. Or rocking the dog.

CONNECT ONLINE

LyssaKayAdams.com/newsletter

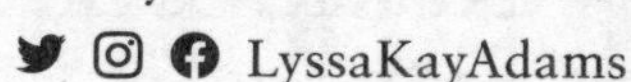
LyssaKayAdams